Praise for William Schiele

"A suspenseful thriller that will have you on the edge of your seat. The very first chapter draws you into the world of David Diegert."
—Kirsty L. Jennings, author of *Soulblade: Forgotten Souls*

"If you like your fiction dark and a little hard-boiled, you'll love *Tears of the Assassin*. Schiele draws us into his clandestine world where we're compelled to follow his hero's journey."
—Jason Pomerance, author of *Women Like Us*

"Deep-seated drama and action, depicting the hard life of someone in the business of violence, *Tears of the Assassin* is an intense and intriguing read."
—Kelsey Rae Barthel, author of *Beyond the Code*

"Gritty and real, *Tears of the Assassin* brings the reader in with stark, real characters, creating the origin of the protagonist David Diegert. The writing is fast-paced and suspenseful."
—Stephen Carignan, author of *The Sleeping Man*

TEARS OF THE ASSASSIN

TEARS OF THE ASSASSIN

William Schiele

Published by Quill, an imprint of Inkshares, Inc.,
San Francisco, California
www.inkshares.com

Cover design by Reid McLachlan
© STYLEPICS

ISBN: 9781942645436
e-ISBN: 9781942645443
Library of Congress Control Number: 2016944263

First edition

Printed in the United States of America

To Schiele A. Brewer and Catherine (Schiele) Brewer,
my father and grandmother,
with gratitude for a lifetime of inspiration and support

The day the power of love overrules the love of power, the world will know peace.

—Mahatma Gandhi

CHAPTER 1

Tattered boots found unstable footing in the snow as David Diegert trudged two miles to his night-shift job at the mini-mart. *Without money life sucks,* he thought as the chill penetrated his coat and the snow-impeded walk numbed his toes. Normally, he passed the time checking e-mail, reading the news, or playing Mobile Strike. On this trip, he was left with only his thoughts, since his service had been cut off for nonpayment.

His job was lousy, but with only a high school diploma in the rural economy of northern Minnesota, Diegert was lucky to have it. Minimum wage sapped his efforts at financial progress. He hated living at home with his parents and older brother, but he hoped the raise he was due would give him enough to get his own apartment. He also hoped to save some money for college, although right now a car would be nice.

Scuffing the snow off his boots on the doormat, which he would later have to clean, Diegert stepped inside. He smelled the pizza cooking and heard the hot dogs sizzling, but his senses had grown numb to it all and it only served to dull his appetite. Barbara, his heavyset coworker, looked up from the counter she was cleaning and gave him a nod. The store manager, Barley Cummings, eyed him quizzically from the door of his messy office. Barley was proud to tell anyone who asked, and even those who didn't, that he was named after the main ingredient for making beer. Cummings beckoned him over with his fingers.

"Hey, didn't you get my e-mail?" asked the rotund manager.

"No," said Diegert, breaking eye contact. "My phone's dead."

"Well, we're downsizing."

"You're making the store smaller?"

"No, I'm making the staff smaller, and I had to let you go."

With a sense of having just been insulted, Diegert replied, "And you told me with an e-mail?"

"Yeah, thought I'd save you the walk. Look, your pass card has been deactivated, and unless you're gonna buy something, you gotta go. You don't work here anymore, Tonto."

Diegert absorbed the news with disappointment, anger and embarrassment rising up at Barley's use of his nickname from high school that he hated.

"I'm due for a raise and so now you fire me."

"It's called corporate cost control," said Cummings matter-of-factly as he put a hand on Diegert's shoulder, nudging him toward the door. Diegert slapped the thoughtless boss's hand away and shoved him up against the soda machine.

"Don't fuckin' touch me."

Cummings's huge belly shook as Diegert pressed him back against the soda fountain. The store manager's wide ass activated the dispensers, which soaked his pants.

"Don't do anything crazy," pleaded the overweight imbecile, who'd never realized that the muscles that bound Diegert's six-foot-two-inch frame were so strong.

Releasing his grip on Cummings and stepping back, Diegert thought about "crazy." He looked at the shelves of chips, the stacks of soda bottles, the cardboard displays of cookies, as well as the refrigerated cases full of beer. He wanted to smash them all, clear the shelves with a sweep of his arm and toss the soda behind the counter where it would crash on the sandwich boards and the pizza oven. Then he would shove a shelving unit right through the glass, bursting the bottles of beer. He wanted to destroy the entire shitty little store where he had wasted so much time. But he did not.

Stepping away from the frightened man, Diegert said, "I'm walking outta here on my own." He turned and left, dropping his employee pass card on the floor.

As he walked away from the store, down a dark country road, Diegert heard the acceleration of an engine and saw his tall shadow cast on the road by flashing red-and-blue lights. He peered over his shoulder at the county sheriff's car, watching as it passed by and pulled in front of him, nose to the snowbank, blocking his path. Officer Paul Tate stepped out of the car and walked back to Diegert.

"Dave, I'm placing you under arrest."

"Oh, come on, Tate."

"Don't give me any shit. Barley called it in, and you have the right to remain silent."

Officer Tate handcuffed Diegert and put him in the car.

At the police station, locked in a processing room, Diegert sat alone for a long time, which allowed his thoughts to wander back to his childhood.

He remembered sitting on the couch—which was really a foam mattress on top of an old door held up by cinderblocks— huddled under a blanket in the cold house while his mother, Denise, read to him from *Harry Potter and the Goblet of Fire*. She cleverly created a distinct voice for each character. David loved the adventures of the students at Hogwarts and was magically transported there by the imagination of his mother.

"God damn it, there's not enough beer in here," bellowed David's father, Tom, as he pulled his head up from inside the fridge.

"I told you to have at least a twelve-pack in here all the time," he shouted as he slammed the fridge door. Denise stopped reading, rose from the mattress, and went to the kitchen.

"You fuckin' injuns can't count past five," Tom said as he shoved the tall, dark-haired woman into the cupboard door. David's fourteen-year-old brother, Jake, quickly left the kitchen and closed the door to his upstairs bedroom.

"Leave her alone," demanded little ten-year-old David. Dressed in pajamas, he stood defiantly between his parents, facing his father with a look of determination.

His father laughed. "Look at the little bastard standing up to protect his slut of a mother. Come on, little man, let's see what you're really made of."

Tom Diegert put up his fists and so did David. Tom flinched his left hand and smacked David's face with his right, snapping the young boy's head and spinning him onto the floor. Blood oozed from David's lips as his mother screamed for Tom to stop. Tom turned his rage on her, slapping her face and shoving her up against the counter.

"This is my house, and you're my wife, and I'll do whatever I goddamn want."

David stepped behind his father, kicking him in the knee. Tom spun and backhanded David across the face, sending him tumbling over a kitchen chair.

"You think you're a tough little guy, eh? Let's see how you like this!"

Tom opened the kitchen door and threw David out into the snow of a Minnesota winter night.

The door slammed, jolting David Diegert out of his recollection of that night over fifteen years ago.

Sheriff Michael Lowery crossed the room and stood before the chair to which Diegert was handcuffed. "It's your lucky day, son. Oh, I know you lost your job at the mini-mart and you beat up your boss for firing you."

"I didn't beat him up, Mr. Lowery," protested Diegert.

"He says you pushed him into a soda machine, but I convinced him not to press charges. You've been arrested, but you're not being charged. You're free to go."

Diegert looked at him untrustingly. "This is the lucky part?"

"Yup, it is," the lawman said as he unlocked the handcuffs. "But that's not all."

As the sheriff of Broward County handed Diegert a business card, he said, "Major Carl Winston, US Army recruiter. I suggest you go see him and consider serving your country instead of assaulting its citizens."

Sheriff Lowery took a seat next to Diegert. "Ya see, I know you've had it rough. I've responded to some of those domestic disputes at your house. But I also remember when you won States in wrestling. You were the first kid from Broward to ever go to States. I felt very proud down at the tournament."

Diegert looked at him, surprised to learn that he had made the trip all the way down to Minneapolis for the State Wrestling Tournament seven years ago. His father hadn't bothered.

Lowery continued, "I want to see you do well in life. Tell Major Winston I sent you, and he'll be very understanding. But, David, if you piss away this opportunity, you will not be walking out of here the next time you're arrested."

Diegert stood up and put the card in his shirt pocket. He hesitated before extending his hand to the sheriff. They shook hands and Diegert walked out into the cold winter night.

The walk home was windy, but the frigid, piercing air was not nearly as uncomfortable as the dynamics of the Diegert household. David had grown tall and strong, so his short, fat father now used his words rather than his fists to hurt him. Stepping straight into the kitchen of the small house, Diegert encountered his father's scorn before he'd even taken off his boots.

"Hey, dipshit, Jake told me you got fired from the mini-mart."

"Well, then, I'm glad I don't have to tell you."

"Don't you give me any of that wiseass shit. If I stop getting calls from them to tow away illegally parked cars, I'm blaming you."

Putting his coat on a hanger in the closet, Diegert replied, "The failure of your business is not my fault."

"Your maternal bitch isn't here to defend you, so you'd better watch your mouth."

Jake interjected, "Barley says you assaulted him and he had you arrested."

"I didn't beat him nearly enough. The charges were dropped and Lowery let me go."

Diegert passed by the kitchen table where his father and brother sat with their brown bottles of beer, a bag of chips, and two cigarettes smoldering in the ashtray. As David opened the fridge, Jake said, "Don't take any of our food."

With a disdainful smirk, David said, "I've got my own."

David stood at the kitchen counter making turkey sandwiches.

"What are you going to do without a job?" asked Tom.

"I don't know. Maybe Jake will let me help him sell drugs," David replied sarcastically.

Jake looked up, sneering at him as he raised his middle finger from his doughy fist.

"Now, dipshit," began his father, "it usually takes a person about two months to find a new job. So I want the next two months' rent up front."

David turned to look at his father with an incredulous expression.

"I'm also raising the rent, so you owe me two thousand dollars."

Pounding the kitchen counter and extending to his full height, David spun to face the table. With a sharp kitchen knife in his hand, David said, "What? A thousand dollars a month to shit in your toilet and sleep in the barn? No fuckin' way."

"Hey, you're lucky to have a roof over your head, and I hate the way your shit stinks, so if you want to live somewhere else, you go right ahead."

Pointing the knife at Jake, David barked, "What about him? He lives in the heat and eats whatever he wants. Why the hell doesn't he pay rent?"

"Look, don't make your problems seem like someone else's." Nodding toward Jake, Tom continued, "He has a very different financial situation from you, so fairness is not the issue."

Jake sniped in, "You ought to try running a business rather than being an employee."

"Yeah, well, most of the time I was with Sheriff Lowery, he was asking me about meth, oxy, and heroin. I don't think your secrets are safe anymore."

"What did you tell him?"

"I told him you're so fucking stupid that it would be real easy to set up a buy and have you show up with enough drugs to put you away for twenty years."

Jake's chair screeched across the floor as he bolted up from the table. David advanced quickly, pinning his brother backward over the sink. He brought the knife to Jake's throat. Jake grabbed his forearm, saying, "Really, you're going to cut me right here in front of Dad?"

Pressing the blade against the skin, David said, "Gladly."

The snap of a hammer being drawn back pulled their attention to their father, whose .38 revolver was pointed at David.

"Let him go. Get your food and get the fuck out of here."

David stepped back, drawing the blade across Jake's throat just enough to scare him. He moved to the counter to finish making his sandwiches.

Jake rubbed his neck, checking for blood, but remained at the sink. "If you snitch, you're dead, you little punk bastard."

The intensity of David's glare conveyed the complete absence of love between them. He put away his food, then slammed the fridge door. His father kept the gun trained on him while he put on his boots and coat. With his dinner in a plastic bag, Diegert left the house and headed for the barn.

David had a small bedroom up in the loft of the old barn out back on the property. The room was defined by two exterior walls and two hanging tarps, which together formed a small rectangle. Since his father used the building as a garage for working on cars, the odor of oil and gas permeated the floor and walls. A thermal sleeping bag and extra-thick blankets insulated Diegert on his single bed. Illumination was provided by a floor lamp, but there was no source of heat. Wearing a wool hat to bed, he often shivered himself to sleep, but it was better than sharing a room with his brother under the same roof as his father.

CHAPTER 2

The next morning, Diegert arrived at the Armed Forces recruiting center in Bemidji. Standing at the counter, Diegert observed a tall, strong-looking African American man dressed in fatigues approach.

"Hello, son, I'm Major Carl Winston," the man said with confidence as he offered his hand.

"David Diegert," was Diegert's simple reply as the two men instinctively assessed one another's strength while gripping hands.

"Oh, Sheriff Lowery gave me a call about you. I'm glad you're here."

Diegert cracked a slight smile as the major directed him around the counter and brought him into the recruiting center. The major's crisp, spicy cologne made Diegert wish he had showered that morning.

"Son, let's address my first question right now. Do you think you're strong enough to be in the US Army?"

"I think so."

The major stepped over to an open area with a metal bar suspended from the ceiling.

"The Army standard is ten pull-ups. Why don't you show me how many you can do?"

Diegert removed his coat, took off his heavy boots, and jumped up, grabbing the bar, pumping out twenty-two pull-ups.

"Well, that's a good place to start," said the major, whose look of surprise revealed he was truly impressed.

The two walked into an interview room and sat down on comfortable chairs. The major offered Diegert bottled water and then asked, "Why do you want to join the Army?"

"Whoa, I never said I did. The sheriff told me to come, and I knew he would call you."

"Alright, so Sheriff Lowery told me you lost your job at the mini-mart."

"So?"

"So what was your mission at the mini-mart?"

The major let the question linger. Diegert looked at him suspiciously.

"Whaddya mean, like exceptional customer service and bullshit like that?" asked Diegert.

The major smiled knowingly, nodding his head, and then asked, "And what is the mission of the US Army?"

Diegert looked at him but wasn't going to answer with something stupid.

Winston continued, "The mission of the US Army is to uphold and defend the Constitution of the United States and to protect this country from all enemies foreign and domestic."

Diegert was underwhelmed; everybody knew that. *Why the question,* he wondered.

"We achieve this mission through the actions of soldiers who go from being lost young people to dedicated military professionals capable of learning, achieving, and leading." Winston stood up and walked over to his desk. "All men need a mission, and there is no better training experience in the world than that of the US Army. We help you find within you the best you can be."

Diegert watched as the major turned from his desk with a picture frame in his hands.

"The Army challenges your sense of self and allows you to bring out the brave person who resides within you."

The major sat back down next to Diegert with the picture frame facedown in his hands.

"David, is there a brave person inside you?"

"Yeah."

"How do you know?"

Diegert stayed silent.

"How do you know what bravery is?"

Diegert stifled a quiver in his lips as he held the major's eyes and sought his answer.

"I'm not afraid."

"OK, you're defining what it is not, but do you possess the courage and resilience necessary to persevere in the face of physical and moral adversity?"

Diegert angled his face to Major Winston but held his gaze.

"I've seen young men like you, David, grow into capable, powerful warriors with integrity and values that represent the very best of our country. These men sat in the chair you're in and then became members of the most formidable fighting force in the world."

Winston spun the frame in his hands and showed Diegert a group of a dozen young men all dressed in combat uniforms with helmets and rifles. He saw the smiles on their faces and the spirit of union apparent in their camaraderie.

"These men are all members of the 1st Cavalry Division out of Fort Hood. This picture was taken upon their arrival in Afghanistan. It was sent to me by this man." Winston pointed to one of the guys, whose broad smile conveyed the pride he felt for what he was doing. "That's Joe Bortle. He came through here after being in a drunken bar fight and getting arrested. He was headed to jail until a judge gave him the same kind of choice Sheriff Lowery gave you. Now he's the sergeant of this squad, and they are one of the best units in Afghanistan. He sent me the picture and on the back he wrote, 'Major Winston, thanks for helping me make the right choice with the most important decision of my life.'"

The major looked squarely at Diegert.

"If there's a warrior in you, David, and I believe there is, then there's only one safe way to let him out, and that's to grow and develop within the US Army. Guys like you make the very best soldiers. You'll become a man of high character."

A smile spread across the young man's face; the recruiter had coaxed out a sprout of pride from the compost of Diegert's dreary life.

"Have you ever considered going to college?"

The question yanked Diegert from his thoughts of becoming a soldier. "Yeah, but it's too expensive."

"After serving two years of active duty, you'll be eligible for the GI Bill, which can pay your college expenses while you earn a bachelor's degree."

"Really? I serve two years and they pay for four years of college?"

"Well, you have to complete basic training, then begin active duty. You also have to qualify for the tuition payments. But if you're smart and serve well in your MOS, I'm sure you'll qualify."

"What's an MOS?"

"It's a military occupational specialty. It's basically a job in the Army. You said you were getting paid minimum wage at your retail job, right?"

"Yeah."

"As a soldier you will not only earn more than that in a salary, but you'll also receive a full compensation package that covers housing and health care, so you get to keep all the money you earn."

"How much will I make?"

"I would estimate your total compensation package would be worth thirty-five to forty thousand dollars."

"Really? That seems like a lot."

"If you're willing to serve your country, then it's worth it for your country to pay you. If you enlist in the next two days, there's also a fifteen-hundred-dollar signing bonus."

Diegert looked at him with suspicious but excited eyes.

"You can start filling out your information on this tablet."

Diegert went to work typing all his personal information into the small computer. As he typed, he started to feel the excitement of moving forward with his life. This was going to be exactly what he needed. When he was done, he handed the tablet back to Major Winston.

"Look, son," said the major calmly and clearly, "you go home and discuss this with your folks. You don't need them to sign anything. You're of legal age to make this decision yourself. But you are volunteering your life for several years, and I want you to talk to them. Call me in two days. If you tell me it's OK, I'll have you processed to Fort Benning, Georgia, to begin Basic Combat Training."

"How long does that take?"

"Basic is ten weeks, then you'll have fourteen weeks of Advanced Individual Training before you'll join the 1st Cavalry Division at Fort Hood in Texas."

"That's a lot of training."

"Wanting to become a soldier may feel natural to you, but it definitely takes a lot of training."

Diegert shook the major's hand with enthusiasm and left the office excited that he was going to become a soldier in the US Army.

CHAPTER 3

Standing outside the Triple Crown Diner, Diegert braced against the cold. His mother's shift ended at eleven p.m., but the single-digit temperatures made each minute as long as the icicles hanging from the gutters. Diegert was too excited to wait at home for her, and he wanted to tell her about the Army without his father and brother around. When her five-foot-eleven-inch frame stepped out the diner door, David approached as she wrapped her scarf around her neck and pulled a wool hat over her lustrous black hair.

"Hey, Mom."

"David, what are you doing here?"

"I wanted to surprise you and walk you home."

"Alright. I just never expected to see you here."

"That's why it's called a surprise."

They started to walk down the road.

"How was your shift tonight?" he asked.

"Same as always. Everyone talking about how cold it is, but they all want ice cream on their pie. I never expected to find you waiting out here for me."

"I've got something to tell you, Mom."

"Something good, I hope."

"I think it is. I'm going to join the Army."

Denise Diegert looked straight ahead, making no reply as she continued striding forward.

"Well, what do you think?"

"I can see why you'd think that's a good choice, but I hate the thought of you going to war."

"Just 'cause I'm joining the Army doesn't mean I'm going to war."

"We are at war all over the world. If you're in the Army, you're going to war."

"Oh, come on, Mom."

They turned the corner onto the dirt road on which they lived.

"I've got nothing to keep me here and no chance for a good job. The Army is going to pay me forty thousand dollars."

"I know there isn't much for you here, but I'll worry about you."

"There's just as much for you to worry about if I stay here. I'm going to call the recruiter tomorrow and commit. Then I'll be shipped out to Georgia for training in two days."

"Two days?"

"It's coincidence. A training class begins next week. It's OK. I'm ready to go."

David stopped walking and held his mother's mitten-covered hands.

"I'll worry about you, Mom."

She sniffed back tears, turning her head away.

"I'll worry about leaving you with Jake and Dad."

"Don't worry about me," she said as she released one hand and held onto the other as they resumed walking. "I have a wife's way of handling him, and even though he and your brother are criminals, I'm not worried about them."

"They're both pathetic jerks who don't deserve to have you in their lives."

"I love our home, David. I've put so much work into it, and it is the only home I've ever really known. When they're not around, it is such a lovely place for me to be."

"Yeah, thinking back on how it used to be and how much you've done to it, I can see why you love it. It's just too bad those two idiots live there too."

As they approached the small two-story house with its snow-covered roof, Denise said, "This house is where my heart lives."

Standing outside between the snowbanks of the driveway, David said, "I'm not saying anything to either of them. Please don't tell them about the Army, but will you take me to the bus station when I leave?"

She looked at him, her dark irises bathed in liquid emotion, then hugged him tightly. "Of course, David. Besides, I have a doctor's appointment in Bemidji on Thursday, so I'm going anyway. Your secret's safe with me, but I'm afraid my heartache may betray me."

"I trust you, Mom, and I love only you. What's with the doctor?"

"Oh, just some routine women's health checks, nothing to worry about."

David let her go and walked back to the barn as she opened the door and stepped into the kitchen.

***

The next morning, Diegert borrowed his mother's phone and got excited when he heard it ringing.

"Major Carl Winston speaking."

"Major Winston? It's David Diegert."

"Well, hello, son. I'm glad to hear back from you. Did you have a talk with your folks?"

"Yes, sir."

"And they're OK with your decision?"

"Yes, sir, they are."

After a brief pause, the major said, "OK, then I will process your application and have a bus ticket waiting for you at the Bemidji station to take you to Fort Benning day after tomorrow."

"Excellent, sir. Thank you, and I'm very much looking forward to getting started."

"Very well, David. Congratulations, and I look forward to hearing about your successful career in the US Army."

"Thank you, sir, thank you for giving me this chance."

"You're very welcome, but it's your country that'll be thanking you for the gift of your service."

After he hung up, Diegert thought about the gift of his service. He would be serving his country, and for the first time, he realized he would be helping others, not just doing things for himself. He felt a flash of pride, and a smile rose from his lips as he thought of himself as a patriot.

***

On the morning of his departure, Diegert had the car warming up as he waited in the driveway for his mother. When the kitchen door opened, his father stepped out into the zero-degree weather wearing dirty sweatpants, a gray T-shirt, and fuzz-lined moccasins. His eyes squinted as he descended the steps and moved toward the car. He rotated his fist and arm, and David pressed the button to lower the window.

"What the fuck you doin' in the car?"

"I'm taking Mom to a doctor's appointment in Bemidji."

"Get the fuck out. I never said she could use the car."

"Look, Dad, I'm taking her. She asked me to, and that's all there is to it."

"Fuckin' bullshit. You can't just use the car."

"Dad, you're gonna freeze out here."

"Fuck you. You sound like your mother, like a scared little bitch."

Denise Diegert stepped out of the house and was intercepted by Tom as she attempted to cross the driveway to the car.

David exited the car and stood by the driver's door.

Squeezing Denise's arm, Tom said, "I didn't hear anything about a doctor's appointment. What's wrong? Why are you going to the doctor?"

Without struggling against Tom's grasp, Denise stood with stoic resolve and said calmly, "I have to see the gynecologist. It's very typical for women to have examinations from time to time, and I would appreciate it if you would let me go."

"Fuck that. You're not going anywhere. We don't have health insurance to pay for this, and unless you're really sick, you're not going."

David grew angry listening to his father's foolishness. He crossed the driveway, grabbed his father's hand, and pulled it off his mother's arm. Tom Diegert swung, striking David in the jaw with a solid right. David's head snapped and he stumbled back against the car. Tom took a fighter's stance, but his self-confidence evaporated since he had just picked a fight with the 180-pound State Wrestling Champ of Minnesota. In spite of his misgivings, Tom's bravado ruled the moment. "Come on, you pussy, let's see what you're made of."

David stepped away from the car and moved toward his pathetic opponent. With lightning skill, David shot low, going to one knee, wrapping up his father's legs and putting him on his back in two seconds. He flipped his dad's legs, holding them perpendicular to the ground so that Tom was stuck on his back like a turtle. With an arm lock, David retained control of both legs, which allowed him to see the fear and the fury in his father's eyes.

"Let him go."

The command came from Jake. Turning, David looked right into the barrel of a Ruger SR22 pistol.

"Let him go and stand up."

David complied, letting the turtle's legs fall into the snow. He stood up with his hands in the air.

"Dad, are you OK?" blurted Jake.

Tom Diegert had to roll over onto his stomach, struggle to his hands and knees, and pull on Jake's outstretched arm in order to stand up.

Jake was so pissed he started shouting at David while pointing the pistol. "You fucking bitch, you little fucking bastard, how dare you treat him like that? You are such a prick. I can't believe you have the balls to treat Dad like shit."

Jake's movements were as unhinged as his words, and he was handling the gun as if it were a toy. He stepped closer and closer, continually waving the gun in David's direction. Backed up against the car, David struck his brother's arm and pushed him hard in the chest. As Jake awkwardly fell back, a shot rang out from the Ruger. The unaimed bullet went wild, striking Tom Diegert in the left hip.

Tom fell to the ground, shocked by the pain and the sight of his own blood. Jake stared with horror at the blood splatters in the snow. He looked at the gun in his hand with utter disbelief. Getting up, he shouted at David, "You goddamn, fucking idiot! Look what you've done. You fucking shot Dad."

"You're holding the gun, genius."

Jake swung his arm into full extension, pointing the gun at David's head. "Die, fucker."

Denise Diegert stepped in front of the gun, putting herself between Jake and David. "Stop it, Jake." She turned to David and said, "Get in the car." David stepped around to the driver's door. Denise lowered Jake's arm, calmly looking him in the eye. "You need to help your father. Take him to the firehouse and have one of his buddies patch him up. I'm leaving with David, and I'll be back in two hours. You need to act now."

Nodding his head, Jake turned to his father, who was groaning in the driveway and clutching his bleeding hip. In spite of his condition, he shouted out at David, "You fucking son of a bitch. You're the son of that bitch!" He pointed at Denise as she opened the car door and climbed in. "You fucking shot me, you shithead."

David, looking over the roof of the car, shook his head at the stupidity of the two idiots as they struggled to get up and make their way into the house. He opened the car door, got in, and backed the car out of the driveway.

CHAPTER 4

On the drive to Bemidji, Denise shook in her seat, reacting to the violence that had just exploded in her family.

"Is he going to be OK?" she asked David.

"He's a tough old lump of shit; he'll be OK. Besides, the gun was only a .22."

"What about the police?"

"I think it's pretty unlikely either of those pseudo felons is going to call the cops."

"But they could do it just to make things difficult for you."

Diegert did not reply as he considered that Jake and his father might very well try to use this against him. He took comfort in the fact that they had no idea where he was really going.

"Mom, you've got to promise me you won't tell them anything about the Army."

"I won't, but eventually they're going to ask about you."

"Don't wait for them to ask. Tell them something stupid, like I was so upset that I ran away. Don't let them know that you know where I am."

"You think they'll buy that?"

"I'll write a note, and you can tell them you found it in the car. It'll keep their anger on me. I'm also going to leave my phone in the car."

"But I want to be able to talk to you."

"I'll get a new phone in Georgia and we can text."

"We can't talk?"

"We'll see, but I'll text you as soon as I get a new phone."

Parking the car in the lot of a convenience store, David scowled at the sight of the Bemidji bus station. In any other city, the station would only be considered a bus stop. Using the back of an envelope he found in the glove box, David wrote a note. He left his mom in the car to read what he'd written to his father and Jake as he walked toward the convenience store.

Dear Dad and Jake,

I'm so sorry for the way I've acted lately, and I apologize for the incident that led to Dad being shot. I know forgiveness is hard, but I ask you to search your hearts for some measure of understanding of how bad I feel about the way things have turned out. I'm going away, I don't know where, but I won't be seeing any of you again. Good-bye.
David

David picked up his ticket in the convenience store, then came back to the car to find his mom crying.

"David, your note made me so sad. I can't believe our family has disintegrated like this."

"Mom, I just wrote the note to keep them from figuring out that I'm in the Army. I'll see you again, and when I do, I'll be a soldier in the US Army. Now give me a hug." She leaned over and embraced him, but the finality of his note left her feeling like this good-bye was for a lot longer than either of them knew.

They didn't have much longer to wait before the bus pulled up to the curb in front of them. There were only two other passengers waiting to board. After getting his duffel bag out of the trunk, David embraced his mother with all the strength of his love.

"I'm trying to be brave for you, David, but I'm gonna miss you."

"Mom, you just did the bravest thing I've ever seen. You stepped in front of Jake, willing to take a bullet for me."

Denise gasped as she averted her gaze to the ground, saying, "David, I did what any loving mother would do."

"You did a lot more than that, and I will never forget it. You saved my life. You also did a great job raising me, and now it's time to show the world who your son is."

"I'm so proud of you, David. I love you so much."

"I love only you, Mom, and I will carry that with me everywhere I go."

Diegert saw the bus driver waving his arm. He kissed his mother on the forehead, slung the bag's strap over his shoulder, and walked backward to the bus. Through the window, Diegert saw his mother still standing at the rear of the car as the bus pulled away and moved down the road.

CHAPTER 5

Twenty-four weeks of training in Fort Benning, Georgia, earned David Diegert the rank of private first class. He distinguished himself by achieving expert marksmanship on the firing range with rifles and handguns, as well as mastery of Level IV in Modern Army Combatives. Diegert paid attention to his instructors and not only learned to become an effective and efficient fighter, but he also embodied the Army's creed of selfless service and teamwork. Now stationed at Fort Hood, outside Austin, Texas, he was a soldier in the 1st Cavalry Division. An enlisted infantryman, whose skills and abilities were broad enough to fulfill many different roles in the Army's vast network of needs.

Through texts with his mother, he learned that Tom did not see a doctor, and although the wound had healed, the slug remained in his hip. The limp in his gait was worse in the mornings, but whenever he was in pain, he had David to blame. Surprisingly, Tom did not let Jake burn the note that David had written them; instead, he folded it carefully and kept it in a drawer. David wondered if it was sentiment or a hope for vengeance that caused his father to keep it.

"Private David Diegert," shouted Sergeant Jesse Rodriguez from the entrance of the barracks.

"Yes, Sergeant," snapped Diegert as he jumped off his bunk and stood at attention.

"Get over here, Diegert. I've got something important for you."

Diegert quickly hightailed it over to his sergeant, who led him through the barracks door.

"Captain Corcoran wants to see you. Head over to his office right now."

Bursting with excitement, Diegert briskly walked to the captain's office. He had applied for Ranger School and was hoping the captain was going to tell him that he'd been accepted. In the captain's office, Diegert stood at attention.

"At ease, soldier," said the dark-haired thirty-something captain. Looking up from a file on his desk, he continued, "David . . . Diegert, you've been here at Fort Hood for four weeks. How do you like Texas?"

"I like it, sir. I love the 1st Cavalry."

"Good, that's what you're supposed to say, and I appreciate a man who knows his role."

"Yes, sir."

"Do you know why I've called you here today?"

"No, sir."

"Care to guess?"

"Well, sir, I did apply to Ranger School, and I'm hoping you're going to tell me I've been selected."

The captain stepped from behind his desk and paced over to Diegert.

"Private Diegert, I'm afraid that is not the case. You are being deployed to Afghanistan."

What? When? Why? The questions raced through his brain, but he had learned not to give voice when receiving orders from an officer.

"You're shipping out tonight, and it's just you."

"Just me? Why . . . ?" The statement burst forth before Diegert could restrain it. "Sorry, sir."

Captain Corcoran stepped closer to Diegert.

"We're the rear detachment for our company in Afghanistan. One of our squads suffered a loss, and through the individual replacement program, you are being sent to backfill the open position."

"Yes, sir."

Stepping out of Diegert's personal space, the captain continued. "You'll be joining a squad from the 1st Cavalry. Fellow soldiers who were stationed here at Fort Hood just like you. You are the only one going, but don't make it sound like we're abandoning you like a lost puppy. Get your shit together and report to transport at 1600."

"Yes, sir."

He sent a text to his mother, letting her know he was being deployed to Afghanistan.

Thirty-six hours later, the hot, dry environment of central Texas seemed like an oasis compared to the even hotter, drier, dustier conditions at Kandahar Airfield in Afghanistan. The heat was oppressive, and the fine sand in the air started to clog David's nose with silica snot.

CHAPTER 6

Private First Class David Diegert reported to his support squad in Afghanistan, where he was immediately treated like the Fucking New Guy and given the shittiest jobs of this unique MOS. Led by Lieutenant Alvin Prescott, this group of enlisted general service soldiers supported the operations of a Special Forces unit referred to as the Syringes.

Opium is to Afghanistan as corn is to Iowa. Right away Diegert became aware of the squad's role in the effort to sustain the progress that had been made in Afghanistan. The squad ran ten tons of opium a month. They moved it onto base, packed it in mislabeled crates, and smuggled it to the United States on return flights of supply planes privately contracted by the Department of Defense. The organization went right up the chain of command, although none of the activities would ever appear in an official report. Little green men like Diegert and the rest of the enlisted just followed orders. Hush money kept their mouths shut, while all the cargo was being transferred to private contractors. The flights didn't return to military bases but to corporate fulfillment centers where the illicit contraband found its way to market.

The Special Forces guys, in spite of all their combat capacity, realized you couldn't build peace if you kept shooting people. So they'd set up the opium network to appease the local tribal leaders. The opium got to market, the locals got paid, and the Syringes made money as the middlemen. The Afghans who were helped became allies. The illicit trade kept the peace, which was the main objective of the entire mission. The rise of heroin on American streets should have surprised no one.

For Diegert, the whole thing was such a disappointment. All the training in the Army focused on mission as defined by combat objectives and enemies overtaken. This was illegal bullshit, appeasing the enemy rather than defeating them. He hated his role as a drug mule supplying opium to the United States, which would end up as heroin being sold by dealers like his brother, Jake! As Diegert contemplated this dissonance of purpose, he heard his name.

"Hey, Diegert," shouted Lieutenant Alvin Prescott.

Diegert stopped packing a crate with burlap bags of fresh opium to see his jerk of a superior officer standing by the entrance of the hangar in which they processed the Afghans' most important export. Prescott motioned for Diegert to come over to him.

"Yes, sir?"

"I just got done inspecting your weapon."

"I'm not due for inspection for two more days."

"Shut up, I can inspect anything at any time, and your weapon was insufficiently cleaned and lubricated."

"That's bullshit."

Stepping forward and looking up at Diegert, Prescott emphasized his point.

"Don't you get insolent with me or the shit you're in will just get deeper. I'm fining you three thousand dollars."

Diegert couldn't believe his ears. This little idiotic officer was using his power to make up for his shortcomings as a person. His latest gambit was to extract outrageous fines from his soldiers' drug hush money for infractions of military protocol. Mixing the "business" and the military was totally wrong, but his greed knew no bounds. Several guys had paid the fines, and this had emboldened their hollow leader to expand his extortions.

"You can't do that," replied Diegert.

"You want to make it five thousand? I know exactly how much money you've got, and if you can't meet minimum 'Army Strong' standards, then a monetary sanction will get your attention."

Diegert stuck his finger into Prescott's thin chest, saying, "You can't mix the business with the Army."

Slapping Diegert's hand aside, Prescott launched into a tirade. "You do not speak to me like that, and how dare you touch me? I'll have you in the stockade so fast you'll think one of those sandstorms sucked you into your cell. I'm your superior officer, and you will submit to my orders and abide by my discipline."

Diegert's boiling temper was not extinguished by Prescott's salivary spray. He pushed Prescott's chest with both hands, forcing the surprised lieutenant to stumble. Diegert grabbed the man by the front of his shirt and punched him twice in the face as he swung the lieutenant's body and tossed him to the ground. Prescott's torso skidded to a stop in the sand and he struggled to rise.

"Hey, you can't . . ."

Diegert didn't wait for the rest of the statement before he front kicked him in the chest, sprawling him onto his back. Grabbing him again by his shirt, Diegert hauled him up off the ground. Prescott swung his fist, striking Diegert in the head with such little force it stunned Diegert how weak this man was. Diegert spun Prescott around, kicked his legs out from under him, and slammed his face into the sandy ground. A group of soldiers started to gather.

Diegert brought his face down to Prescott's and growled, "You are a prick, and I will not take your shit."

Having stood up and started to walk away, Diegert was tackled by four military police officers. The MPs cuffed him and took him immediately to the stockade. Prescott stood up and brushed himself off while limping to medical. None of the soldiers under his command stepped up to help him.

***

Captain Dylan Reeves from the Army Judge Advocate General's Corps was assigned to serve as Diegert's lawyer. He conducted the requisite defendant interview in Diegert's stockade cell.

"So, reading this report doesn't reveal much for me to use in your defense. You wanna tell me why you beat the shit out of your commanding officer?"

Diegert looked at the clean-cut captain, but the tone of the question made him feel like he was not talking to someone who was on his side. Diegert knew that ratting on the opium operation was not an option. If he spoke against them, the Syringes would see to it that he was KIA in a couple of days. That's what happened to Emmitt Stilchus, the guy he replaced. The official report listed his death as the result of an improvised explosive device, which was true, but the Syringes set up that IED when Stilchus stupidly told everyone he was going to blow the whistle if he didn't get more money.

"The situation between Lieutenant Prescott and me was a personal issue."

"Were you and your superior officer having an inappropriate sexual relationship?"

"No!" replied Diegert, bristling at the accusation within the question.

"If you're not going to tell me about the incident, then how about you tell me a little bit about yourself."

"Like what?"

"Well, I know you're from Broward County in the northern part of Minnesota, you have a black belt in karate, you were a state champion wrestler, and you've earned skill level four in Modern Army Combatives. You're assigned to the 1st Cavalry Division out of Fort Hood, and back in high school you were referred to as 'Tonto.'"

Diegert's annoyed expression suddenly turned more agitated at the use of his hated nickname.

"Back in the day, you didn't like that name, did ya? Now you'd beat up anybody who called you that, wouldn't ya?"

Diegert felt the pain of his heritage once again tearing at his heart. His mother's mix of white and Native American blood made her an outcast of both the white and Ojibwa cultures of northern Minnesota. Even though his mother had married a white man, making Diegert only a quarter native, he was still referred to as an Ojib-white by the kids in school. They constantly taunted him, reminding him to stay in his place.

Reeves continued. "It's amazing what you can find out about someone with a Web search. How about you tell me a little bit more about your family? What was your father like?"

Diegert's contempt was hard to hide as he recalled the fool who was his father. Tom Diegert was short, fat, bald, perpetually dirty, and regularly drunk. He ran a tow-truck business in a rural area where everyone had four-wheel drives. He treated his wife like shit, making worse their mismatched marriage. She was taller than he, lean with long black hair and an exotic face. To Tom Diegert, she was the squaw he married so she wouldn't be homeless in the dead of winter. Tom Diegert had been in the Army as a young man, and even though he hadn't done shit with the rest of his life, he was proud of his military service. For Diegert to tell his father that he'd been dishonorably discharged was really going to suck, especially since Tom didn't even know he was in the Army.

"My father is a proud military veteran; he'll be angry with me if I'm dishonorably discharged."

"I could see that being uncomfortable. What branch of the service was he in?"

"The Army."

"Where was he stationed?"

"I don't know."

"What was his rank?"

"I don't know that either."

"So did you and your dad discuss your commitment to serve?"

"No."

Reeves sat quietly, waiting for more information, which Diegert did not provide.

"How about your mom?"

Diegert's mother was the person he admired most in the world—the one person he truly loved. She was hardworking, dedicated, and thoughtful. She had issues with fear and lack of self-confidence, remnants of growing up in foster homes after her own mother committed suicide when Denise was twelve. Despite her difficulties, she showed David a mother's love and made sure the home was a comfortable sanctuary for her second son.

"My mom is a beautiful, loving woman who always puts others before herself."

"Sounds lovely. Was the marriage between her and your father a happy one?"

"Not really."

Again Reeves let the silence linger, but Diegert added nothing.

"You know the process of getting to know someone benefits from explanations that are longer than just two words."

"Oh really?" was Diegert's only reply.

Reeves grew impatient. "Any brothers or sisters?"

His brother, Jake, was just like his father, short, loud, and focused on himself. He played football, which his dad loved, followed, and supported. He, too, was a half-breed but crossed the line and hung with the cool kids by being their drug dealer. At first, he'd sold stolen beer, then pot and pills, and then heroin and crystal meth. He made sure David's life remained miserable. Often when Diegert was working at his job at the minimart, Jake and his friends would smash jars and make a mess in an aisle just so they could laugh at him while he cleaned it up.

"My brother, Jake, is a jerk. I don't talk to him very often."

"Sibling rivalry?"

"He doesn't have anything I desire."

"How about growing up? Was he someone you could trust and confide in?"

"Definitely not."

"I see. Why did you join the Army?'

"For the college benefits. I want to do my active duty, get out, and go to school on the GI Bill."

"Wouldn't a student loan be a better idea?"

Diegert tilted his head back and cast an unappreciative look upon his lawyer.

"Anyway—I don't see a sense of patriotism in you, a desire to serve your country, or the motivation to fulfill a family tradition. The Army is simply a means to an end for you, and I think you're now finding that the role of a soldier requires a lot more work and sacrifice than any semester in college. What do you want to study in school?"

"Math. I'm pretty good at math."

"I'm glad to hear it, but I have to tell you that your defense is not adding up to an acquittal."

Reeves watched Diegert's face as the statement sank in.

"You will most likely be convicted of this crime and dishonorably discharged. I don't believe Lieutenant Prescott is pressing any additional charges, and the final sentencing is up to the judge."

"As my lawyer, what do you advise me to do?"

Reeves tapped his pencil on the table while contemplating his reply.

"I don't think you're committed to the military life," said Reeves as he slid his papers into his briefcase, stood up, and placed his JAG officer's cap securely on his head. He crossed the small space of Diegert's cell, then looked back as he stood in the doorway to say, "I see your future outside the US Army, but I'll see you at the court-martial on Monday."

CHAPTER 7

The courts at the military base at Kandahar Airfield in Afghanistan were located in the commandant's area, where legal proceedings were only conducted on Mondays and Fridays. After an uncomfortable weekend in the stockade, where the ventilation was so bad that the body odor rivaled that of a bag of hockey pads left in a hundred-degree car trunk, Diegert sat quietly with Captain Reeves as they waited for the court-martial proceedings to begin. The earlier consultation with his lawyer did nothing to raise Diegert's confidence; nevertheless, he had to move forward with this unfortunate conclusion to his short military career.

Diegert shuffled in his seat and quietly ground his fist into his palm, feeling the regret of his actions as his thoughts moved on to what lay ahead. At first, being in the Army had been so cool, training at Fort Benning and being stationed at Fort Hood were both good times, but in Afghanistan, everything was totally fucked up.

"Private David Terrance Diegert," shouted the MP serving as court bailiff. The lawyer and the accused entered the room, which was used for many functions but today served as a court of military justice. Seated behind an eight-foot folding table was Colonel Reginald Hayes, fulfilling the role of judge. Next to him was the plaintiff, Lieutenant Alvin Prescott, with his lawyer, Captain Patricia Stokes.

At Judge Hayes's direction, Captain Stokes presented her case, which implicated Diegert as insubordinate to his superior officer before violently assaulting him and causing bodily injury. Captain Dylan Reeves's presentation recounted the incident and concluded with an admission of Diegert's guilt and an apology. With nothing more from either member of counsel, Judge Hayes pronounced Diegert guilty as charged and commenced with the process of dishonorably discharging him from the US Army.

Returning to the stockade, Diegert had time to think about how much it sucked to be powerless in a system that allowed the Special Forces personnel to do what they wanted while sidelining the enlisted who spoke out, took action, or threatened to disrupt the status quo. Diegert thought about how the Army had been a new beginning where people didn't judge him for what they heard about his family or thought about Indians. But now he was learning that it didn't matter who or what you were if you were one of the powerless. People in power would fuck you over without even meaning to. He had no idea what he was going to do now.

***

Back at Fort Hood, Diegert completed the processing of his discharge by being informed of all the privileges he would not have. No GI Bill, no outplacement employment assistance, no veteran's benefits. He was also disallowed to own a firearm, take a position teaching in a public school, or become a police officer or security agent. A dishonorable discharge was almost as bad as a felony conviction. He took a bus from the base with his stuff in a duffel bag and got a room in a cheap place on the outskirts of Austin called the Single Star Motel.

In the motel room, Diegert dumped out his duffel bag, put his clothes in the dresser and closet, set his toothbrush and shaving stuff in the bathroom, and returned to the bed. Lying there were three items he had received from his mother a few years back. She had acknowledged his eighteenth birthday as his coming-of-age day, and to her it signified him becoming a man. She marked it by presenting him with three gifts that were part of the ritual for young Ojibwa men who were coming of age. A ritual Diegert had never heard of or expected. The first gift was a leather amulet on a leather necklace. The necklace was beaded with colors that signified the seven values of the Ojibwa: wisdom, love, respect, bravery, honesty, humility, and truth. The amulet was a circular piece of leather. On the front, the top half was white and the bottom dark black. In the center, spanning both the top and the bottom halves, was the imprint of a human foot. The back contained an Ojibwa inscription, which stated: *A man must travel through darkness to find the light.*

The second item was a hunting knife. The knife had an antler handle, a six-inch blade, and a leather sheath. The blade had a razor-sharp edge and point. The back side of the blade had serrated teeth extending from the hilt for an inch and a half, and the rest was a sharpened edge designed for scraping and planing. Inscribed on the blade in Ojibwa was the phrase: *The blade is both a tool and a weapon; let it work for you and defend you.*

The final item was a woven wool blanket his mother had made for him on her loom. Its intricate pattern of stripes and diamonds was in tones of brown, yellow, and red. In the top corner of the blanket, she had embroidered an Ojibwa mother's prayer: *Your mother's love will be with you always, covering and comforting you no matter where you journey in life.*

She'd presented these gifts to him at home while his father and brother were out getting drunk at the Moose Jaw Inn. Of the three gifts, Diegert thought the knife was really cool. The amulet and blanket were nice, but he really didn't care about them. After presenting him with the gifts, his mother had begun to tell him about Ojibwa customs for young men coming of age. She said, "David, these gifts symbolize the transition you are now making from a boy to a man. They can help you on your journey to find your purpose in life. You can find your spirit through a vision quest." Diegert had never heard his mother speak of the Ojibwa customs before, and it freaked him out that she suggested he find meaning in life by communicating with a spirit. She continued, "Ojibwa young men let the spirit in and it guides them to their life's destiny. As an Anishinaabe, one of the good beings, you can let the spirit help you live a full and rewarding life."

Diegert's brow furrowed and his eyes narrowed. *An Amish-nobby? What was she talking about?* Diegert looked at his mother with a sidelong glance as he thought that maybe she had gotten into some of Jake's drugs. His mother smiled at him as she placed a mocha maple chocolate cake, his favorite, on the table. Her baking was exquisite, and Diegert's smile returned as she cut a piece of birthday cake, saying, "I want you to have the very best life, and a vision quest seeking your Ojibwa spirit will get you there."

"Thanks," said Diegert as she handed him the cake.

His mother, who was always the most practical and down-to-earth person in his life, was now speaking of spirits and journeys and the meaning of life. She was also saying that happiness lay in his Ojibwa spirit. In fact, Diegert felt the Ojibwa part of him was the root of all his problems; the ostracism, the taunting and fighting, and the just plain being ignored by all the cool kids were because of being an Ojib-white.

He looked at his mother. "Thanks for the cake and the presents, I really like the knife, but an Ojibwa spirit quest, I don't think so. Why are you dumping all this on me now?" Denise Diegert slid the fork out of her mouth and began to chew a bite of cake. She placed her gaze directly on the eyes of her son, who continued speaking. "Having Ojibwa blood in me is the worst part of my life. People in town, kids at school, and even the Indians on the reservation all hate me and you for being half-breeds. I hate the Ojibwa part of me, and I'm certainly not going to seek out any Indian spirits to guide me. I want them to stay the hell away from me."

Swallowing her cake, Denise began, "You're young and you need time to realize the importance of accepting who you are and embracing those things which make you unique."

Scoffing, Diegert said, "Did you memorize that from a lousy self-help book, because it sounds like psychobabble bullshit. I don't need a spirit to guide me, and I'm sure not impressed with where the spirit led you. So if this is the best an Indian quest can do for me, you can fucking forget it."

Diegert never swore at his mother, but the sudden infusion of Ojibwa culture and the lifelong pent-up frustration at the bigotry and prejudice he lived with brought out feelings he had long suppressed.

His mother replied, "I'm sorry you feel that way, but if you don't seek the spirit with respect, it will find you in your darkest hour, where you will then be compelled to face the spirit's wrath."

"Oh yeah, right. Now the spirit is a great big threat." Diegert grabbed the knife off the table. "If the spirit is going to come get me, I'm not going to be unarmed." With his new weapon in his hand, Diegert walked out of the house and into the night.

Recalling all this discourse with his mom, Diegert found his motel room to be a claustrophobic cell. He caught a bus for downtown. Austin was a city alive with diverse young people, techies, bikers, college students, musicians, artists, and especially weirdos who kept the city as it wanted to be. Whoever you were, there was a bar for you in Austin. Diegert entered the Dark Horse feeling like the name reflected his place in life. The ten-dollar cover got you all the honky-tonk music you needed from the band at the back of the bar. The bouncer was huge, six eight, and had to weigh over three hundred pounds. The big man smiled and told Diegert to have a good time. At the bar, Diegert took a stool, spun around, and leaned against the bar, looking at all the country western people. Guys were wearing Stetsons, Wrangler jeans, and Frye boots. Diegert wondered if the bar had a stable out back for their horses. The women did the big-hair thing with the tight, checkered blouses, and several of them had barely enough denim to cover their asses. Having not seen any women while in Afghanistan, Diegert literally couldn't avert his eyes from the feminine beauty on display at the Dark Horse.

"Hey."

He nearly fell off his stool when a female voice startled him out of his staring. She spoke as he turned his head.

"The ten dollars covers the band. If you want a titty show, you're going to have to go down the street to one of the strip clubs."

Diegert spun his stool around, placing his forearms on the bar. She was cute and feisty, and since it was still early, she was energetic and ready for a busy night of tending bar.

"You want a Star?"

Diegert looked at her like she was a third-grade teacher handing out stickers.

Realizing he didn't comprehend, she asked, "You want a Lone Star beer?"

Chuckling at his foolishness, Diegert replied, "Sure, thanks."

Placing the tall brown bottle on the bar, she said, "I haven't seen you here before."

"I've never been here."

"You don't seem like a cowboy. What kind of pickup do you drive?"

"I don't have a truck."

"You're definitely the only guy in here who'll say that."

Diegert tilted his head and smiled at the precocious brunette who held his eye contact with confidence. "What's your name?" he asked her.

"I'm working, and I'm not here to flirt."

"Of course not, I just asked for your name?"

"Taurus . . . like the bull."

"That's your last name?" Diegert asked hesitantly.

"Uh-huh," she said with a nod to the obvious.

"Well, what's your first name?"

"Collette," she said.

"Collette Taurus." The instant he said the name, she burst out laughing and several patrons at the bar started cracking up at the guy using such an intimate term in such a public place. Diegert, realizing he had just been played for a fool, retorted, "My name's Mike."

The bartender replied, "Well, I wasn't asking, but if you're going to tell me that your last name is 'Hunt,' then you really are a cunt, and that makes me especially disinterested in you."

The embarrassing rejection was abruptly interrupted when furniture and bodies crashed to the floor at the entrance of the bar. All attention turned to the fracas between the bouncer and some rowdies at the front door.

The big man, who had been so friendly to Diegert, had pushed one of a group of four guys to the floor, knocking over a table and chairs. Two of the others were punching and kicking the giant, with each blow to the face producing a spray of blood. The bouncer went down, the guy who was pushed was helped up, and the four leather-clad men entered the bar, led by the tallest man, who wore a sleeveless black leather vest over a white T-shirt. The leader sported a gray Van Dyke around his mouth and chin. Like the others, he looked a little too old for such delinquent behavior.

The commotion brought the manager from an office behind the bar. A thin man with wide eyes and a nervous look surveyed the scene and muttered, "Not again." Diegert watched as the uptight man struggled to help the bleeding bouncer to the kitchen.

People were filing into the bar without being checked or paying the cover. The four rowdies took a table in the back corner of the bar, and the feisty bartender was now playing cocktail waitress and taking their orders. When she returned behind the bar, Diegert said to her, "I bet you wouldn't have come to get my order if I sat over there."

"Damn right, you're not Igor Dimitrov . . . Russian mobster," she said while mixing the drinks and opening the beer bottles on her tray.

Diegert gazed over, observing the muscular silver-haired man, dressed up as a biker with his gang of goons, and remarked, "You'd think he owns this place."

"Better than that, he owns the loan that got this place started." The bartender hefted the tray to her shoulder and left to deliver the Russians their drinks.

The nervous manager came through the kitchen door. He smoothed his shirt and adjusted his glasses as he stepped toward the bar. Diegert called out to him.

"Excuse me."

The manager stepped over to Diegert.

"I know things are happening fast here tonight, but it looks like you could use a man at the door."

They both turned to see a crowd of confused people entering the door while not paying a cover charge. Diegert turned to the manager and offered his hand.

"David Diegert."

Taking his hand, the manager introduced himself.

"Terry Buscetti. Do you have any experience?"

"Yup."

"If you steal any of the cover money, I'll have those guys who roughed up the other guy beat the shit out of you."

Diegert didn't avert his eyes as he said, "I won't steal from you, but you've got to pay me thirty dollars an hour to sit at that door."

"That's a lot."

"What happened to that other guy will never happen to me. That door will be secure."

"Come on back, and I'll give you a shirt and you can get started."

Back in the kitchen, the big guy's facial wounds were still bleeding. Buscetti said, "His ride is on its way."

Buscetti pulled a black polo shirt with the bar's horsehead logo from a hanger. "Put this on and remember it's ten dollars per person."

As he was leaving the kitchen, Diegert stepped over to the injured man and patted him on the shoulder. "Those are some nasty wounds."

"That fucker had brass knuckles."

They looked at each other as they searched for words they could not find. Diegert gently slapped him on the shoulder again before he left the kitchen.

At the door, Diegert did the job and collected the money without incident. At one point, the bartender, on her way to the Russian table, swung by the door to say, "You've got to be brain damaged to be taking this job."

Diegert just smiled and thought she was probably right, but he needed a job, and this one would do.

For the next two weeks, he was at the door every night and eventually learned that the bartender's name was Tracy Vandersmith. She was a premed student at UT and never lingered when her shift was done. She gave Diegert a ride home one rainy night, and when she saw he was living in a cheap motel, she shouted at him out the car window, "We work together, that's it. That's all it will ever be. You got that?"

Diegert's legs were soaked by the spray off her tires as she pulled away.

CHAPTER 8

The High Note Drifters commanded a fifteen-dollar cover charge at the Dark Horse. Igor Dimitrov and three guys from his entourage were not charged as Diegert cleared the way for them to enter the bar. As Dimitrov passed, he stopped and told Diegert, "Uri Pestonach was supposed to meet us here. You know which one he is, right?" Drawing his finger across his forehead, Dimitrov continued, "The guy has just one eyebrow." Diegert nodded. "Since he's late, I do not want you to let him in."

Diegert's gaze centered on the big Russian's eyes. Dimitrov produced a hundred-dollar bill and handed it to Diegert, repeating, "Don't let Uri in."

Diegert signaled his compliance, accepting the hundred.

Thirty minutes later, Uri Pestonach arrived, pushed his way through the line, and proceeded to enter. Diegert had to place his hand on the guy's chest to impede his entrance. The furrowed forehead and narrowed eyelids were overshadowed by his unibrow, but they projected the man's displeasure with being handled. Standing in front of Uri, Diegert tried to explain.

"Sorry, man, you can't come in tonight."

"What the fuck is this?" bellowed the insolent Russian.

"Tonight you are not allowed in. Perhaps another night would be better for you."

Uri slapped Diegert's hand from his chest, and his incredulous expression found its voice.

"You can't stop me from coming in, and if you're worried about the fifteen dollars, you can fuck yourself."

Diegert saw Uri's hand slip into his pocket, and he watched as the angry man withdrew his hand in a fist. The dull yellow of the brass caught Diegert's eye as the fist was thrust at his head. Diegert tipped his head back as the fist blazed by. He grabbed the man's forearm, twisted it behind his back, and pressed on the median nerve. The pressure on the nerve forced Uri's fist to open. Diegert swept the man's hand, stripping the brass knuckles off his fingers. He shoved the man forward into a cigarette machine. The angry man awkwardly spun around to face Diegert, who now had the brass knuckles on his fist and a *fuck you* smirk on his face.

Diegert dropped into a balanced stance and gave no sign of retreat as he squared off against the Russian, who was now armed with only his skin. The patrons at the door formed a ring around the two combatants. Diegert said, "You can leave now and come back another night."

The Russian's angry expression showed the fear of embarrassment as his situation had become the center of attention for a growing crowd. He circled Diegert, seeing the brass knuckles on his enemy who seemed to be without fear.

Diegert stood up out of his fighting stance. "You are free to go." He extended his hand in front of him, motioning toward the door.

Uri's brow formed into a *V* as his angry eyes peered at Diegert. Realizing the Russian wouldn't be taking the gentleman's way out, Diegert dropped his right foot back and brought his left hand up. Uri put his weight into a swing with his right. Diegert leaned back and grabbed the big guy's arm, pulling him off balance while delivering a bone-crushing strike with the brass knuckles to the temple of the belligerent bar crasher. Uri's consciousness vacated his brain as his bulk fell to the floor. Diegert grabbed the back of the big guy's leather coat and dragged him outside.

Igor Dimitrov was stunned to see how quickly his best muscle had gone down at the hands of Diegert. The economy of movement and the lethality of force the young man displayed impressed the mobster. He couldn't recall ever seeing a one-punch knockout in a bar fight. *Skills like that could be very useful,* thought the boss of the local Russian Bratva.

The next day when Diegert showed up early for his evening shift, Tracy Vandersmith told him, "Hey, slugger, Terry told me to send you to his office when you got here."

"Thanks."

"Don't thank me, he didn't look happy."

Knocking on Buscetti's office door, Diegert called out softly, "Hello."

"Yeah, get on in here."

Buscetti got up and closed the door as he directed Diegert to sit down next to his cluttered desk. "Listen, about last night—"

"Hey, he had it coming."

"I'm not worried about fucking Uri. No, Mr. Dimitrov has asked that you . . . rough up a guy here tonight."

"Rough him up?"

"Yeah—put a beating on a guy who's been encroaching on the business, you know."

"The business?"

"Come on . . . you know Dimitrov runs the Russian Bratva. He's pushing meth and heroin into Austin, and he's putting the squeeze on the Mexicans."

"Oh . . . yeah."

"Well, he wants you to beat up the spic the Mexicans send here every night to spy on 'em. I sent his picture to your phone. Keep an eye on him, and when he goes outside, put a beating on him. Dimitrov has a thousand dollars for you when it's done."

A quizzical look crossed Diegert's face as he thought about assaulting someone for money.

"Come on—come on, I need you to do this, and you need the money," said Buscetti impatiently.

"Alright . . . but I get the money up front."

Pulling a thick envelope from his desk drawer, Buscetti said, "I got the money right here. When the job is done, it's yours. Now go get ready. The High Note Drifters are playing again tonight, so it should be busy at the door."

As he left the office, Diegert checked his phone to see a picture of a medium-size Mexican guy smoking a cigarette while leaning against a Camaro.

As Diegert walked out into the bar, Tracy shouted, "Hey, Mr. Tough Guy, if you can go beating up people for the entertainment of the bar, how about you help me by stocking the fridge with beer?"

"If it will entertain you, I certainly will," said Diegert as he opened the case and began filling the shelves.

The High Note Drifters' loyal following filled the bar by the end of their first set. Diegert noted that the Mexican guy's name was Miguel Lopez, or at least that's what his Texas driver's license said. Lopez had paid the cover without incident and eventually got a stool at the far end of the bar. From time to time, Diegert would observe the guy, and it really appeared like he was doing nothing. He drank his beer slowly, smiled at people, but didn't talk much and was otherwise easily forgotten.

As the evening wore on, Lopez crossed the bar, exiting right in front of Diegert while shaking a cigarette out of his pack. Buscetti appeared at his side and told Diegert, "I got the door." He nodded toward the exit, and Diegert followed Lopez outside.

Lopez had his cigarette burning as soon as he stepped onto the sidewalk, the nicotine sending a wave of relief to his stimulant-deprived nerves. Exhaling, the tension from his craving dissipated as fast as the cloud of smoke. He was shocked when Diegert shoved him into the wall.

Diegert slapped the cigarette out of Lopez's hand. He pushed the Mexican around the corner and into the alley back by the bar's dumpsters.

"Hey, what the fuck?" shouted Lopez.

Diegert said nothing as he pushed Lopez again, this time knocking him against the wall between two dumpsters.

"What the fuck you doing, man? I know who you are, you're the bouncer."

Diegert's first punch was lightning fast, striking Lopez on the cheek. The Mexican stumbled backward but remained standing.

"Fucking A," said Lopez as he put his hand to his face. "You don't know who you're fucking with. The Quinoloans are going to hunt you down and—"

Diegert's next combination struck Lopez three times in the face, leaving him with a bleeding nose. Using the dumpster for balance, the man still stood but was dazed. The smeared blood from his nose on the back of his hand made it clear he was not going to talk his way out of this. Straightening himself, he tried not to wobble as he put up his fists. Diegert saw the vulnerability and exploited the guy's weakness by throwing a fake. The instant Lopez reacted, Diegert struck with a combination that included a second punch to the bleeding nose. The Mexican crashed into the back wall, falling to the ground in an awkward pile. Diegert stepped to him and kicked him twice in the ribs. Lopez coughed up blood and desperately extended his hands to fend off the next kick.

Seeing the man defenseless and covered in blood, Diegert stepped back and watched him struggle. He felt powerful in a primal, dominant way. He had beaten his enemy so swiftly and completely that he felt like the king of the pride. He also felt foolish. He had assaulted this man for money, with no indication that Lopez deserved this. Even Lieutenant Prescott had deserved what he'd gotten. Diegert had to admit to himself that he had violated the ethics of martial arts and had used his skills to instigate violence. He could feel the point turning. *Fuck it,* he thought, *I need the money, and this fucker is a drug dealer playing a dangerous game.* He snapped a picture of the defeated Lopez, who gurgled through his bloody lips, "You're gonna get yours." Diegert walked away, listening to the defeated man, who raised his voice and said, "I'm gonna kill you, motherfucker. I know who you are."

After washing the blood off his hands, Diegert showed the picture to Buscetti and collected his envelope of cash. He resumed his post at the door and soon found himself opening it as Igor Dimitrov and his crew departed. As he passed, Dimitrov stopped to shake Diegert's hand. Clapping his big paw on Diegert's shoulder, he said, "хороший удар." Good punch. It was an unusually friendly gesture, which Diegert didn't understand and to which he did not reply. Strangely, he felt both a sense of camaraderie and revulsion. After the group left, a feeling of foreboding crept over him.

The next morning was a bright, dry Texas beauty with the fragrance of bluebells and oleanders mixing with the diesel exhaust that hung in the air around the Single Star Motel. The flowers made him think of home, and Diegert recalled how his mom had always put so much effort into keeping the house neat, tidy, and attractive. She did all the gardening, and although he had mowed the grass, she made the place look real nice with flowers and her well-tended berry bushes. She kept the chicken coop secure, repairing the damage from attempted incursions by foxes and coyotes. She painted the house, washed the windows, and pulled the weeds. His mom took pride and pleasure in keeping their small, simple home, which was fronted by a dirt road, looking like a place that was loved and appreciated.

At this time of day, she would be home since she worked the evening shift at the diner. He smiled as he waited for her to answer his call.

"Hello," she said.

"Hey, Mom."

"David, I didn't expect a call from you."

"Yeah, well, they finally gave us phones over here. How ya doin'?"

"Fine, I'm fine. How about you?"

"I'm doing OK, although the Army isn't everything the recruiters tell you. I'm supposed to be home in eight months."

"Eight months? That long?"

"Yeah, I might get some leave for a week or two, but I don't know when that's going to happen." Diegert turned out of the wind so he could hear better. "I tell ya, Mom, Afghanistan is really hot this time of year."

"Oh, that's too bad. I miss you, David."

"Yeah, I miss you too, Mom."

"Without you, I have to do everything around here."

"How are Jake and Dad?"

"They're fine. Usually drunk. Jake's still dealing drugs. I don't let them bother me."

"But you're OK, right?"

Through the phone, Diegert got only a muffled response. He listened carefully, and he could hear the soft gasp of a cry escaping from his mother.

"Mom, what's wrong? Tell me what's going on."

Her sobs were being stifled, and he could hear that she was struggling to speak.

"Come on, Mom, talk to me; tell me what's happening."

"I'm scared."

"Is Dad hitting you?"

"No, no, no, it's not that."

"Then what? What are you afraid of?"

"I'm afraid we're going to lose the house."

Diegert thought about the house and property and figured it wasn't even worth a hundred grand. They'd been living in it for more than twenty years, so surely it should be close to being paid off.

"What do you mean, lose the house?"

"The bank is threatening foreclosure."

Diegert's thoughts flashed through his head. Although she was smart with money, his father had bought the house before he'd met his mom, and Diegert had no idea how the mortgage was being financed.

"Tell me what the bank said."

"A man came to the door and gave me some papers. They said Dad hasn't been paying the mortgage, and he took out an equity loan some time ago. We owe a hundred and sixty-seven thousand. David, I don't know what to do," sobbed his mother.

Diegert dropped the phone from his ear as the number passed through his mind. The small house and his father's beat-up old barn were worth nowhere near that much. Blinking his eyes, Diegert slowly shook his head as the problem became clear.

"How much money do you have?"

Snuffling back her tears, Denise Diegert said, "Fifteen hundred in my checking account, that's it. I've no idea what Dad has. He's never told me about how he handles his money, but it obviously hasn't been good."

"Mom, how much time did the bank give you?"

"Two months, but the entire amount is due by then. Apparently they've been sending Dad notifications for a while, and they're now at the point where it's pay it all or lose the house."

As the predicament settled into Diegert's thoughts, his mother continued, "David, I don't want to lose the house. This is the only home I've ever had and, you know, I do all the work, keep it nice, and I feel safe here. If I have to leave, then the fear starts all over again. Please help me."

Imagining her there in the small, tidy kitchen, tears flowing over her high cheekbones with a feeling of desperation and abandonment welling up inside her, Diegert wanted to reassure her.

"Mom, I will help you get that money, and I will keep you from losing the house."

"How, David? How are you going to do that?"

"I'll find a way. You just hang in there, and I'll find a way. My time is up. I've to get off the phone. Bye, Mom."

"Good-bye, David. I love you."

When the call disconnected, Diegert gazed across the parking lot of the Single Star Motel and realized he had no idea how he was going to get that much money.

CHAPTER 9

The Austin Police Department encircled the alley behind the Dark Horse in yellow tape as soon as the bullet-riddled body of a Mexican man had been reported between the dumpsters. They confiscated Buscetti's video surveillance recordings and began the long process of interviewing all the patrons and employees who had been working the previous night.

Buscetti texted Diegert: *Tune into the news.* Diegert brought up a local news app and saw the video of himself pushing Lopez through the alley to the dumpsters. The view of what happened between the big trash bins was blocked, but after a few minutes, the video showed Diegert walking out of the alley, alone. The grainy image made it hard to identify the man on the screen, but Diegert certainly recognized himself.

Diegert replied: *I need a place to hole up.*

Buscetti texted back: *1370 Valencia Drive. Go there and stay put.*

The address wasn't too far away. Diegert pulled his hood over his head and walked to Valencia Drive, which was located in an upscale suburb. The house had a winding drive leading to a nice house set back thirty yards from the road. When he knocked on the door, it opened right away, surprising Diegert, who looked up into the heavily bearded face of a large Russian man who introduced himself as "Peotor Vladak." Diegert was nearly yanked through the door by the powerful man, who didn't release his hand until the front door had closed.

"I know your name, and I know your crime," said the man, who stood six foot five inches tall and weighed over two hundred fifty pounds. "But you are safe here. This is a safe house."

Peotor nodded his head and gestured for Diegert to follow him into the next room.

Diegert remained rooted in the foyer. "I didn't kill that guy."

Peotor's smile crept out from under his beard. "I saw the video, and you wouldn't be here if you didn't earn your entrance with a murder. Come. Follow me into the kitchen."

Peotor trained his gaze on Diegert's face as he held his arms out and proceeded into the kitchen.

"Sit here, friend."

Diegert sat on a stool at the raised counter as Peotor called out, "Sam, come down here, we have a guest."

Rapid footfalls on the stairs preceded the entrance of a thin, wiry young man with close-cropped blond hair and wide-set hazel eyes. From the bottom of the stairs to the kitchen, the guy checked his phone screen twice. His finger stroked the screen until satisfied with the effects before looking squarely at Diegert. Peotor spoke, "This is the guy from the video who killed the Mexican."

The wiry man's eyelids narrowed as a slight sneer distorted his otherwise inexpressive lips.

"I didn't kill him," offered Diegert. "I only beat him up. When I left him, he was alive and shouting." Diegert felt like he was pleading to the police. The thin man raised his sleeve, revealing a tattooed bicep depicting a combat dagger from which four distinct drops of blood fell off the blade toward his elbow. Leaning forward, the man said with clarity, "Don't let anyone take credit for what you've done."

Diegert swallowed hard as the proud murderer stepped back, dropped his sleeve, extended his hand, and introduced himself. "I'm Sam Klemczar. How long will you be with us?"

Diegert felt the cold of Sam's hand pass into him like a winter's draft.

"I don't know." The question forced Diegert to face his situation and realize he had no idea what to do. His answer passed by the ears of Sam without being heard, since the thin man's phone had buzzed and the screen once again had his full attention.

As the young man's climb up the stairs drummed through the house, Peotor told Diegert, "You can use the refrigerator but don't take anything from the bottom shelf or the one above that. You can use anything in the door."

So it went for two days, with Sam almost never coming downstairs and Peotor constantly talking about Russia and all the exploits of the Russian mob all over the world. At one point, Sam had returned to confiscate Diegert's phone for "safety reasons." Without communication, Diegert began to get paranoid. He wanted to talk to Buscetti and check in on his mom, but Sam's insistence that his phone could be tracked and the safe house blown forced him to be incommunicado. Not being able to do what you want for even the most basic things can make anyone edgy. Diegert, however, had the Austin Police Department, the Quinoloan cartel, and probably the FBI all looking for him. Not knowing if he was really safe or just being set up to be turned over was very aggravating.

Peotor's laptop became the only conduit to the outside world, and Peotor's worldview was dominated by the exploits of assassins as depicted on the darknet. The underground Internet required the installation of Tor software, which rerouted digital signals so they couldn't be traced. It presented a means of worldwide communication that couldn't be tracked or controlled by law enforcement. Peotor told Diegert the original software was designed by the US Navy. It had been adopted by criminals and served the needs of drug dealers, human traffickers, fences for stolen merchandise, and contract killers. The killers fascinated Peotor. Assassins seeking employment posted their exploits, including graphic pictures of the people they'd murdered. The more audacious assassins posted GoPro videos that showed not only the kill but the process of breaching security to execute the target.

Watching all this with Peotor at first shocked Diegert, then intrigued him, and finally numbed him as the bloody images became routine and the videos that were just simple shaky shots of dead bodies were no longer entertaining compared to the more complex depictions of the entire process. Diegert, though, was amazed by the money; the going rate was about a hundred thousand US dollars for a human life. In addition to the assassins' postings, there were several pages of contracts to kill being advertised.

"One day, you will see my page on the darknet, and I'll be the most sought-after assassin in the world." Peotor's boastful statement did nothing to impress Diegert, but what he said next was more chilling.

"An assassin must commit to the kill. When the pistol is pointed, the trigger must be pulled, and then the assassin must walk away." Diegert's doubt of Peotor's capacity to kill was weakened by his lethal pronouncement. The big guy continued, "I can do this. I can shut my emotions down in order to become as cold as Sam. He has four kills, you know."

"Yeah . . . he showed me his tattoo."

After a rapid flurry of keystrokes, Peotor brought up a screen to show Diegert.

"Look at his website; you can see his kills."

On the computer, Diegert saw four grisly posthumous portraits, all with entrance wounds in the forehead.

"One day I will have many more tattoos than that guy," said Peotor as he gestured upstairs to an unconvinced Diegert.

"Then why are you just sitting here babysitting me?"

"Babysitting? There are no babies here. What do you mean?"

"What are you waiting for? There are contracts right here with all the information you need to carry them out. Why aren't you doing one of these jobs?" asked Diegert as he tapped his fingers on Peotor's screen.

Peotor's round face turned to Diegert. "I need to lose weight, and I need to get my knee fixed." Peotor slapped his right knee. "I hurt it playing rugby, and I need surgery to fix the ligaments. I can't run on it. Hey, since you killed the Mexican, we can use him to set up your profile."

"No way, I don't want a profile."

Later, for dinner, Sam cooked himself up a soup with sausage, noodles, lard, and butter. It looked to Diegert like a liquid heart attack with several different layers of fat fighting to remain separate from the broth. Peotor stared enviously at the fatty meal while he peeled back the foil on his cup of lite yogurt. Diegert finished fixing a turkey sandwich, but before he bit into it, he asked Sam, "Can I use your phone to call Buscetti?"

Sam's gaze snapped at Diegert, and he instinctively snatched his phone off the counter. "No, you can't."

"When am I going to get to speak with Buscetti and get out of here?"

Sam replied, "According to Mr. Dimitrov, you're to stay here. He specifically said you aren't to leave."

An unnerving chill trickled down Diegert's spine as Sam's revelation of who was in charge registered within him.

"You're to remain as our guest," said Peotor, the smiling bear.

"I appreciate the hospitality, but I would like to move on and get back to my life."

"Your life," said Sam coldly, "is safer here than out on the street. You will remain until I hear from Dimitrov."

Peotor added, with a smile that included yogurt at the corner of his beard, "I'm glad you're staying here with us."

Diegert wondered if Peotor was really as dumb as he looked, but he felt the cold from Sam's icy stare and realized his predicament might have far more dire consequences than he'd originally thought.

***

On day four, Peotor asked Diegert to fire up the laptop, telling him the password was "RUSSIA." When Diegert signed in, the screen immediately opened to a site displaying gay porn.

Diegert sensed Peotor's bulky body coming up behind him.

"Hey, let's watch some of this . . . together."

The scene on the screen of one man fellating another turned Diegert's stomach, but it turned Peotor on.

"No, that's not my thing," Diegert said as he stood up, handed Peotor the computer, and moved to the other side of the room.

"Come on, I thought you'd like it."

"You thought I was gay?"

"What's wrong with being gay?"

"Look, I'm not saying there's anything wrong with it, but I'm not gay. I don't want to watch gay porn."

"What . . . you're too good for gay sex?"

"No, man, I'm just not interested."

Peotor's face became a hard scowl as he turned his attention to the screen, watching the porn with the sound up high. Diegert distracted himself with a magazine, but it was like trying to find peace and quiet at a Dionysus orgy. As Peotor's excitement intensified, he undid his pants and pulled out his erection. "I want your wet lips on my cock. Get over here," he commanded in an authoritarian tone Diegert had not heard him use before.

The Russian reached to his right, taking his Makarov 9 mm pistol off the table and pointing it at Diegert. The incredulous American got up and walked over to the couch.

"That's right, kneel down and suck it." With the gun in his hand, Peotor proclaimed, "Power and pleasure."

On one knee in front of the big guy, Diegert encircled the man's cock with his fingers and gently stroked it up and down. Loving the pleasure, Peotor leaned his head back and closed his eyes. The instant the big guy's lids fell, Diegert crushed the erection in his grasp and grabbed the gun from the stunned man's hand. Peotor's painful holler alerted Sam, who bounded down the stairs into the living room. Keeping the squeeze on the big guy's dick, Diegert pivoted and put two bullets into the skinnier guard as he entered the room. Letting go of the guy's prick, Diegert plunged his knee into the bellowing man's crotch. Diegert pulled Peotor's head back by the hair and put the barrel in his face. He pulled the trigger, shattering Peotor's cranium, splattering the carpet with blood and brains.

CHAPTER 10

With two dead bodies and a bloody mess in the Russian safe house, Diegert was stunned at what he'd just done. Shooting two men so quickly left him gasping for breath. The adrenaline rush was like none he'd ever felt, and he was afraid he was going into cardiac arrest. With his heart bashing against his sternum, he stepped back and fell into a chair on the opposite side of the room. He sat there realizing his life would never be the same. The eerie quiet was unsettling, but it was broken by the sound of blood dripping to the floor from Peotor's head. Being trapped, not communicating, and worrying that he'd be killed by these mobsters, Diegert had reacted with a survival reflex.

The sound of thumping and dragging drew him into the kitchen. Sam had two bullet holes in his chest and was sucking air through pursed lips as he reached back with his elbows to pull himself across the floor. The blood exiting the wounds in his back smeared across the floor as he struggled to make his way toward the stairs. Diegert stood by the granite-topped island looking at the pitiful four-time assassin as he desperately sought to escape.

When their eyes met, Diegert saw the fear and felt a jolt of power he hadn't expected. This man, who had struck Diegert as so cold and ruthless, now had fear radiating from his face. This man, who had killed several others, now displayed the weakness and desperation of a wounded quarry about to be killed. The powerlessness and the abandonment of hope for mercy played across Sam's face and filled the vector between his and Diegert's eyes. Diegert felt triumph. He felt like he did after beating Miguel Lopez in the alley, but this sensation was even more powerful and primal. This man was going to die, and Diegert was going to look him in the eye as he shoved aside his humanity to end Sam's pathetic little life with explosive violence. Sam's eyes widened until his irises were ringed by the bright-white sclera as Diegert raised the pistol, squaring the sight bead on the point between the eyes where the nose began. Sam stopped shuffling and pleaded, "Please don't." The bullet imploded the nasal and frontal bones while producing an instantaneous splash that spread across the hardwood floor when the back of Sam's skull was pulverized by the force of the close-range projectile. Diegert did not flinch after firing the weapon. He gazed upon the dead man while the anger and frustration of his being a captive mixed with the sudden liberation he felt now that there was no one to hold him hostage. The feeling was more than that, though. The capacity to inflict death by his will and hand heated his blood, engorging his muscles with an animalistic sense of power. The adrenaline was huge, and Diegert felt so alive and energized for having shot these men to gain his freedom.

If Diegert were to become an assassin, then a killer he would be. The abuse he had endured from his father and the servitude of his lousy old job as well as the disappointment of his service in the Army all left him feeling weak, lost, and rudderless. In contrast, here now was something that made him feel powerful, in control, and free of himself.

In the Army, he was trained as a soldier to kill enemies for the sake of the mission as well as to protect his fellow soldiers. He had done that today. His willingness to cross the line, to become the killer, grabbed his thoughts and expanded his sense of self with an unexpected realization. He enjoyed the kill. This moment, this internal experience, extended from his head to his muscles to his soul, filling him with an unprecedented sense of personal power.

After washing the blood off his face and hands, he gathered up useful things: guns, ammo, some cash, car keys, his phone, as well as his Ojibwa knife. He was wearing his amulet while he looked at the blanket his mother had made him. Using the knife, he cut out the embroidered prayer, folded it up, and stuck it in his pocket. From Peotor's computer, he downloaded the Tor software and verified that he could access the darknet on his phone. Exiting the back door, he came around where the cars were parked and drove away in a big black BMW 738i.

A stolen Bratva vehicle would quickly become a liability. Diegert found refuge in the interior of the third floor of a downtown parking garage. He accessed the darknet and read through a number of contract offerings for assassinations. He figured he was accused of one murder he didn't commit, and now he was guilty of taking two lives, so if convicted, he would go to jail for life or a spot on death row. He reluctantly realized that the best thing to do was go all in. It was scary and messy, but he admitted to himself that he felt charged by the power of the experience. Shooting those two guys had left him with a strangely liberating sense of relief. This was a feeling he would never admit to anyone, but he couldn't deny to himself. His emotions were raw, confusing, and powerful.

Out of all the advertisements he reviewed, he was attracted to one that was a two-part job. A successful hit in Miami got you a private jet out of the United States to perform a second job in Paris. This seemed like just what Diegert needed, the money was good, a hundred thousand dollars, but the flight was more important. If he could escape the United States, he would be able to establish himself in Europe and remain free and unpursued.

His reply to the ad went secretly to the computer of Aaron Blevinsky. Blevinsky was employed as a special operations manager for an elite group known as Crepusculous. All of Blevinsky's communication was sent blindly. No one knew the real identity of the person with whom they were communicating when that person worked for Crepusculous. This elite organization, comprised of four men, represented the smallest percentage of the world's wealthiest people. Their combined wealth encompassed 75 percent of the world's resources. Their ability to influence governments, markets, and the global economy made them the most powerful people on earth. All four of the men were practically unknown in the media, largely because they owned most of the media outlets in the world and made sure that tawdry gossip and investigative news stories were focused on the few competitors they had. "Crepusculous" meant "in the shadows," and from their clandestine positions, these men controlled the world.

As director of special operations, Blevinsky was tasked with ensuring that Crepusculous had a private military. Blevinsky kept ready a group of men and women, from battle-hardened commandos to stealthy assassins, who could carry out missions deemed necessary by the four Board members of Crepusculous.

With the ad that attracted Diegert, Blevinsky was fishing for a fresh operator, someone young yet confident and ready to prove himself. A prospect for the future who had very little past and could be groomed for a special mission he was planning for the Board.

Blevinsky read Diegert's message, which was sent under the online ID Next Chance: *I'm interested in the opportunity you're advertising.*

He replied under the online ID Darkmass: *What experience do you have?*

Next Chance: *I have three recent completions against narcotic organizations.*

Darkmass: *Were there complications from law enforcement?*

Blevinsky's questions kept Diegert on the line, which was essential for the success of a reverse tracking worm designed in a Crepusculous tech lab that was able to move through Tor and identify the source of a signal. Each message Diegert sent led Blevinsky closer to identifying him.

Next Chance: *I was never arrested or clearly identified.*

Darkmass: *You're free of convictions?*

Next Chance: *Quite.*

Darkmass: *Do you have a profile on the darknet?*

Next Chance: *No, I do not, but the recent completions are news in the Austin area.*

Blevinsky kept Diegert waiting while he looked for news stories on the Web, allowing the worm more time to work. Once the worm was able to find the signal's path, it was able to move through the various servers the Tor software had hopped between. Within minutes, Blevinsky had Diegert's phone under surveillance. From it, he was able to identify him as David Diegert, extract his e-mails, and locate him by GPS. He learned that Diegert was twenty-five years old from Broward County, Minnesota; had been dishonorably discharged from the Army; was a reasonably handsome guy with dark hair and features; had $2,604 in credit card debt; and was currently located in

Austin, Texas. If he kept mining, he would find more, but for now, he had what he needed.

Darkmass: *I see the news from Austin, a Mexican outside a bar and two guys in a suburb. Be in Miami in two days. When you arrive, you will receive instructions.*

Diegert was surprised how quickly Sam's and Peotor's deaths had made the news. The bus station was only two blocks away. In the trunk of the car, he found a black reusable shopping bag into which he placed his useful items, tied the top of the bag, and walked to the station.

After a twenty-two-hour bus ride through most of which Diegert slept, he stepped into the blazing sun and heavy afternoon humidity of Miami. As he walked away from the bus, his phone buzzed, and the text from Darkmass instructed him to take a cab to the Blue Pearl Restaurant and Nightclub in Miami Beach. En route, his screen revealed a photo of a large, mustachioed Hispanic man named Victor Del Fuentes. The accompanying text read: *This is your target. Send a message when the job is complete. Make it look like an accident.*

"An accident," muttered Diegert after he paid the cabbie and approached the Blue Pearl. As he got closer, the expensive nature of this club became obvious. Dressed in casual clothes and carrying his shopping bag, Diegert simply passed by while gathering visual intel. The outdoor diners enjoyed a fabulous view of the ocean while an army of waitstaff attended their every need. Through the windows, more tables could be seen, along with a bar and a large open dance floor. Diegert surmised that when the dinner crowd left, the Blue Pearl transformed into a partying nightclub. Farther down the street, he came upon Ocean View Park with its quiet public space next to busy Ocean Drive. From a food truck, he got a chicken fajita. It felt good to eat, and he sat looking out at the water, waiting for darkness to fall.

Blevinsky tracked Diegert's phone signal across a map of Miami. He was impressed that the young man had so quickly located the theater of operations, and a dangerous smile scrawled over his lips as he hoped he had found what the Board required.

During the long bus ride and now sitting through the sunset, Diegert thought about what he had done and what he was going to do. Killing the two Russian guards was self-defense. A reactionary act anybody would have done, given the threat. Beating up Miguel Lopez was different; getting paid meant instigating the attack. There was no threat, no need, just an opportunity and a greedy reward. Whoever killed Lopez, and it was obviously Dimitrov, had set Diegert up, and that bad choice pinned him with three murders. Without intending to, he had become a killer and was now being hired to do it again. The experience of committing the murders was thrilling, but now it was also guilt inducing. *Do I just walk away from this and forget it?* Diegert thought. *I can't really do that, because I'll eventually be caught, convicted, and executed. If I complete this job and leave the US, I will have enough money to live in Europe and get away with this. I'll live cheap, earn more money, and send it back to Mom. God, this sucks! I can't believe I'm in this shit.*

His mind went blank as contemplating the intractable situation failed to produce a better solution. His thoughts turned to how he would kill Victor Del Fuentes and make it look like an accident. Making a plan and thinking about the future as only a matter of hours was far more comforting than worrying about the rest of his life. Focusing on the Del Fuentes mission kept him from being paralyzed by the consequences of his earlier actions.

Darkness fell as the sun set, and he left Ocean View Park. Passing through the pools of light projected on the sidewalk by the streetlamps, Diegert could hear the sounds of a party coming from the Blue Pearl. He was attracted to the thump of music, the din of a hundred conversations punctuated by bursts of laughter and the kinetic waves of a crowd in motion. He knew the transient sense of camaraderie that formed as people were relaxed by alcohol and tacitly agreed that they were all having a good time.

Twenty bucks got him inside the party, and he began his reconnaissance. Del Fuentes was not hard to find. The big, handsome gentleman sat at a corner booth with a beautiful young woman beside him and several couples surrounding the table. He was gregarious and animated and clearly in control of the evening. The waiter would approach him from behind, speak directly into his ear, and then walk briskly away when Del Fuentes waved his hand. He looked like the king of this court and someone who relished the servitude his money and power were able to buy. His bodyguard stood off to the side with a .45 under his summer-weight suit coat.

From his seat at the bar, Diegert was able to observe his target. As the evening progressed, Del Fuentes eventually rose from his seat and forced his considerable bulk out of the booth and down the hall. The bodyguard was instructed to stay put with a wave of the hand. Diegert followed, observing as the big man bypassed the men's room where all the rest of the guys went and entered a room farther down the hall marked "Private." The king certainly wasn't going to piss with the pawns, and Diegert knew he had found his opportunity to stage an accident.

Diegert got a cheap motel room in Overtown for which he paid cash and falsified the registry. He showered and slept, but he was buzzing on adrenaline now that he had a plan to kill Victor Del Fuentes. In the morning, he went to a hardware store and acquired a screwdriver with multiple heads, needle-nose pliers, electrical wire, and an aerosol can of ignition starter fluid. From a consignment shop, he purchased black pants and a black shirt. Combined, the two garments dressed him like all the waitstaff at the Blue Pearl. After passing the day avoiding being burned by a sun that was almost as hot as in Afghanistan, he entered the kitchen of the Blue Pearl looking like a new guy on the waitstaff. Del Fuentes was in his booth with a different young lady and a new set of couples enthralled with the king's every word. Diegert stepped out of the kitchen in his waiter's attire, went straight down the hall, and entered the room labeled "Private." The toilet was to the right, the sink to the left. The room had soft lighting, which gave the space a gentle glow in which to complete your business. Stepping to the sink activated a sensor that illuminated an overhead unit. The brighter light conveniently lit the sink for the washing of hands. Diegert smiled, as his plan had found the perfect situation for execution.

Using his tools and the canister of ignition starter fluid, Diegert turned the overhead sink light into an automatically activated explosive device in a matter of minutes. Stepping out of the room, he heard, "Hey, you're not supposed to be in there." The young waitress had a tray of meals in her hands and cast Diegert a scornful look as she continued out to the dining room. Diegert just looked at her, smiled, and shrugged his shoulders. For thirty minutes, Diegert blended in with the staff while observing the booth. The young lady with Del Fuentes was very disinterested in the paunchy man and seemed to be much more enamored with the cleavage of the wife sitting next to her. Del Fuentes's bladder eventually asserted itself, and the big guy exited the booth. Diegert moved toward the restaurant's exit. The explosion was immense, blowing the door of the private bathroom right off its hinges and across the hall. Del Fuentes's dead body lay in the doorway as a grisly decapitated corpse. The crowd grew hushed for a second, contemplating that perhaps there was an accident in the kitchen. The situation turned into a panic when a waitress, seeing Del Fuentes, screamed like a victim in a horror movie. By this time, Diegert had already taken his leave and was walking down the street, turning the corner, and leaving the scene of his first "accidental" assassination.

The text Blevinsky received from Diegert had only one word: *Completed.* Checking the news a few hours later, Blevinsky read a post from the *Miami Herald* announcing the death of Victor Del Fuentes in what appeared to be a freak accident in the men's room of the Blue Pearl. Blevinsky's reply gave Diegert the address of the Miami Executive Airport southeast of Miami. The text included the tail number of the plane and a boarding code to show the plane's crew.

When Diegert arrived, the sleek design of the Gulfstream G650 made him feel out of his element yet eager to move forward. As he boarded, his initial impressions were surpassed by the luxury appointments of the interior.

"Welcome aboard, Mr. Diegert," came the voice through the cabin speakers. "I am your captain, Edward James, and your cocaptain for this flight is Robert Allen. We are ready for departure as soon as you're comfortable. Our flight time to Paris is seven hours and forty-three minutes. Amber, your cabin attendant, will be serving you as soon as we reach our cruising altitude of thirty thousand feet. Please press the green button on your armrest when you are ready to fly. Thank you."

As he sat in the broad, soft leather seat, Diegert's smile revealed his pleasure to be receiving such service and respect. Amber was a gorgeous young woman whose continuous smile told him she was ready to please. After one last satisfying breath and a look at the cherrywood trim of the cabin, Diegert pressed the green button and left America behind.

The comfortable seats, the serene sky, and the sense of secure quiet lulled Diegert into contemplation. His reaction to killing Sam and Peotor was so intense he realized that the time he felt most powerful was when he was fighting. In high school, the only place he felt competent and confident was on the wrestling mat. The intensity of the matches had cleared his thoughts, allowing him to detach from his regular life and use his skills on the mat to gain a sense of power. The success of thrashing guys into submission filled a void in his day-to-day life. The minute practice was over, returning to the hallways or the bus or pretty much anywhere else, he was filled with doubt and self-conscious judgment. In the Army at Fort Benning, he'd felt good when training. The full-pack marches, low crawling through the dirt, and practicing Modern Army Combatives had given him a sense of accomplishment. He was able to detach from the pain of the struggle and push through whatever was asked of him. But in the barracks, the mess hall, or the PX, he'd felt empty, hollow, and without purpose. These recollections came back to him with unsettling clarity. He had just killed three men while emotionally detached from the experience. To kill was a powerful catharsis, a forceful expression of his anger and frustration finding a release in a spasm of violence, but he did it out of a necessity to survive. He experienced an adrenaline rush during the action, but it was followed by a deep crash, and soon Diegert felt like shit. He was doing the work of others, who, through their power and money, were forcing him to comply with their demands or suffer the consequences. In spite of the luxurious surroundings, Diegert realized he was in a cylindrical jail cell financed by those who were ordering him to kill. How far was he willing to go to fulfill his employer's requests for death? He willed himself to hold onto the feelings of guilt and recrimination that surfaced after killing. He didn't want to become someone addicted to violence, a junkie seeking a kill to get a thrill. He held the guilt in and nurtured it, swallowing its poison. He would crush any thrill with the guilt of having killed. Caught between the power of taking a life and the emotional consequence of having committed the ultimate sin, Diegert hurtled forward at six hundred miles per hour into an uncertain future.

CHAPTER 11

The stairway of the Gulfstream opened at Le Bourget, a private airport in Paris. David Diegert descended to the tarmac, where he was met by a chauffeur who did not introduce himself before ushering the American into the rear compartment of a Renault. A smartphone, on the seat beside David, chirped when the car door closed. Instructions on the phone indicated the target was named Gunther Mibuku. There were no other details about the man, but in his photo, he looked biracial. Diegert was to meet one of Mibuku's female consorts, whose cooperation was making this mission possible. Next to him was a gray fedora, which he was to wear while sitting at a table in a street-side café. The nameless chauffeur dropped Diegert at the sidewalk.

Wearing the hat, drinking coffee, and seated at a sidewalk table, Diegert took in the view of Paris. The lively movement of people and the strange lack of tall buildings seemed a bit incongruous for a large urban city, not at all like Minneapolis and definitely not like small Broward County, Minnesota. "May I join you?" asked a strikingly attractive Asian woman. "Certainly," said Diegert as he looked up at the surprisingly tall, dark-haired beauty.

As she sat down, she placed her smartphone on the table. The screen displayed an alphanumeric code, "A12B14C18," and the pretty woman said, "Please confirm."

Diegert was confused for a moment and sat still just looking at her. "With your phone," the lady urged.

Pulling out his phone, he saw the same code and showed it to her: "A12B14C18."

"Chateau Lambert Room 316. I will be meeting him at seven p.m. You'll receive a text from me when the time is right. The guard in the hall is your problem."

"OK."

She got up and left, and David's eyes were not the only ones gazing at her lovely feminine form as she walked away. Before he could take another sip of coffee, the chauffeur in the Renault pulled up and Diegert was whisked away.

As they drove, the nameless chauffeur pointed out the Chateau Lambert and took Diegert to an apartment that he referred to as a safe house. In the apartment, Diegert found the equipment he would need. A hotel photo ID, which was also a room keycard, an MK 23 pistol with a suppressor and two extra clips of ammunition, latex gloves, and a rubber mask. He put the mask on and looked in the mirror. The rubber panels covered his cheeks, forehead, chin, and nose. He still had good visibility. The thing was not uncomfortable, and it would fulfill its role of distorting his face for the surveillance cameras. There was also a paper map of the neighborhood with indicated routes to the hotel, one to walk there and a different one for coming back. Diegert put both in his phone. In the kitchen, there was bread and cheese, and on the television, a soccer game.

As seven p.m. approached, Diegert took the longer route to the hotel. Dressed in black so he would blend in with the service staff, he attracted no attention on the street. At the hotel, he found a linen closet and acquired a set of towels.

Diegert walked the halls and rode the elevators, carrying his towels and looking like he belonged. One British chap on the elevator, heading to the pool, took one of the towels and gave Diegert a polite nod. At seven forty-five p.m., he received the Asian woman's text. Withdrawing his pistol and attaching the suppressor, he placed it between the first and second towel. As he walked down the hall approaching Room 316, he stopped perpendicular to the guard, pressed the barrel into the man's chest, and fired a muffled shot. The failed protector slumped forward with Diegert breaking his fall. Using his keycard, Diegert opened the room, dragged the man inside, and laid him on the floor. A second bullet to the head assured the guard would no longer be an obstacle.

Locking the door behind him, Diegert saw the Asian beauty getting dressed and pointing the way into the suite's bedroom. The target was on the bed. A magnificent specimen of a man, very fit looking, all muscle covered in smooth skin. He was sexually spent and contently stretched out on the king-size sheets. Diegert stepped to the side of the bed, and the slightest look of confusion crossed the man's face as he opened his sleepy eyes before two bullets entered into his head. Aside from the slight moment of surprise, it seemed to Diegert that he died a happy man, having just had sex. As instructed by his employer, Diegert used his smartphone to send video confirmation of the hit. He received an immediate reply, which acknowledged the completion of the mission, but the message had an additional component, stating: *$100,000 has just been placed in your account, for an additional 5%, take out the girl.*

Checking his account, he could see the money was there. Diegert thought of helping his mom, and even though five thousand dollars wasn't much, every dollar he earned got her closer to paying off the house.

The girl was throwing the last of her belongings in a shoulder bag and beckoning him to hurry so they could leave together.

He didn't know this woman. Maybe she wasn't an accomplice but a criminal like Mibuku. Maybe she was going to turn him in as soon as they stepped out of the room. Why would the employer want her dead? Was she an ally or an adversary? As she approached him, Diegert raised his MK 23, placing the laser sight on her chest. She stopped in her tracks and looked him squarely in the eye.

"Really, you're gonna shoot me?"

Waving his phone in his hand, he said, "Our employer is asking me to. Why would he do that?"

"Fucking cheap bastard."

"Or maybe I'm being warned not to trust you."

"Oh, come on. I'm just a girl with habits in a town full of customers. I'm no threat to you."

Gesturing toward the dead body on the bed, Diegert asked, "What's the story with this guy?"

"We don't have time to play kill and tell. Let's get out of here."

Killing Mibuku was easy, it was intended, it was the plan. Killing her was not. His employer had given him no explanation, and she didn't feel like a threat. Diegert definitely did not want to kill a woman. He hadn't really thought it through, but facing the issue right in front of him, he could not bring himself to shoot her.

"Alright, but you're coming with me."

"That's stupid."

"Stupid is not controlling the situation, and until I feel it's right, you're staying with me."

Diegert put on his facial distortion mask and a black baseball cap.

"What, no disguise for me?"

"Sorry, you're leading the way."

They exited the back of the hotel and took the short route to the apartment.

The streets were not too busy, and with a fast pace, they made quick progress on the sidewalks. Rounding a corner, they came upon the scene of a car accident. A Peugeot driven by a mom with two small children had rear-ended a Fiat that belonged to a middle-aged couple. The man yelled at the police officer as he pointed at the damage to his car while gesturing about the mom's distracted driving. Diegert kept his head down for fear the distortion mask might attract attention. The tall prostitute put a little more sway in her hips, exaggerating her stride, drawing glances from both the cop and the irate motorist. Diegert placed a tight grip on her arm as they continued down the street, turning the corner onto the final lane and into the apartment building. Climbing the stairs, Diegert kept looking behind him, fearing that the cop might follow them into the building. He knew it was paranoia, but killing someone can bring that out in a person.

The apartment was small, but Diegert realized just how cramped it was when the prostitute had to sit on the bed while he occupied the one kitchen chair.

"How did you get this job?" asked Diegert.

"Through an e-mail, I never spoke to anyone. All instructions . . . electronic," she said, cocking her head to the side and drawing out her last word.

"So tell me about Mibuku."

"Aren't killers supposed to do their homework before they pull the trigger?"

"It was a short-order contract, and I was given very little information."

"And now you're questioning your actions. I do that all the time after I fuck somebody I probably shouldn't have."

"What about Mibuku?"

"What about him? He was a drug dealer and always had the best stuff. The kind I like. He had a big, hard cock and an arrogant personality. He liked Asian women because he thought our cunts were smaller . . . tighter. What a narrow-minded fool."

"You had a regular thing with him?"

"We had an occasional recurring thing, but as you can see, I sold him out for a big payday. Your employer has promised me good money for helping you."

They sat quietly contemplating their places in life. Diegert thought about how they were both hired to provide a service. She provided the pleasure of the flesh, associated with the creation of new life, and he deliberately and violently brought lives to an end. Their occupations cast them outside of society, their work, unacceptable. Yet there was no shortage of demand for their services. Realizing that a prostitute was his closest ally made Diegert shake his head. The woman broke his reverie.

"If you want to fuck me, it's five hundred. Otherwise, I'll be leaving."

He could see her hands twitching in a soft but constant tremor; she needed a fix.

"Where are you meeting for your payoff?"

"We're not meeting. The money is going into an account."

Diegert nodded knowingly, but his long pause brought an *I'm out of here* look to her face. Diegert abruptly commanded her, "Dump your purse on the bed."

"What?"

"Dump it all out or I will."

She grabbed the bottom of her large bag and raised her long, slender arm over her head. The contents spilled onto the bed. All sorts of typical items were in the pile, but Diegert's eyebrows rose when he saw the strap-on dildo and three types of vibrators. He grabbed her wallet and extracted her driver's license. Crossing to the kitchen table, he placed it on the surface and took a picture with his phone. Handing it back to her and returning to the chair, he changed his tone, asking her, "Where around here could a guy go for some nightlife, Miss Shei Leun Wong?"

Returning her belongings to the bag, she replied, "A guy like you, looking for some free sex, I'd tell you to go to Luna-Sea on Rue Chea Remiur. They party hard there and hook up pretty easily."

Holding the dildo up in the air with the straps dangling around her wrist, she twirled the plastic cock and teased, "You sure you wouldn't like to try something a little different? My treat."

"No. You can take that and go."

She stood up, slinging the bag over her shoulder. They continued to look at each other with curious but suspicious eyes. Their mutual moment of infatuated mistrust was broken by the sound of sirens wailing from the southerly direction of Chateau Lambert. Shei Leun Wong spun on her heels and exited the tiny apartment.

He sat with his conflicted thoughts. Pulling off the hit was exciting, exhilarating, a primal rush. He was becoming more comfortable with it, which concerned him. He didn't want to lose his sense of self; he had to control his willingness to kill and not let it become an urge. What was his employer going to do, he wondered, now that he hadn't killed the girl? Had he passed or failed the test? His disconcerting thoughts gave him no peace.

After two hours of solitude in the safe house with no disturbance at his door, Diegert figured he could go hang out in a club for a while. Shei Leun's suggestion, Luna-Sea, was only fifteen minutes away, and the videos on his phone made him feel like he was holding the coolest party in town in the palm of his hand. A quick stop at an ATM put five hundred euros in his pocket. Twenty euros got him past the bouncer and to the coat check girl, who collected another twenty, even though he didn't check a coat. Entering the cavernous space of Luna-Sea, he was struck by the décor, which was a clash of new-age gauche and postindustrial distress. The pulsing beat of the electronic dance music permeated every space and penetrated every structure so that the music was not only heard but felt. Surveying the room, he looked beyond the gyrating bodies on the dance floor to see a group of East Indians gathered in a large booth in the far corner of the club. He also noticed a mixed group of young people hanging out in a smaller booth much closer to the dance floor.

Making his way to the bar, he had to wade through the crowd of dancers, some of whom were grinding their hips in time with the beat, creating an erotic scene from which Diegert had trouble looking away. Without colliding into any of the randy couples, Diegert approached the bar and soon had the tender's attention. Gesturing to the unoccupied corner booth beyond the bar, Diegert said, "I'm going to take that booth. Please deliver a bottle of Grey Goose." Diegert's vodka request cost him 250 euros, but the order got the bartender to nod at the bouncer manning the posts and ropes. In the booth's minibar, Diegert found drink glasses, an ice bucket, and enough juice and soda mixers to keep the vodka interesting. After mixing his first drink, he looked up to see five young ladies lined up along the braided ropes like a murder of crows perching on a wire above recent roadkill. Diegert dispatched three of them with a wave of his hand. Pointing and then moving his fingers, he invited two of them into the booth. The two girls' pretty faces degraded as they stepped from the inky haze of the club floor into the soft light of the booth. The one with short punky hair didn't say anything as she grabbed a glass and reached for the vodka. Diegert quickly got his hand on the bottle so he could pour the pricey alcohol for her. Her eyes never left the glass as she swilled the drink without a mixer. The one with longer hair held out her glass saying, "Hey, I want some too." Diegert held the bottle of vodka vertically. "Yeah, but you and your friend aren't staying." The long-haired girl looked at Diegert with desperate bloodshot eyes.

"What?"

"Get out."

Diegert nodded to the bouncer and watched as the big guy escorted them out of sight.

The night's big spender asked his waitress to tell the group crowded into the booth by the dance floor that the next round was on him. The news turned all heads his way, and he nodded and raised his glass. Several of the women cast long glances at the dark-eyed, dark-haired man whose complexion was just a shade lighter than soft buckskin. His looks were intriguing and somewhat mysterious because he could pass for an Argentinian, Arab, or Italian. Women who liked dark, rugged men found him attractive, while others felt a sense of danger.

Diegert had mixed his vodka with orange juice, which made it easy for him to consume several quick drinks. Watching the dance floor, he was entertained by the thrusting hips and the back extensions of girls whose breasts were pressed outward and skyward as they undulated with their partners. He was mixing his next vodka with apple juice when he noticed a tall woman with a short skirt approaching the booth. Diegert nodded and the bouncer unsnapped the rope, allowing her to pass.

She held a long-stemmed martini glass and lifted it toward Diegert. "I want to thank you for the drink. Everyone appreciated it, but I wanted to thank you personally." In the soft glow of the booth's lighting, Diegert was taken by the woman's beautiful Asian face. Her eyes were large, round, and brown and her cheeks dimpled when she revealed her perfect white teeth with a friendly smile.

"It looks like your martini is nearly empty. Sit down and let me fix you another."

Stepping into the booth, the beautiful lady sat next to Diegert, whose eyes couldn't help but notice the extra length of leg revealed as her skirt slid up when she sat down. The young lady offered her hand. "I'm Jung Hwa." Her hand was delicate but firm.

"I'm John Sullivan," Diegert said. "So what's in your martini?"

"Pineapple juice and cassis along with the vodka."

"I don't think I have any cassis, but I do have pineapple juice."

Gulping what was left in her glass and flashing an enthusiastic smile, Jung Hwa handed her glass to Diegert. "Do you live here in Paris, Mr. John Sullivan?"

"Please, just call me John, and no, I'm here on a business trip. How about you, are you in school?"

"Yes, I'm studying art at the Sorbonne. I'm from Seoul, my program will have me here for two more years."

Diegert handed her the drink. "Let me know if this tastes any different." Jung Hwa took a generous sip, and her eyelids widened as she swallowed her mouthful. Recovering from the surprise, she waved her hand in front of her mouth. "Whoa, it is very good."

"But it is much stronger than the one from the bar?" Diegert asked.

Jung Hwa nodded as she emptied the rest of her drink. Diegert refilled the glass again, going heavy on the Grey Goose.

"Is your business going well?"

"Yeah, today was especially good."

"What business are you in?"

"The stock market. I made a killing today."

"So now you're celebrating?" Jung Hwa raised her shallow glass and swallowed its contents in one gulp. As Diegert was mixing another, the music changed to a dance version of a popular song. Jung Hwa squealed with excitement. Diegert could see what she wanted. "How about we get out on the dance floor?" he asked. Slurping down her refreshed drink, Jung Hwa grabbed his hand, leading him onto the crowded dance floor. As the floor filled up, Diegert could not deny the eroticism of the grinding hips that surrounded him. Jung Hwa faced away from Diegert as she backed into him, pressing her hips into his. Diegert picked up the rhythm and soon they both found the experience absolutely hypnotic. As the lyrics of the song faded away and the techno beat intensified, Jung Hwa turned to face him without reducing the contact at the hips. While they danced the coitus simularis, Jung Hwa leaned into Diegert's ear. "Get me out of here."

Out of the club, into the cab, and into her apartment in less than fifteen minutes. In that time, Diegert had kissed the Korean beauty so enticingly that when the apartment door closed behind them, clothes were shed and they recreated their carnal dance moves. In the bed, they found a passion neither of them had expected. Their libidos were driven by lust, and their bodies sought pleasure with a fervency neither had experienced before. Their intensity held up for nearly two hours, until they fell asleep entwined in each other's limbs.

Diegert slept soundly until the sunlight streamed onto the bed, shining in his eyes. The sound of sizzling and a soft voice humming brought a smile to his face as he woke up. From the kitchen, the aroma of fresh coffee and eggs tantalized him out of bed. Poking his head into the small kitchenette, he got a smile from Jung Hwa, who wore a thick robe and had her hair tied in a bun on the top of her head. The glasses she wore gave her an intelligent look, which was, Diegert figured, probably well deserved.

"Good morning. Have you ever had *gyeran mari*?"

"Good morning to you too. No, I haven't. What is it?"

"It's a Korean rolled omelet. You're going to love it. Do you want coffee?"

"No . . . I—I don't drink coffee."

She gave him the strange look he often received when he refused coffee. The caffeine-dependent didn't trust the unaddicted and couldn't fathom why anyone would deny themselves the earth's most popular stimulant.

"Some orange juice, then?"

"Thanks," said Diegert as he poured himself a glass and looked over her shoulder at the rolled omelet cooking in the skillet.

"I like to make them for my guests. It's a little bit of Seoul right here in Paris."

As Jung Hwa lifted the finished *gyeran mari* from the pan to the cutting board, Diegert's gaze was drawn to the small TV across from him. The news broadcast grabbed his attention. On the screen, the police were lifting a dead body from the river. In the corner of the screen appeared a headshot of a young woman; it was Shei Leun Wong. Diegert nearly sprayed the kitchen with his mouthful of juice. He coughed loudly as he choked down the juice.

"Are you OK?" asked Jung Hwa.

Waving his hand and nodding his head, Diegert replied, "Yeah—yeah, I'm fine, but what's happening on the TV? I don't understand the French."

Jung Hwa had not been paying attention to the news but now focused for Diegert's sake.

"They're reporting that the body of a prostitute was pulled from the Seine this morning."

"Oh," said Diegert as his cheeks flushed. He didn't know how to respond, but Jung Hwa was looking at him curiously as she sliced the rolled omelet into pieces, revealing their concentric rings. The broadcast now displayed the anchorwoman speaking. Diegert concentrated on the television while Jung Hwa instinctively provided the translation.

"They say there is some evidence that the woman pulled from the river may have been involved in a murder last night at the Chateau Lambert."

"Really?" said Diegert as a tingle of tension traversed his spine.

"Being a sex worker is so dangerous," observed Jung Hwa as she served Diegert a plate of hot, fresh slices of rolled egg with a filling of vegetables and cheese. Lost in thought, Diegert considered the unexpected news as he hungrily filled his mouth with the delicious *gyeran mari*.

He wondered if Wong had said something about him before being killed. Was whoever killed her now after him or was the employer simply accomplishing what he had failed to do?

"Whaddya think?"

The simple question confused Diegert as he continued looking at the TV's display of a well-dressed Gunther Mibuku. Did Jung Hwa know what he had done?

Realizing he was still engrossed in the TV, Jung Hwa clarified, "I don't mean about that. How about the *gyeran mari*?"

Diegert was embarrassed and relieved when he realized she was talking about her cooking and not his killing.

"This is the most delicious breakfast I've had in a very long time. I love the blend of the filling and the egg. The rolled-up slices make each bite full of flavor. I love it." Diegert could hardly believe himself for being so effusive, but it refocused Jung Hwa away from the television.

"Well, thank you, I'm glad you like it."

They finished their breakfast together, and Jung Hwa told Diegert about her sister and two brothers in Seoul. She described to him the courses she was taking, and Diegert lied about his international business. Checking the time on his phone, Diegert said, "I've got a noon meeting and then I catch a late flight back to the States, but I've really enjoyed myself, and if I could have your number, I'd love to see you again when I come back."

Jung Hwa hesitated and pushed her glasses up her nose before saying, "I will give you my number but no guarantee I will see you when you come back."

Recognizing the implications of their quickness to intimacy, Diegert replied, "Of course, I understand. There is no requirement here, but if you are available, I'd be happy to have dinner with you or tour an art gallery or anything else you'd like to do in Paris."

Jung Hwa's smile spread across her pretty face as her dimples tucked into her rosy cheeks, and she gave him her number.

CHAPTER 12

Walking back to the safe house, Diegert received a message on his phone. His employer wanted another hit. The job was a Greek politician, Constantine Stavropoulos. The contract was worth fifty thousand dollars. The hit had to be public, preferably during a speech. The text on the phone directed Diegert to a secure website where the specifics on the job were laid out. In Athens, he would be put up in a safe house and supplied with a compact sniper rifle equipped with a remotely controlled automated sighting and firing system. He would be able to operate the weapon from a distance using his smartphone.

In the Gulfstream, on the flight to Greece, he discovered that Stavropoulos was giving two speeches in the next two days, then had no scheduled public appearances for the next four weeks. The first speech was in the atrium of a newly renovated hospital. The second was at a soccer stadium during a rally for the upcoming World Cup bid. Greece wanted to host the soccer World Cup tournament in four years. It seemed they'd forgotten all about the debt they still owed for the 2004 Olympics and the fact that the country was currently bankrupt.

Once he arrived in Greece, Diegert visited the hospital and checked out the atrium. It was a big space, but it was enclosed, and the vantage points to place the weapon were either too far away, requiring shooting through glass, or too close inside and would surely be observed. At the soccer stadium, a small stage was being constructed on the front steps. Across from the stadium and to the south was an apartment building with a roof that proved to be an excellent vantage point. Thirty-six hours remained before the speech.

Diegert was very impressed by the rifle. It was a compact sniper design with a long barrel imbedded in a wooden stock. Since the rifle was designed to be operated remotely, the firing chamber made up the rearmost area of the unit. The triggering mechanism was pressure sensitive and operated by a servo. The sighting system fed digitally into Diegert's smartphone. The sighting and firing mechanisms were integrated, so when the rifle was in optimal firing position, the trigger was engaged. Tiny movement-sensitive gyroscopes detected and corrected subtle variances from the ideal firing position, adjusting for wind or vibration. The feed to Diegert's smartphone allowed him to set the process in motion, but once it was engaged, it couldn't be altered. On the secure website, there was a video game–style training program; Diegert used it to teach himself how to operate the system. After a few hours with the program, he was ready.

He wished he'd had such a system in Afghanistan. If the Army deployed this technology, a lot of American soldiers wouldn't be dead. Putting computers behind the rifles would have been not only safer but more effective.

The speech was scheduled for three p.m. Early that morning, Diegert was on the roof positioning the rifle. His employer was amazingly thorough, having included in the mission package everything he would need to pull off the positioning of the rifle. He used the digital sighting mechanism to aim at the point on the stage where his target would give the speech. He concealed the rifle in a foldout metal box that looked like an air-conditioning unit. Only someone who knew the building well would be able to recognize that the box was a phony. Inside the box, he planted enough C-4 to destroy the rifle and all its components beyond recognition. He set up a pressure-sensitive wire mesh network on the gravel rooftop, fanning it out so that anyone who stepped on it would ignite the C-4 and destroy the weapon. After setting, concealing, and booby-trapping his weapon, he went and had a nice brunch at a café with a view of the Parthenon, up on the Acropolis.

At two p.m. a few early birds showed up, by two forty-five a crowd had formed, and by three p.m. Stavropoulos was late. No one was surprised or concerned except for Diegert. He wondered if Stavropoulos was even coming. *All the setup and training on the system, and if this guy doesn't show, I won't have another chance,* worried Diegert.

At three thirty Stavropoulos was introduced by the director of the local soccer federation, and he walked onto the stage and started speaking. Having no idea how long the speech would last, Diegert wasted no time activating the system.

Diegert stood in the middle of the crowd and blended right in while he looked at his phone throughout the introduction. On his screen, he saw the reticle squarely on the politician's chest. He engaged the system and instantly the rifle fired, the bullet hitting Stavropoulos. His chest imploded and the bullet exited his back, ripping out his vertebral column. Lung tissue splattered the dignitaries behind him, and a quivering chunk of his heart fell onto the stage.

The panicked crowd stampeded. All video on his phone instantly disappeared, and his smartphone disconnected from the Internet. Diegert tried to ignite the C-4, but it wouldn't work. He left the crowd and returned to the safe house. The

Web filled up with amateur videos of the hit, and Diegert stopped watching.

A few hours later during the police investigation of the shooting, they found the equipment on the apartment roof and triggered the C-4, destroying the weapon and themselves. Three officers were killed and a building maintenance man was wounded. Diegert grew angry. Their deaths were unnecessary. He should've been able to detonate the C-4 remotely. Why did his employer disable his phone? If he could have detonated the weapon, the police officers wouldn't have been killed.

His account now held a hundred and forty-five thousand dollars, but the unintended consequence of the police deaths weighed on Diegert's mind and forced him to recognize the violent risks he brought with him to an area of operation.

The disabled phone chirped back to life, displaying his next assignment, a hit on Mohammed Farooq Arindi. The job was worth another fifty thousand. Diegert replied, beginning his message with: *Why was my phone disabled? I could have destroyed the weapon on the roof so no one else got hurt.*

Darkmass: *Your phone is obviously back to being operational, your concerns are tactical, not strategic.*

Next Chance: *What if I don't want to do this next job?*

Darkmass: *We'll turn you over to law enforcement.*

Pausing to consider the negative consequences of that, Diegert replied: *Where do I report for transport?*

The reply sent him to the commercial freight side of Athens International Airport, where he found the plane with the tail number NB7845. It was a large transport plane designed for freight—not people. His phone vibrated, and on the screen was the face of a man he had noticed when he'd first arrived. The instructions indicated he was to show the man the document now on the phone's screen.

The big, gray-bearded man said not a word to Diegert after inspecting the document. He walked him out to the plane, climbed up the back cargo ramp, and folded down a hard plastic seat from the wall.

"You'll sit here. Your parachute is right there."

The man slapped his hand on a large dull-green backpack that was affixed to the wall of the fuselage by some straps.

Adjacent to the seat was a door. "Pull the door latch. You'll have thirty seconds to jump before the door closes."

Diegert put on his best *no problem* face, but the bearded man's expression was doubtful.

"There are some printed instructions for the parachute in the outside pocket of the pack, and I'm sure you'll be instructed through your phone for everything else. Good luck to you." The man offered his hand. As Diegert shook it, he was informed, "This craft is airborne in twenty minutes."

His phone screen instructed him to lift the thin padding on the fold-down seat. There he found a large envelope with documents for his cover as a foreign aid relief worker. He was also instructed to inspect the contents of a duffel bag he found to the left of his seat. Inside he found a kit that included weapons, climbing gear, and tactical clothing. On the outside of the bag, three words were printed in black letters: "Duty, Honor, Mission."

During the flight, he was instructed that on the ground he was to meet a man who would inform him of the target's vulnerability. When the job was done, this same man would drive him two hours away to a small airstrip, and he would be flown to Cairo. Arindi was the financier for the pirates of Mogadishu. He controlled the money by leading the negotiations for the ransoms, and Diegert's employer wanted him dead.

Diegert familiarized himself with the parachute, since he had never used one before. His time in the Army included no airborne training. This being his first jump, he needed to learn what to do before leaving the plane. He remembered what his wrestling coach, Mr. Oliver, would say: *"Learn by doing."*

Two hours into the flight, Diegert found himself staring at the three words printed on the tactical bag: "Duty, Honor, Mission." Honor stuck in his mind, and he thought about his time in Afghanistan. On a night raid, his unit had invaded a family compound. Rousing everyone from bed, they'd gathered them outside in the courtyard. The tall, heavily bearded man of the house kept telling the interpreter that this was not being handled with honor. Lieutenant Prescott ordered that the house be torn apart to look for "evidence." Guns and money were found, but it wasn't what the lieutenant wanted. When he confronted the family man, the interpreter said the man was angry about what a dishonorable thing the soldiers were doing. Prescott hit the man across the face, knocking him down, and shouted at him as he lay on the ground. The man went totally silent and argued no more. It was too dishonorable to argue and lose face in front of his family, so the guy shut down like an honorable man. The lieutenant ordered the soldiers to ransack the entire home. *High moral standards of behavior, are you fucking kidding? This was war,* Diegert had thought at the time. *You get honor for going to war and coming back, especially if it's in a coffin. But while you're there, while you're fighting, there was no honor in any of it. Honor was for the parades, balls, and barbeques back home, not the battlefield.*

Diegert had to ask himself, *Was there honor in what he was doing now?* There sure weren't going to be any parades or barbeques. The thoughts annoyed him, and he turned the bag so the words were no longer visible.

CHAPTER 13

Crepusculous was the power behind the curtain, but the name on the front of the corporate curtain was Omnisphere, the world's largest private equity firm. The corporation was so massive that many of its holdings were publicly traded companies with their own stock market icons and boards of directors. Brand names and companies that people used and interacted with every day fell under the broad umbrella of Omnisphere. Through its holdings, Omnisphere profited from energy, communications, agriculture, retail, insurance, financial services, entertainment, and health care. Through clandestine means, the huge firm also benefited from drug trafficking, arms sales, gambling, and money laundering. If there was a profit to be made, Omnisphere would develop a subsidiary to penetrate the market and gain the advantage.

The face of Omnisphere was its CEO, Abaya Patel, an Indian-born, Harvard-educated businesswoman whom Klaus Panzer had personally picked to run the megacorporation for Crepusculous.

The board of Omnisphere was comprised of retired CEOs of the many companies that existed within the firm. It was an insular society that kept the business of Omnisphere powerful and private. Crepusculous, however, held the true power. Klaus Panzer and his three associates secretly and insidiously maintained control of all that Patel and the board of Omnisphere were allowed to do. Panzer was a devout practitioner of the adage, "That which is unseen is the most powerful."

Abaya Patel received the meeting invitation from Klaus Panzer: *Thursday 2 p.m. Innsbruck*, as the summons that it was. In spite of her perch atop the world's largest corporate conglomerate, she felt like a naughty child remanded to the principal's office.

On Thursday at two p.m., Panzer anticipated her arrival at his home in Innsbruck, Austria. The mansion had thirty-five rooms on the shore of a private lake surrounded by a meadow at the base of a mountain. The building was divided into the residence and the business area. Panzer would receive Patel in his office, where he sat in the comfort of a leather chair at a massive oak desk. The wood-paneled walls featured the taxidermy conquests of his Alaskan hunting trips and African safaris. Through eyes of glass, the silent beasts peered with menace at the room's inhabitants. The fully maned African lion leaping from the wall above and behind the desk intimidated all but the strongest of hearts that sat across from Klaus Panzer.

Patel brought her admin assistant, her chief of counsel, and her COO with her. They waited patiently in the ornate foyer, which was furnished with a rich leather couch and a marble-top table with a massive bouquet of fresh flowers, and upon the walls hung the works of the German painters Hermann Anschütz and Johann Jakob Dorner the Elder.

Seated on the edge of the couch, Patel recalled Panzer's manipulation of the Telexicon retirement fund problem four years ago. Telexicon was a holding of Omnisphere. Throughout the 2000s and up until 2012, the company was a major manufacturer of cell phones, the flip phone variety, with dedicated keypads and small screens. The phones seem quaint when compared to today's more versatile and powerful smartphones, but in their day, they were revolutionary and profitable. As technology and the market changed, Telexicon was unable to respond, and the business languished. While losses mounted, Omnisphere stepped in to close the business. A review of the books revealed a tremendous debt obligation to retired workers of both Telexicon and its parent company, United Telephone. The retirees were entitled to payments and health care coverage equaling ten billion dollars per year. The fund had barely eight million dollars in assets. Corporate finance had been borrowing from the retirement fund to float the company against the losses. Omnisphere was going to feel this pain.

It was against this backdrop that Patel had first been summoned to the Panzer mansion. Abaya recalled how Panzer had greeted her with warmth and hospitality. His charming grace was disarming, and his confidence emanated more powerfully than his Clive Christian 1872 cologne. After making her comfortable, he asked her opinion of the Telexicon problem. He listened carefully as she described a plan to spread the pain across the broad business entities of the Omnisphere global portfolio, allowing the company to service the Telexicon debts.

Panzer, with his chiseled face, full sweep of gray hair, and penetrating ice-blue eyes, listened carefully and nodded agreeably throughout her monologue. She finished and waited for Panzer's response. The man cleared his throat, placed his elbows on the desktop, steepled his hands, then interlocked his fingers before thumping the leather desk blotter with his unifist. He informed Patel that he had a different perspective, which did not involve bailing out Telexicon. He instructed her to invoke the cellular financial model that Omnisphere had outlined in all corporate contracts. This clause allowed

Omnisphere to sever any aspect of the conglomerate that was deemed to be no longer financially viable. Like a tree shedding deformed leaves or the human body sloughing off dead skin cells, Panzer was in favor of excreting the people of Telexicon and divorcing their debts from Omnisphere.

Patel protested, claiming they had a corporate responsibility to all the people whose lives were dependent on their retirement incomes. Panzer glanced away as he waved off the annoying gnat of a concern she had just expressed. He countered with a requirement that she was to fulfill his request, shed Telexicon, and report back to him in one week. His closing statement to her now reverberated in her mind. *"I can see this is going to be difficult for you, but let me assure you the rewards will surpass the inconvenience."*

The dumping of Telexicon was a shit storm right from the start, and Patel was the face the media was given to hate. Panzer was right; the capability to leave the losses behind was built into the corporate agreements. It was legal, even though it impoverished thousands of retirees. Patel suffered the public's ire, the social media assault was brutal, and she was saddened by all the hurtful headlines to which her children were exposed. The employees, retirees, and their families turned to her for help, and when she offered none, they turned on her like injured animals. These people had no chance to restart their careers and no safety net to keep them from drowning in debt. They had no lifeline, and their former employer didn't care. Following the "shed," Omnisphere posted one of their best financial years ever.

After facing the wrath of the public and the failed lawsuits brought on by opportunistic lawyers, Patel received a video from Klaus Panzer. The images displayed the most beautiful property in Europe, a villa on Lake Lucerne in Switzerland. The house was magnificent, the grounds immaculate, and the view spectacular. She sat transfixed by the serenity of the lake nestled within the surrounding Alps. She thought it was almost thoughtful of Panzer to send her this mini mind vacation after the hell she'd gone through for him. When the video ended, a deliveryman knocked on her office door and entered with a small tray in his hand. He stepped up to her and bowed, placing the tray within reach. On the tray was a small box upon which her name was embossed. She picked up the box, opened the hinged lid, and there lay a golden key. A card with the address of the lake house sat on a tiny velvet cushion. On the reverse side of the card, in scripted handwriting, it said, *Thank you and enjoy. K. Panzer.*

The house was hers. Had the rewards surpassed the troubles? Wasn't that why they paid the executives the big bucks, because they had to make the tough decisions? Business was business, and the objectivity of money didn't allow for the vagaries of the human condition. Those people would find a way, they always did, and the government bailouts would support them. This rationalization played in Patel's head as she lifted the key from the cushion and hit replay on the video. Watching it a second time, she felt a surge of excitement to think this magnificent residence was now hers. Screw the guilt; savor the rewards. Patel booked the corporate jet to Switzerland for the next day. Panzer's seduction had corrupted her morals in a most delightful way. Patel relocated to Lake Lucerne and ran the business from the villa for the next six months, which was plenty of time for the Telexicon story to fade from the media's memory. Soon she was once again heralded as the world's most powerful executive, leading Omnisphere, the world's wealthiest company. She was the visible, public entity of corporate stewardship, assuring shareholders of profitability. Oh, how sweet was the success of corporate power.

Her palms were sweating as she wondered what Klaus Panzer would request of her this time.

After announcing her through the intercom, Panzer's administrative assistant, Marta, escorted Patel and her entourage into Panzer's office. She and her group stood quietly for a moment, taking in all the animals. Panzer had grown accustomed to the pause his collection created in newcomers and sat quietly enjoying the head-swiveling effect of his trophies. After a moment, he rose from his seat. "Abaya, I'm so glad you were able to make it."

Panzer crossed in front of his desk to warmly shake her hand.

"Thank you, Klaus. Allow me to make introductions," Patel said as she turned to her people.

"Oh no, no, no, we don't have time for that. Marta, could you see to it that these fine folks are served refreshments and made comfortable in the foyer?" directed Panzer as he graciously extended his arm toward the door.

The three people, who considered Abaya Patel to be one of the most powerful people in the world, just had their perceptions adjusted by the person who was, in fact, the most powerful.

Panzer ignored Patel's look of consternation as he gestured for her to sit in a leather-cushioned wooden chair under the head of a wildebeest. Craning her neck to inspect the ugly gray antelope, she took her place with some reluctance.

With feet on the floor and hips leaning on the front of his desk, Panzer began questioning her.

"Abaya, are you happy in your position?"

Offended by this direct and unexpected question, Patel answered quizzically, "Why, yes, I am."

"Good," said Panzer, "because we are about to embark on something truly remarkable."

Patel's confusion was now set in the wrinkle of her brow.

Panzer continued, "The financial sector of Omnisphere, at my direction, has developed a digital currency known as Digival."

"Yes, I am aware of it."

"Good. I want Digival to be in place and functioning even if, at first, it only has a very small penetration. I want it all set up so, when the economy is right and the dollar collapses, Digival will be the go-to currency for people concerned about the evaporation of their wealth."

"You're planning to profit from the financial ruin of the economy?" Patel said with a chuckle.

"Don't worry, you will too. With the system already in place and the public aware, a digital currency backed by the world's wealthiest corporation will be better than a government that is insolvent."

Realizing there was no jest in Panzer's proclamation, Patel said, "You really think you can change the world's monetary system?"

"I absolutely do, and you will help me. With banking, payroll, and payment systems already set up, we will make the transition during the time of crisis and recovery less disruptive."

"What crisis, and did you say payroll?"

"Yes, Omnisphere employees who choose to be paid in Digival will receive an automatic ten percent raise."

Patel looked at Panzer with a dropped jaw, which she quickly closed into a frown.

Panzer continued, "It will be a voluntary program, but with over five hundred thousand employees, I'm sure many will switch, and their success will bolster others. Digival will be seen as a haven for wealth, and people will be eager to transfer their finances rather than lose it all to a devalued dollar."

Patel now found herself snickering. "You really are going to pull this off."

"The world changes every day; we are just going to change the way money works for people. We launch Digival now, saturate the Web with information about how it's accepted at all the places people shop, and make transferring to Digival easy and worthwhile. We can offer a ten percent increase in the value of money transferred from dollars to Digival."

"You're making money out of thin air."

"We don't even have to print a thing, but you know as well as I that our vast holdings are more than enough to support this venture. Make no mistake about it; we will destroy the value of the dollar and replace it and all world currency with Digival."

"This is unprecedented."

"Thank you."

"That was not meant as a compliment; I'm concerned about all the fiduciary responsibilities we are taking on by trying to be the world's only currency."

"Abaya, I expect you will soon realize that the benefits of controlling the entirety of the world's money far outweigh the risks and responsibilities. We must think big. Consider all the inequities in the markets due to fluctuating currencies. How many times have we seen whole countries starving and struggling to survive because their money has inflated to worthlessness?"

"The US economy is the strongest in the world; you're not taking out some tin-pan despot!"

"Why must we bow to the United States, a country that is basically bankrupt and unable to pay its debts? It has no intention of paying what it owes. It arrogantly continues to borrow while dominating the planet with its mortgaged military."

"We draw a great deal of profit from the United States and have significant holdings throughout it," Patel said as she removed her glasses and, with a small cloth, polished the lenses.

"Of course, I know that, and we will continue to occupy the majority role in the US just like we have for the past two decades, but now we'll be supplying the currency. The old saying goes, 'Those who control the dollars control the men.' Please excuse the gender bias, but the new saying will be, 'Those who control the currency will control the world.'"

Patel tilted her head forward, returning her glasses to the bridge of her nose and looking over them at Panzer, whom she considered brilliant, but this time she knew he was out of control.

The world's most powerful man hoped his words would get her to yield to his passion. Uncertain he had done so, Panzer made it plain. "Omnisphere will be the organization, Digival will be the mechanism, and you will be the competent, capable, trustworthy CEO orchestrating it all."

"And you will be back in the shadows calling the shots."

"I will remain discreet, but I have great faith that you will oversee the successful launch and eventual globalization of Digival."

"How is it that you are so certain the dollar will collapse?"

"The Crepusculous Board has a plan, which is being conducted on a need-to-know basis; therefore, I'm afraid I cannot tell you anything more."

"So I should just have faith that the four of you are doing the right thing?"

"Absolutely." Standing up and checking his Rolex, Panzer was ready to conclude the meeting. "I'll have finance get in touch with you, and I'm sure your associates are ready for your departure now."

Patel, realizing her audience with Panzer had just ended, stood and, after shaking his hand, headed toward the door. Her gaze caught the gleam of green eyes in the jet-black face of a snarling panther. The big black cat's sinewy body slunk around the leg of an overstuffed wingback chair. Gasping with a start, she reflexively pulled her hand to her mouth as a slight screech escaped. Turning, she saw a devilish grin on Panzer's face, who was so pleased to have frightened her with the unexpected placement of the rare and deadly panther. Patel, annoyed at being the source of his amusement, straightened herself as she exited the room.

CHAPTER 14

After four more hours of flying, Diegert's plane made a gradual descent and his phone alerted him to prepare for the drop. Dressed in the tactical clothing he had earlier changed into, he secured the duffel bag in front of him and the parachute on his back. Putting on his helmet, he stepped to the door. He thought about the fact that thirty seconds after the door opened was all he had to make his jump.

He pulled up on the latch, the door popped open, and the force of the slipstream sucked him out of the airplane. He tumbled and rolled while falling ten thousand feet above the most poorly governed country in Africa. The darkness and the rush of the wind disoriented him, but he was able to stabilize himself by extending his arms and legs. It was a strain against the force of gravity, but the extra surface area slowed his fall and stopped his rolling. With his right hand, he grabbed the release and pulled the cord. The chute unfolded and yanked him forty feet up in the air, or at least that's how it felt. He grabbed the lines above him, stabilizing his movements as he began descending at a gradual pace.

From his skyborne position, he saw a very dark earth below. In fact, he could see nothing below him at all. It was disorienting because the lack of any distinguishing characteristics in any visual plane left him with only his internal balance system for an indication of which way was up.

As he struggled with his lack of orientation, a cold, wet mist plastered his face. Droplets of water condensed on his warm skin and clung to his hair and clothes. He was passing through a cloud.

When he emerged from under the bank of suspended vapor, his sense of alignment to the world returned. Although he still had eight thousand feet to fall, he could now see lights below, and every minute he was able to see more and more distinguishing features of the earth's surface.

Soon the shoreline was clear, and the intermittent lights of Mogadishu twinkled, evidence of an urban population. Certainly nothing compared to the city lights of an American or European city, but it was his target from the sky. As he floated past Mogadishu, Diegert realized he would land in the desert northwest of the city.

Darkness distorted Diegert's sense of both speed and distance. He hit the rocky ground hard with both feet, and a gusty surface wind filled his chute and yanked him farther north. He struggled to pull the parachute down, but instead, it dragged him through the brush and thickets that dotted the sand and rock surface of this little piece of Africa.

While being dragged, Diegert undid the buckles of the parachute pack, and the wind ripped it off, sending him tumbling into a patch of thorny bushes. Watching his chute blow across the scrubland, Diegert was grateful he still had his duffel bag. He changed out of his tactical suit and put on his khaki relief-worker costume. Following his compass, he hiked into town.

Diegert had never seen a place more chaotic and dangerous than Mogadishu. All the men and boys were armed, and his white skin attracted unsettling curiosity. Even the stray dogs were threatening. This city, which had endured decades of warfare and civil strife, was on the rebound—at least parts of it. Coastal areas of the southern section of the city were benefitting from foreign investment, with several new hotels being built by the beaches. The north, though, was under the control of al-Shabaab, an Islamic organization that was at odds with the Somali federal government and used terrorism to advance its agenda. The northern part of Mogadishu hadn't changed much in the past twenty years, and Diegert's mission took him deep into an area known as Shibis, where conflict and tension hung in the air along with the stench of rotting garbage.

Although it was past ten p.m., he was to meet his contact in the dusty bar of the Hotel Curuba. This establishment catered more to the locals than international travelers, so Diegert's light-brown skin, often the darkest in the room in Minnesota, looked as pale as the dingy white tablecloth in front of him. He was seriously questioning the wisdom of his contact in selecting this bar as their meeting place. The contact's name was Charles, or at least that was his English name. Charles approached Diegert cautiously but quickly sat down and informed him that Arindi lived in the old Hotel Duprie, which, on the outside, looked dilapidated and uninhabited but inside was well appointed and comfortable. The structure had an enclosed inner courtyard, and every morning, Arindi spent fifteen to thirty minutes quietly secluded in a private retreat enclosed by large palm fronds and tropical ferns. This is where he would be most vulnerable. Charles gave Diegert the address where he would meet him for extraction when the job was done. Their business concluded, Charles took a quick exit, leaving Diegert to the uncomfortable stares of the well-armed men chewing khat in the Hotel Curuba. Within minutes, he realized it was time to leave.

The Hotel Duprie was heavily guarded in spite of its decrepit appearance. At night, though, so many of the men in Mogadishu were spent from chewing khat that, as guards, they were worthless. Diegert climbed the farthest outside wall of the four-story building, using the foldout grappling hook and strong paracord from his kit. On top of the roof, he changed into his tactical suit, ate a beef burrito MRE, and prepared to lay low for the night. The desert night was clear and surprisingly cold. Diegert put on a black tactical jacket and a dark knit hat. As he lay on an eight-foot slab of concrete set within the stone-covered rooftop, he could hear the barking of a distant dog, the crying of a hungry baby, and frequent bursts of automatic gunfire from guys he figured had more bullets than brains. In the short time he had been in this strained urban part of Africa, he had seen more abject poverty than he ever imagined existed. It made his American life, with its solid roof, public school, and clean running water seem like more than one should expect to be granted. To the west, he could see the illuminated concrete skeletons of coastal hotels under construction. They represented a glimmer of hope for the future and a reminder that many would continue to be ignored in this tropically attractive yet tragic place. He never really slept but rested with his MK 23 pistol in his hand, in case others sought to take in the depressing view from atop the Hotel Duprie.

In the morning, with his pistol holstered on his right and the Ojibwa knife on his left hip, Diegert crept to a position where he could see down into the courtyard. Arindi had women and children living with him. They talked and played on the balconies facing into the courtyard as the day began. Suddenly, the children were pulled back into rooms and the women cleared the balconies. Arindi emerged on the ground floor and strode around the courtyard, stretching his arms and legs. He followed a little path into the grotto of large green plants. Diegert seized his opportunity.

Dropping a rope into the courtyard, Diegert descended to the ground floor. Withdrawing his silenced pistol, he walked quickly down the little path. Inside the grotto, Arindi had a water fountain making a peaceful bubbling sound. Where Diegert expected to find the financier of thieves sitting like a cross-legged Buddha, he found only empty space.

From the right a tremendous force cross-chopped Diegert's forearm, knocking his pistol to the ground. Diegert was struck in the face with a powerful punch. Dazed and off-balance, he was kneed in the gut, doubling him over. Arindi was strong and hit hard. Diegert anticipated the next strike and blocked it with his right arm. Using his left hand, Diegert grabbed Arindi's throat and squeezed with all his might. Diegert wanted to disable him, but he also wanted to keep him from calling for help. Grasping the antler handle, he drew his knife. Arindi grabbed Diegert's right arm with his left hand, and the struggle became a stalemate. Unable to fully ventilate, Arindi surprised Diegert at how powerful he remained. Diegert kneed him in the groin, and although the pain shone in his eyes, the African hung on to Diegert's arm. Diegert drove him back through the plants until he collided with the wall. Diegert smacked Arindi's head repeatedly against the concrete wall until the African's grip on the assassin's arm slackened. Yanking his right arm free, Diegert plunged the knife into Arindi's chest, forcing the inscribed blade up and dissecting the aorta from the heart. Blood poured out of the African financier's chest as he slumped forward into Diegert's arms. Arindi looked at Diegert as he was laid down, but the expression was so bewildering that the assassin had no idea of the dying man's final thoughts. Diegert made a quick video of the corpse and sent it to his employer.

Covered in blood, he went over to the water fountain to wash his hands and arms as well as rinse some of the blood off his sleeves. The water turned dull crimson as it mixed with the blood in the recirculating fountain. Diegert had picked up his pistol, put on his dark-brown facial distortion mask, and adjusted his dark knit hat when a piercing shriek blasted down from the balcony. He instinctively turned to the sound, seeing two women at the rail of the second-floor overlook screaming and pointing. Turning his face away, he quickly walked out the front door of the old hotel. Two lazy guards were surprised when this man in black walked out of the building they were supposedly protecting. The mask made his face look weird, which confused the two guards. Diegert shot the first one in the forehead. The second tried to raise his AK but failed when Diegert shot him in the chest and then in the face. Rounding the corner of the building, he moved briskly down the street. He grabbed a large white sheet off a laundry line, wrapping it around him in Mogadishu fashion.

At the address Charles had given him, Diegert found the door open. He knocked and stepped down the hall, expecting Charles to greet him. At the end of the hall, he turned the corner to see Charles's body seated in a chair with his severed head on the floor.

The hallway darkened as a figure blocked the light. Diegert didn't hesitate, firing two rounds down the hallway, which dropped a body at the door. The hallway lit up with automatic gunfire as Diegert backed into the opposite room hoping to find another door. Charles's wife and two children were huddled in the room. She looked at him with dread and simply pointed at the window. It had no glass but was a large square hole in the wall covered by a curtain. He climbed out the window, knowing the next men to enter that room would be getting the same directions. He ran down the alley, tucking in behind a large rain barrel. Peering down the alley, he saw three men exit the window. One turned and went in the opposite direction. The other two came his way. Placing a fresh magazine in his pistol, he racked the slide as he pulled back against the wall. He could see their long shadows preceding them as the morning sun shone from behind. When the head of the shadow crossed the plane of the barrel, Diegert rose and fired into the face of the first man. The second was surprised, but he had been carrying his AK-47 at the ready and immediately pulled the trigger. The shots whizzed past Diegert, ricocheting off the barrel and pockmarking the walls. Squatting behind the barrel, Diegert fired his pistol low, shattering the Somali man's legs. As the thin, dark man crumpled to the ground, Diegert rose and killed his attacker with a lethal shot.

With both men down and the whole neighborhood awake, he sprinted out the alley and onto the street. He had no idea where he was except that the ocean was to the east.

Everyone on the street was an informant, and Diegert knew he needed a safe place to hole up. He just kept moving, knowing that very shortly the whole town would be looking for him. Fortunately, the northern part of "The World's Most Dangerous City" had a lot of dilapidated buildings where a hiding place could be found. The trick was that each bombed-out building was fully occupied by the desperate residents of this city of despair.

The façade of the building Diegert finally found said only "OTEL" in sandblasted letters. He climbed to the second floor and found an unoccupied room. The sparse furnishings included an old couch and nothing else. He took some cord from a utility pouch and tied it to the door, running it around a bare water pipe in the corner of the room. He positioned himself behind the couch, removed his mask and the sheet he'd been wearing, and waited to see if his location had gone unnoticed.

Several hours passed, and Diegert's hopes to escape in the darkness grew. As he formulated a plan to exit the city at night, there was a delicate knock on the door. He pulled the string, opening the door and revealing a young boy with a bottle of water to sell. The boy was small and undernourished. Diegert could see he had recently skinned one of his knobby knees. He was dressed in baggy gym shorts and a T-shirt that read, *Denver Broncos, 2013 Super Bowl Champions*. When the boy smiled, his lips revealed a pair of buckteeth and a lack of oral hygiene. Diegert smiled, though, to see the friendly little water merchant whose bright eyes expressed his hopeful anticipation of making a sale. As the boy stepped inside, a metal canister was tossed in. The explosion ripped through the room, tearing the door off its hinges and vaporizing the poor little boy. Automatic gunfire followed the explosion, and the room became a maze of flying bullets. The couch offered minimal protection as it was being torn to shreds.

Several men entered the room, and Diegert took two of them down. He had to fight or they would overwhelm him. Rolling across the floor, he grabbed one of the AKs. He fired out the doorway, driving back the attackers. From the window, he looked outside to see a Somali man on the back of a pickup truck with a mounted machine gun, known in Mogadishu as a "technical." The driver of the armed vehicle pointed to the window, shouting at the other man to fire his weapon. The man with the gun fired a series of staccato rounds through the open window and into the surrounding walls. Diegert ducked down as splinters of wood and chunks of plaster flew through the room. Suddenly, the rounds from the truck ceased, and gunfire again filled the doorway. Diegert returned fire at the room's entrance, looked out the window, and realized the gun on the truck had jammed. He quickly shot the man who struggled with the incapacitated weapon. Diegert leapt out the window onto a heap of garbage. The truck's driver struggled to get a pistol out of his pants pocket. Diegert struck the man in the face with the butt of the AK, grabbed him by his flimsy shirt, and dragged him out of the truck, tossing him to the ground. In the dusty road, the driver managed to extract his pistol, but not before Diegert perforated his chest with a spate of bullets. Off the dead man's belt, Diegert unpinned a grenade and tossed it into the second-floor room. Jumping into the technical, he sped down the street as flames and smoke exploded out the second-floor window.

CHAPTER 15

Diegert drove the pickup truck, dodging donkeys, goats, merchant stalls, old men, and young kids. The lack of signage forced navigation by landmarks, Diegert using the ones that oriented him to the sea. Soon he was at a northern seaport in an area known as Abdiaziz. Decades ago, this port had welcomed Europeans coming to enjoy the fabulous beaches, tropical temperatures, and the beauty of the Indian Ocean. Today, the port was home only to vessels that had been captured by pirates and brought there to be held for ransom.

Diegert drove along the packed sand track that ran parallel to the waterfront, then brought his vehicle to a stop. Doing a quick self-assessment, he wiped blood from a gash on his forehead. His ears ringing, he extracted a small piece of white shrapnel from a wound on his forearm. Inspecting the curious object drew the buck-toothed smile of the small water merchant to his mind as he realized he held in his fingers one of the little boy's front teeth. Diegert's stomach turned as he tossed the tooth out the window.

He was surprised at the variety of boats secured to the aging docks: cabin cruisers, fishing vessels, and sailboats with their masts removed. Thin Somali men with large weapons occupied the boats and the entrances to the docks. Their hard stares made Diegert anxious, especially when they leaned toward one another, exchanging questioning gestures. As a white man driving a technical, he knew any interaction with these AK-47-wielding land pirates would be fatal.

Diegert continued along the waterfront until he came upon a sailing yacht with its mast still in place, beach headed away from the other boats. Two Somalis guarded the vessel. One was asleep on the sand. The other was grooving to the music in his earbuds. Diegert exited the truck and used his silenced pistol to allow the sleeping guard to enjoy permanent slumber. He stepped onto the yacht. The second guard was on the deck of the stern, dancing and singing as if the whole ocean was his audience. Diegert stood behind him, raised his pistol, and quietly used a bullet to end the distracted guard's career as an entertainer. The body landed with a splash. Diegert stood still for a moment, relieved that he hadn't drawn attention to himself. Returning to the pickup truck, he tied the steering wheel with a rope and placed a rock on the gas pedal. The truck accelerated off the end of an ancient concrete break wall and plunged into the channel passage. Diegert quickly returned to the yacht. He pulled up the mooring lines and the sand anchors, started the engine, and quietly backed the vessel away from the beach. He knew there was a risk he would encounter pirates as soon as he left the port, but the alternative on land was no better. This mission's original extraction plan had gone to shit. Diegert reasoned, however, that if any pirates attempted to take the yacht back, he was going show them what it meant to defend a vessel by all means possible.

The power of the engine delivered him away from the port. His first priority being escape, he now realized he should check his fuel supply. Throttling the engine back, he went below for the first time. In the dining area next to the galley kitchen sat a gray-haired, weather-beaten old man. Diegert flinched when he saw someone else on board. The man's hands were bound and leashed to the table. A rag, tied around his head, gagged his mouth.

The old man's eyes went wide with surprise, and his startled look actually calmed Diegert, who could see the old guy was sizing him up. At six foot two and 190 pounds, Diegert was lean, strong, and very fit. His black tactical outfit, with vest and boots, was dirty and sweat stained. The old man's gaze lingered at the splotches of dried blood on his pants. Diegert needed a shave, but his dark stubble only made him appear all the more imposing.

He untied the rag. The grizzled guy made a series of awkward faces as he tried to bring comfort back to his lips. Diegert looked at him squarely. "Is this is your vessel?"

"Aye," the old man said, looking at his replacement captor. "What now?"

"Now I go check the fuel."

The old man shouted after him, "The gauge is on the far right, near the anchor chains."

Returning from the engine room, Diegert told him, "There's less than half a tank."

"It'll be enough if we start using the wind." The old man lifted his tethered hands, yanking on the leash that held him to the table.

Diegert looked at him wearily. "What's your name?"

"Barnard Pinsdale, this vessel is the *Sue Ellen*. She's named after a beautiful girl I knew when I was young. I've been captive for five days. The fools think I'm rich, and they're hoping for money. What are you doing in Somalia?"

"Never mind."

Diegert knew he could not sail the boat himself, and this man didn't seem like a threat, yet he was hesitant to free him and allow him to take charge of the vessel. He went up on the top deck and looked out. The shore was receding, and all around was vast distance. The great expanse made him uncomfortable, and he realized he would need the old man's help.

Diegert freed the man from the tether and untied his hands. The old man rubbed his wrists as he slid out of the galley booth. He rose on wobbly legs, and Diegert could see the wiry man was paunchy, but his forearms were taut bands of muscle under deeply tanned skin. The old man extended his weathered hand.

"You can call me Barney."

The two shook hands, but Diegert didn't offer his name. Barney held on longer than Diegert expected, but it had probably been awhile since the old man had been touched without violence. Barney shut the engine off and directed Diegert to drop the anchor.

"What? We've got to get out of here. We're not just going to sit here and let them come after us."

"Listen, darkness is falling; we'll keep our lights off. The winds are doldrums; we can't sail. In the morning, we'll catch the warming winds and soon be far away from here. Besides, I haven't been in my bed for five nights. Now come over here and let me show you how to release the anchor winch."

The two men remained separate through the night with Diegert on deck and Barney stretched out on his bunk below.

As the sun rose, Barney directed Diegert on how to control the sails and handle the sheets, and soon the yacht was on a true course. With good wind and calm waters, the two passengers rode in silence as the boat delivered them away from a place they were happy to leave behind.

CHAPTER 16

As the day passed, they traveled nearly a hundred nautical miles. Barney commented to Diegert, "We're making good progress. The winds are being kind to us, and you sure are a quiet fella."

Diegert looked at him, smirked, and said nothing.

"So why won't you tell me what you were doing in Somalia?"

"I was doing hunger relief work."

"With which agency?"

"Ahh . . . the International Association for Hunger Relief," replied the younger man while continuing to look out at sea.

"Never heard of 'em."

Turning to face Barney, Diegert addressed his inquisitor. "We're a new agency, and I was doing the lead work of establishing relationships and securing facilities for our operations."

"How'd that go?"

"Not well. The Somalis are very short on trust and have long memories for disappointment."

"You sound like a do-gooder, you just aren't dressed like one. Speaking of hunger relief, let's eat."

Diegert's face lit up with the mention of a meal.

"When the Skinnys were here, they fed me uncooked pasta and raw canned meat."

"Well, what do we have now?"

"Now I'm going to cook it."

Barney stepped down into the galley. Diegert sat on the stairs. Barney got out the pot and pulled out a bag of egg noodles and a can of ALPO "Stew with Beef and Vegetables" dog food. The can had a picture of a handsome yellow lab, and Barney set it next to the noodles. He handed Diegert a large cooking pot. "Go fill this half-full with water."

"From the ocean?"

"No, why don't you go pump some from the well?"

Diegert rose and returned with the pot half-full of seawater.

Once the water was boiling, Barney put in the noodles.

"The Skinnys didn't like pasta. Of course, they never figured out you had to cook it. They tried it raw, and that's how they fed it to me."

"You never told them about cooking it?"

"I wasn't going to be their Julia Child. It's the small victories that help you survive being a captive."

"Who's Julia Child?"

Turning away in disgust, Barney checked the boiling noodles and used a can opener on the dog food.

"What's with that?" asked Diegert.

"This is our meat."

"That's dog food."

"Yeah, the Skinnys couldn't read; they took one look at the picture and thought it was dog meat."

The old man was laughing as he recalled the Somalis' reaction to the canned food.

"In fact, that's what they called me. They'd say, *'Hey, Dog Meat.'*"

Chuckling again, Barney drained the boiling water, mixed the contents of the can with the noodles, and returned the pot to low heat to simmer.

Diegert was incredulous as he watched the meal being prepared.

"Who's Julia Child? Come on! You don't even know the greatest chef to ever have a TV show. Why don't you Google her?"

Diegert pulled out his smartphone.

"I don't have a connection."

"Of course you don't. Your generation doesn't know shit. You think intelligence is being able to manipulate technology. You know how to look stuff up, but you can't remember a thing. You've traded knowledge in your head for gigabytes in your hand, and when your technology fails, you're left with a brain that ain't worth shit."

Diegert wasn't listening; he was torn between the rumbling in his stomach and the realization that the only relief of hunger was Barney's canine cuisine.

"I cook; you clean." Barney handed Diegert a plate of warm, tender noodles in a rich, beefy gravy with generous portions of cubed meat and finely chopped vegetables. With a shake of Parmesan, it actually tasted good, and Diegert eagerly emptied his plate and looked up for seconds.

"One serving is all you get. There is no more."

Barney finished his meal and pulled out an old disc player. He put in a CD, pressed a button, and a symphony came forth from the speakers. He leaned back, closed his eyes, and waved his hand with his index finger pointed as if he were conducting the musicians. Diegert listened to the classical music and felt like he was at the movies with no movie. Even though Barney was enraptured, Diegert asked, "What kind of music is this?"

Barney, pulled from his reverie, said, "You don't recognize this?"

"No, I never listen to this kind of music."

With a critical scowl, Barney informed Diegert, "This music is the most beautiful and complex in the world. All modern music owes a debt of gratitude to this work."

"Oh, come on, all music?"

"Yes, the work of Mozart revolutionized the way music was written, played, and appreciated, such that any musician who does not recognize his contributions to the art form has no sense of historical significance."

The symphony hit a high note just as Barney concluded his statement. The musical accompaniment to the diatribe spewed forth by Barney forced Diegert to feel the impact of his words with a silencing effect. He struggled to say only, "OK."

As Diegert literally licked his plate, he watched Barney close his eyes and return to conducting Mozart's Symphony no. 1 in E-flat Major. Diegert wondered if he would one day like this music when he was old. His mind wandered to another question, though, and he interrupted Barney again: "Hey, what happened to your dog?"

Opening only one eye, Barney replied, "I've never had a dog on board the *Sue Ellen.*"

"You mean, you meant to eat the dog food?"

"It's way cheaper."

Diegert couldn't hide his disgust as he gathered the dirty dishes and went below.

"Use seawater for washing. Don't waste any fresh."

Barney sat on the deck as the sun, augmented by Mozart's symphony, slowly set.

After cleaning the kitchen, Diegert came back on deck.

"Night watch," said the old man. "We've got wind tonight, so we'll each take a six-hour shift, during which it is your responsibility to maintain course and report any equipment problems or severe weather changes. I'll go first, so you go below and get some sleep."

Diegert went belowdecks and found two berths. One had obviously been used by Barney; the other had become a repository for junk. Diegert moved the boxes of canned dog food as well as various towels and tarps covering the old mattress upon which he was going to sleep. Once he was lying on the mattress, he found it very uneven and uncomfortable. Getting out of the bed, he pulled up the mattress, uncovering a case. It wasn't his business to know what was in the case, but the latches gave way with a soft snap. Lifting the lid, he could see black foam formed into the outline of a rifle stock. Other areas of the foam were specifically cut out for the barrel, ammunition magazine, and a high-powered scope. Encased in foam on the top of the lid were two pistols with sound suppressors as well as more mags of ammo. Diegert looked at the arsenal and thought again about Barney Pinsdale and the Somali pirates. Could this set of weapons have belonged to the Somalis, or was Barney something more than just a wandering sailor? He closed the lid, facing the same storage difficulty that led to it being stored under his mattress. There was nowhere else to put it. He set the case on the floor and piled the tarps, towels, and boxes of food on top of it. He stretched out on the old mattress and put his head on the dirty pillow, and even though he had made this perplexing discovery, he was so fatigued that he instantly fell asleep.

The *Sue Ellen* had made its way into the commercial shipping lanes, which were the best routes through the ocean. The ships sought efficiency in their transit, and corridors through the ocean could become busy and dangerous places for smaller vessels, especially at night. Barney had the *Sue Ellen* outfitted with solar-charged lights on the bow, stern, and atop the main mast so that she could be illuminated all night long. This was an appropriate precaution, but it also presented a risk. Pirates traveled without lights, and finding a lit vessel at night was easier than searching through the day. All day while they sailed, Barney had known they were still in dangerous waters but had hoped for the best. In addition to the wind and the weather, Barney was keeping his ears alert for the sound of any approaching outboard engines.

After six hours, Barney's watch had passed without incident. Below in the cabin, he woke Diegert and waited up top to review the change of the watch.

Diegert found it hard to wake up; he could've easily slept longer. At the top of the stairs, he was impressed with how dark the night was. He could see by the light from the boat's illumination, but otherwise, the ocean was a very black place on this moonless night.

"The winds are light without much variation, but we're still making progress under sail. Keep the tiller within the range I showed you, and we'll stay on course. Not many stars out tonight, so just hold the line."

"Right."

"One last thing, lad, keep an ear out for sounds of motor engines. If you hear the running of an outboard engine, I want you to wake me."

"Why, what is it?"

"We're still in pirate waters. They cruise around in skiffs. You can hear them before you can see them. These devils are smart, though; they've learned to muffle the engines very well. If you hear something, wake me up."

Sitting alone on the deck in the dark, Diegert looked suspiciously into the blackness, imagining approaching pirates. Over time, this gave way to thoughts about his family. His father and brother didn't garner much reflection. He knew they were in the middle of deer season, hunting every day and spending every night at the Moose Jaw, drinking too much beer and talking too much bullshit. His father never took him deer hunting. Excluding him was the highest form of rejection in northern Minnesota.

His mother would be working long, hard hours at the Triple Crown Diner. Taking orders, serving meals, and cleaning tables, she had to do it all, and she only knew one speed, full bore and wide open. She worked herself so hard so that she didn't have time to think about a different life. She was the one who would be missing him. She would be thinking of him, and it hurt that he hadn't talked with her in such a long time.

Diegert had never met his grandmother, but he knew she'd been raped by a white guy, and that's how his mother was half Ojibwa. Denise was born but not accepted by the Ojibwa as a true native. As she grew up and went to school, the white kids called her half-breed and treated her like shit. After high school, short, fat, bald Tom Diegert asked the tall, statuesque, but socially crippled beauty to marry him, and she did. Her own mother had committed suicide years before, so she was alone at the Justice of the Peace ceremony. She moved into Tom's dump of a house, and within a few weeks, she had it cleaned up, painted, and looking pretty good, even though the small two-story house lacked an efficient furnace and any real furniture.

Physically, she was out of his league. From time to time, he would have to take the joking insults that flew around the Moose Jaw. The guys called him "chief" and asked if his "squaw" was good in bed. He would drink away the embarrassment and go home to fuck her with anger. Eventually, she got pregnant, and Jake was born and grew up to look just like his dad.

She would like being out on this boat. She had never seen the ocean, but every vacation he had spent with her was a camping trip. Just the two of them, hiking or canoeing to a remote, beautiful place in Minnesota's Boundary Waters. They would set up camp, and only after she had done the work of making their site homey, would she sit down and relax. She would say, *"It's a real vacation when it's cheaper to be away than it is to stay at home."* Spending time with her in the wilderness, he'd developed an appreciation for independence. He learned a lot from his mother, and although not all the lessons were good, he found in her a person he knew loved him and took pride in his accomplishments.

What would she think of what he was doing now? Killing people and running away. Grief rose in him and made him feel as dark and lonely as the ocean was, without light and seemingly without end. He thought about those he had killed, both the targeted and circumstantial. He wanted to shed the tears he felt were forming behind his eyes, but they wouldn't flow. He couldn't find a way to release the guilt for his violent acts, and therefore, he retained the pain in his soul. It was a long, dark, lonely night, and Diegert began to fear that the night and his life were becoming indistinguishable. An assassin lived a sad and singular life.

Six hours later, Diegert's watch ended without incident and with a beautiful sunrise.

Barney's disheveled hair and sleepy face appeared in the stairwell.

"Well, we survived another night," Diegert said, greeting his shipmate.

"Survival—your generation doesn't know shit about it," Barney replied as he continued up the stairs onto the deck.

In a mocking voice, the old man began, "Oh my God, I survived college, or I don't think I will survive the holidays. What bullshit. You people mistake effort and a moment without complete comfort as something to endure. You think it's a great virtue to have succeeded where there was very little chance of failure and absolutely no threat to your life."

Diegert caught Barney's wrinkled stare and looked away from the old man's scorn.

"Come out here," Barney said, sweeping his arm out over the ocean. "No grocery store, no police, no hospital . . . no fuckin' Internet, and then you can talk about survival."

Diegert looked at the exasperated old man and waited to see if he was finished. He gazed across the empty horizon, then brought his eyes back to Barney's, saying, "Yeah . . . like I said, we made it through the night. What's for breakfast, Milk-Bones?"

Barney pulled from his pocket a foil-wrapped Wild Berry granola bar and tossed it to Diegert.

"Eat your fruit. The Skinnys stole all my oatmeal and sold it to some guy to feed his donkey."

With breakfast over, Barney set a large plastic bucket on the deck. From behind the door of the cabin, he pulled a toilet seat and placed it on the bucket. He dropped his pants and sat down.

Diegert's expression couldn't hide his surprise.

"I've seen you piss off the stern, but this is where you shit." Barney leaned to the side and tapped the toilet seat. "And this is a luxury. I expect you to appreciate it."

Before long, a whiff of the wind told Diegert the old man was done and it was his turn.

Barney informed him, "Make sure you clean it when you're done."

"I gotta clean your shit?"

"I'm the captain. This is my home. I'm very comfortable out here. Clean the rags too."

"Rags? You mean there's no toilet paper?"

"No."

A short time later, the bucket was clean, the toilet seat was on its door hook, and two rags were drying in the wind.

CHAPTER 17

And so it went for several days. Diegert withstood Barney's criticism of his generation and ate dog food, while the old man taught him about life at sea and how to sail. Diegert fleshed out his lie about the relief agency he worked for, but he felt that Barney was not convinced. As the days passed and they crossed great stretches of ocean, Diegert found himself humming to Mozart and developing a bit of trust in the old man. On an evening following a particularly tasty dinner of ALPO Prime Cuts, Diegert decided to share the truth with him.

"I'm not a relief worker."

"Well, that's a relief, because I've been waitin' for a helicopter to drop a crate of food and old clothes on us."

Diegert's eyes turned to the old man as he fought the urge to curl his lips into a smile.

"So now you're gonna tell me what you really are, besides a liar."

"The truth is as fluid as this ocean," Diegert said, gesturing with a wave of his hand over the gunwale.

"Just like the wind and the water are taking us northwest," said Barney, "the truth is the only thing that's going to get you through this journey."

Diegert looked at the old man, realizing that the isolation of the ocean and having to rely on each other allowed him to relieve himself of his secrets.

"I was a soldier in the Army, but it didn't work out, and I was dishonorably discharged. Then I got a job as a bouncer at a bar in Austin, but that didn't go so well either, and . . . I ended up killing two guys."

"Murder or self-defense?"

"Definitely self-defense. I had to escape, so I went on the darknet and found a job as an assassin."

"Dare I ask, what is the darknet?"

"It's an underground network on the Internet. It uses software originally developed by the US Navy called Tor to keep information private and anonymous. I loaded the Tor software on my phone, got on the darknet, and replied to a posting looking for someone to do a two-part job. One hit in Miami and the other in France. A clean job in Miami got you a free flight to Paris on a private jet. No airport security on either end. It was just what I needed, and I was relieved when I got an immediate response."

"Wait a minute, you decided to become an assassin after killing two guys in self-defense?"

"Look, it was self-defense, but the guys were mobsters and there was no going to the police. I had to get out of Austin or I would've been killed. I completed the job in Miami and hopped on the plane to Paris. From there, it was a job in Athens and on to Mogadishu."

"Hold on a second, you were all alone on the flight from Miami, no one to explain anything or brief you regarding the next mission?"

"Well, there was a flight attendant. Her name was Amber and she was gorgeous. She provided food and drinks and was very happy to talk with me. She asked the right questions and didn't question any of my answers. As the flight continued, she told me she would like to have sex with me and that the cabin at the back of the plane would be an ideal place for us to be together. We went into the cabin, with its huge bed, and she started undressing, and so did I. She stepped over to me completely naked. I wrapped my arms around her and hugged her and we had sex." Diegert grinned as he quietly dwelled on the memory.

"Whoa, whoa, whoa . . . you can't stop there. You're talking to a guy who hasn't been with a woman for months and months."

"Months? Come on, you look like a guy who hasn't been with a woman for years and years."

Barney's face hardened as they looked at each other. Diegert realized he'd crossed a line, but he didn't care. "Oh, wait, I wasn't thinking about women who get paid."

"It's true that female companionship has become a commodity in my life, but it has only been a matter of months, not years, since my last transaction."

"Whatever . . . Amber was beautiful. Sometimes you fuck the girl; other times you get laid. Amber was an erotic artist. She had me feeling pleasure like I had never felt before. She had the right pace, fabulous rhythm, and she performed pleasurable acts in ways I will never forget. The sex was incredible, and when it was over, she lay down next to me and hugged me. She kissed my neck, and I began to sob. She said 'shh' in my ear, and I started crying like a baby. She said, 'There, there, just let it out, don't be embarrassed, just let yourself cry.' I cried uncontrollably for a long time. All the killing, all the running, all the looking over my shoulder every minute just built up until I couldn't take it anymore. Being up that high with such a beautiful woman on a clean, soft bed, I just had to let it out. She was so soft and warm; I was able to find peace like I hadn't for weeks. She never asked me to explain what I was feeling; she just used her body to comfort me, and in the state I was in, it was better than the sex. I fell asleep and had the deepest rest I'd had for weeks. When I woke up, she was still there. She told me we would be landing soon and that she hoped I would always be able to find peace when I needed it. I thanked her for giving me what I needed when I needed it. She slipped on a robe and left the cabin."

Barney blinked his eyes several times before turning and looking up at the sky. "I don't know if that is the sexiest or saddest story I've ever heard."

"Let's keep it private. It was a very personal thing, and it taught me a lot about coping with this life."

"Whaddya you mean?"

"Killing for a living. It takes an emotional toll for which you must atone or you'll go crazy. Other guys just bottle it up and try to be tough, but they will emotionally implode. They drink too much and become very sanctimonious and judgmental. I've seen it in the Army. When you kill someone, you hurt inside. You know it's wrong on many levels, but you justify it; even if the circumstances require it, it's wrong and it hurts. If you let that out and express the grief, you can process it and move on. Letting it out allows me to continue."

"You sound like a priest trying to sell the confessional."

"I've never been in a confessional."

"Maybe you'll get the chance someday. But crying is what helps you?"

"It's the coping mechanism I discovered with Amber at thirty thousand feet."

"Look, that was quite a bedtime story. I'm gonna let you take first watch, and I'll see you in six hours."

CHAPTER 18

Barney went below to sleep and Diegert stood on the deck, looking out into the inky blackness. Diegert kept himself from falling asleep by pacing around the deck. The pacing also kept the chill of the night from penetrating his cotton T-shirt. After two hours, Diegert heard the low rumble of an engine. He looked out to sea in spite of the futility of searching the darkness. The sound was growing closer, but he had no idea from which direction. He stepped down into the cabin to wake Barney. He gently shook the old man's shoulder. "I hear an engine."

The old man's eyes opened with an expression of dread. "Let me speak with them."

"What? Let's kill the fuckers before they even get on the boat."

"They're already on the boat."

At that moment, Diegert heard footsteps along the gunwales, and then men were shouting in Somali as they descended into the cabin. Armed with AK-47s, they poked the barrels into the chests of the two sailors, forcing them up onto the deck. The pirates went about the business of taking over the boat as if it were so very routine. Diegert was ready to snap. None of these skinny guys looked like they could withstand even one body blow, let alone the kind of strike combinations he would deliver. It was as if they expected no resistance.

"Just remain calm. They may not take anything or find us very interesting."

"These guys are pussies. Let's kick ass."

"Oh no, you don't. You start a fight with them, and they will simply scuttle the whole boat, leaving us without even a life raft."

"Bullshit."

The Somalis shouted for them to stop talking. There were three pirates on board and three more in the skiff. The small size of their open-hulled, rundown old boat surprised Diegert. It wasn't more than ten feet long, and Diegert wouldn't have wanted to cross a Minnesota lake in that thing, let alone the Indian Ocean.

One of the pirates went belowdecks and searched for valuables. The other two stayed above and kept their AK-47s in their hands. The pirate belowdecks let out a loud ululation and rejoiced for whatever he had found. The pirate guarding Barney shouted down to him, and when the other pirate shouted back, he couldn't stop himself and went down below. The single pirate on deck was also distracted by what was going on below. Diegert seized the moment. He elbowed the pirate in the chest, bashed him in the mouth, grabbed the back of his head, and drove his face into a cleat on the mast, splitting his cranium on the rigid piece of metal.

Barney motioned for Diegert to stop, but the younger man stripped the AK off the dying pirate and descended into the cabin. The two pirates belowdecks were so amazed with the case of guns they'd found that, when they turned to see who was coming, Diegert struck the first one in the face with the AK's buttstock. The second received a hand blade strike to the larynx. Both were dazed, and Diegert wrapped the strap of the AK-47 around the first guy's neck and backhauled him over his shoulder. The force of the maneuver broke the pirate's neck, and Diegert knew it when he heard the vertebrae snap. The second guy was coughing and struggling to breathe. Diegert noticed a knife on the man's belt. He grabbed the man's knife, slashed his throat, and plunged the blade into his chest. The pirate crumpled to the floor as blood bubbled out of his neck.

Three down, three to go. Diegert took the AK-47s and ascended the stairs. He tossed one to Barney and proceeded to the stern where the pirates' skiff was tethered to the *Sue Ellen*. The men in the skiff were confused by the commotion on board. Diegert took full advantage of their lack of communication and their expectation that sailors wouldn't fight back to open fire with the AK. The volley of bullets cut down two while striking the legs of the third.

With the dull illumination of the stern's safety light, Diegert could see the third man was wounded, having fallen onto his back in the boat. Diegert's weapon had a flashlight taped to it. Turning it on, he could see the remaining pirate better. The guy was young, maybe fifteen or sixteen, yet he had a rifle and was pointing it in Diegert's direction. The defender of the *Sue Ellen* hesitated to see if the boy made any gesture of surrender. When the wounded pirate leveled his barrel at Diegert, he sealed his fate. With a rapid burst, the young sea robber's life ended with bullets to the chest and head.

From the moment the second pirate went down into the cabin until the last shot was fired, barely two minutes had passed and six lives had ended. Diegert's adrenaline was on full blast, and he was still on point, making sure there were no other threats.

"Relax," said Barney. "They're all dead and we're OK."

Diegert stepped back for a better look at the skiff, where he saw no evidence of life. Barney looked down into the cabin. It was a bloody mess with the two bodies heaped upon one another. He sat down on the bridge with slumped shoulders. Diegert came up along the port side and stepped into the cabin entrance to stand next to Barney.

Neither man knew how to begin the conversation. Diegert thought some statement of gratitude from Barney might be in order, or at least an "attaboy." He knew Barney had wanted to handle it differently, but this outcome allowed them to continue their trip without interruption. Barney stood quietly as his breathing returned to normal.

"Well, lad, you certainly know how to handle yourself. I have never seen a man use violence with such precision and speed. Maybe I'm just getting old, but I could barely see what was happening, let alone assist."

"It's how I've been trained."

"Well, apparently you haven't been trained to follow orders. I'm angry that you disobeyed me," said Barney, stepping onto the deck to look Diegert in the eye. "I'm the captain and I run this ship. If I tell you to do something, or not to do something, I expect your compliance."

Diegert let out a long sigh and chose his words carefully. "I will obey your orders. I'm sorry to have disrespected your authority."

Barney looked at Diegert, quite taken aback by such a humble reply. "We've got a mess to clean up, and we may still face consequences, so let's get busy before the sun rises. I'll keep the sails set so we can ride these winds as fast as possible."

Diegert dragged the bodies up from the cabin and laid them on the deck. He also moved the pirate from the base of the mast so all three were lined up together. Barney boarded the skiff and found fuel, weapons, and ammo, as well as grenades, food in the form of dried fish and coffee, fresh water, and a battery-powered drill with a huge bit on it. In the pocket of one of the men, Barney found a satellite phone. He and Diegert transferred the items to the *Sue Ellen*.

"We have to perforate both the chest and the abdomen of each man so the bodies will sink," Diegert said. "I have the knife that one of them was wearing. I'll do the job and jettison the bodies." Diegert went to work. He stripped them naked, viewing the tattoos and scars on each man. These bodies had not had easy lives but were now committed to the sea and on their way to the bottom of the Indian Ocean. All the clothing, worn out and tattered, was placed in a bag and sealed so it had no air. It was then tied to the outboard engine, which Barney and Diegert, both standing in the skiff, removed and sank.

"What about the boat itself?"

Barney hoisted the heavy drill. "We'll scuttle it. That's what this is for. If a vessel gives them trouble, they drill holes below the waterline and soon the boat is a relic on the ocean floor. So we'll put holes in the vessel of these devils and send it to the bottom along with everything else we've sunk."

Diegert took the drill from the old man, saying, "I'll do it, you climb back on board."

Wearing a life vest and tethered to the *Sue Ellen*, Diegert started in the stern and put several holes through the hull of the skiff. Soon the whole boat was underwater and Barney cut the rope. The craft made a slow descent, fading out of sight.

As Diegert floated on the surface watching the skiff sink, the image of the last pirate to die played across his mind, a boy who should've been in high school. Then the face of the little boy blown up in Mogadishu appeared in the placid water, haunting Diegert with his toothy smile.

Diegert hauled himself up the tether and back on board the yacht. As the sun rose, the only remaining signs of the night's events were the bloodstains. Barney and Diegert spent the morning quietly cleaning the bloody splotches off every part of the *Sue Ellen*.

CHAPTER 19

Breakfast was more granola bars, and Barney supplemented his with Somali dried fish. They both appreciated the coffee, hoping the caffeine would supplant the lack of sleep. With their course set, Barney picked up the satellite phone. "This phone is GPS equipped, so the pirates could be tracked as well as be able to communicate while on the ocean. I have no idea if they communicated what was happening out here. When I found it in his pocket it was on, but who knows if a call had been placed."

"Check the record on the phone?"

Barney had that look of technology ignorance that defines people of different generations.

"Let's have a look." Diegert took the phone from Barney. "We used these phones in Afghanistan."

Pressing the keypad, Diegert brought up the phone's call history. "Look, they placed a call shortly before midnight, and that was the last one."

"Midnight would make it just before they came aboard. So their cohorts on land know they encountered a vessel. Hopefully, they didn't get our name."

"So what if they did? They couldn't catch up to us."

"No, but they could task another skiff to come looking or they could use an aircraft."

"Aircraft?"

"Yes, all that money they get for ransoms buys old airplanes, so they can patrol the skies and direct their skiffs more efficiently."

"I can't believe they are that sophisticated."

"Why not? The ransoms corporations pay to get their cargo ships released are in the tens of millions. That kind of business attracts a lot of very smart criminals; please don't be so naïve. You must realize your violent actions may not be the end of our troubles."

"Throw it in the ocean so they can't track us with the phone."

"The phone has been off since I found it."

"You can turn the phone off, but the GPS will still connect with the satellite. Bottom line, the phone can be tracked."

"Very well, then." Barney snapped open the phone, pulled out the battery, and tossed the device overboard. "Now we are in a race to the Red Sea."

Barney got out a map and showed Diegert where they were and where he felt they would be safe. "It'll be about two days of sailing to round the Horn of Africa and enter the Gulf of Aden. Pirates operate in the gulf, but the US Navy has a very big presence. I think we'll be safe. To sail across the gulf will take another day, and then we'll enter the Red Sea."

Diegert reviewed what was described on the map and nodded with understanding.

"We've got a good wind coming up. Let's unfurl the jib and really capture its strength."

When the jib sail was fully engaged, the *Sue Ellen* flew across the ocean faster than Diegert had yet experienced.

When duties returned to refinement and adjustment of the sails, Barney asked, "So you told me about leaving America because of killing two men, and last night you killed six. When was the first time you killed a man?"

"The first thing I ever killed was a frog. My dad was a hunter. He was always hunting, with deer season being the most important. He and my older brother, Jake, would go on hunting trips all the time. When I was seven or eight, I begged him to take me hunting. He got out a BB gun and we went frogging. We waded into ponds and waited for their big-eyed heads to surface. My dad shot the first two, right between the eyes. They just floated there dead for him to scoop up in a net. He handed me the gun and reminded me to only shoot big ones."

"Sounds like a good old American bonding experience."

"Yeah, we spied one that was big enough, and I sighted the gun on the head and fired the tiny metal BB, hitting the frog but not killing it. The frog started flopping around, splashing in a circle. My dad was quick with the net and scooped up the frog, which entangled itself in the net.

"We waded ashore, and I could tell he wasn't happy. He stepped over to a big stone in the woods and said to me, 'Now you have to finish him.' I cocked the BB gun. He said, 'Not with a BB.' I looked up at him confused about what he meant. He said, 'Whack his head on the stone.' He handed me the net. I untangled the frog and could see that I had hit him on the side of the head near his ear, debilitating but not fatal. I held the frog by the legs and looked at my dad, who made a powerful downward thrust with his fist."

Diegert demonstrated by forcefully slapping the back of one hand into the other.

"The stone had a jagged edge. I raised the frog over my head and brought him down as hard as I could. When the frog struck the rock it started screaming." Diegert paused. "You'd be surprised at how frogs can scream. The sound was shrill and the pitch turned my stomach. I started crying, and my dad told me, 'He's suffering, boy. You've got to finish him.' Through my tears, I struck the frog on the rock again and again and again until his screaming stopped and his body went limp."

Diegert's face was sallow, his head and shoulders slumped, and he couldn't meet Barney's eyes.

"I dropped the frog and turned away from my dad, choking back my tears. I swallowed the pain and wiped my tears on my sleeve. 'Quit cryin' like a girl,' my dad said, 'we gotta clean these frogs.' I picked up the frogs, and he showed me how to clean them, cutting off their legs and stripping the skins. We ate them that night, and my dad never took me hunting again."

"Were you disappointed about that?" asked Barney.

"Yeah, but I learned what I was capable of and how I would react."

"Whaddya mean?"

"I mean, I was capable of killing, but it hurt. I could do it, but I'd feel it," Diegert said forlornly.

"But the feeling didn't stop you."

"I wanted to go hunting because I wanted to be with my dad. Killing frogs wasn't really what I was after. I figured the killing would be fine. He and Jake killed animals all the time. I was unprepared, though, for my emotional reaction to the struggle and suffering of something that's trying to hold on to its life."

"The fight for survival," spilled almost absentmindedly from Barney.

"Absolutely, the desperation and despair that even a frog experiences all because you chose to kill it. It's tough, but if you deal with your emotions, you can get through it and continue."

Diegert looked at Barney, who held his gaze while pressing him with his next question.

"What about the first man?"

"The first time I ever killed men was those two guys in Austin."

Barney's eyebrows rose as he glanced at Diegert.

"I was being held hostage by the Russian mafia, and my captors were going to rape me. I snapped, fought back, got a gun from one of them, and shot them both."

Barney, caught in thought, paused to form his next question. "Why were you being held hostage?"

"Because they used me to make it seem like I'd killed a guy three days earlier. They were holding me so they could eventually turn me in."

"And they figured as long as they're holding you, they might as well man-rape you."

"Yeah, so I wasn't having any of that shit. Once you start fighting with guys like that, though, it's to the death. The one guy already had four assassinations to his credit."

"The situation sounds somewhat like the pirates. Disarming men and using their weapons to kill them."

Diegert reacted with a slight chuckle. "I guess so."

Barney kept his gaze on Diegert, who stared down at the deck of the boat.

"So you began killing in self-defense, and you've progressed since then."

"I'm not sure I'd call it progress, but I have . . . diversified. I've also learned the value of a good clean head shot."

CHAPTER 20

In the afternoon quiet, Diegert was concentrating while sailing the *Sue Ellen*. He paused for a moment, feeling a shift in the wind.

"Hey, did you feel that?"

Smiling, Barney replied, "Good for you, a shift from the east, and it's now coming offshore. Trim the sheets and I'll bring the boom around."

Diegert pulled on the main sail's sheets while Barney used the tiller to change the boat's angle. They ducked as the boom passed overhead to the port side of the vessel.

"We're secure," said the ship's captain.

As they sat on deck working the sails and enjoying the speed of the boat, Diegert asked, "Who was Sue Ellen?"

"Sue Ellen? We all have a Sue Ellen," Barney began. "The girl you fell in love with but only you knew. Or maybe some others knew, but she didn't, and if she did, she never let you know she knew."

"Was this a real girl?"

"She's as real as love and as thrilling as lust. She's the delight of attraction and the disappointment of unrequited advances.

She's the reason your heart took flight and the reason your heart is broken."

Barney's semi-poetic words struck Diegert as maudlin. "I don't have a Sue Ellen."

"If you don't, I worry about ya and I feel sorry for ya, but I can't say I admire ya."

"So you named your boat after a disappointing girl who broke your heart?"

"No, I named her after youth, beauty, hope, and the heart-pounding excitement of loving someone special."

Diegert held his gaze upon Barney as if he were looking at an oddity in the zoo. "Weird."

"I certainly hope you don't grow old without having a Sue Ellen in your life."

The sudden realization that he might one day be as alone and lonely as Barney hit Diegert hard. Nevertheless, he replied with, "Whatever."

Diegert felt hesitant, but he was compelled to ask Barney something more. "I have another question for you."

Barney eyed the younger man from under his bushy gray brows.

"Tell me about the guns in the case?"

Barney looked out over the ocean and gazed across the expanse of the sky. "They're not mine."

"Then whose are they?"

"I can't tell you."

"Why not?"

"I have been entrusted with them, but they are deadly. They bring a curse upon this vessel and its occupants. I hate the contents of that case, and it's all I can do not to throw them overboard."

Diegert sat quietly with the uneasy feeling of having intruded, while at the same time, being even more curious about why the weapons were even on the *Sue Ellen*.

"I prefer not to talk about it again. Now go tighten the halyards and keep her on course." Barney descended the stairs into the cabin below.

Diegert had learned a lot about sailing in his time at sea with Barney. Still, he was a bit surprised the old man just left him to skipper the boat under the current strong winds. Necessity enhanced learning, and Diegert didn't want to slow the boat, so he worked the sails to keep the pressure on the windward side. The course Barney had set brought them closer to shore, and off the port side, Diegert could gauge progress as landmarks on shore passed by. If the guns in the case were a curse, Diegert took comfort in the fact that the dolphins off the starboard side were a blessing. A school of eight dolphins raced alongside the *Sue Ellen*. Their speed and power were awe inspiring and their interest in the boat and desire to stay by her side thrilled Diegert. Just having these beautiful creatures nearby took away the boredom and loneliness that were such a difficult part of life at sea. Having alienated the only other human on board, Diegert appreciated the harmonious relationships represented by the pod. Even if it were only in his mind, he felt a kinship with these high-speed mammals. He wondered what it would be like to live your life in such a huge expanse of water and need nothing but your body in order to thrive. Humans always needed stuff to live. Even if you adhered to a strict code of poverty, you couldn't survive in any environment with nothing but your body. He also wondered if the dolphins were curious about life outside the water or if they contemplated what life must be like sailing on a boat. All this thought was suddenly brought to an end when Diegert looked off the starboard gunwale and the pod of dolphins was gone.

Just as unexpectedly as they'd appeared, the group of fast-moving gray bodies had disappeared. He checked back again and again, but they were gone. The fleeting kinship left him feeling lonely again.

Barney resurfaced, but Diegert didn't tell him about the dolphins.

"You've really learned to handle her well. We're making good progress, skipper."

Barney's compliment got a big smile out of Diegert and went a long way toward reestablishing their camaraderie. "It's OK that we're so close to shore?"

"Yes, the waters are deep. Plus, the hot air rising off the land draws in the cool air from the ocean, producing these powerful winds that are ushering us up the coast."

"I didn't realize that, but it makes sense."

Barney stretched out the map to show Diegert that they were only about fifty miles from rounding the Horn of Africa at Cape Guardafui. They would soon be in the Gulf of Aden as they continued making progress on the powerful offshore winds.

CHAPTER 21

After it rounded the Horn of Africa, the strong westerly winds guided the *Sue Ellen* across the Gulf of Aden and into the smaller Gulf of Tadjoura, where she made port at the city of Djibouti. Going ashore for the first time in so many days was a refreshing experience for both men. Being able to pace more than a few feet awakened muscles and joints to ranges of motion not possible on the boat. The central market was a crowded and busy place, but it gave the two mariners an opportunity to buy fresh fruit and meat. Barney was negotiating for a leg of goat while Diegert was inspecting mangoes. The stalls were full of produce, some of it delicious looking and enticing while other vendors' wares were rotting on the stands. A very friendly vendor stepped out from behind his stand to shake Diegert's hand. The two did not share a common language, but their smiles spoke for them. The friendly man brought Diegert over to his juice bar. The vendor's stall had a counter at the front, and the man had several electric blenders in his work area in the back. Hanging from the ceiling were nets filled with fruit. A very pretty, dark-skinned young lady indicated that she would make a juice drink with whatever fruits he chose. This woman had a dazzling smile and perfectly straight white teeth. Diegert enjoyed the twinkle in her eyes that glimmered each time she smiled. He couldn't understand a word she said, even though she spoke French as well as her native language. Diegert just kept smiling. The young lady eventually selected the fruits for him, cut them up, and blended them into a thick, juicy beverage. Even before his first sip, the tropical aroma of the blended juices tantalized Diegert's nostrils. When he sipped the drink, it was exquisite both in flavor and texture. His enjoyment of the drink was obvious to its creator, and she touched him on his forearm, communicating that she understood his pleasure. Diegert finished the entire drink, paid the pretty lady way too much, and happily kept looking back at her as he walked on through the market.

Barney had gotten some grains that could be made into porridge on the boat and had also filled their fuel cans. He had negotiated for the leg of goat to be cooked and he would pick it up later. Diegert had purchased two dozen eggs and a bag of flatbread. The two shoppers rejoined at one of the night-clubs that served lunch during the afternoon. Over their meal of hummus, sprouts, and goat meat wraps, Barney laid out his plan to stay in port one night and sail into the Red Sea tomorrow. That plan was fine with Diegert, who was curious to see if Saturday nights in Djibouti were anything like those in the States. After finishing their food, they drank a couple more beers and observed all the activity of the market from their café seats.

"I had a juice drink from the vendor just down there by the corner. It was great, and the girl at the shop was real friendly."

"When you've got money to spend, everyone here is friendly."

"I know, but I recommend their juice drinks."

"I'm going to go get our leg of goat, and I will meet you at the dock so we can take our stuff to the boat. You can stay on the boat tonight if you want, but I'm going to stay in a room here in town."

"Really?"

"That berth I sleep on may look comfortable, but tonight I'm going to sleep in a big bed with clean sheets on a solid floor."

"OK, I'll be on the boat."

When they returned from stowing their provisions, it was six p.m. The sun set fast in the tropics. When darkness fell, the markets closed, tarps were drawn, and some stalls even chained guard dogs in front of their businesses. The hustle and bustle of the vendors and shoppers was gone, but the volume of sound increased as the clubs started playing French and American rock music. Cars, trucks, and SUVs started pulling into places previously occupied by donkey carts. French and American military personnel from Camp Lemonnier flooded the strip of nightclubs to mix, mingle, party, and, for a lot of the guys, pay to get laid. Diegert recognized the camaraderie of the guys as they swaggered into the bars and were as loud and boisterous as they wanted to be. Having worked on base all week, they felt it was time to cut loose.

In addition to the gaggles of partiers, there were also the familiar MP jeeps. The Military Police had the assignment of ensuring that, although the peace might be disturbed, it was not destroyed. Mickey's seemed to be the bar of choice for the first arrivals.

Diegert thought back to times when he and his squad mates got to go on leave from Fort Hood. They would drive to Austin and help the city fulfill its request to "Keep Austin Weird." They would dance with girls and get rejected. They would get in fights and get arrested by the police, who would call the MPs and turn them over. What fun to be young, off duty, and out with friends with a handful of dollars to drink.

Even though these guys were Navy, Diegert was drawn to hang out with them and have some fun. His hair was kind of long, and he wasn't clean shaven, but that shouldn't matter. He hoped he would be welcomed, since he was American and a long way from home.

Barney had rented a room from one of the cheaper hotels away from the waterfront. A view of the water was nothing special to him, and he was more concerned with the quiet for his night's sleep. Of course, Barney was lonely too—lonely for female companionship, and for a price, any guy could pay a woman to spend the night with him. Barney took a center bar-stool at Mickey's and started drinking whiskey fast and hard. Soon several Ethiopian women were vying for his attention and using the simple English they knew along with their smiles and plunging necklines to seduce him into making a selection. Barney was the happy king of his own pathetic harem.

When Diegert walked in, he caught sight of Barney and his competing concubines. He shook his head, stepped to the far end of the bar, and ordered a beer. When the bottle was served, the young man was soon also surrounded by willing women who wanted to be his for a cheap price. Diegert did not engage them and instead walked over to observe the game being played on the pool table. The Navy men controlled the table as their regular turf. They were drinking beer and were largely ignored by the ladies of the night. Diegert stood leaning against a chest-high counter with his beer in hand. After performing several impressive shots, one of the sailors stood next to Diegert.

"Nice shooting," Diegert said.

"Thanks. What are you doing here? I didn't think there was a cruise ship in port."

"I'm not on a cruise."

"Well, what brought you here? We don't see many American tourists."

Diegert offered his hand. "Gary Nelson, I'm on a sailing vessel heading for the Mediterranean, but I used to be in the Army."

"Don't say that too loud." Taking Diegert's hand, the Navy man introduced himself. "I'm Andrew Clark, but people call me Clarky. My buddies and I are stationed at Camp Lemonnier."

Clarky shouted out, drawing the attention of his friends. "Hey, fellas, we got ourselves a real live Army man here. I know he's not green and carrying a bayonet rifle over his head." At that crack, several of the guys raised pool cues over their heads, posing like the classic plastic toy. Everyone chuckled. Clarky continued, "But let's show this fellow American some good old Djibouti hospitality, even if he did choose the caveman's branch of service." Clarky lifted his beer and everybody banged their bottles together. Diegert was in with the group for the evening, and although it felt good, he worried that he would regret making friends.

Barney's whiskey was taking over his brain. He was firmly planted on the barstool, or he might very well have been on the floor. The ladies around him were realizing that they would be able to get money from him with no sex at all.

Diegert and Clarky teamed up to play pool, and Clarky told him that his squad mates were all aeromechanics who kept F/A-18s and Predator drones flying. It was steady, regular work with lots of it to do. They all lived in container barracks, no windows, one room, three guys. The structures were air-conditioned; otherwise, they were literal ovens in the desert sun. Each time Diegert went over to the bar, he checked on Barney.

"Hey, man, I think you've had enough."

"You think I've had enuff . . . I'm the one who'll decide when I've had enuff. Scroow you!"

"OK, but just watch your money; you've got a lot of pretty little vultures circling."

"This isn't the first port-side bar I've been in. I know what those ladies want."

"Just keep your money in your pocket."

"Just mind your own fucking business."

Having grown up with his father, Diegert recognized an angry drunk. He knew it was the right time to make an exit.

Over at the pool table, they faced their opponents, Omar and Moe. Omar Pascal was a special agent with the Naval Criminal Investigative Service, and he observed Diegert with unusual interest. He was in Djibouti completing training for the Foreign Area Officer Program. His ability to speak both French and Arabic, in addition to his Middle Eastern heritage, provided the Navy with a highly qualified special agent who assisted in the interdicting of piracy.

Omar stepped over to Diegert. "How ya doing? I'm Omar Pascal."

Shaking the hand that was offered, Diegert introduced himself. "Gary Nelson, and Clarky says he's gonna run the table."

"We'll see about that."

Clarky only sank one ball, allowing Omar to put his cue to work. The dark man quietly and efficiently sank four balls before missing the ten in the side pocket. Diegert was lucky to knock in three before turning the table over to Omar's partner, Moe.

Commenting on Omar's shooting, Diegert said, "You shoot pretty well. Are you a mechanic like Clarky?"

"No, I work with computers. What division of the Army were you in?"

"1st Cavalry out of Fort Hood."

"Oh, really? Maybe that's why you look so familiar. I think I've seen your face before, but I couldn't place the name Nelson."

"Oh yeah," is all Diegert said as a cold chill ran down the back of his neck.

"I did my undergrad at UT. Did you ever get down to Austin for South by Southwest?"

"Yeah, we'd go to the fest. Austin's a cool place."

Diegert eyed Omar warily as they watched Moe take his next shot. After he sank two and missed the third, Clarky was back on the table. With three balls left before the eight ball, the slightly inebriated Navy man had difficulty deciding which ball to focus on. When he finally took his shot, three balls and the eight ball remained for Diegert.

"Damn it!" shouted Clarky.

Omar had only the eleven and the eight ball left. He placed the eleven securely in the far right corner. The eight ball lay against the bumper, but Omar had a suitable angle from the cue ball's position. Using simple geometry and a steady straight cue, Omar sank the eight ball in the far left corner to conclude the match.

"Nice game," said Diegert. "You got winner?"

"Nah, I'm done. Moe's gonna find somebody else."

Omar walked away from the pool table, heading toward a window seat.

As he walked away, Diegert watched him tapping on his phone.

"Hey, Clarky," said Diegert. "Where does Omar work?"

"Omar? He's with NCIS. He's doing some foreign regional training thing. He got hot on the table, didn't he?"

"He certainly can shoot." Diegert turned slowly to observe Omar from below his raised eyebrow.

Diegert could see that Omar was engrossed in his smartphone. Getting two fresh beers, Diegert walked over to where the NCIS officer was sitting. As he approached, Diegert could see Omar's phone screen. Upon the screen, Diegert saw a picture of his face underlined by his real name on an Austin Police Department website.

"Hey, Omar."

The dark man nearly fumbled his phone to the floor when he heard Diegert's voice.

"Sorry to scare you, but I just gotcha a beer." Diegert handed the cold bottle to the man, who had hurriedly stuffed his phone in his pocket.

"Ah, thanks, but I don't drink."

"Oh, I didn't think that was allowed in the Navy."

"Maybe not the Navy of the past."

Feeling the rising awkwardness, Diegert said, "Well, you shot a great game, and I just wanted to get you a . . . something."

"Thanks, but I bet you can get Clarky to drink that beer."

As they both looked at their goofy friend, who was trying to balance a pool cue on a single finger, Diegert said, "Definitely."

Extending his hand, Omar said, "Look, I'm gonna get going. It was nice to meet you Dav . . . Gary."

Diegert looked at the man through narrowed eyelids, saying, "You take care," as he relaxed the tension in his grip on the Navy man's hand.

Omar moved to the entrance of the bar and went outside. Diegert watched the entrance, and within five minutes his concern was warranted; in came the MPs with Omar right behind them. Diegert set down his beer and stepped over to Barney. He grabbed his arm and pinched him hard. Barney yelped and looked at Diegert like he was crazy. "Listen very carefully, my cover is blown, MPs are coming to arrest me, I'm leaving now. Don't say anything to them about the boat. Get back to it, and we are outta here." Diegert stepped past him and ducked through the back kitchen to leave the bar.

The noise, the crowd, and the music all made moving and seeing through the bar very difficult. The MPs were taking directions from Omar, but by the time they got to the pool table, Diegert was gone and Clarky was confused, until Omar showed him the wanted notice posted on the Austin PD's website. As the MPs looked around, Barney was attempting to leave by the front door. His harem of competitors was down to just two women. One of the women pulled the hair of the other from behind while taking her out at the knee, knocking her to the floor. Screams erupted, and the woman on the floor kicked out, knocking down both her competitor and Barney. The two women began to fight on the floor, punching, scratching, and pulling hair. The commotion impeded the MPs. Barney fell hard on the floor and struggled to get to his feet with the assistance of friendly patrons. He brushed himself off, thanked his helpers, and staggered to the door.

The two Ethiopian women were tossed out by the bar's bouncers and continued their argument as they strode down the street. Clarky and Omar were at the door of the bar, and they pointed Barney out to the MPs as he exited. The MPs, two male, one female, stepped over to Barney. The leading male officer said, "Excuse me, sir, but could we ask you a few questions?"

Barney continued walking, and Omar stepped next to him. "Sir, would you please stop walking?" With Omar standing next to him and the MPs nearby, Barney couldn't avoid acknowledging them. He certainly was drunk, but he was going to play it up for all it was worth.

"What . . . what . . . whaddya want?"

"Sir, we just have a few questions for you," Omar said.

"What questions? What do I have to do with you?"

"Sir, back in the bar you were seen speaking with a young man. Do you recall that?"

"I recall speaking to some young ladies, which I enjoyed, but I'm not interested in young men. I'm not that way."

"Sir, you don't recall speaking with a male in the bar?"

"Do you mean the bartender? He was male."

"No, sir, this male was white."

Barney put his hand to his chin, stroking his stubble. "I don't think I talked to any white guys, but I'm not prejudiced, you know."

"Yes, sir. Are you attached to a vessel here in port?"

"I was . . . but the ship left without me, and now I'm looking for a new one."

"Sir, do you have a place to stay?"

"An old sea scallop like me is always able to find a shell for the night."

"Sir, if we would like to talk with you again, is there an address where we could find you?"

"I appreciate you calling me 'sir,' but I do not have an address. If you want to talk, I will be at Mickey's. I'm not in the Army, and I haven't done anything wrong, so good night and good-bye."

The three MPs and Omar watched as Barney staggered into the shantytown of local residences. A place no member of the US military would ever walk, especially at night and drunk. When he was out of sight, the MPs went back to their jeep.

"Thanks, guys. I appreciate the backup," said Omar, who then looked at his phone again at the list of crimes of which Diegert was accused.

***

After exiting the kitchen at the back of Mickey's, Diegert walked down the alley and toward the waterfront. He wanted to go straight out to the *Sue Ellen*, but he also wanted to assist

Barney if things went bad. He went to the rowboat they'd used to come ashore. He found an old tarp covering a nearby collection of lobster traps. He dragged the tarp over to the rowboat, which had three benches in its interior. The oarlocks and oars were at the middle bench. Diegert climbed in and tucked himself into the space behind the last bench and the stern wall of the boat. He covered himself with the tarp, held onto his pistol, and lay quietly, waiting and hoping that Barney would recognize the rowboat and use it to get out to the *Sue Ellen*.

Eventually, closing time came, and those who were not spending the night with a prostitute made their way back to the base, with the MPs dutifully following the sailors' vehicles back to Camp Lemonnier.

CHAPTER 22

Looking at his watch, Barney could see it was past closing time and it was safe to make his move out to the *Sue Ellen*. For the past two hours, he'd wandered the slums of Djibouti and had slowly begun to sober up. He'd also got angrier at how Diegert's problems had ruined his plans for a comfortable sleep in a bed for which he had already paid. He returned to the spot where the line of bars, the waterfront, and the entrance to the slums converged. Looking through the darkness, he recognized the rowboat they'd used to come ashore. He lifted the bow of the boat and began pushing it out into the water. From the back end of the boat, the old man heard his name. "Hey, Barney . . . Barney, it's me under the tarp."

Barney stopped pushing.

"Diegert?"

"Yeah."

"Stay there. We'll be offshore in a second."

Barney heard a voice behind him on the shore. "Excuse me, sir . . . Sir, I'd like to speak to you." Turning around, Barney faced Omar Pascal, who seemed intent on continuing his investigation. "Sir, I'm sorry to approach you like this so late at night, but I saw you in the bar tonight speaking with a young man who it turns out is a fugitive and is wanted for murder."

"*Murder?* I guess there's all kinds of criminals here in Djibouti."

"I saw the two of you arguing at one point, and I just want to make sure you're safe."

"Well, that's mighty kind of you, but I don't recall talking to a young man. I remember the ladies, though."

"I saw you drank an awful lot, and so I was worried you might be vulnerable."

"As you can see, I'm fine." Continuing to push the boat, Barney stumbled and nearly fell into the bow. Awkwardly righting himself, he said again, "I'm fine, really, I'm fine."

Omar stepped forward while Barney stumbled, offering, "How about I row you out to your boat and make sure you get there safely?"

"No . . . no, that's not necessary. I'll be fine."

Diegert stepped out from under the tarp, pointing his pistol at Omar.

Barney shouted, "What are you doing?"

An agitated Diegert quickly stepped forward. "Shut up. He's NCIS. I can't let him go."

Diegert grabbed the agent, pointed the pistol at his head, and frisked him for a weapon. Omar was unarmed.

"Get in the boat."

Diegert forced Omar to row the boat. When they reached the *Sue Ellen*, the rowboat was brought next to the ladder so Barney could climb out.

"Attach the dinghy's line to the mooring," Diegert commanded Omar.

Omar did as directed, while an ashen pallor took the color from his skin.

"Now climb up."

On board, Diegert took Omar belowdecks, tied his hands behind his back, secured him to a bolt eye in the wall, and gagged him with a thick piece of cloth. Barney untethered the boat, started the engine, and began motoring out of the port.

From Djibouti, the Red Sea was north by northeast. Its gateway was a strait known as Bab-el-Mandeb. Under the cover of darkness and with the motor running at full speed, the *Sue Ellen* was quickly in the open waters of the Gulf of Tadjoura. As they left port, Diegert removed the battery from Omar's smartphone, snapped the SIM card in half, and dropped them in the water.

"What now?" asked Barney.

"A few miles out, I'll take care of him."

"Will that resolve the problem?"

"Did you ever mention the *Sue Ellen* to the MPs?"

"No, I told them I had been left behind by a merchant vessel and was hoping to get on another."

"Good. Then here's the situation. I was sighted in Djibouti by US servicemen. My presence was never confirmed by the MPs or corroborated by other reliable sightings. I was never seen again. Coincidentally, the NCIS agent who reported seeing me has gone missing. If you were the investigator, you would certainly put those two things together and then you would find nothing to support your hunch. The last known position of his smartphone will be the Djibouti port, where he spent the night partying."

"It's not much to go on."

"It sure isn't, so poor Mr. Pascal is going to the bottom of the ocean so we get away scot-free."

"You really think he must die?"

"If we let him live, he presents an uncontrollable risk. He's a lawman, and everything he represents will work against us."

"I leave it to you, then."

Diegert went belowdecks and untied Omar from the bolt eye. He pushed him up the stairs. On deck, Omar saw that they were far out to sea. It was a dark dawn, and no land was in sight. Barney never even looked at the man as Diegert directed him to the stern of the boat. With the gag still tied, Omar's attempts at speech came out as pitiful moans. Tears spilled over his lower lids, and their streams were absorbed by his gag. Diegert was in kill mode as he forced Omar to face the ocean off the stern deck. He kicked him in the back of the leg so the man fell to his knees like a good Catholic about to receive communion. Even though they were miles from shore, Diegert rotated the suppressor onto the end of his pistol. He placed the barrel on the occipital of the NCIS agent's head and pulled the trigger. Omar's suffering was over and Diegert stripped the clothing off his body. He thoroughly perforated the abdomen and thorax so that Omar's body would remain on the bottom of the ocean. Using buckets of seawater, he rinsed the deck clean. Omar's clothing was placed in the boat's burn can, doused with petrol, and ignited. When the clothing was reduced to ash, the contents of the burn can were dumped in the ocean, leaving a black trail in the wake of the *Sue Ellen* as the sun rose with spectacular beauty over the Gulf of Tadjoura.

CHAPTER 23

The Red Sea began after the Bab-el-Mandeb Strait. The sea was long but not very wide. Sailing south to north was preferable because the winds were more favorable. Barney had traversed this body of water before, and although it was deep in the center of the sea, there were shallow shelves off both coasts. The *Sue Ellen* didn't draw too deeply, so Barney was confident of their safe passage.

Djibouti demonstrated the worldwide reach of the Internet. Even on the other side of the earth, Diegert's identity and crimes were just a Google search away. The reach of modern technology had led to Omar's death. Killing a US serviceman disturbed Diegert and Barney both, but leaving Omar alive would've certainly brought a search and their eventual capture. Diegert realized that if he were to remain free, it would cost other people their lives—not only by continuing his work as an assassin, but also because killing others would surely be necessary to keep from being captured. *Fuck it,* he thought, *no one but Barney knows I killed Omar. There is no evidence and no one to accuse me.*

The stable winds and good weather allowed the *Sue Ellen* to traverse the Red Sea in two weeks' time. Diegert and Barney ate well and relaxed between watches. They passed by the tremendous luxury yachts of the Saudi royal family. They saw beautiful sunsets bathing the water in a deep-crimson glow, the phenomenon that gave the sea its name. When they arrived at the northern end, they passed through the Suez Canal and entered the Mediterranean. The history of this body of water was ancient, and on its shores, the most dominant civilizations on earth had found their birth. After they cleared the canal and set a northeasterly course, Diegert asked, "Where are we headed now?"

"Greece."

"What part of Greece?"

"We're headed to the northwestern port city of Alexandroupoli. I have some business there, and you'll be safe."

They sailed past the island of Crete into the Aegean Sea. An extensive archipelago delineated the Aegean from other waters of the Mediterranean, and sailors had to navigate carefully to avoid running aground on the many islands and shoals. Barney Pinsdale was very familiar with the region and slowed the pace, paying close attention to guiding the *Sue Ellen*. Diegert felt like he was back at day one. The movement through this region required a lot more adjusting of the sails, according to Barney's directions. As they continued north, passing the islands of Naxos, Lesvos, Chios, and Limnos, they would soon drop anchor at the port of Alexandroupoli. Barney slowed the pace and kept the boat out on the open water. The winds were calm, the air was balmy, and a bright half-moon hung in the sky, casting shadows across the deck.

Following their evening meal, Barney played the Brahms Violin Concerto in D Major, which put them both into a contemplative mood. Barney took advantage of the tranquility, saying, "Son, there's something I have to tell you."

Diegert looked at him with surprise because, although Barnard Pinsdale was a very kind sea captain, he had never called Diegert "son" before.

"This whole trip may have seemed to you as a chance encounter, but I was, in fact, in Mogadishu to pick you up."

Diegert turned his head, wrinkling his brow as he intensified his gaze at Barney.

"Do you believe fate or chance has more to do with determining the events of your life? Do you think all that has happened to you was simply a series of random events?"

Diegert could detect the rhetorical nature of these questions, and he folded his arms across his chest and remained silent.

"The contact you made on the darknet, his name is Aaron Blevinsky, and he's the operations manager for Crepusculous, a secretive and very powerful organization. Your actions in Paris and Athens, as well as your adaptability, perseverance, and improvisation in Mogadishu, impressed those who are watching."

"Wait a minute. I found you with a gag in your mouth chained to the galley table."

"An unfortunate occupational hazard when you sail into a port full of pirates. You can now imagine how glad I was to see you."

"This doesn't make sense."

"Was I not the only sailing vessel in the port with its mast still intact?"

"Yeah."

"Was it not fortunate that the two men guarding my dear boat were nowhere near as committed as the thugs on the docks?"

"True, they did go down awfully easy."

"I arrived a little early and underestimated the pirates' perceived value of the *Sue Ellen*. I thought they were only interested in large commercial vessels now. I can assure you, however, that I wouldn't have been in those waters were I not assigned to your extraction."

Diegert was getting angry; he didn't like the idea of being a pawn in someone else's game.

"Who's behind all of this? Who are the people watching me?"

Barney raised his hands in order to calm him. "Please let me continue, and it will all make sense. Did I not listen to your stories without interruption?"

Diegert rolled his eyes and looked away before returning his attention back to Barney.

"Once contact was made on the darknet, it allowed Blevinsky to directly influence your actions. The jobs in Miami, Paris, Athens, and Mogadishu were all sanctions that were authorized and orchestrated by the Board of Crepusculous."

Barney stopped talking and let the last word sink in. Diegert sat quietly feeling both angry and naïve. Shouldn't he have realized these were all connected? Of course, the hits carried out for the employer were connected, but being observed and selected without notification was both flattering and disconcerting.

"What is Crepusculous? It sounds disgusting."

"'Crepusculous' means 'in the shadows.' It also refers to twilight at the beginning or end of the day. I can't tell you who they are, but as an aggregate, they are the most powerful people in the world."

"The world?"

"Yes, they possess tremendous wealth and control global corporations; they are a select few who cooperatively influence governments, markets, and the worldwide economy. We like to think that no one is above the law, but that is not true. The Board of Crepusculous follows its own code and conducts its business as it sees fit to preserve the world order as it deems appropriate. Their influence infiltrates all aspects of government on every continent, and the most important thing to them is power. They stay in power by being unknown."

"And I'm one of their hit men."

"You have been a contract agent for them, but they also train and maintain their own squads of special service operators. You've been selected to undergo training at their facility in Romania."

"Romania?"

"Yes, we'll dock at Alexandroupoli in the morning. You will be met by a vehicle that will take you across Bulgaria into Romania and on to a Crepusculous training facility."

"Do I have a choice in this?"

"Of course, you have a choice. You can choose not to go with them, and you'll be a free man in Alexandroupoli, Greece. You'll no longer be a passenger on the *Sue Ellen*. You'll have to avoid apprehension on your own, because you're a wanted man all over the world."

With his chin in his hand, Diegert shifted his gaze away from Barney.

"I can't be certain, but the instructors in the facility could use you as a training target."

"What?"

"Capturing or killing you would be the type of mission that would put the skills of developing operators to the test."

"Do they have it in for me?"

"Not at all, but your rejection of their interest would change the nature of the relationship. Hunting you down and taking you out would be a challenging mission and would assure that what I'm telling you is not broadcast."

"Will you tell them to kill me?"

Barney's wan smile revealed his recollection of Diegert's lethality. "Not at all. I won't be asked to make any suggestions. The instructors plan the training, and they won't speak to me about it at all. I'm just telling you this because of things from the past."

"So I really don't have a choice," Diegert said with his gaze fixed across the deck of the boat.

"Your choice to be independent will result in capture, conviction, incarceration, and probable execution. Or you can join a program designed to support and enhance the lethal capabilities you've already demonstrated." Without turning his head, Diegert shifted his eyes to meet Barney's. "You've told me that you plan to make your living by killing people," Barney continued. "Since I have seen what you can do, I believe you will find Crepusculous to be an ideal place for you to practice your chosen career."

"I'll become one of the horses in a stable of assassins."

"You, my friend, will be a stallion. Besides, don't they owe you some money?"

Recalling he was owed for the Mogadishu job, Diegert nodded.

Raising another question he had been holding onto for some time, Diegert asked, "Whose guns are those in the case?"

"They belong to you."

Diegert looked at him quizzically.

"I mean they belong to you now," Barney said.

"Well, I suppose I should thank you, but to whom did they belong before now?"

"You're not the first assassin to be a passenger on the *Sue Ellen*. I have worked for Crepusculous for many years as a courier of operators. A free-moving ocean vessel is an ideal insertion and extraction vehicle to deliver and retrieve operators to and from missions. That case of weapons belonged to a previous operator, Shamus McGee. A fun-loving and funny Irishman who, like you, had a killer's instinct. He and I traveled extensively; he learned to sail, like you, and he became conflicted about what he was doing and found the big open space of the ocean a good place to contemplate the role he was playing. One night, we went ashore in Tunis, and as we were heading back to the boat, we were ambushed. I was hit with a Taser and drugged. When I came to, I was back on the *Sue Ellen.*"

"And you think it was Crepusculous? There could have been many people who wanted an accomplished corporate assassin dead."

"Aye, you're correct, but there was a note stuck in the cabin door. It said Shamus had been killed and I was to set sail before morning or the *Sue Ellen* would suffer a drone strike. Only Crepusculous has the capacity to strike with their own drones."

"What have they got on you that keeps you working for them?"

"We all have our secrets, which others can exploit. It's best you not let anyone know yours. You can grow close to someone when you're together out at sea. I used to think of Shamus as the son I never had, but I've learned not to grow close to you guys anymore."

Diegert looked to the floor of the deck.

Barney continued, "Shamus's weapons will serve you well. He'd like to know they went to the right person, even though you and he are very different."

"How so?"

"Shamus would've let Omar Pascal live, and he would have set those pirates adrift. He was a good Irishman, he loved his Guinness, and he was a hell of a lot funnier than you. You seem more suited to this life. I don't think Shamus ever found a way to absolve himself like you have."

Diegert lifted his gaze and held the old man's stare as Barney delivered the next statement.

"I think you have a very dark future in this dirty business. You seem to be free of remorse."

The quiet of the half-moon night enveloped them, and Barney suggested that Diegert go below and get some rest before they switched the watch. Staying up on deck, the old man thought of why he still worked for Crepusculous. His own attempt at being an assassin had failed miserably, but not without criminal guilt. His skills at sailing provided a reliable option for the movement of assets. Barney, a man who loved the sea, had found a way to make his living sailing the waters of the world. He'd learned to accept the compromises that allowed him to be the constant captain of the *Sue Ellen*.

CHAPTER 24

On the dock the next morning in Alexandroupoli, Diegert stood at the side of the *Sue Ellen* with his MK 23 in his pocket, his bag slung over his shoulder, and the case of weapons. He shook Barney's hand, saying, "I hope to voyage with you again one day."

Barney took Diegert's hand, firmly replying, "It would be an honor to have you as a passenger again, no matter what the circumstances."

The two men smiled, and Diegert turned and walked off the dock and into the parking lot of the marina.

Two big guys dressed in black with their pants tucked into their tactical boots were standing next to a vehicle that looked like an Eastern European version of the Hummer. Diegert eyeballed them, anticipating their indication that he was to ride with them. The two guys ignored him completely. As he walked, Diegert kept looking back at them, convinced that they would soon recognize him. "Ahem . . . Mr. Diegert?" said a voice that startled the assassin and made him step back to look at the person in front of him. "Are you David Diegert?"

"Yes, I am."

"I am here to give you a ride to Videle, Romania."

"OK."

"The truck is over here." The young man walked over to a Derways Plutus dual cab pickup truck. The guy looked to be maybe twenty-one, with long, dark curly hair and an unkempt, scruffy beard in need of a shave. He was wearing oversized khaki cargo pants right out of the nineties and a T-shirt with Super Mario brandishing a shotgun and an assault rifle. He had a cigarette in his hand, from which he took a long drag as they approached the truck. "You can put your stuff in the back."

When they were both seated in the truck, Diegert drew his pistol and grabbed the guy by the collar, pulling him across the cab. The guy looked at the pistol inches from his face and didn't say a word, although his lips were quivering and he was breathing in shallow, ragged gasps.

"Tell me about Crepusculous," said Diegert.

"I don't have a disease . . . I don't know what you're talking about."

"What's your name?"

"Oh, I'm sorry, I should've told you before. I am Beduna Lucianus. My uncle owns a cab company in Bucharest. Usually I just give people rides around the city. We use this truck to move stuff, refrigerators, washers, stuff like that. Please, you put the gun away now?"

"I will decide when the gun goes away."

Diegert loosened his grip on the young man's shirt. His obvious fear and complete lack of any defensive actions told Diegert this kid was just as he appeared, a slacker cab driver. They both sat back in the seats of the truck, but Diegert held the gun on Beduna.

"All I know is my uncle tells me to drive down here and pick you up. Why you cannot take a train or a bus, I do not know, but now you're getting a cab ride all the way to Videle, over seven hours of driving. You tell me what is so special?"

"Where's your GPS?"

Holding out his smartphone, Beduna replied, "On my phone."

"Let me see it." Diegert scrolled through the GPS route and saw it was indeed the most direct route between the two places. Placing the phone in the center console cup holder, Diegert said, "Do not vary from this route. We only stop to piss, eat, and get gas. Understood?"

"*Da.*"

Placing the pistol in the plastic map pocket of the truck's passenger door, Diegert instructed the young man, "Let's go."

Two miles into the trip, Beduna pulled a cigarette from his pack. Diegert reacted immediately. "No smoking."

"What?"

"I said no smoking—I do not want you smoking cigarettes while you're driving."

"But I smoke all the time."

Grabbing the cigarette from his hand and the pack from where it lay on the console, Diegert lowered his window and threw them out. Beduna slammed on the brakes.

"That pack was practically full. I'm going to get it."

Diegert picked up his pistol and pressed it into Beduna's ribs.

"You're not smoking in this truck today, and if you don't have cigarettes, you'll not be distracted. Now get your foot off the brake and continue driving."

"FUCK," shouted Beduna.

Leaning forward and getting right in the angry man's face, Diegert said, "There'll be no fucking swearing either. Now drive."

Fifteen minutes passed, during which Diegert said nothing and Beduna grew more angry and agitated. The Romanian driver turned on the radio, which loudly blared heavy death metal. The guitars screeched, the drums boomed, and the vocals were relentless, incoherent screams. Diegert let it go for two minutes, after which he turned the radio off and pulled the control knob from the panel. Beduna looked at him with even more anger when he realized Diegert had disabled the radio and placed the knob in his vest pocket.

"I hate that shit."

"I thought you said no swearing?"

"I said no fucking swearing from you."

One hour later, which was quiet and peaceful for Diegert and aggravating and annoying for the nicotine-deprived driver, they approached the border. Diegert checked their position on the GPS. The Greece-Bulgaria border was just a kilometer ahead, and the first city on the other side was Svilengrad.

"When we cross the border, let's find a place to stop in Svilengrad."

"*Da.*"

The gas station where they stopped had a convenience store just steps away. Beduna filled the truck with gas while Diegert used the restroom and bought a bottle of water. Beduna paid for the gas and got a large coffee and a pack of cigarettes. Diegert, standing outside the store, stretched his stiff back. Beduna came out, saying, "Look, I will smoke only when we are not driving. You can hold the pack while we drive."

"OK, but give me the keys so I can move the truck and let other people use the gas pump."

Beduna, with a cigarette already in his mouth, handed Diegert the keys and gleefully lit his smoke. The nicotine hitting his nerve endings felt so good that it took him a few seconds to realize that Diegert had pulled the truck onto the road and was driving away. The dumbfounded Beduna fashioned a belief that Diegert must be doing something and then coming back. A full five minutes passed before it sank in that he had been abandoned.

Diegert smiled, having rid himself of the annoying, drug-dependent wastrel. He had the GPS on the phone and a full tank of gas, and the kid knew nothing about Crepusculous and couldn't provide him with any useful intelligence, so the whole trip would be better without him.

CHAPTER 25

The drive across Bulgaria took Diegert four hours through rural countryside and small villages. After he crossed into Romania, another hour and a half brought him to Videle. Videle had a few stores, a pub, a petrol station that also served as a mechanics shop, and several areas of mixed housing. "Mixed" meaning some of the places looked nice with lots of European charm, while others looked like impoverished hovels. The address Diegert was looking for was a couple more hilly kilometers outside of Videle. The building was a three-story gray structure with peeling paint and green slime water stains running down from the flat roof. It looked to be abandoned and in disrepair. It certainly was out of place in the forested land that surrounded it. Diegert checked the GPS; the phone indicated he was in the right spot. He thought to himself, *I've come all this way for this? It must be better than it appears.*

Diegert turned off the road onto the gravel drive and stopped at the gate. He opened the driver's side window and looked at the camera with an exaggerated smile. The gate opened, and he drove to a small parking lot next to the building's entrance. Two burly guys dressed in black combat fatigues and boots came out of the building and approached. Both men had sidearms on their hips. The first one said, "Welcome, please follow me." Diegert motioned to the back of the truck. The second man stepped up to the truck and lifted the case out of the back. The three of them entered the building.

Inside, things were different. The place was clean, well lit, Spartan in its interior design, but solid and functional. Diegert was escorted to a counter behind which stood a man who appeared to be in his midfifties. He was of medium height and looked to weigh about two hundred pounds, with at least forty of those protruding out of his abdomen. He was bald on top with a crescent of gray above his ears and around the back of his head.

"Hello, I'm Aaron Blevinsky, I'm the director of this facility, and I'll be your host during your stay. We refer to this facility as the Headquarters, and it includes both learning centers and living quarters for individuals undergoing training. Today we'll complete the intake process, get you situated in your quarters, and introduce you to your training officer. Where's your driver?"

"He's in Bulgaria."

"What happened to him?"

"I last saw him smoking cigarettes in Svilengrad. He's OK, here's the key."

Diegert placed the truck key on the counter, and Blevinsky looked at him quizzically, expecting more to the story. Diegert said nothing more about his ride to Videle.

"Is there a bunch of paperwork for me to fill out?"

"No, we have your data in the system, but you will need this."

Blevinsky handed Diegert a magnetic swipe card with his picture already on it. He then snapped open the long case and looked at the rifle and two handguns.

"Personal weapons are not allowed in the living quarters. All personal weapons are registered and held at the armory. Do you have any other weapons?"

"No other guns, but I do have a knife."

Blevinsky motioned with his hand. "All sharpened blades are to be registered."

Diegert placed his bag on the counter. Unzipping the bag, he stuck his hand in, searching for the knife. As he felt inside the bag, he was unable to locate the knife his mother had given him. He started pulling everything out of the bag, making a mess of all his stuff. With the bag practically empty, it became obvious to everyone that Diegert didn't have a knife.

"Damn, I'm sorry, but I must have lost it." Diegert thought that Beduna had taken it, but that kid was never near the bag. No one else had touched the bag, and he never used the knife during the whole trip. Could he have left it on the boat? God, what a careless idiot, how could he lose something so special? He struggled to recall the Ojibwa inscription: *The blade is both a tool and a weapon let it work for you and defend you. Great,* he thought, *you can remember that, but you lost the fucking knife.*

"If you do not have a weapon to register, then I'll introduce you to your instructor."

Blevinsky and Diegert walked down a hallway with doors spaced every thirty feet. They turned a corner, and the hallway was half glass, so Diegert could see about a dozen men practicing hand-to-hand combat in a padded room. After traversing the hallway, they turned down another and stopped at a door. Blevinsky knocked. The name "Fatima Hussain" was engraved on a plastic nameplate. The door opened to reveal a Pakistani woman with jet-black hair and eyes. She was taller than Blevinsky, and Diegert figured she was not yet thirty. She looked strong and fit. She wore the same black combat pants, boots, and black T-shirt that everyone wore, but her clothes, especially the T-shirt, did not conceal her feminine form. With her terse look and her hair pulled back into a tight bun, she revealed no softness; instead, she seemed sinister, potent, and deadly.

"David Diegert, I would like to introduce you to your training officer, Fatima Hussain."

Diegert extended his hand but said nothing; she shook his hand with an assured sense of strength and said nothing as well. Blevinsky said, "Fatima, will you please show Mr. Diegert to his quarters and the mess hall? Dinner begins in an hour."

"Of course," replied the strong, confident woman.

As Blevinsky left, Fatima turned to Diegert, saying, "Give me a minute to finish what's on my computer."

She closed the door, and Diegert stood in the hall. As the time dragged, Diegert recalled the caption of a cartoon on the single restroom in the diner where his mother worked: *The length of a minute depends on which side of the door you're on.* Diegert's watch revealed that a "minute" for Fatima Hussain was more than eighteen minutes long. When the door opened, she stepped out, closed it behind her, and began striding away. Diegert stepped quickly to catch up and maintained a fast clip to keep pace with her. She turned down halls and climbed stairs, turned down several more halls and climbed more stairs, until all Diegert knew was that he was on the third floor. At Room 365, she stopped, swiped the lock with her card, opened the door, and walked in. Diegert followed her in to find quarters designed for single occupancy. The room was sparsely furnished but adequately appointed: bed, dresser, closet, desk with a chair, and a computer, as well as his own bathroom.

"See you in the mess hall in thirty-five minutes."

"But where is the mess hall?"

"Follow the signs."

"I didn't see any signs."

Fatima took a step closer to him, intensifying her words. "Then let's see how good you are at reconnaissance. Follow the smell and make sure you're wearing the right clothes."

She stepped back into the hall and walked away. Diegert stepped to the door, watching her depart, imagining her hips under those dark pants as she strode down the hall.

Diegert changed into his black uniform, which was all there was in the closet. He left his room and used the time to walk around, familiarizing himself with the facility. He found the armory and indoor shooting range, the garage, the fitness center, the pool, and the locker room, which led to the outdoor training facilities. He was slightly concerned that the food might be bad since the medical center was located next to the cafeteria. Diegert got in line, got a tray full of food, and sat down by himself at a table in the mess hall. The dining room had a dozen large, round tables, and there were about twenty-five people eating. The majority were men, who looked fit and strong. The few women in the room looked matronly and clerical. After sampling a few bites and finding the food to be pretty good, he enjoyed his meal. Fatima set a small plastic box down on the table and sat next to him.

"I can see you were able to find your way."

"Oh, yeah . . . I've been around. In the Army: Afghanistan. I've also been to Miami, Paris, Athens, Somalia."

"Don't forget Djibouti," interrupted Fatima. "I know all about you, where you're from, what you've done, and what I don't know I will learn in your training sessions."

She opened her box and took a small bite of a spinach salad.

"When do I get to learn about you?" asked Diegert.

"You don't. I'm the teacher; you're the student. I'm the expert; you're the newbie. You do what I say, when I say, and in the manner in which I instruct you. Thinking about and talking about who I am is a waste of time neither of us can afford. When you're finished eating, report to the outside training area."

Fatima ate the rest of her salad without discussion. Diegert did the same. When she finished and left the cafeteria, Diegert found that not thinking about Fatima was going to take a level of self-discipline he doubted he possessed.

Diegert returned to the locker room, which led outside. He noticed the lockers were large and wide. They were fronted by pressed metal screening through which Diegert could see heavy jumpsuits, boots, wet weather jackets, climbing gear, and helmets. He got the impression the outside training occurred regardless of the weather and probably involved heights. Outside, he found Fatima. "I sure hope finding the exit isn't your best quality."

"I was just looking around."

"Come on, I want to show you some areas you won't find on your own."

They walked down a trail and covered about a quarter mile before she turned onto another trail and continued a half mile deeper into the woods. Diegert observed that she had a pistol in an integrated holster sewn into her pants. The carrying mechanism allowed the weapon to remain concealed, yet it was firmly held in place by strong webbing and could be conveniently deployed through the extra-large pocket slit that ran parallel with her seam. That she was carrying a weapon was not surprising, but it was unsettling since he didn't have one.

When they arrived at the corner of a chain-link fence that ran through the woods, Fatima opened the sliding gate with her swipe card. They stepped inside and the gate closed. They walked a bit farther, and there was a second fence. This one was higher and topped by rolls of razor wire. Again, Fatima swiped the card and opened the gate. Within the woods, several structures of different sizes and shapes appeared. It looked like a ghost town or, more accurately, a movie set for a post-apocalypse sci-fi adventure. Some buildings were just façades, supported only by scaffolding. Others were fully framed with skeletal interiors. Still others looked like the abandoned apartments one would expect to find in a war zone. Fatima continued the silent tour, showing Diegert an area with dozens of concrete blocks five feet high by five feet wide. The blocks were bullet-pocked and worse. They had suffered many gun battles, and the dark-crimson splotches were evidence of the human toll taken in this training area. Finally, Fatima brought him to a swamp that was filled with high reeds and murky water. Through the swamp was a series of narrow bridges that were the only means of traversing this treacherous area. Fatima led Diegert across a bridge until they reached a dry stand of pines.

"Is this the end of the tour? Can we go to the souvenir shop now?"

"Not funny," replied the humorless, dark-haired lady. "Your training here is serious business. You will demonstrate a number of skills and abilities and accomplish several difficult missions, and when you survive all of that, you and other trainees will be placed in here to compete in a tournament."

"A tournament? You never showed me the tennis or shuffleboard courts."

Without a hint of a smile, Fatima narrowed her eyes. "This is a tournament to the death. As your trainer, I want you to win that tournament and show the boys that I'm better than them. The only way that happens is through you. I read all the dossiers of potential trainees, and yours was the only one that impressed me. I fought to be your trainer. Don't let me down or show me I chose poorly. I want you to win, and I will help you do that."

"So we're a team?"

"No, you are my trainee, and you must win. Do not cloud your mind. You must win in here or we both fail. There is no team in the tournament."

"I take it you've won this tournament?"

"All instructors here are tournament winners."

"Then when do we begin training?"

"No training is allowed in here, and technically I shouldn't have shown you this place. So your first test is to keep this tour secret—tell no one you were here. Let's go."

When they returned to the compound, Diegert entered the men's locker room. Inside were two guys who had just finished a practice session. They were dressed in tactical suits that were like nothing Diegert had seen before. The suits were a woven material that seemed to move easily as the guys were stowing their equipment. The outfits were formfitting without baggy or bulky parts. They had built-in harnesses for attaching climbing lines. The chest and back armor plates were flexible and appeared to be made of composite foam that hardens on impact. The suits made the guys look invincible, and Diegert hoped he might get fitted for one soon. One of the two guys said, "Hey, new guy, what are you doing down here?"

The guy was taller than Diegert, perhaps six foot four, had a beard, and spoke with a Russian accent. He weighed at least two hundred pounds, and sizing him up gave Diegert reason to pause.

"I was just touring around, trying to get the lay of the land."

"Oh, I'm Alexi Strakov, and this is Curt Jaeger."

The other guy didn't have a beard but was practically the same size as Strakov. Diegert could see that these two would be a formidable team, and he hoped he would be on their side. They both shook hands with him, and Strakov said, "You really shouldn't be down here without your trainer."

"My trainer is the one who was taking me on the tour."

"I don't see your trainer," remarked Strakov as he pulled off his outer shell, revealing the padded under-portion of his suit.

"Well, she's not going to come in here."

"SHE!" exclaimed the big bearded guy. Both men began laughing.

"Where did you go wrong to get the girl as your trainer?" asked Strakov.

"Blevinsky must not think much of you if he assigned you to her," said Jaeger, who had also removed the composite foam piece of the tactical suit.

"Hey, maybe you get to fuck her."

Jaeger chuckled at the Russian's comment, saying, "I never got to fuck my trainer."

Laughing, Strakov said, "Maybe you're just the perfect guy to take orders from that bitch."

Diegert felt angry and embarrassed, but he didn't reply to the joke except to turn and leave the locker room.

"What's wrong with the new guy?" asked Strakov. "Was it something I said?"

CHAPTER 26

What a fucking idiot I am, thought Diegert. He hadn't given the fact that he was being trained by a woman a moment of consideration. Training with her already put him on the wrong team from the rest of the guys. *I have to change this.* On the way back to his quarters, he stopped at Blevinsky's office and knocked on the door. "Can I speak with you, sir?"

Blevinsky was engrossed in his computer. Without moving his head, he raised an eyebrow and directed his pupils at Diegert. Returning his gaze to the computer screen, he said, "What can I do for you?"

"I was curious about the process by which trainees are assigned to instructors."

"Are you really interested in the process or are you concerned that you have a female trainer?"

"Umm . . . yeah, I was wondering why I have the girl trainer."

Blevinsky took his hands off the keyboard, leaned back in his chair, and looked at Diegert.

"What's the matter, did someone make fun of you or are you just having a chauvinist moment? Fatima Hussain is one of the toughest, most resourceful operators I have ever seen. Whatever deficit she has in strength, and it ain't much, she more than makes up for in intelligence, cunning, and perseverance. Her willingness to risk her own safety in order to accomplish missions is far greater than any man in this facility."

Blevinsky paused to let that assessment sink in before continuing. "No one rises to the position of trainer without fully earning it. As an instructor on my staff, she has proven herself, and for you to question her is absolutely insulting and will not be tolerated. Do I make myself clear?"

"Yes, sir."

"You should tell Strakov and Jaeger to go fuck themselves," said the tired and agitated man. "I want you to know that I will be right here when your training is done and you want to thank me for assigning you to Fatima Hussain."

Diegert swallowed hard but didn't respond.

"Hey, another thing," said Blevinsky. "That girl you failed to kill in Paris. You actually did me a favor. I got rid of her for less than half of what I was gonna pay you."

"I won't kill women."

"Yeah, right, Mr. Gender Restriction. Yet here you are, bitching about your trainer being a woman. Fuckin' get out of here and figure yourself out."

Back in his room, Diegert tried to figure himself out. Killing bad men, criminals, those who knew they were playing dangerous games but took the risk anyway, he could justify that. But killing women just didn't fit. Blevinsky could assign him whatever he wanted, but if he wanted him to shoot a woman, Diegert decided he just wouldn't do it.

It was still early, only nine p.m., but the clean, comfortable bed beckoned to Diegert, who was looking forward to a good night's sleep. He got himself ready and climbed into bed. He thought about his family, his father and his brother and especially his mother. It had been such a long time since he'd spoken with them, and it seemed as though it would be a long time before he spoke with them again. As he thought about them, he realized missing his father and brother was an emotionally hollow experience. They certainly weren't thinking of him. Missing his mother hurt, though, because he knew that without him she was all alone in her own family.

Suddenly, he realized he hadn't sent her the money. Jumping out of bed, he used his phone to check his account, which held $204,500. He transferred $167,000 to his mother's account. He sent a text to let her know the money was there. Feeling good about himself for helping her pay off the debt on the house, he got back in bed and fell into a deep sleep.

After too short a time, the door to Diegert's room opened and someone quietly stepped in. "Don't be alarmed," said the pretty voice of a woman. "It's me, Fatima."

Diegert opened his bleary eyes and saw her silhouette outlined by the light of the door. "It's time to begin your training."

"What?" asked Diegert as he struggled to wake up.

Raising her voice and slamming the door behind her, Fatima shouted, "Get up. It's time to start your training."

Fatima hit the light switch, blinding Diegert with the fluorescent glare of the overhead rectangles. Disoriented and confused, Diegert remained under the blankets. Fatima grew furious. She forcefully extended her arm, snapping a collapsible baton to its full length. Diegert was alarmed by the loud, metallic snap, but he was shocked by the strike across his thighs as Fatima shouted, "Get out of bed now. Stand up and get ready for training."

Diegert complied and stood next to the bed, wearing only his boxer shorts. He eyed her with derision and contempt. Fatima stepped right up to him, placing the end of the baton under his chin and lifting his face away from her eyes and into the blinding brightness of the ceiling fixtures.

"Don't you look at me with such contempt. I'm your superior, not only in rank but in ability. We are not some weak-willed government agency. You will survive this training or die; there is no other option."

Pointing to the closet with her baton, she instructed him, "Put on the outfit marked 'Street Clothes.'" Diegert dressed in front of her, and she directed him to the desk chair. She handed him a dossier, saying, "Find this man and get him to give you two hundred euros."

She handed him a Jericho 941 9 mm pistol and suppressor. That she would equip him with an Israeli firearm was surprising, but then again, the gun was only a tool. "You have twenty-four hours to complete the mission."

"What, no push-ups or pull-ups?"

"If you need to increase the strength of your body, do it on your own time, but I don't want to see you back in that bed."

Fatima left the room much more abruptly than she had entered.

CHAPTER 27

Diegert noted the time, 11:05 p.m., as he opened the dossier on Sebastor Sbrebetskov. The man was a midlevel mobster of the Bucharest underworld in an organization headed by the notorious Michka Barovitz. It turned out Sbrebetskov's appetites were bigger than his abilities, and he was in debt to Barovitz for a large sum of money. Furthermore, Barovitz was not entirely happy about the sideline businesses Sbrebetskov was running in Bucharest. Sbrebetskov was extorting protection money from local merchants, and the speculation was that he planned to establish himself independent of Barovitz. The risk he was taking was significant; either he would become his own boss or a corpse.

Barovitz's criminal empire extended throughout Romania and beyond. He was at the top of a self-made criminal pyramid, which he preserved with bribery and force. It was reported that he viewed Sbrebetskov as an interesting plaything, which he controlled through puppet strings. Diegert's mission was to find Sbrebetskov and convince the mobster to give him two hundred euros. He would begin at a pub called the Loyal Dog just over the Ialomita River in Bucharest.

Diegert signed out a Saab from the motor pool and drove into the night. The bridge over the Ialomita was closed to vehicle traffic for repairs; however, foot traffic was allowed. Diegert parked and crossed the bridge. The pub faced the river fifty meters from the bridge. Diegert took a stool at the bar and ordered a beer. Soon he was talking with an older man sitting next to him. Diegert steered the conversation to Sbrebetskov. The old man said, "Everyone knows that man is in debt to Barovitz, and I believe he has a price on his head."

"You mean, they want him dead?"

"I think the price is more reflective of the debt he carries."

"Is this the kind of debt that can be repaid or is there something more Barovitz holds over him?"

"Barovitz surely has much to hold over him, but Sbrebetskov wants to have his own organization. Right now, he only has two men. He would need a lot more to challenge Barovitz. Even the men he has are actually being paid by Barovitz. He's on thin ice."

"Tell me more about Barovitz."

"Ah, the Scorpion. He's ruthless, and his rise to power has been paved by executing the competition."

"Sounds tough."

"Well, he's older now, more refined, but as a young man, he removed his rivals with a revolver. He was called the Scorpion because he also used poison. He would give those who didn't follow his rules the option of drinking poison or being shot."

"Unfortunate choices."

"He would also offer the choice to business people who didn't want to pay protection money."

"Is he still around town?"

"No, he has a villa on an island in the Aegean. He conducts his business through associates. He doesn't have to twist arms himself anymore. What Sbrebetskov needs is a settlement."

"What do you mean?"

"I mean, he needs Barovitz to offer him a deal that will allow him to save his hide and save face. Partial payment on his current debt and a percentage of future business, that sort of thing. Sbrebetskov isn't foolish enough to pass up a settlement from Barovitz, but he hasn't been offered one yet."

The old man pointed to an empty booth in the back corner of the bar.

"That's Sbrebetskov's booth over there. It's the last place in town where he has any clout. I imagine he'll be here later, but I will not."

The man swilled the last of his beer and offered his hand to Diegert, saying, "An old man needs his rest, while a young man seeks excitement. Good night, stranger."

Looking down at the coaster under his beer, Diegert noticed it had a scorpion insignia. Wiping the coaster dry, he ordered another beer and a shot of Romana Black Sambuca di Liquore, to be served over at the empty booth in the corner. Diegert sat there for twenty minutes before Sbrebetskov and two men arrived. The two thugs preceded Sbrebetskov to the table.

"Hey, get out of that seat," said the first one, who had a flattop buzz cut.

"This booth is ours. You must leave," the second guy, who sported a dark goatee, offered, sounding almost polite in comparison.

Diegert raised his silenced Jericho just above the tabletop and placed the red laser on the forehead of the more belligerent thug. Speaking directly to Sbrebetskov, who stood behind the two men, Diegert said, "I'm here to talk to you. Tell your men to wait at the bar or climb into a grave."

Sbrebetskov, not wanting a public spectacle, gestured to the bar. "Have a seat and a beer."

Sbrebetskov was a big man, very heavy, with a large sloping abdomen. He was dressed in a tailored suit because he wouldn't fit well in anything off the rack. His full head of dark hair was only beginning to show the gray, which would likely be the color of all his hair should he live long enough. He slid his bulk into the booth and made himself appear comfortable. The waiter brought him his beer in a tall glass with an embossed Ursus logo. Diegert wasted no time. "I'm here to offer you a settlement."

Sbrebetskov's eyes widened.

"Ten percent of your debt buys you six months to come up with the balance."

Sbrebetskov's look of surprise caused Diegert to go on.

"Barovitz believes in you, and he's taking the long view that you will do well for him in spite of your current setback."

"How do I know you represent Barovitz?"

Diegert placed the coaster with the scorpion on the table and then set the shot glass with the dark-black liquid on the coaster. Placing his pistol on the table, Diegert folded his arms in front of him.

"Ten percent of your current debt, and I will leave you to celebrate your good fortune this evening."

Sbrebetskov pulled out a roll of cash and counted it. "A thousand euros, this is all I have tonight."

He handed the money to Diegert. Returning his gun to its holster and putting the cash in his pocket, Diegert stood up.

"I will be back tomorrow night for the rest."

Diegert picked up the shot glass of dark fluid and poured it on the floor, saying, "We wouldn't want an accident." He stashed the scorpion coaster in his coat pocket.

Stepping outside the pub, Diegert walked along the river and started to cross the bridge. He counted out two hundred euros, placed it in his jacket pocket, and put the rest in the pocket of his pants. Glancing back, he noticed the two thugs exiting the pub and pointing at him as he ascended the bridge. Over its span of the river, the bridge rose to a height of fifteen meters above the water. The thugs sprinted after him, and as he reached the peak of the bridge, he slowed his pace, and the thugs closed the gap.

As they approached, guns drawn, one shouted, "Hey, stop right there!"

Diegert halted, grasped the handle of his Jericho 9 mm, and withdrew it as he spun to face his attackers. His first shot pierced the frontal bone of the flattop thug just above the right eye. As the man's body began to drop forward, Diegert kicked him into the second thug. The force of his comrade's body knocked over the man with the goatee. Diegert fired, striking the guy's right arm, causing him to drop his gun. Diegert grabbed the shattered forearm, and with ligament-tearing force pulled it behind the guy's back. The thug swung wildly with his left and cracked Diegert on the cheekbone. The blow stunned Diegert, who dropped his pistol and stumbled backward. The thug stood up and punched Diegert repeatedly in the ribs. With the wind knocked out of him, Diegert fell to the deck of the bridge. The thug reached for his fallen pistol, and when he turned back, Diegert delivered a kick to the guy's right knee. Falling on the damaged knee, the man with the goatee held on to his pistol. Diegert reached behind him, grabbed his gun, and both men pointed at one another. Diegert flipped on his laser sight, dazzling the thug's vision as the muffled spurt of the bullet permanently ended the henchman's struggle to survive.

Diegert rose to his feet. Quickly assessing his situation, he heaved the two bodies into the river, with every tug of his muscles on his rib cage causing intense pain. He pocketed the pistols while descending the bridge to his car and drove back to Headquarters.

***

Diegert had cleaned himself up when Fatima came to his room at 2:33 a.m. "Here's your two hundred euros," said Diegert, extending the cash.

"Is he dead?"

"No, but his two thugs are. I thought we had a gentleman's agreement, but it seems I overestimated Sbrebetskov's commitment to a pact made in honor."

Folding the money and placing it in her pocket, Fatima stepped to the door, turned, and looked over her shoulder just soon enough to catch Diegert checking out her ass.

"I'll see you at 0700 for tomorrow's training brief. I hope your dreams are satisfying."

His dreams were not satisfying; sadness and grief had built up inside him. All the deaths—Paris, Athens, Mogadishu, the pirates on the *Sue Ellen*, Omar Pascal, and now the two thugs—were exerting their psychological effect. Barney, whom he considered a friend, was now out of his life. He needed to express the grief and release the sadness, but when he tried to, he just couldn't. He relaxed in the privacy of his little room, and with his face pressed to the pillow, he opened himself to his painful feelings, but tears wouldn't come. He thought of the hurt and the pain, the violence and the loss, but the expression of those emotions needed something more to come to the surface. He needed to cleanse his soul and perform penance for his actions. He was frustrated at not being able to purge these feelings. Tossing and turning, he eventually fell asleep but awoke to his five thirty a.m. alarm feeling lousy.

CHAPTER 28

Arthur Cambridge was a successful real-estate developer in England. His company, Cambridge Holdings, owned property worth over eight hundred million pounds. The apartment and office buildings produced rental income in excess of five million pounds a month. His father, Sinclair Cambridge, had developed the business with the assistance of Dean Kellerman, a member of the Board of Crepusculous. Through wise investments and reinvestments, Cambridge Holdings grew until it was a self-sustaining real-estate entity. Kellerman remained an investor but didn't take part in the operations of the business. Arthur learned the business while completing his studies at Oxford, and Sinclair gave him a prominent position in the company upon his graduation. So it was no surprise that, upon the elder man's death, his personal estate worth over twenty-five million pounds was turned over to his only son, who was now president of Cambridge Holdings. With such a large volume of money now at his disposal, Arthur had to invest it quickly or lose most of it to taxes. He and his investment assistants looked at the Eastern European market for a suitable place to purchase large housing stock at very low prices. With their past success, they were certain they could keep the properties occupied as they did in England, the Netherlands, and France. The twenty-five million pounds bought forty buildings in Romania. Each building had one to two hundred apartments per unit. The income potential from rent was enormous, and Cambridge Holdings was poised to become a force in the Romanian real-estate business.

Government regulations in Romania were significantly less complex than British bureaucracy. The lawyers of Cambridge Holdings completed the necessary paperwork, putting Arthur Cambridge in business in the Balkans within a month of inheriting his father's wealth. Cambridge visited the country and toured several of the buildings he had purchased. He realized the numerous structures were in various states of repair. Some were in good shape with charming features, while others needed to be condemned and would take a substantial investment to restore. Like a bushel of apples, there were some bad ones. Cambridge directed his business planners to take a complete inventory of the entire purchase and put together a restoration plan for him to review. Upon his return to England, Cambridge prepared to celebrate Christmas with his family on their thirty-acre country estate.

***

The e-mail arrived in the inbox of Nigel Flannery, director of finance for Cambridge Holdings. The document laid out in extensive detail the payment expectations of Michka Barovitz. The payments were required for protection, and fees were listed for every building the company had just purchased in Romania. Nigel thought for a moment but couldn't recall any contracts with security companies for any of the buildings. Security was handled through keyed doorways and neighborhood watch efforts. Spending extra money on security was not a practice of Cambridge Holdings, except for special residents who purchased such services. In the contracts written to purchase the assets in Romania, no security fees were included or required. What also struck the Oxford-educated financier was the use of the word "protection" rather than "security."

Corruption and bribery were part of the history of the Balkans, and Nigel had read about such circumstances in the news and in spy novels, but he certainly never expected the fine company of Cambridge Holdings to be faced with thugs demanding bribes. The thought was so repugnant that he hesitated to bring it to Arthur Cambridge's attention, especially during the Christmas holidays. Barovitz's note, though, demanded a reply and stated that lack of protection payments might result in criminal activity affecting the properties. Nigel gave it some thought and realized he would have to reply to this e-mail in an unequivocal manner.

December 22

Dear Mr. Barovitz,

Regarding your e-mail of December 21, I am afraid we will not be fulfilling your demand for payment. Cambridge Holdings has made the purchase of the Romanian properties without establishing building security contracts. Building security is handled through lock-and-key mechanisms as well as good relations with local law enforcement. Your demand for "protection" payments strikes me as nothing more than extortion, and we simply will not be held hostage to such requests. I request that you never contact our company again, and furthermore, a copy of this notice and your request for extortion payments will be forwarded to

*the local police in the areas where our buildings are
located. I trust this will conclude our correspondence
and that you understand that your draconian ways of
doing business will no longer be tolerated or indulged by
Cambridge Holdings.*
Sincerely,

Nigel Flannery, Director of Finance,
Cambridge Holdings

Nigel sent the e-mail to Barovitz. He also forwarded copies of
the e-mail and the request for payments from Barovitz to the
police headquarters of every district in which they held buildings. Feeling as though he had thoroughly addressed the issue,
Mr. Flannery turned his attention to other business.

CHAPTER 29

David Diegert moved through the line of the cafeteria, collecting his breakfast. As he slid his tray on the metal counter, he looked at the soft hazel eyes and gentle smile of Elena Balan. Elena was a charming young woman with wispy blonde hair pulled back into a ponytail. Diegert hadn't seen her in the cafeteria before and was captivated by her plain but pretty face and her smooth, soft skin. He looked at her without expression until her smile faded and she asked him, "What do you want?" Diegert pondered how he could tell her that he desperately wanted to hug her and hold her in a private place and share with her the passion that was erupting inside him. She looked at him quizzically and repeated, "What do you want?"

Diegert snapped out of it and replied, "Eggs, please, and some sausage." Elena spooned his request onto a plate and slid it under the glass guard. Her smile returned, but she looked at him rather strangely as he stepped down the line. Out in the eating area, Fatima, dressed in the black uniform of the day, directed him to sit at a table with her. "I want to brief you on today's training assignment while you eat."

With only the two of them at the table, Fatima asked, "So how is it that you got the two hundred euros last night, but Sbrebetskov is alive and his two body guards are dead?"

Diegert was not paying attention to her question as he poked and picked at his meal.

"Hey, I asked you a question," the dark-haired trainer snapped.

"What?"

"I asked how is it that Sbrebetskov is alive and his two body guards are dead?"

"You asked me to get him to give me two hundred euros, you didn't assign me to kill him. I convinced him to give me the money, and then his dudes tried to jump me and get it back. My ribs are killing me, by the way."

"Do you need to go to medical?"

"Thanks, but there's nothing they can do for injured ribs."

Diegert dug into his eggs and took a big swallow of orange juice.

"Very well. Our training today isn't so physical as intellectual. I'll develop your skills as a hacker."

"Computers?"

"Of course. We may be assassins, but our ability to infiltrate, acquire, and sabotage information is our greatest asset, and that's what's going to give you longevity in this business."

"Is hacking part of the tournament?"

Fatima looked over her shoulder, returned her gaze to Diegert, and lowered her voice. "Never mind the tournament. You have many other tests to pass before you concern yourself with that."

Folding his toast over his last sausage link and consuming his impromptu sandwich, he asked, "Are you going to make me a lethal geek?"

"I will first try to make you a competent code breaker. Report to Room 278 at 0800."

Leaning forward and locking eyes with him, she said, "Don't be so obvious staring at my ass when I get up and walk away." Diegert forced himself to look down at his empty plate until she'd left the room.

When she was gone, he took his plate and went for seconds. There was no one in line, and Elena stepped up to serve him. From the other side of the glass guard, he handed her his plate, and she asked, "More of the same?"

"Yeah, thanks." He smiled wanly at her and tried to convey a friendly nonverbal message. It might have worked, because she smiled back at him, but he didn't know if that was special or just the way she interacted with everybody. He read her name tag as she filled his plate and handed it back to him.

Diegert didn't know what to say, so he said, "Your name is so pretty. What does it mean?"

Her smile lit up. "Thank you. Elena means . . . bright, shiny . . . like sunlight on water."

"Wow, that's beautiful! My name's David . . . David Diegert."

Diegert set his tray on the metal counter and looked at her and then started to feel awkward and unsure what to say next. Elena seemed to feel the same and asked, "What does David mean?"

Diegert had never considered the meaning of his name and had no idea how to answer. He pretended to ponder for a moment and then said, "I'm afraid I don't know."

This made the awkwardness all the more palpable, and he picked up his tray and said, "I gotta go. Thanks for the seconds."

She just smiled sadly and waved her hand. He walked out into the eating area feeling like a jerk.

***

Room 278 had no windows and a lot of computers. Its fluorescent lighting, numerous workstations, and powerful air-conditioning made it a cold and serious place. Fatima was already there, wearing a thick zip-up hoodie—black, of course.

"It's just you and me in here?" Diegert asked.

"For now, but in my opinion, this is one of the most underutilized facilities on the campus."

"Campus? Now I really feel like I'm back in school."

"You are in school, only this time if you fail you die."

"Wow," Diegert said sarcastically.

"Information is our most crucial commodity. That's been obvious for decades. All information is now in a digital form. That's convenient; it allows for large-scale storage and retrieval, and it lends itself to easy analysis. None of this is news. Information, though, is vulnerable to being observed, copied, altered, stolen, or destroyed. When a system can be breached using remote electronics, then the infiltration happens from a room like this."

"Keyboard spies of the future."

"Right, no one is in actual danger. But when critical data can only be accessed by direct infiltration, then we come into play. The danger is something we're already trained to deal with, but you're of no value if you get in the building but can't get into the data."

"Alright, the keyboard is mightier than the AK-47."

"Definitely. Everyone around here has their big guns and can't wait to use them. But with the right information, you can disable an enemy just as effectively as shooting him." Fatima smiled at Diegert, and it appeared to him that she was just as happy to hack as shoot someone.

"The first thing you have to understand is code. All computer information is coded, and the code allows the information to be specific and unique as well as portable, compressible, and, in many ways, permanent. Think of how government spy agencies collect all that data and sift through it, looking for terrorists. It's through manipulating code that they can identify what they are looking for from all the rest of the tons and tons of data they collect. Using code, you can put yourself on the other side of the firewall and see what's going on in the network. Here, let me show you."

Fatima took her smartphone from her pocket, activated an app, and scrolled through some screens. "I have a program that allows me to bypass the firewall on the Headquarters network."

"Are you supposed to have that?"

"I have it. Once inside, I can access things like personnel files, after-action reports, construction plans, even Internet browsing histories. Care to know what some of the guys were entertaining themselves with last night?"

Diegert met her mischievous gaze with a curious look. Fatima proceeded to tap on the screen of her smartphone. "Here's someone who was on Hulu watching *Mission: Impossible II*, as if we don't get enough of that around here. Someone else was watching *The Outlaw Josey Wales*, a Clint Eastwood movie from 1976! Here's Bassmaster.com, where someone was watching "The Greatest Places for Bass in South Carolina." I guess someone is planning a fishing trip. Gunsandammo.com with the search "Decibel Reduction without Loss of Velocity," the best sound suppressors being made today. Now that's someone doing their homework."

"Can you tell who?"

Smiling again, Fatima replied, "I was wondering when you would ask that. Every log-on to the Internet requires an IP address. This piece of code identifies which computer is using the Internet. You may not always know who's using the computer, but you do know what computer is using the Internet. We may have to make some assumptions or gather evidence about who is actually using a computer, but there are ways of doing that with user IDs and passwords. People think that a user ID and password makes their access secure. It does, but it also is their personal identifier. So our subject interested in silencers is, no surprise, Carl Lindstrom, the Headquarters armorer."

The two snoopers looked at each other, shrugged their shoulders at the innocuousness of it, and moved on. "Now here's an interesting Internet address: Gayboy.com. Not that we're concerned with that, but the video that was watched was "Suck It Long and Strong." This was being watched on the computer registered to . . ."

Fatima held her finger over the screen, not yet scrolling the information into view as Diegert's anticipation built. "See, this is why I want you to learn about data and be able to manipulate code. You can see how powerful this capability is and how much can be learned by knowing how to access information."

"Alright . . . alright. Who is the gay boy?"

Fatima touched her finger to the screen and scrolled up the name assigned to the IP address: Alexi Strakov.

"No . . ." gasped Diegert.

"Come on, now, we aren't supposed to care about that anymore."

"No way . . ." continued Diegert incredulously.

Fatima left Diegert in Room 278 with some basic coding exercises that would allow him to learn rudimentary elements of code design and the interface process. The exercises required Diegert to write some simple programs to get the computer to do some calculations and store the data in specifically identified files. The tutorials provided step-by-step instructions, allowing students to progress as they succeeded. Fatima didn't think the work was very complicated, but given the number of assignments he had, she anticipated Diegert would be at it all day.

CHAPTER 30

Barovitz was not amused by the e-mail from Nigel Flannery.
"Fucking British pricks! They have no respect for how business is done here. They think we'll just do things the British way. Well, bollocks to them."

Barovitz had risen to his current position of power and prominence through strength of will and persistence. Of course, for him to be so successful meant that others were intimidated and threatened into paying him regularly and consistently from the proceeds of their labor. A mobster like Barovitz extorted money from all businesses in the country and kept law enforcement officers on his payroll. His business required him to create no product or service; he only had to siphon payments from those who actually contributed to the economy. The Balkans had functioned in this way for so long that Michka Barovitz actually had earned the respect of many for his rise to power and his ability to stay in power for so long. His business was the envy of many, and young boys were told to dream of growing up and being Barovitz.

In consultation with his most loyal and ruthless assistants, Barovitz made a plan to show the wealthy bastards that they didn't just buy their way into Romania without respecting the business culture. They met for an hour, and Barovitz felt satisfied that their plan would bring the Brits into line and give them a new appreciation for Balkan business practices.

* * *

Diegert found the code difficult to follow, and he was frustrated by the complexity of the number and letter patterns. In the Army, he'd used programs all the time but never had to write one. His smartphone had all sorts of apps, but he didn't have to create them. He patiently tried to accomplish the first simple task but was stymied each time a new pattern had to be mastered. Even though he was good at math, he was failing at coding. The tutorial required progress before opening the next challenge, and Diegert was getting angry at not being able to move forward.

In the afternoon, he abandoned his first unfinished trial and opened a different tutorial, which presented him with a file to be opened without knowing the password. Diegert spent two angry hours trying to open the file, and he cursed at his inability to do what was asked. The tutorial informed him he had one last chance and it would close in fifteen minutes if he remained unsuccessful. A quarter hour later, Diegert was swearing out loud at the computer and angry at his failure to learn the password.

The next tutorial provided a lesson on establishing a firewall against a virus. Diegert found the whole concept of digital defense mystifying. The program instructed him to create a digital barrier that would thwart the program's virus. Try as he might, each code combination he created failed to prevent the virus from corrupting the files he was to protect. The trial was the most frustrating of all, because each time he failed, he had to reread the instructions he didn't understand in the first place. He felt he was put in a no-win situation, with insufficient instruction to be able to do the things expected of him. He imagined getting through the tournament would be easier than this.

By the end of the day, he had accomplished nothing. It was dinnertime, and he was hungry. He was relieved Fatima hadn't come back to check on him, although he figured she was probably keeping track of him remotely. It was stupid that she thought he would just be able to learn all this stuff on his own. From the printer station, Diegert took out a piece of paper, folded it, and put it in his pocket as he left the room.

The cafeteria was serving spaghetti and meatballs, and there were a lot of guys who were much more physically fatigued from their day of training, waiting in line ahead of Diegert. While he waited, his phone buzzed. The text was from Fatima: *Pretty lousy work on the coding. I thought you were smart.*

When Diegert came through the service line, Elena smiled to see him and gave him an extra meatball. Her beautiful smile made him feel a bit better about his crappy day. While he ate his dinner, he took out the piece of paper and wrote:

Please visit me, Room 365
David

He watched the exit of the service line until no one had come out for five minutes. He then went back for more to eat. Elena smiled when he entered, and as he approached, she said, "Beloved."

"Excuse me?"

"Beloved," repeated Elena. "Your name means 'Beloved.'"

"Oh," said Diegert.

215

"David is a name of Hebrew origin that has been adopted by almost every culture in the world, and it means 'The Beloved One.' So you are Beloved."

Reaching her hand under the glass guard, she said, "You want seconds?"

"Yes, please."

Elena placed the food on his plate, again giving him an extra meatball. She slid the plate under the glass guard, and Diegert slid his paper note to her side of the guard, saying only, "Thank you."

After eating his fill, he placed his dirty dishes in the cleaning area and went back to his room. He figured Elena was off duty in the next hour, and if she was going to come, he wanted to be there.

In his room, he sat alone on his bed, where thoughts of his violent acts plagued him. He saw the bullet strikes and the blood splatters in vivid color. He felt the thud of the falling bodies and the terror of the frightened mothers caught in the crossfire, risking themselves to protect their children. He recalled the fading light in the eyes of his victims, whose final gaze was upon the face of their killer. The emotions he felt left him sad and dejected. They preoccupied him as if the garbage can were full and had to be emptied before one more piece of trash could be put in it. Yet he couldn't breach that container and get it to tip over and dump its noxious contents.

These dreadful feelings were juxtaposed by the attraction he felt to Elena. She was kind and friendly. Her smile so genuine, he melted when she looked at him with her bright eyes. Her service uniform hid the outline of her body, but Diegert imagined she was femininely curvaceous, and he was eager to find out. Being emotionally and sexually attracted to this young woman gave Diegert a jolt of life, making him feel energized and excited. His conflicted state, though, clouded his thinking and occupied his mind.

It was while he was jumbled in turmoil that a knock on his door reverberated through the room. He opened the door and looked into the warm eyes and sweet smile of Elena. She stood at the threshold with her smile masking her apprehension. She knew she was breaking a protocol she had been trained to obey.

"Thanks for coming," said a grateful and anxious David Diegert. "Please come in."

He stepped aside so she could enter the room and closed the door behind her.

"First, thanks so much for coming to see me."

"Thank you for inviting me."

"I've thought about you a lot since we first met, and I was hoping we'd be able to become friends."

"Friends or lovers?"

Diegert was taken aback by her forward question, but it was exactly what was on his mind.

"Lovers, I hope."

He looked into her kind, gentle eyes and was captivated by the soft feminine features of her caring expression. He held out his hand, and she took it. He slowly pulled her into him and hugged her lovely body. He was embarrassed but unable to stop as the first tears crested his eyelids and rolled down his cheeks.

They moved onto the bed, and lying by her side, he burst into tears, crying bitterly, angrily, and forcefully, letting all the pain, sadness, anger, and grief come out of his body, his soul. She was taken aback by this unexpected encounter, yet she could feel how much he needed it. She brushed his hair, stroked his neck, and quietly said, "Shhh . . . let it all out, sweet David the Beloved."

Diegert poured it out for twenty minutes, during which he relived the tragedies of the deaths he had created. When the memory of Omar's death came up, he was especially tortured. The serviceman was a brother in arms and just trying to do the right thing. Diegert deeply regretted killing him and was now facing the emotions of his wicked act. The exit from his heart was punishing. Elena held him tight as he suffered the disemboweling sensation of exorcising his guilt. Having saturated the pillow as well as the shoulder of her blouse, he was exhausted. She had never seen a man cry like this, and it struck her as deeply intimate. This man entrusted her to see him at his weakest moment, with his most painful emotions on unshielded display. She was awestruck.

He lay quietly with her, opening himself to make certain the trash can was empty and he was able to be himself again. As he lay there with her, he had to admit to himself that this need for emotional catharsis was part of him. He was grateful for the comfort this lovely woman shared with him, and now he had no idea how to discuss this with her. He hoped she wouldn't ask for an explanation. He went for the simplest phrase: "Thank you."

She caressed his hair and face, saying, "I'm glad I could be here for you."

Diegert looked into her eyes and saw her desire. He moved forward, bringing his lips to hers. She pressed forward as well, and the pressure of their mouths ignited their sense of pleasure. Diegert pulled her closer in his arms. Elena slid her leg between his, allowing their hips to exert an erotic pressure. Elena opened her mouth, and their tongues intertwined, dancing in a flurry of exquisite pleasure. Diegert's hands ran down her body, feeling the sweep of her rib cage into her narrow waist and then the sensual curve of her hips. Diegert rolled her to the side, sliding his hand up until he caressed her clothed breasts.

Elena moaned as Diegert gently squeezed her sensitive chest and started unbuttoning her blouse. Elena's excitement exploded, and she broke from Diegert to strip off her clothes. Diegert used the moment to do the same, and then the lovers were back on the bed, naked and enthralled with the sensation of skin on skin.

Elena's breasts had never been exposed to the sun and looked like soft alabaster with rosy nipples. Diegert hungrily took one of her sensitive buds into his mouth, and Elena responded with an erotic moan and intense thrusts of her hips. Diegert's shaft was fully engorged, and Elena pressed herself against the stiff member. She broke Diegert's nipple kiss and slid down his body so she could take his erection into her moist mouth. Diegert looked to the ceiling and gave himself over to the pleasure she was providing. She stroked his shaft with her lips, altering her actions according to his pleasurable responses.

Diegert enjoyed her sensual pleasures, but he wanted to share the climax. He guided her to straddle him and inserted himself into her. The lovers found their rhythm, thrusting their hips in time with their mounting desire. Their timing was just right as Diegert reached the peak of pleasure a moment before Elena's body exploded into a transcendent orgasm that lasted longer than any Diegert had ever witnessed. She crashed down on top of him, pressing her body against his.

They lay quietly, comfortable in their mutual silence. Diegert heard the swipe of plastic through the door's electronic lock. The latch popped open with a loud snap, and the room filled with the bright light of the hallway, causing both of them to shield their faces.

Entering the room, Fatima was shocked to see two bodies entwined on the bed. She stopped abruptly and gasped at the sight before her. Diegert got up, stepped past Fatima, and closed the door. Elena swung her legs to the floor and struggled to get dressed. Diegert stepped into his boxers while Fatima caught her breath and formed her next statement.

"This is not supposed to happen."

"Calm down, I don't have to explain this to you."

"As a matter of fact, you do."

"You can mind your own fucking business."

"When you're fucking a Headquarters employee, that is my business."

"We're adults who don't need your approval."

"One of your points can't be argued, but on the other, you're clearly wrong."

Returning next to her on the bed and grabbing her hand, Diegert told Elena, "You're the kindest, most gentle woman I've ever met, and I'm so grateful for the time you spent with me."

Fatima blurted out, "Shut the fuck up." Turning to Elena, she said, "Get out of here right now before I call security."

Elena glanced at Diegert with a quiet smile, stood up, faced Fatima with eyes like daggers, and walked out. Diegert sat on the bed, looking at the floor.

Fatima sighed, saying, "This is over. You are not to fraternize with Headquarters employees. I'll see you at 0700."

CHAPTER 31

To be a member of the choir of Westminster Abbey, you not only had to be a boy between the ages of eight and fourteen with the gift of voice, but you also had to be fully committed to the schedule of daily performances and enroll in the abbey's choir school. The school was specifically designed to allow the boys to complete their educations while fulfilling the performance requirements of the choir. The choir's schedule included daily participation in services at the abbey as well as state and international performances.

Andrew Cambridge was eleven years old and one of the principal voices in the choir. His parents, Arthur and Elizabeth, were so very proud of his participation, and their generous sponsorship allowed the choir to stay at some of the finest hotels in the world when they traveled to perform. Andrew thought all the songs were kind of old-fashioned, but he was so accustomed to being with his friends in the choir that the very uniqueness of his privileged but demanding life didn't even occur to him. Even at the age of eleven, he enjoyed the fantasy of Christmas. He and his family made the most of the story of Father Christmas and his chimney-sliding habit of bringing gifts on Christmas morning. The choir of Westminster Abbey performed at the classic midnight mass as well as the morning services, but in between, Andrew Cambridge and the other boys were allowed to go home and have Christmas morning with their families. Andrew was so very excited about the holiday that the butterflies in his stomach flapped all day.

Midnight mass was a tremendous affair, attended by the royal family and a thousand other parishioners. The cathedral, dressed in lights and decorations for the holiday, had a magical feel for this special season. Andrew's parents, as well as his older sister, Victoria, were all in attendance at midnight mass, so Andrew was a little surprised when a dark-suited man approached him after the performance and informed him he would be providing Andrew transport to the Cambridge estate. But Andrew's excitement wasn't diminished by the fact that he was riding separately to the family's home in the country. As a member of the choir, he was always being driven to one place or another. The car certainly looked right, a big black Rolls-Royce. The man opened the rear door, Andrew climbed in, and the man followed. The car immediately drove off the grounds of the abbey and turned in the direction of the estate.

Andrew asked, "Was Victoria with my parents?"

"I'm sure she is," replied the man in the seat beside him.

"She is becoming such a bother to Mum and Dad. She's doing the teenage thing really badly, rejecting everything Mum and Dad want her to do. I wouldn't be surprised if she just pissed on midnight mass and stayed home."

The man remained silent but smiled weakly and looked out the window. Andrew looked out the window as well, and it looked like they were getting on the freeway, which was certainly not the route to the estate. When Andrew turned to question their route, he was startled to see the man had a small mask over his nose and mouth. He looked to the driver, and the window between them was closed tight. The man held a small spray bottle. Andrew put his hands up to defend himself, but the vapors found their way into his lungs. Within a minute, he was unconscious, and the man opened the moonroof to aerate the cabin. The driver continued on to the airport, where Andrew was loaded on a private plane and flown to Bucharest, Romania.

When he received notice that the abduction had succeeded, Michka Barovitz sent an e-mail to both Arthur Cambridge and Nigel Flannery.

Gentlemen,

Apparently you have some lessons to learn about doing business in the Balkans. I will instruct you to make the payments I outlined in my earlier e-mail or your son will suffer the consequences for nonpayment. Hopefully, he will learn early to abide by the cultural practices of different regions of the world. When payment in full has been made and a consistent payment history has been established, your son's tour of the Balkans will conclude and he will be returned. Until then, his location and well-being will be at my direction. I wish you a Happy Christmas.
Michka Barovitz

When they got the e-mail, it concluded the two hours of worry about the disappearance of Andrew, but it extended an already long night. Elizabeth Cambridge was hysterical. She cried inconsolably, hyperventilating to the point of fainting. Arthur felt powerless yet was resigned to resolve this with dignity. Nigel Flannery was at the family estate. He explained to Arthur the earlier correspondence with Barovitz and was so very apologetic, though he could never have imagined that this would be the consequence for refusing to be extorted. News of the boy's kidnapping spread quickly, and the British online tabloids feasted on the story, speculating on all sorts of dreadful possibilities and probable suspects.

When Dean Kellerman heard the news, he was taken by the plight of his friend and business associate. Being a parishioner of the abbey and a member of the same exclusive golf club as Arthur, he felt compelled to offer his assistance. Unlike so many people, who offered to do whatever they could even when there was nothing they could actually do, Dean Kellerman's wealth and position were substantially greater than the rest of London's elite. As a member of the Board of Crepusculous, he played on the world stage and belonged to the small group of the world's most influential people. In spite of his lofty position, he could feel the pain and sorrow his friend's family was going through. It certainly wasn't pity he was offering, and he was aware of Cambridge Holdings' new properties in Romania. With that knowledge, he speculated the problem emanated from the Balkans, although no such information had left the mouths of either Arthur or Nigel.

When Kellerman's name appeared on Arthur's phone, he wisely took the call. "Hello, Dean."

"Arthur, my dear chap, this is a dreadful situation. Let me save us some time and share a speculation with you."

"Thank you for calling. I appreciate your concern."

"Right, my good man. I'm curious to know if this has anything to do with your recent acquisition of properties in Romania?"

Arthur's shocked response was audible through the phone. "Why . . . yes."

"I was afraid so. Dreadful buggers, those Balkan businessmen. Extortion is such a part of the culture that they don't even perceive it as wrong. Did they say which country he's being held in?"

"I believe Romania, but the message said he will be on a tour of the Balkans."

"OK, here it is. I have assets in the Balkans that are trained to deal with situations like this. They are Special Forces types who work for me as mercenaries when I need them. I'll deploy them to find and retrieve your son, but I will ask that you do not tell the police, the press, or your family of this arrangement. I do hope you can appreciate the sensitivity of training and maintaining such resources?"

"Yes, of course, I will tell no one."

At that instant, Arthur turned and looked at Nigel, who was hearing only half the conversation.

Kellerman broke back in. "Arthur, you certainly can inform your good man Nigel, but no one else. I'll call you on this number with news as things develop in the theater. Keep up your spirits and Happy Christmas."

"Yes . . . thank you, sir."

Kellerman hung up the phone and called Blevinsky. He informed him of the situation and tasked him with locating the boy and assembling a team to retrieve him. Fortunately, Barovitz operated with such brazen impunity in Bucharest and kidnapped whomever he wanted, that his locations were known in the underground community. Blevinsky put together a reconnaissance plan, tasking three operators to infiltrate and investigate Barovitz's most likely locations. He informed Fatima of the situation and told her he wanted Diegert to be one of those operators.

CHAPTER 32

It's Christmas time, and this fucking place doesn't even have a Christmas tree, thought Diegert as he ate his breakfast. Fatima appeared and, as usual, didn't eat any cafeteria food. "Why don't you eat anything?" asked Diegert.

"Because I choose not to poison my body with the junk they serve."

"What have you got? A hot plate, bean sprouts, and a teapot in your room?"

"Never mind, I'm here to task you with a mission."

"You got rid of her, didn't you?"

"What?"

"Elena, the girl in the service line, you got her fired, didn't you?"

"That's right, she doesn't work here anymore, and her husband's not too happy about it. It's going to make it a lot harder for them to feed their two children. But I suppose you never thought about that?"

Diegert drew a long breath as he looked down at his plate. Turning his gaze to Fatima, he said, "You didn't have to get her fired."

"Employees are not to fraternize with trainees and vice versa. It was her or you. So you're lucky you're still here."

"Yeah, lucky me."

Fatima sprang up, grabbing Diegert's right hand in a wrist-lock and twisting it behind his back. She picked up his fork and placed it against his neck. "I have told you this is serious shit, and I'm not going to fuck around with you. If I kill you right now, no one will care and I'll suffer no consequences, you understand?"

She pressed the fork until blood ran down from the four tines. She kept going deeper until Diegert spat out an answer. "Yes, I understand."

She took her hand off the fork, leaving it embedded in his flesh, released the armlock, and stepped back. The cafeteria grew talkative again after the passing of the dramatic moment. Diegert reached up and extracted the fork.

Fatima instructed him, "Meet me in Room 240 after you're done poisoning yourself."

The bleeding wouldn't stop. Diegert had to go to medical, where an antibiotic ointment was applied and the wound was covered by a large bandage. The medic said it was a good thing he came, because impalements usually got infected, especially when egg and saliva penetrated the skin.

Room 240 was behind a windowless door. When Diegert stepped inside, he noticed all the walls were padded and there were no windows at all. The floor was also padded. Fatima stood across the room dressed in her black combat uniform and tactical boots. Her dark hair fell below her shoulders in lustrous waves. She looked at him and giggled. "You look like you're trying to hide a hickey."

Diegert didn't reply, but his furrowed brow told her he did not find her amusing. With a playful, seductive smile, she bounced over to him and asked, "Do you know why I brought you here?"

Diegert was disarmed. He had never seen Fatima show her sexy side, and it was very sexy indeed. She approached him looking into his eyes with hers wide and her smile broad and appealing. "I brought you here because I can't stand it any longer. You really turn me on."

"I do?"

"Yes, of course. You may have misinterpreted the way I've been treating you, but it's because I want you so bad," Fatima said as she reached out and stroked his dark hair.

"Bullshit! This is total bullshit."

"You don't believe me? Why wouldn't you believe that I'm hot for you? You don't find me attractive?"

"You just stabbed me with a fork, and now this?"

"You didn't answer my question. Do you find me attractive?"

"No . . . no . . . I mean, yes, you're very attractive. But what about all the other shit you've been doing to me?"

Stepping close to him and placing her hand on his chest, she said, "I have to keep up appearances around here, you know." She turned from him and walked a few paces, moping sadly. Looking back over her shoulder, she said, "I was really jealous of that other girl. The one you had in your room."

"And you certainly fixed it so you won't have to worry about her anymore."

"I thought, doesn't he see how much I want him, how sexy I think he is, and how much I want to be with him? So I brought you here, to the most private room in the whole place, so we could . . . share some passion." Standing with her feet in a wide stance and her hips turned and tilted, Fatima pulled her T-shirt over her head, revealing her black sports bra.

Diegert was amazed, and this woman was hot, even though it was so unexpected. If she wanted to have sex, he was more than willing to take pleasure from her body.

"Why don't you come over here and I'll give you a real hickey to hide."

"I don't believe this. You're fucking around with me so you can get me in more trouble."

"You're being a silly boy," she said as she dipped her head and strode over to him. "I'm not fucking you, not yet, but I want to." She trailed her hand around his neck, across his chest, and over his shoulder while circling him.

Diegert's face revealed his conflict and confusion, but he stood fast as she finished her circle and drew herself close to him.

"Honestly, what has a girl gotta do to show a guy she's hot for him?" She held his gaze, exuding sexual desire. Stepping back one pace, she undid the belt of her combat pants and lowered her zipper, revealing white panties with a red waistband and a little yellow flower on the front. She reached out and pulled his hips to hers. She smiled up at him with warmth and assurance. She squeezed his butt with her left hand, and with her right, she hit him in the chin with a palm heel strike.

Diegert's head snapped. She grasped his right arm, kicking him in the hip, sending him sprawling on his back to the floor. She stepped on the biceps of his right arm, causing his hand to lie flat on the floor, palm up. She slid her foot out to his hand and placed her heel on his palm.

Diegert was shocked but quickly realized what a fool he had been. The pain in his palm was more intense than he'd ever imagined. Fatima dropped her right knee into the meat of his thigh; he rotated the leg, and her weight exerted extreme pressure on his femur. This, too, was far more painful than Diegert had expected. From her position, Fatima easily punched

Diegert in the ribs. The excruciating pain of the injured bones took his breath away.

"Do I have your attention now? Do you recognize who your superior is? Will you realize that I'm better at what we do than you are? I have tools you will never have, and I know how to use them to disarm those who should be able to recognize a ruse."

Diegert was in so much pain from so many places he was having trouble listening to her. She reached down and slapped his face. "Hey, are you paying attention? Do you realize how vulnerable you are?"

She slapped him again. "Answer me."

Diegert had both his left arm and leg free. His eyes darted to her right side, planning a countermovement.

"I see . . . you want to try to get free."

Fatima pressed her weight into his right palm and drove her left knee into his groin. The searing pain from the sudden strike on his testicles sent Diegert to a place of agony he had never experienced before. He was about to lose consciousness when she struck his ribs again. He thought she was speaking, but he could no longer hear her, and his world was closing in, his mind going gray. His face was slapped again and again, but he could no longer feel it, and soon he was in a black world of nothingness.

Fatima realized he was unconscious when every muscle in his body went limp.

"What a pussy," she said as she stood up and stepped off him. She looked at her watch: 0742. She squatted back down next to him to confirm his heartbeat and breathing; he was still alive. She stood again and stepped away from him. She realized she had gone a little too far as she did up her pants and put her T-shirt back on. She reminded herself she was authorized to expose trainees to harsh treatment simulating that which they might encounter in the field. She reasoned he would now know his limits and operate accordingly. When he came to, she would treat him nicer and brief him on the upcoming mission. 0745. She had to admit that she had never applied this much abuse before. She was certain that waterboarding and stress positions were worse, but the sustained application of pain, with escalation on areas that had already been traumatized, could be considered excessive in a training program. *Yeah . . . this was bad,* she thought. 0750. She gently tapped his face and rubbed his forearm, softly saying, "Diegert . . . David."

When he remained unresponsive, she stepped away and crossed to the far side of the room. She nervously brought her hand to her chin as she thought that she would have to keep a lid on his reactions so that the full story never left the room. Perhaps he'd have amnesia. 0754.

Diegert coughed. He brought his hands to his face and rolled onto his side. He tucked into a fetal position.

Fatima asked, "Are you OK?"

"Fuck you."

"OK, well, if you're all better, I want you to sit up and listen to the mission briefing I have for you."

Diegert propped himself on his right elbow, saying, "What the fuck was that all about?"

"You're vulnerable to the seductive powers of women. You need to be able to see beyond the end of your prick and realize how disarming a woman can be. If you and I squared off directly, you would never end up like this. But throw in the possibility of getting laid, and you turn to putty."

"You're a fucking bitch."

"Yeah, I know. Don't ever let another woman do this to you. And don't tell anyone what happened here today. Now if you're ready to focus, there is a mission coming up, part of which is going to be assigned to you."

"Whoa . . . whoa . . . whoa. You just treat me like shit with your backhanded seduction, and now you're going to brief me on a mission?"

Fatima's fiery personality ignited, and she exploded at Diegert. "You want to cry about your treatment, go right ahead, but there is no one to listen to your complaints. If you are not able to produce what's requested, there are plenty of law enforcement agencies that would love to get their hands on you. Do you understand me?"

Rolling back onto his side so he wouldn't have to look at her, Diegert said, "What part of the mission do you want me to do?"

"Reconnaissance. A British national, a young boy, has been taken hostage and brought to Romania. Barovitz, the mob boss in Bucharest, is holding him. We've been tasked with locating the subject and then formulating a rescue plan. Obviously we don't want the boy hurt, and it will be a team mission to retrieve him."

"You mean we do hostage rescues as well as assassinations?"

Raising her voice, she said, "When we have the opportunity to do something that will directly help an innocent person, we'll do it."

"How do we know he's innocent?"

Stepping over to him and rolling him onto his back, Fatima's fiery eyes locked on his as she said, "He's an eleven-year-old choir boy. I think that qualifies as innocent."

"Alright, what have I got to do?"

"Blevinsky has identified three likely locations where the boy might be held. You will perform reconnaissance on a casino. The schematics of the building have been sent to your phone. When the boy's location is known, his extraction will be carried out by a strike team. Why don't you go rest up; the recon mission is tonight. Study those schematics and learn them a lot better than the shitty job you did learning code."

Diegert looked at her with disdain and distrust as he struggled to his feet and left the room.

CHAPTER 33

In the free-weight area of the fitness center, Blevinsky addressed Strakov, "Alexi, I want you to make certain all the men on the strike team realize that the mission is to rescue the hostage. You must use restraint. Your team is not to fill a room with dead bodies."

"When do we deploy? Do we have time to practice?"

"You have time. I have reconnaissance missions underway to locate the boy and gather intel."

"Alright, we'll practice selective shooting."

"Good, I'll keep you updated."

Blevinsky left Strakov, but the big guy cut his workout short so he could get his team prepared.

***

As darkness fell, Diegert was driven to Barovitz's Casino Placere. The gambling establishment, located in an ancient palace, had long since lost its luster. The place was big and old with two floors of gambling. Roulette wheels, blackjack tables, and slot machines dominated the first floor, with the noise, lights, and smoke giving it both an exciting and a depressing feel. The second floor had poker and other high-stakes card games, which were played on well-lit tables in darkened rooms. Barovitz generated huge profits from this facility, and although there were occasional winners, the house dominated, and the mobster used both the profits and individuals' debts to his advantage.

If a person was unable to pay, Barovitz often found some dirty job for them to do or took whatever property or valuables they had as payment. Barovitz considered young women an acceptable commodity. Several daughters of debtors now worked for Barovitz to pay for the losses of their fathers. The period between Christmas and New Year's was an especially busy time as people celebrated the holidays by feeding their desires for easy money.

The parking lot was full, and people were dressed in their best for an evening in the old palace. Diegert entered the casino with the rest of the gamblers. He was not interested in trying to win money. His objectives were far riskier than losing a couple hundred euros. On his smartphone, he checked the schematic of the area in the basement he was to reconnoiter. At the far end of the corridor, near the men's room, was a door to a staircase that led to the basement. Diegert found the door locked, but using a pick tool, he opened it and stepped inside. Descending the stairs led him to another locked door. Using his tool, he had it open in thirty seconds. Before entering, he reexamined the diagram on his phone, which revealed that on the other side of the door was a very large storage space. There was also a ground-level exit door on the opposite side of the building. The intel he was given indicated that this was the place where Barovitz held hostages.

Diegert opened the door a crack, peering into the cavernous space. In one corner, there were dozens of aged slot machines stacked horizontally and covered in plastic. There was no movement, but a light shone from the far side of the large space. Diegert withdrew his HK45 tactical pistol from its holster. The gun was equipped with a laser sight and a flashlight. He affixed his suppressor and was now armed with his favorite weapon. Very cautiously, he stepped out from behind the door. On silent feet, he crossed the room and proceeded to the end of the row of slot machines. From this vantage point, he could see an area lit by several hanging fluorescent fixtures. In the center of the space was a table with four chairs. The table was littered with food wrappers, cards, ashtrays, and liquor bottles. Flanking the table in an *L*-shaped arrangement were two dingy couches. Beyond them was a curtain strung between two hooks that were attached to the ceiling. The place showed signs of recent occupation, but at the moment it was deserted. Diegert, dressed in black, carefully crossed the space, passed the table, and peered behind the curtain. There was a boy with his hands tied through the back of a sturdy chair. He was dressed in navy slacks and a white shirt, with a red tie and a dark-blue blazer displaying the shield of the Westminster Abbey. His right eye was bruised, and he had a cut on his left lower lip, but his eyes made direct contact with Diegert's from under his tousled mop of blond hair. Although this mission was reconnaissance only, Diegert couldn't turn away and leave the injured boy.

Stepping forward, Diegert said, "I'm here to take you home."

Diegert unraveled the duct tape binding the boy's wrists. The instant the bonds were broken, the boy took off running. Diegert chased after him into the open space and saw the boy rush around the corner of the stacked slot machines. When Diegert turned the corner, he was confronted by a very large, very bald bodyguard who held the struggling Andrew Cambridge by his right arm. The boy kicked and punched the big man. Annoyed by the boy's violence, the guard backhanded the lad across the face, turning him into an unconscious heap. The guard faced Diegert, who pulled the trigger of his HK45, firing a sound-suppressed bullet into the big man's chest. The round delivered a solid body blow, but the guard's Kevlar vest stopped the bullet, and he came forward, bringing the fight to Diegert. Stepping behind the slot machines, Diegert eluded his enemy. He sprinted back to the table and behind the curtain, drawing the guard away from the boy. Listening carefully, Diegert could hear the angry guard coming. When the big bald man lifted the curtain, Diegert's laser sight marked the spot on the guard's forehead where the bullet entered his brain. The big guy's body collapsed with a powerful thud, and Diegert sprinted back to Andrew Cambridge.

Lifting the unconscious boy over his shoulder, Diegert headed for the exit down the hallway on the south side of the building. As he moved down the hall, Diegert texted Fatima.

I have the boy. I need extraction at the south end of the casino.

Fatima's response was immediate; she called, saying, "God damn it, you were only supposed to do reconnaissance. What the fuck is going on?"

"We'll argue later; right now I need help getting the boy out of here."

"There is no help. Nothing is organized."

"Fuckin' get it together. Call me back."

***

The elevator descended and opened up not far from the door that Diegert had used to enter the basement. A second body-guard exited the elevator, stepped around the defunct slot machines, and walked to the area where he was to relieve his associate. When he entered the area formed by the table and couches, he did not see his comrade and shouted, "Boris?"

When there was no reply, he moved to the curtained-off area, pulled back the cloth, and saw his dead associate. Dismayed as he was by the scene, the boy's absence quickly rose to prominence, and he began searching for the missing prisoner.

***

Fatima realized she had to do something, but deploying a rescue team was out of the question and would certainly fail without thorough planning. Checking the map, she noticed a large water tower south of the casino that was serviced by a dirt road. If Diegert could get there, she could extract him with a vehicle. She texted him the plan.

Extract at the water tower in 30 mins.

Diegert checked the map on his smartphone. The water tower sat on a hill across from the parking lot surrounded by thin woods and a fence. He recalled seeing a toolbox on the floor near one of the couches. He made Andrew as comfortable as possible, turned off the hall lights, and went back to get a cutting tool for the fence.

After searching all the many hiding places in the big room, the bodyguard headed down the south hallway. Diegert could see the long shadow cast by whoever was backlit as he walked down the hall. From the cover of darkness, Diegert sprinted forward, placing a vicious choke strike on the trachea of the bodyguard. The shock and force of the strike cracked the man's larynx, triggering a disabling coughing fit. Diegert slugged the guy in the gut and then chopped him on the back of the neck, felling him.

Diegert didn't want to shoot this man in front of Andrew. He stepped back down the hallway to check on the boy. When he turned on the lights, the brightness startled the boy, who was suddenly awake and aware. Diegert approached Andrew in a manner he assumed was friendly and reassuring. "Andrew, everything is going to be OK. Stay here, and I'll be right back to take you to safety. OK?"

To the boy, none of it made sense, and Diegert looked like just another tough guy dressed in black.

Diegert drew his pistol and returned to the sputtering guard. He hauled the guy to his feet and pushed him back to the big room. He made him open the toolbox and dump the contents on the table. A hammer, screwdrivers, nails, screws, washers, but the closest thing to a cutting tool was a pair of needle-nose pliers and a wood-handled rasp. He stuck these two tools in a pouch pocket and looked back up to see the bodyguard reaching for the hammer. Diegert pointed his pistol at him, saying, "Touch it and I nail you."

Suddenly, a blaring alarm startled both men. The bodyguard looked past Diegert down the hallway. Diegert turned instinctively to the sound, giving the bodyguard the moment he needed to grab the hammer and swing at Diegert's right arm. The strike on his radius was intense, and Diegert lost the grip on his pistol. The bodyguard swung the hammer at his head, and Diegert leaned back as the head of the hammer passed within millimeters of his face. Diegert stepped in and used his arm to block the bodyguard's return swing. He struck him in the temple with three quick jabs. The bodyguard stumbled to his left, and Diegert delivered a full-force kick to the hip. Having fallen on his left side, the bodyguard flung the hammer at Diegert, striking him in his already injured ribs. Diegert gasped for air as the cage of protective bones was once again tested.

The bodyguard got to his feet, grabbed a screwdriver, and slashed at Diegert. The boy's would-be rescuer dodged the swipes and swings the big guy made with the pointed tool. Diegert stepped back up against one of the couches and felt the rasp he had in his pocket. The bodyguard thought he had his enemy trapped against the furniture and strode forward to impale him. Diegert flipped backward over the couch, extracting the rasp from his pocket. Holding the wood handle, he watched as the bodyguard prepared to climb over the couch. The moment the big guy's foot was on the unstable cushions, Diegert rushed forward and slashed the rasp across the bodyguard's face. So destructive was the sharp surface of the rasp that the guy's right cheek flayed open, revealing his molars. The blood poured out of his lacerated face, escalating his anger. Diegert stepped out into an open area and squared off with his determined foe. With the screwdriver held forward, the bodyguard lunged at Diegert, who was able to avoid the thrusts. Eventually, the frustrated attacker charged, and Diegert struck him with the rasp on the back of his arm, shredding his shirtsleeve and turning it crimson from his ripped triceps. Diegert quickly struck again, this time hitting his opponent on the back of the head. The bodyguard was stunned from the blow, and Diegert hit him again and again with the rasp until the vertebrae in his neck were severed and blood erupted from the spinal arteries. The big bodyguard's body slumped forward, collapsing on the floor as his life-sustaining fluids pulsed out of his neck.

Diegert found his HK just as the elevator doors opened and two more men stepped out. With the slot machines as a barrier, Diegert turned and sprinted down the hallway. Andrew was no longer there, and he raced through the open door. Outside, he noticed a pile of pallets. Grabbing one, he wedged it under the doorknob, making the exit inoperable from the inside.

CHAPTER 34

From the door, Diegert saw tracks leading to the parking lot. The poorly plowed gravel space had at least a hundred cars in it, and Diegert had no idea where Andrew might be. He started searching the lot, looking down the aisles between cars. Finding nothing, he wondered if Andrew would've taken off into the woods, but there were no tracks in that direction. As his frustration grew, Diegert heard a group of kids shouting and laughing not far away. He moved in their direction and could see a group of six teens standing in a circle. The hoodlums surrounded Andrew and were taunting and teasing him. The boy was standing his ground as his tormentors threw snowballs and insults at him. Diegert stepped in front of Andrew and told the punks, "Get the fuck out of here." One look at the menacing face of David Diegert was enough to give them pause, but the gun in his hand made the group of troublemakers quickly disperse.

Diegert turned to Andrew, saying, "I know you don't know me, and you've been through some terrible things, but for your safety and survival, you have to come with me. Now."

Frustrated with the impassibility of the southern exit, the two men went back upstairs, gathered two more guys, and went outside looking for the boy and whoever took him and killed the other bodyguards.

Diegert had moved to the fence at the base of the water tower hill. The wire-cutting jaws on the pliers were completely inadequate to cut through the fencing. Diegert used them, though, to untwist the chain-link diamonds. As he struggled with the metal, the men from the casino spotted them and came running. The guys were taking pot shots at Diegert, and he had to stop untangling the fencing and return fire. Each time they stopped firing, he went back to work dismantling the barrier. Soon he could hear the men's voices growing closer. The chain links were almost untangled enough for them to slip through.

Diegert looked back to see one of the men ten meters away, sighting his assault rifle on them. Covering Andrew, he looked up to see the man's head explode off his shoulders. The beam of a laser sight was briefly visible in the bloody spray before the lifeless body collapsed to the ground. The next man in the lot was similarly vanquished, and Diegert quickly pulled the fencing apart so that he and Andrew could crawl through.

They ran a short distance through the woods and began ascending the hill. The other two men were firing on them as they were exposed on the hillside. The sniper fire was not able to take them out but did keep them pinned down long enough for Diegert to pick Andrew up and shoulder haul him up to the top of the hill. Fatima directed them to the SUV while she placed an incendiary round into the chamber of her rifle. She aimed carefully at the gas tank of the car the men were hiding behind. The shot entered the tank, igniting its contents and taking out the last two men who knew where the boy had gone.

Diegert sat in the driver's seat, and Andrew was buckled in the back. Fatima put her rifle in the back of the vehicle and jumped into the front passenger's seat. She reluctantly handed

Diegert the keys, saying, "You're in deep shit. What the fuck were you doing? I had to pull a favor to get the rifle, and you owe me."

"Thanks for coming. I'd like to introduce you to Andrew Cambridge, but I request that you control your profane tongue."

Fatima's anger hung on her face until she turned to Andrew. When she looked at the traumatized boy, she became warm and gentle. Her smile was loving and comforting. Diegert drove down the hill, heading back to Headquarters. She spoke to Andrew softly. "It's all over, you're going to be OK. You're going home to be with your family. Don't be frightened, Hamni, we'll be in a safe place very soon."

She reached her hand back and caressed the boy's forearm. He closed his eyes, and the tears squeezed out from under his lids and down his cheeks. Fatima pulled a handkerchief out of her pocket, unbuckled her seat belt, and climbed in the back to hug Andrew in her arms. "Shhh . . ." she said as the boy took comfort in her embrace.

When Diegert neared the Headquarters, he looked back and saw that Andrew was asleep in Fatima's arms. She looked content and more peaceful than he had ever seen her. With less than a mile to go, Fatima told Diegert, "I don't want you telling anyone about my involvement with this operation. You understand?"

"Who's Hamni?"

"What?"

"Hamni? You called him Hamni when you spoke to him. His name is Andrew."

"I know his name, and I didn't call him anything else." Her pissed-off face was back, but it now had shades of surprise and perplexity.

"I'm just saying, you called the kid Hamni, so I was just asking who that is?"

"Shut up, just make sure you don't tell anyone I was involved at all."

"You sure? Because you were awesome."

"Tell no one anything. Pull the car over here."

Diegert parked the SUV on the side of the road.

"You're going to get out of the car and carry Andrew into Headquarters. I'll return before you. Using the car is no big deal as long as I return without you. Returning the rifle, I have covered, but I owe Lindstrom a big favor, which you are going to repay."

Diegert looked at her and shrugged.

"Now think up a lie about how you got away and how you got back here with the boy and stick to it. Don't mention me."

"Yeah . . . yeah, I got it, you were never there."

Diegert stepped out of the vehicle, opened the passenger door, and lifted Andrew into his arms. Fatima drove away, and Diegert was left to walk the three-quarters of a mile to Headquarters.

The gate opened automatically as Diegert approached with the boy. Inside he went straight to medical, as people in the halls and offices looked to see what was going on. A child in the facility was a very rare occurrence. Once Andrew was secure in the hands of the medical staff, Diegert reported to Blevinsky's office. The terse bald man stood in his doorway watching Diegert's approach. As the younger man got closer, Blevinsky stepped back into his office, never breaking eye contact until he was on the other side of the door. Diegert walked in as Blevinsky rounded his desk and took a position standing in front of his chair.

"Close the door. In some sappy Hollywood movie, I would be saying something to you like, 'Even though you broke protocol, you saved the day, you little rascal.' But this is not Hollywood, and the only thing that concerns me is that you broke protocol. I don't care about the outcome; you disobeyed, and now your training requires additional supervision."

"Sir, I was just trying to improvise as the situation developed."

"Improvisation! This is not some fucking comedy club. Is that what Fatima is teaching you?"

"Sir, aren't you even interested in what transpired before you judge it as wrong?"

"No, I am not. I was developing an extraction plan that was waiting on your intel. But your dangerous and careless actions have made that plan obsolete while exposing the hostage to even greater danger."

"He was already in great danger that he may not have survived if I just gathered intel and left him there."

Blevinsky shouted, "That's your judgment, and you are not qualified to make such assessments. In the future, you will follow orders when they are as explicit as these were." The angry man slammed his fist on the desk.

"Now you're dismissed. Tomorrow, Alexi Strakov will have a training mission for you."

Diegert rolled his eyes and let out a sigh before leaving the office.

On the other side of the door stood Alexi Strakov. Diegert was surprised and had to step around him to keep from colliding with the big Russian.

"Guess you just can't wait, eh, Liberace?" Diegert said.

Looking around, Diegert realized the hall was full of Strakov's strike team. Strakov pounced on his statement.

"What the fuck was that? Are you insulting my homosexuality?"

Diegert looked at the imposing man and the expectant stares of the guys in the hall. He was reeling from the fact that his insult was not at all disarming but rather infuriated this combat-capable man, who was backed up by a group of the toughest men Diegert had ever seen.

"That's right, I'm gay. You got a problem with that, then you got a big fucking problem."

"No, man, it's cool."

"You fuckin' phobe. The training session I have planned for you tomorrow will be just right for a single superman like you. You don't need anyone's help? You don't need to be part of a team? We'll see tomorrow how well you operate all by yourself."

"Hey, I'm sorry if your assault plan didn't happen."

Gesturing to the men in the hall, Strakov said, "You hear that? He's sorry we didn't get to be part of a well-planned and practiced operation. Well, your apology makes all of us feel so much better. We're really grateful you saved the day, even if it almost got that little kid killed."

Diegert looked at him quizzically.

Strakov went on, "Be ready for the mission at 1600 tomorrow, you selfish puke."

Strakov walked down the hall, passing between the six men leaning against the walls. As he passed, each man looked disapprovingly at Diegert and fell in line behind his leader. Diegert wondered to himself, *Are they all gay?*

CHAPTER 35

As Diegert left his office, Blevinsky took a call from Kellerman. "My good man, do update me on the situation."

"Sir, I can report that we have Andrew Cambridge safe and secure here at Headquarters."

"What?"

"Yes, sir, he was recovered just an hour ago."

"That's splendid; that's incredible. Arthur and Elizabeth will be so relieved. However did you manage it? Were there casualties? How many men were on the team? I must see to it they are rewarded."

"There were no casualties on our side, Mr. Kellerman. We were lucky to locate the boy quickly, and he's a tough little guy."

"Why, I'm sure he had to be. Give me details? How did the team extract him?"

Blevinsky ran his fingers through the gray band of hair on the back of his head and struggled to find a way to answer the questions. "He was . . . extracted from the location where he was found."

"Yes, of course, but how many men took part? Was there fighting?"

Blevinsky squeezed his eyes shut and banged his fist against his head as he listened to the question. Throwing his head back and tilting his chair, he fought against his reticence to tell Kellerman the truth. "Sir, there was no team in the rescue of Andrew Cambridge."

"No team? What do you mean? How many men were involved?"

Tapping the phone against the crown of his smooth head, Blevinsky answered, "Just one man."

"A single man . . . against a Michka Barovitz crew? That's incredible. Who is this man?"

"His name is Diegert, David Diegert."

"Well, very good for you, Aaron, training men who can operate on their own. I'm so very pleased. I'll see to it that Mr. Diegert is financially rewarded. You and he have returned the holiday spirit to the season along with young Master Cambridge. Thank you, old chap."

"Certainly, sir, I hope you and your friends can get back to enjoying your festivities."

"Oh, very well, good man. I thank you again and good night."

When Blevinsky hung up, he dropped his head in his hand, let out a sigh, and thought how unfair luck could be.

***

Back in his room, Diegert was watching *Mission: Impossible III*. His phone rang, interrupting the movie just as Tom Cruise was sliding down a glass building.

"Hello?"

"Is this Mr. David Diegert?"

"Yes."

"Good evening, sir, my name is Wendall Bishop. I am your account manager from the Royal Bank of the Caribbean in the Cayman Islands. I'm calling you regarding your account."

"OK."

"Sir, I'm calling, as stipulated in our customer service policy, to inform you that there has been a substantial deposit into your account. We have checked the depositing agent's source and confirmed the transfer. We suggest you check your account and verify the activity. Please contact us with any issues you may have with the account. Good night, sir."

Diegert stared at his phone skeptically, as if what he'd just heard had to be a prank.

Before he could check his account, his phone rang again, and he saw it was Fatima calling. "Yeah," he answered.

"You didn't let my involvement slip, did you?"

"No, everyone thinks I did this on my own, and it pisses them off."

"Too bad. This is the way I want it. Tomorrow morning, 0730, you're to report to the armory where you will do what Lindstrom tells you. You'll be fulfilling the debt I owe him. The armory is in Room 135. You know where that is, right?"

"Yeah, I know. I'll be there. Hey, are all the guys here gay?"

"No ... Why does that matter? Some are, I suppose. Strakov is, but you already knew that. What are you pursuing?"

"Nothing. It was just on my mind from some things I've observed."

"Look, you gotta crawl out from under your year 2000 rock and recognize that people don't care about that anymore. We're not the ridiculous US military. If Strakov gets the job done, then who cares if he loves men. I'm glad he's gay; it's one less guy staring at my ass every time I walk by. Be at the armory at 0730."

After hanging up, Diegert had a hard time believing that such an obvious Alpha male, who led the men so powerfully, was gay. The values, or rather the prejudices, of his rural Minnesota upbringing just didn't allow for that combination. It seemed as though it was time to update his perspective. *Update,* he thought, remembering to check his account. There on the phone screen was his account balance with an additional ten thousand dollars in it. He now had $47,500 in his personal account.

CHAPTER 36

The armory was placed away from the living quarters not only because of the noise of the shooting range, but also so that its remote location could reduce the danger associated with the storage of several tons of explosive gunpowder. Diegert liked the armory. It was clean and orderly; Carl Lindstrom, a man of Norwegian ancestry, made certain of that. Carl was a thin, wiry, energetic man in his early sixties. He spiked himself with a constant cup of coffee, using the caffeine to fuel his management of the ordnance and arsenal of the Headquarters. The six foot, 150-pound man with a full head of gray hair and glasses greeted Diegert's arrival. "Good morning. You must be David Diegert."

Shaking his hand, Diegert replied, "Yes, sir."

"So you're here to fulfill Fatima's debt?"

"Is that really how it works? If you supply us with what we need for a mission, we owe you?"

"If your mission is official, I will receive a requisition with a detailed list authorized by the administration, and I'll provide you with everything you need. But if you arrive at 2230, wake me up with a desperate demand to be given a sniper rifle, and ask that the release not be logged, then yeah . . . you owe me."

"OK."

"Fatima can be a very forceful person, but she's also very fair. I knew she would keep her word, and I trust her with weapons. I know she helped you get the kid, but apparently I'm the only one."

"That's how she wants it."

"Appearances are very important to her, and she walks on eggshells because she's the only woman operator in the whole facility. Frankly, we would be more effective with more female operators, but it's a rare woman who can kill and live with herself."

"What do you want me to do?"

"Bullets!" said Lindstrom as he turned and walked through the armory into a workroom. Diegert followed, though he lagged as he passed the gun lockers and the fascinating arsenal of assault rifles, submachine guns, combat shotguns, handguns, and sniper rifles. Within the metal mesh lockers were all the accessories that gave the weapons greater lethality. Scopes and laser sights, extra ammo clips and enlarged ammunition dispensers, different styles of buttstocks for the assault rifles and the submachine guns, and a wide variety of sound suppressors, sights, and integrated lighting systems for the pistols. The hardware excited Diegert, and when he infiltrated areas where discovery meant death, these weapons gave him the confidence to proceed.

"We shoot a lot of bullets in this facility. Training new guys and keeping the active operators sharp require a lot of practice, both in the range and out in the field. So I keep a very active inventory of ammunition. I like to assure quality in the projectiles we work with, and I don't like to see resources wasted, so I collect the spent shells and lead from the range and reload bullets."

Lindstrom had been moving while speaking, and now he positioned himself in front of a workbench with a large wooden box filled with shells, a smaller box filled with formed projectiles, and a large, funnel-shaped canister with a hose leading to the work space at the center of all these items.

"My dad believed the same thing, and he had me reload ammo all the time."

"Excellent! Then I'll just familiarize you with the process and let you get reacquainted with a part of your well-spent youth."

Diegert was very aware of what a boring and repetitive job this was, and now he knew why Fatima was so eager to subjugate him for the payback.

Soon Diegert was well into the six-step process of resizing the shells, decapping the old primer, expanding the inside neck of the shell with a small lathe, repriming with a new cap, loading the powder, and seating the new projectile. When all six steps were complete, the bullet was placed in a large tray that held a hundred individual rounds. Lindstrom was cleaning and repairing weapons that had been used recently and looked like they'd been dragged through dirt, mud, and sand. He had a workbench on wheels, so he was able to roll it over to where Diegert was doing his boring job. "Hey, what happened to that case of weapons I gave you when I arrived?" asked Diegert.

"Those are some very nice weapons. I have them down here."

"Did you know the guy to whom they belonged?"

"Shamus McGee? Yeah . . . he was the nicest guy. Always smiling and laughing, he was such a funny guy. Not really telling jokes but just adding humor everywhere he went. He was the best shot I have ever seen. Calm and steady. He could place the bullet exactly where he wanted it over and over again. His accuracy and consistency were absolutely deadly."

"What happened to him?"

"I can't tell you. I mean, I don't know."

"Which is it? You can't tell me or you won't tell me?"

"I won't tell you. But I will tell you the rifle you brought in was the rifle I gave Fatima to help you last night. Since you just brought it in, it's not really in my inventory. That's why I could loan it out without having to falsify any records."

Looking at the big box with thousands of shell casings, Diegert asked, "So maybe I don't have to do all these bullets?"

"Yes, you do. You and she still owe me; besides, I don't get much company down here."

"Can you tell me what you know about Crepusculous?"

"The men of Crepusculous are so wealthy that they finance this whole operation on the lint from their pockets. Money is so available to them that expenses we incur represent the smallest decimal point on their balance sheets. I don't even know if they bother with balance sheets. Wealth is not the most important thing to them, though; they seek and desire power. They want to influence the world to turn in their direction, and then their wealth is assured without having to chase dollars."

"You seem to know a lot about them."

"I know a lot about their intentions and philosophy. I know what they're after, although I don't always know the means to their ends. I know life on their side is so much better than it would be fighting them."

"This all sounds diabolical and mysterious."

"It is, and it is also deadly. Be sure to conduct yourself carefully now that you're in the shadows of Crepusculous."

"Do you know the members of the Board?"

"No," deadpanned Lindstrom before posing his own question. "Was your father a big-game hunter?"

"Ahh . . . he was a deer hunter. Three or four a year to fill the freezer. We ate venison in so many different ways. God, I haven't had venison in so long."

"What did he hunt with?"

"A 12-gauge Remington on a drive, a Winchester 30-06 from a tree stand."

"Did you hunt with him?"

"No, but my brother did."

"Was he an older brother?"

"Yeah, three years older. His name is Jacob . . . Jake actually. He and my father just got along so well. He looked, acted, and sounded like my father: round, foolish, and loud. They were more like best friends than father and son. I just wasn't invited—ice fishing, snowmobiling, hunting. There was no explanation for it; I was just left home with my mom. She got me into other things, karate and strength training at the Y. I was on the wrestling team at school and did pretty well. My dad never came to a single match. Jake wasn't that big, but he played football. My dad was in the booster club. He never missed a single game."

"That doesn't seem fair," said the thoughtful armorer.

Diegert continued, "Jake would pound on me whenever my mom wasn't around, which was quite a lot, because she worked as a waitress in a busy restaurant. Eventually, the weight lifting, karate, and growing paid off, but when he couldn't physically dominate me anymore, he would harass me in other ways."

"Sibling rivalry, sometimes it never ends."

"One time, he asked me to go fishing. I didn't have my own rod, so he told me to use my dad's. I knew Dad was very protective about his equipment and would be angry, but I took it anyway. We walked on the train tracks toward Sandy Creek. The creek is at the bottom of a steep ravine. The train tracks cross over on a very high trestle. Jake told me we should cross the trestle because the hillside was not as steep on the other side. The trestle has holes between each railroad tie. You must walk very carefully, and there are no rails on the sides. I was very frightened of the height and the holes and the whole thing."

Diegert set his tray of completed bullets to the side and placed a new tray in position.

"Out in the middle of the trestle, he stopped and grabbed my dad's rod from me. He took it and started pulling the line out of the end of the rod. He pulled out about ten feet of line. Then he said, 'Let's see how brave you are.' With the ten feet of line lying coiled in front of him, he tossed my dad's rod over the side of the trestle. I saw the line quickly uncoiling over the edge. I knew my father would kill me if the rod was damaged. As the line disappeared, I knew I needed to stop it from falling, but I was frozen with fear. At the last second, I lunged for the line, but it was thin and slick and so hard to get a hold of. I was on my knees at the edge of the trestle extended over the side, but the thin plastic line slid through my fingers, and the rod plunged down into the depths of the creek. As I was hanging over the edge, Jake grabbed my feet and lifted them off the rail ties and scared the shit out of me. Only my chest was in contact with the rail. I grabbed the end of the ties to keep myself from falling. He dropped my feet and ran off the trestle back to the side we came from. He said, 'I don't really feel like fishing. I'll see you later.' He started walking away. I got up, got off the trestle, and ran after him with the intent to kill. He heard me coming, and as I approached, he spun around with his fish knife in his hand.

"He said, 'Go ahead give me the reason to cut you out of this family. Do you know why Dad hates you? Because he's not your father. Mom was fucking some guy from the Deerfield Lodge when she was catering and got pregnant. Dad didn't kick the bitch out like he should have, and then you were born. You're a bastard. The product of a fucking affair, and Dad should've drowned you like a runt pup. Now he's gonna know how you lost his rod, and I'm glad you know the truth about yourself."'

Diegert stopped for a moment from his process of reloading bullets. When he realized he'd stopped, he quickly started up again.

"My brother turned and walked away. I sat there a while, then went home, got all my money, went to the tackle shop, and bought the best rod and reel they had, and when Dad came home, I told him I lost his rod in Sandy Creek. I was sorry, and I gave him the new one. He was surprised I'd taken his rod, but I told him Jake had invited me to go. He was even more surprised and pleased to see the brand-new rod I'd bought him. He recognized it was the best rod they had in the shop. He wasn't pissed, and he forgave me.

"When he and Jake were next out of the house, I went to my mother and hugged her. I started crying, and I just kept crying. All the pain and sadness and rejection I had felt for so long had to come out. She soothed me and caressed me and asked me what was wrong. I looked at her with my tear-filled eyes, and said, 'I know, Mom. I now know the truth about me.' Her eyes grew round as saucers and she hugged me closer so she wouldn't have to see my face. I cried till I fell asleep, and when I woke up, I was alone on the couch and she was in the kitchen. We never talked about it again."

Diegert turned his half-filled tray of bullets around so he could fill the other side.

"That's a real sad story," said Lindstrom. "But all you guys got sad stories. I often wonder if it's the sadness that lets you kill like you do."

"What I find sad, Mr. Lindstrom, is to have lived so long in a world of deception. Perhaps not lied to, but to live with . . . without the truth."

Diegert sat quietly for a moment, contemplating the impact of his realization. He reached into his shirt and stroked his leather amulet between his thumb and forefinger. Lindstrom sat quietly as well, not running away from Diegert's emotional turmoil.

"It's three o'clock, Mr. Lindstrom. I got a training mission at four, and I'd like to get something to eat."

"Alright, you've done enough. Good luck on your mission. It was nice having you down here."

CHAPTER 37

Fatima knew there was no one at Headquarters who cared less about her success as an operator, a trainer, or any other role than Strakov. She wasn't surprised to find him in the weight room.

"What have you got planned today for my trainee?"

"Trainee? What a dorky word. You mean, what am I going to do to your superman?"

"Look, I'm his trainer, and you should consult me before you do anything with him."

"That's not what Blevinsky told me."

"Regardless, you know you should consult me."

"I think I should ignore you. I think you've been doing a lousy job training a guy who already has a lot of skills but no discipline. I think he needs to be reminded of the importance of teamwork. Blevinsky thinks so as well. So if you got a problem with that, take your sweet ass and go complain to him."

Strakov lay back down on the bench press, lifted the bar over his chest, and started another set. Fatima stood there fuming and counting Strakov's repetitions. When he approached ten and started to struggle, she stepped forward and put her hand on the bar. She pressed down as he strained to keep the bar moving up. Eventually, he could no longer resist her and the bar. His arms gave way, and the bar, with 230 pounds on it, collapsed onto his chest. He howled in agony as she walked away, leaving him screaming for help.

Diegert went to the locker room after getting something to eat. At his locker was a bag with a pair of padded punching gloves. As he inspected the gloves, Gregor and Pierre, two of the guys who were part of Strakov's strike team, entered the locker room. Gregor was from Sweden and Pierre from France. Gregor continued a story he had been telling Pierre. "Then she climbs on my lap in the hot tub, even though there are three other couples in the tub. She pulls down my suit, slides her bikini bottoms to the side, and inserts me into her. Her movements were very gentle, but eventually, I explode. Two of the couples leave, one couple stays, and we were all fucking in the hot tub for quite a while."

The guys visually acknowledged Diegert and started changing. Pierre said, "The wildest sex I ever had was with this Belgian girl. We were driving to Nice, and she said she wanted to suck my dick, while driving! She started in, and it felt great. We had to go through a tollbooth. I told her to stop, but she refused. All these booths are automated now, and they have cameras. The camera caught us with her head in my lap. The person who watches the cameras sent a message to the police with my license plate number. So we are driving along, she's still sucking me, and I look over to see a cop driving right next to us, watching. He turns on his lights and pulls us over. She makes me come just before the cop steps up to the window. He tickets me for distracted driving and her for public lewdness. He tells her, 'I got your number.' She says, 'Call me.'"

"What about you, Diegert, ever have any wild sex?" asked the Frenchman.

"A drive-in movie in a convertible, doggie style. We were in the backseat with her bent over the front passenger seat. She was moaning so loud that we attracted a lot of attention away from the movie. Someone shone a flashlight on us, and I shouted I was going to charge them double the admission price if they didn't shut off the light. Management came and kicked us out. She was really wild and loved the public spectacle of the whole thing."

"Women . . . How quickly we are willing to help them with their strange sexual desires," observed Pierre.

After they changed into shorts, T-shirts, and sneakers, they walked up to Room 240. In the padded room, Enrique, Jaeger, and Strakov were stretching and warming up. Diegert started limbering up and watched as the rest of the guys joked around, smiled, and basked in their camaraderie. Strakov was particularly jovial and inclusive of his team members.

"Alright, guys, bring it in."

When the guys had gathered around their leader, Strakov began.

"As a strike team, we know the value of teamwork and that when we work together we can achieve things we could never do on our own. Today, we are going to share that lesson with Mr. Diegert as we practice our defensive tactics."

All eyes cast looks upon the new guy. "Mr. Diegert's individual accomplishments are well known, but he will never be a member of a strike team without learning and practicing teamwork. Later this week, Mr. Diegert faces a mission in the Urban Zone."

All the guys chuckled and shook their heads at the memory of this training mission. Diegert was surprised by the reactions of such a tough bunch of men.

"You all know the challenges of the Urban Zone, but let's see how Mr. Diegert does with DTs."

Again the men laughed, sighed, and looked at Diegert with pity.

"To demonstrate the value of teamwork, this is what we are going to do. Mr. Diegert will assume a defensive stance, and we'll attack him in a serial pattern. Each of us needs to take Mr. Diegert to the mat."

Diegert stabilized his feet, tugged on his new gloves, and faced Curtis Jaeger.

Jaeger stepped forward, throwing a flurry of high punches. Diegert defended them, but Jaeger utilized the focus to sweep the legs out from under his opponent, flattening Diegert on his back. He concluded his attack by placing near-fatal force on his opponent's throat. When he released the choke hold and stepped back, Diegert coughed and sputtered but stood up to face the next attacker.

Pierre had long legs and used them effectively. He threw a series of roundhouse kicks, landing blows on Diegert's hips, thighs, and ribs. His fourth strike was a spinning kick that struck Diegert in the head, snapping his neck to the side, sending him crashing into the wall before he crumpled to the floor.

Enrique was a very solid man with powerful muscles, which he used to generate painful blows to Diegert's head and face. The strong man drew blood from above Diegert's eye as well as his nose and mouth, before a right cross to the jaw put his opponent back on the mat.

Diegert felt like a foolish punching bag and resolved to get some strikes of his own in on the next opponent. Gregor stood ready as Diegert brought the fight to the big Swede. Diegert's first combination was deflected, and Gregor nimbly switched his position, causing Diegert to have to shift his stance. The frustrated American threw a jab, and the Swede grabbed his arm and, with just enough force, pulled Diegert off balance, pitching him face-first into the mat. Diegert's battered face left a bloody imprint on the mat. Pain shot through his nose and teeth.

Strakov was next. Diegert wiped the blood from his face and found a renewed strength for the opportunity to hit the big Russian. Strakov moved forward while Diegert stepped to the side to avoid him. The big guy's movements were awkward, and Diegert saw winces of pain each time Strakov threw a slow, ineffective punch. Like a wolf that selects the injured member of the herd, Diegert realized his opponent was hurt. He aggressively took the fight to Strakov, moving fast and landing punches on the face and body of the big Alpha male. Diegert saw the panic in the face of his nemesis but was unprepared when the big Russian bull-rushed him, tackling him like a linebacker. Strakov groaned when Diegert hit the mat with him on top, but he had fulfilled the requirement of taking Diegert down. As he struggled to his feet, Strakov said, "This phase is over."

Diegert stood by himself while Strakov handed weapons to the rest of the operators.

"Now," stated the big Russian, "if Mr. Diegert disarms one of us, he does not have to complete the mission in the Urban Zone. Ready? Attack."

All five operators, armed with weapons, attacked Diegert simultaneously. Enrique had a two-foot truncheon with which he struck Diegert on the shoulder blade as the American ducked to avoid a blow to the head. Jaeger, armed with a knife, stabbed at Diegert, who had to twist his torso to evade the sharp blade. He countered Jaeger's strike with a punch to the temple, stunning the German enough so that he could focus on Gregor's attack with a six-foot staff. As the Swede swung the big stick, Diegert took the hit, grabbed the shaft, and shoved it forward, impaling Gregor in the abdomen. Pierre stepped forward, swinging a length of chain. The first swing was inches from Diegert's head, and the return required Diegert to jump above it. For the next swing, Diegert positioned himself so that when he ducked, the chain collided with Strakov's ribs. The big Russian gasped for air as the metal links concussed his chest, making it easy for Diegert to grab the pistol from his hand. As the leader of the strike team reinflated his lungs, Diegert kicked him in the hip, knocking him to the ground, and stood above him with the pistol, saying, "Too bad it's not loaded."

Strakov was furious. The situation was awkward, since no one, least of all Diegert, had expected this outcome. Strakov was in serious pain but struggled to his feet. He was gasping and at a loss for words, but his anger was visible, and Diegert told him, "I'm still gonna do your Urban Zone mission. I don't want to become an operator just because I beat you assholes."

Strakov wasn't prepared for this reaction, and with a look of disdain, he said, "Meet at the armory tomorrow at 1800."

Strakov, wincing in pain, walked away, not wanting the guys to see just how badly he was injured.

Pierre came up to Diegert, saying, "Very clever. I hope I get to work with you on a team someday." Pierre punched Diegert in the shoulder and went to the locker room.

***

Outside the locker room, Fatima was waiting for Diegert and walked with him as he headed back to his room. "I heard about your self-defense training."

"I heard about your failure spotting Strakov on the bench press."

"Looks like we are always finding ways of helping each other."

"Yeah, what can you tell me about the Urban Zone?"

"It was a very gutsy call, and a wise one, because you don't want to have the reputation of being excused from the tough stuff. Strakov's arrogance just backfired on him, and it'll take a long time for him to live it down."

"What I meant was, what do you know about the details of the mission?"

"Just roll with it—they change them all the time—and be very skeptical of anything that looks obvious. I think you'll do fine, which is to say, you'll survive."

"Have there been others who have not?"

"Of course, how many times do I have to tell you? We don't train by the sissy safety rules of the US Army. If you don't win out there, you die. That's why your decision to do the training when you had a pass was so gutsy."

Fatima smiled at Diegert, punched him lightly on the shoulder, and left.

Holy shit, thought Diegert.

CHAPTER 38

The next day at 1800 hours, Diegert reported to the armory.

"Back so soon?" said the wiry Lindstrom.

"Is this my stuff?"

Laid on a table in the armory was the equipment being issued to Diegert.

"The Urban Zone mission has several demands and hazards. This equipment will help keep you from becoming a casualty."

Diegert surveyed the equipment on the table.

"First you should put this on."

Lindstrom picked up the top piece of a protective body suit.

"This Kevlar-weave combat suit won't make you bulletproof, but it is bullet resistant. If it can resist bullets, then just imagine how good it is at resisting everything else." Diegert thumped the Kevlar with his knuckles, and Lindstrom continued, "The pants have reinforced panels on the thighs and around the hips. Here are your Viper tactical boots. We think they're the best. You also have Viper gloves. Scissors are here too, should you want to customize your gloves with an exposed finger or two. This outer shell vest will protect you from shrapnel and other projectiles. It has pockets filled with useful things such as explosives, listening devices, and other items. Take some time to check out each pocket."

Diegert counted the pockets with his fingers.

"This belt also has many items that you will find helpful. Your vest, belt, and body suit integrate to form an internal web harness so that this clip ring here on the belt can be used to secure you when climbing or rappelling. For a weapon, you will have the HK VP9 tactical pistol. You can see it has the under-barrel flashlight and laser sight. There is a silencer, which will be in a pouch on the holster."

Diegert held the gun and felt the weight and balance of it. He nodded approvingly before setting it back down.

"Go put it all on and come back for a systems check."

When he returned, Diegert looked like a deadly operator capable of stealth and violence. The suit was snug and form-fitting, projecting an appearance of fitness and mobility. Its shades of gray and black would allow Diegert to disappear into the shadows of the night.

"Looks good," said the experienced armorer. "Very crepuscular."

He handed Diegert a black backpack. "This is your climbing kit. I want the contents returned."

"OK."

Dressed and ready to go, Diegert sat outside the room from which his mission would be controlled. Strakov arrived with a sour look on his face. "Let's review your mission. In the Urban Zone, you're to ascend the building marked 'H7.' You will then rappel to the fourth floor, recover a laptop that contains critical information, exit the building, commandeer a motor vehicle, and return here to base. You must accomplish this mission in twenty minutes. We have transportation for you to the Zone. I don't care if you have questions. I'm not answering them." With a shake of his head to the right, he said, "Jaeger will drive you."

Diegert and Jaeger climbed into an open-topped jeep and drove down the road from the armory. After the first turn, the jeep encountered a row of orange cones across the road. Puzzled, Jaeger brought the vehicle to a stop. From the bushes on the driver's side, Fatima stepped out with her Sig Sauer P320 pistol pointed at Jaeger.

"Get out" was all she said. His hesitation produced a drawback of the hammer on Fatima's pistol. Jaeger released the steering wheel and put his hands up as he stepped out of the jeep.

Fatima took Jaeger's position in the driver's seat, and flattened the rubber cones as she drove over them, leaving Jaeger behind.

"Is this my rescue?"

"Shut up. I'm here to warn you that Strakov has a hit planned on you. He's using your mission as a training mission for a counterstrike team. The team's mission is to prevent you from completing yours, and they are authorized to kill."

"I'm walking into a trap."

"Yes, you are, but if you didn't know this, you'd be walking into your grave." Fatima brought the jeep to a halt and looked beyond Diegert.

"There it is. It's totally wired with closed-circuit TV so they will be watching everything, and the clock starts when you first come into view. You'd better survive."

Diegert stepped out of the jeep. Fatima accelerated and left him standing in the dirt road on the edge of the Zone. The place was like an abandoned city block being reclaimed by nature. Just beyond the tall pine trees around him was a high chain-link fence with a gate marked "Urban Zone." The gate was unlocked and had an eight-foot crossbar above it. Diegert recalled what Fatima had said about things that looked too obvious, and he did not walk through the gate; rather, he stole through the woods adjacent to the fencing. As he moved, he pulled a folding multi-tool with wire snips from a vest pocket. He cut through the fencing and entered the Urban Zone away from the gate.

When he stepped through the hole, he set his watch for a twenty-minute countdown. It was uncanny how urban the Zone looked. It had city streets, manhole covers, streetlights, traffic signs, and buildings of various heights and architectural designs. The eerie thing was, there were no people. These streets looked like they should have people on them, living the urban life, but there were no inhabitants. When he found building H7, it was a six-story apartment building, gray concrete with rectangular windows. He pulled the climbing gear from his backpack and used the folding grappling hook and a length of rope to climb the side of the building from one floor to the next until he was on the roof. There he could find no suitable place to anchor the rope. He had to use valuable length to secure it to the back side and run the rope the width of the building so he could rappel down the front side. Once it was secure, he clipped in and rappelled down to the fourth floor.

The fourth floor was illuminated, and like the rest of the building, the hallways were exterior balconies. He stepped onto the balcony hallway. As he did so, he was ensnared in micro-mesh netting, which clung to him like a spider's web and entrapped him more and more as he tried to get out of it. His struggling triggered a mechanism that cinched a system of cords, retracting the netting, with Diegert in it, pulling him thirty feet to the western wall and depositing him on the floor. The netting had him entangled, and there was no way he could reach his knife. He was, however, able to reach a cigarette lighter in a pocket on his outer vest. He struck the lighter, and the netting ignited quickly, burning to ash with very lit-tle flame. His tactical suit protected him from harm, and he was free of the netting and surrounded by gray ash. He looked to the ceiling and saw the cords that ran through a tracking mechanism and were designed to entrap trespassers.

He drew his weapon, aware now that activating the trap would alert the hit squad to his location. A check of his watch indicated that he had seventeen minutes and thirty-five sec-onds remaining. He moved down the hall, searching for the target. The first door he tried was locked, and so were the second and the third. The fourth door was unlocked. Diegert gradually eased the door open; looking in, he saw four men sitting at a table, playing cards beneath a bare bulb. He entered the room, firing lethal shots. As the bullets entered, stuffing flew out of the men. Plastic shells cracked and facial expres-sions remained unchanged while no blood spilled. The men were mannequins. On the far wall, there was a doorway lead-ing to another room, also occupied by a mannequin. A laptop sat on a table in front of the mannequin. On the floor was a computer case. Diegert used the keyboard to shut the com-puter down. As the shutdown began, a message on the screen read: *25 seconds to explosives activation.*

Diegert's eyes grew wide, as he did not know if the message meant the computer would explode or the building. He ripped the cord out of the computer and placed it in the case, zipped it shut, and slung the strap over his shoulder. With the com-puter case across his back, he headed back to the hallway. His watch read 16:45. As he proceeded down the hallway, passing one of the locked doors, it exploded with a concussive force that blasted Diegert against the opposite wall, spraying him with splintered wood and plaster dust. Once again the tac suit saved him, but his hearing was shocked. He stumbled forward, disoriented and confused. The dust and smoke made vision unreliable, but he knew he had to keep moving to the western part of the building to access the staircase.

At the stairwell, Diegert grasped the outside railing with his left hand and descended the darkened staircase. He rounded the landing, continuing to the third floor. Crossing the third-floor landing, he stepped forward and his foot dropped into open darkness. As he fell, he twisted his body 180 degrees, catching the edge of the landing with his fingers. He struggled with his grip, desperately holding on as his legs helplessly flailed in the air. Realizing what was happening, he raised his left elbow onto the ledge. Looking up, he could just make out the position of the handrail about three feet away. He pressed hard with his left arm and reached for the handrail. He was so surprised when he missed it that he almost lost his entire grip on the stair ledge. Regaining his left elbow position, he swung his left leg up and got his knee on the stair ledge. With both a leg and an arm over the edge, he rolled himself onto the flat surface of the landing. "SHIT!" he shouted as the frustration and relief combined into an emotional outburst.

Rolling onto his stomach, he peered over the edge. In the patchy darkness, he could see that the stairway had collapsed and all the material was in a pile of rubble three stories below. Climbing back up the stairs to the fourth-floor balcony, he found his rappelling rope was gone. Stepping back from the balcony, he realized that others were in the field and someone had removed his rope, making his precarious position even more dire. He remembered the micro-mesh netting and the cords in the tracks on the ceiling. He reached up and pulled the lines out. He kept pulling until he had all the available line. He knotted the sections together into a substantial length of strong cord. Deploying the line from the edge of the balcony left about a twenty-foot gap between the end of the line and the ground.

Dejected, Diegert rolled up the cord and descended the stairs to the dark abyss of the third floor. Securing the line to the handrail, he rappelled down to the rubble pile of the old stairwell. The darkness and the uneven surface of the pile made it a struggle to find secure footing. Soon, though, he was standing in the entrance to the stairs on the first floor. He stepped through a door that opened into the entrance lobby of the building. Light filtered in from the street, and Diegert pushed on the crash bar located on the front door. The bar was inoperable and the door wouldn't budge. Looking at the casement and the surrounding structure for the door, he realized it was load bearing and blowing it open would destabilize the front of the building. The adjacent window was thick double-paned glass, but the casement was not load bearing. C-4 charges at all four corners blew out the window, shattering it into thousands of shards of sharp glass.

Diegert peered out the hole and looked across the weed-infested parking lot to see four vehicles. He also noticed the movement of a dark figure taking cover near the vehicles. Holding his position, he waited and saw the first figure make a hand signal, and two more weapon-carrying personnel moved forward into shooting positions around the parking area. He had 8:38 left to complete the mission.

Taking stock, Diegert had a full clip of twelve rounds in his pistol. Attached to his vest, he had four more twelve-round magazines, two flashbangs, and two frag grenades. As he inventoried his equipment, a canister flew in through the window, clanged off the back wall, and landed on the floor in front of him.

Instantly, Diegert dove back to the entrance of the stairwell. Just as he crashed through the door, the explosion ripped apart the area between the window and the front door, and a great fireball erupted from the front entrance, propelling the door ten feet from the building.

Diegert was fortunate the force of the blast went in the opposite direction of him. The kill team was sure to come forward. Trapped in the stairwell, he found a piece of metal handrail in the rubble and used it to barricade the door. Holding his pistol ready for whoever broke through the door, he stepped forward, peering through the wire mesh–reinforced glass window of the stairwell door to see if the hit squad was coming.

The three men approached the building cautiously, seeking to confirm Diegert's status. The first looked in the window and could see the crater in the floor the grenade had made, but he didn't see Diegert's body. He signaled to the other two to move forward and check through the front door. As they approached, the load-bearing walls buckled and six floors of concrete facing sheared off and collapsed. The two operators were crushed as tons of material fell on top of them. The third operator was partially buried in debris. Both of his legs were trapped, and his left arm was impaled by a piece of rebar that pierced his biceps and pinned his arm behind him.

Diegert was fortunate to have been in the stairwell, which was constructed independently of the front wall and had withstood the collapsing debris. He removed his barricade and climbed over the rubble of the front wall. To his left, he saw the third operator. He was a pitiful sight and would not survive many more minutes. Diegert looked at him and mercifully removed his combat helmet. The guy was delirious and suffering incredible pain. David Diegert stood back, aimed his weapon, and fired a round that brought peace to the wounded warrior's tortured body. He had 4:04 left.

Beyond the debris field, parked in a row were a motorcycle, a Hummer, and a sedan. Diegert approached the Hummer first. He opened the door and heard a faint growl. In an instant, the growl erupted into the vicious snarling of a ferocious dog. Diegert slammed the door shut as the powerful beast lunged into the truck's door. With a sigh of relief, he stepped away from the Hummer as the dog continued to attack the window with intent to get blood from any intruder.

Diegert straddled the motorcycle and kicked the starter. He noticed an electric crackle as an overloaded wire sent a surge of electricity from the starter to the gas tank. When the gas tank exploded, the force hit Diegert directly in the protective chest plate of his outer vest. The force lifted him clear off the motorcycle, propelling him through the air until he ended up sprawled on his back in the dirt. Debris from the motorcycle lay all around him. He struggled to get his bearings. His face was burned, his hair was singed, and his ears were ringing. He sat up and wobbled to his feet. He stepped over to the sedan to find the front passenger tire pierced by a metal shard from the motorcycle. 3:15 remaining.

Back to the Hummer. He grabbed a shaft with a twisted metal end on it from the motorcycle debris. He climbed on the Hummer's roof and used the elongated metal piece to open the driver's door. The dog blasted out the door, ready to attack. He ran forward snarling, but there was no one to bite. The dog realized Diegert was on the roof and launched into a relentless assault on the side of the Hummer, leaping up, trying to reach Diegert. After watching for a moment, Diegert drew his pistol and fired a bullet into the dog's chest. The beast staggered and fell to the ground. Diegert descended and stepped toward the wounded animal, which continued to snap and snarl. Sighting down the length of the barrel, he fired into the dog's head, permanently ending his aggression. He slipped the computer case off his shoulder, climbed into the truck, and drove the Hummer back to the armory, arriving with fourteen seconds remaining.

Strakov, Jaeger, Blevinsky, Lindstrom, and others had been watching on the television monitors. They saw it all, and still Strakov sat stunned when Diegert pulled up to the armory and walked into the monitoring room.

"I guess you're going to have to do a little building reconstruction, and you'll need some body bags." Diegert placed the computer case on the table and took off his backpack.

Turning to Lindstrom, he said, "You'll have to ask one of these guys what happened to the contents, because I sure as hell didn't lose them."

Pulling his gloves off and removing his outer vest while looking at Strakov, Diegert said, "You couldn't beat me in DTs, and now you've failed to kill me."

Strakov stood up. "You still have to survive the tournament."

Diegert stepped right up to his face, saying, "I'll not only survive but win the fucking tournament, you shadow of a man."

The two men stared into the hate simmering in their souls. Diegert stepped back without breaking eye contact, wiped the blood from his head, and said, "I'll be in medical."

CHAPTER 39

As the adrenaline wore off, the shock from the trauma began to eat away at Diegert's strength and even his consciousness. The medical staff recognized the symptoms of slowed speech and an awkward gait. They immediately got him out of the tac suit and into a gown and on a hospital bed. Using IV sedation, they forced his injured body to rest. Fatima arrived and sat by his bed for a long time. Eventually, the medic had to leave the clinic, saying, "I have to go for about fifteen minutes. Will you be staying with him?"

"Yes, I'll stay until you get back, and maybe even longer."

When the medic had left, Fatima went to the medicine locker, picked the lock, and searched until she found a vial labeled, "Multisystem Performance Enhancer." The medicine was a booster. It enhanced neural function, increasing strength and reaction time. It improved sight and hearing while facilitating faster reflexes. It improved aerobic capacity, allowing for greater endurance as well as anaerobic energy supply, creating greater speed. The fluid also had the capacity to reduce the experience of pain by blocking pain receptors in the brain. The medicine would give Diegert an advantage and allow him to recover quickly. Fatima filled a syringe and injected it into the side port on Diegert's IV. The fluid flowed unimpeded into his bloodstream and was distributed throughout his body. For Diegert, there was no sudden reaction; in fact, he didn't wake up. The influence on his systems would create no visible changes in appearance, and the performance enhancements would only be functional as a result of use. If he didn't practice, the stuff wouldn't make any difference. He wasn't going to become Captain America, but with practice, he would be a better David Diegert.

Fatima closed up the medicine locker and disposed of the syringe. When the medic returned, she was sitting right where she had been. She stayed another thirty minutes and then said to the medic, "I have to go, but please call me as soon as he wakes up."

Walking down the hall, she was pleased with herself for giving Diegert an advantage. In this dangerous business, any advantage had to be utilized.

When Diegert awoke two hours later, Fatima was called. She stepped into the room and drew the privacy curtain around the bed, shielding them from the medic's view. She had a very happy, energetic, and, Diegert thought, sexy smile. She seemed genuinely glad to see him. She could still turn him on with her beauty, energy, and charm, even though he had been so wronged by her beguiling ways before. She picked up on his reactions, saying, "Keep your gown on, big boy. I'm not here for any of that. I'm just glad you did so well in the Urban Zone."

"You make it sound like I just won a blue ribbon at the fair. Three operators died while trying to kill me, and a building is lying in ruins, and I'm supposed to celebrate this as a success? It's fucked up!"

"Oh, stop your sniveling. You were brilliant. You got by every obstacle they threw at you. Maybe no one else is telling you how well you did, but I am."

Looking at her, he didn't know if he should thank her or call the medic for a psych consult. He just looked down and asked, "When do I get out of here?"

"Right now," replied the bossy dark-haired lady. "Medic!"

The startled medic rushed in. "*What?*"

"Please remove the IV and release the patient." The medic looked bewildered. Fatima provided clarity, snapping, "Now!"

After a late meal and a comfortable night's sleep in his own bed, Diegert felt good the next morning. Following breakfast, Fatima had a full day of activities for him: shooting in the range, including both sniper rifles and mobile handgun practice, and hand-to-hand combat, using defensive tactics against assailants with weapons. Pierre served as his opponent, and he showed Diegert some very effective takedown maneuvers, using the legs while on the ground. Diegert practiced the moves, and Pierre was very surprised by how quickly Diegert was able to learn and master them. Diegert was surprised too. He wasn't one to tire easily, but today he felt like he was never going to get tired, and it felt great. Pierre attacked with knives, clubs, a hatchet, and even a long-handled pike, and Diegert learned quickly how to respond to the variety of weapons.

Finally, Pierre shared some methods of disarming an assailant with a gun. The key to success was proximity. If the assailant was within six feet, then the probability of success went up. Diegert practiced moves that allowed him to strip the gun from the assailant and use the weapon against him. None of this was new to Diegert, but practicing the techniques refreshed his reflexes, improved his reactions, and boosted his confidence. He spent the rest of the week practicing the skills of combat using the extensive facilities and with the guidance of the expert personnel of the Headquarters.

"You've spent your time well," remarked Fatima. "The tournament is in two days, and I can tell you a little about your opponents."

"Oh yeah, are they some of the guys who've been training here?"

"No, these men are arriving from other facilities. I don't know how extensively they've been trained, but presumably they have the same skills and abilities you do."

"So what's the point?"

"The tournament's goal is to expose operators to the challenge of facing opponents who are as deadly and lethal as they are. This gives each operator the chance to see if they can face the most dangerous and violently skilled assassins in the world and prevail."

"How many guys are in the tournament?"

"There will be four of you in total."

"So four of us go into the area you walked me around, and then we try to kill each other."

"You and your three opponents will enter the Proving Grounds, where you will kill them all and win."

"OK, tell me what you know about these guys."

"Brutus Orilius is a Bulgarian who completed his army service and was a decorated security officer. He wants to work for the Crepusculous Board as a bodyguard, and his military background got him into the program. He's big, six four, two hundred thirty pounds, and he was the Bulgarian army's judo champion for three years."

"That's it? An MP who knows how to grab you by your shirt and roll you to the ground?"

"Hey, these guys could've gone through the same training program we put you through."

"Well, if they did, it wouldn't make any fucking difference. This program sucks; it's not about learning, it's about surviving."

"You want to hear about the next guy?"

Diegert nodded.

"Shioki Wong is a former member of the Chinese special forces."

"The People's Liberation Army Special Operations Forces," clarified Diegert.

"What a mouthful. He was an explosive specialist, and apparently he mistakenly killed some comrades with charges. He was court-martialed, but his sentence was purchased by a powerful individual, and Wong has been trained for service with Crepusculous."

"OK, now we got a guy who can't safely light his firecrackers, and his admission to this death match has been purchased by some rich prick?"

Fatima looked at him and didn't want to acknowledge his sarcasm. "The third participant is Deiobo Mogales. He comes from Brazil, where he was convicted of murdering two sons of a cocaine cartel boss. In prison, he killed three more men who were apparently instructed by the boss to kill him. For a sum, his sentence was purchased, and he was released to a member of the Board. Deiobo is skilled in capoeira, the Brazilian martial art. He killed the cocaine sons with a gun, but the three men in prison were killed with his hands."

"Alright, this guy sounds like a challenge. Someone worth going up against."

"You can shove that arrogant attitude. If you underestimate your opponents, you're sure to lose."

"Did you read that on the bumper of a truck or a car?"

"You fuck this up, and all that I've invested in you will be for nothing."

"I see. You want all that's been invested in these other guys to be for nothing. Training operators and then sending them to be killed seems stupid and wasteful. Why do they do this?"

"Failing on a mission is the real waste we are trying to avoid. The Board has enough resources that it can afford this process to develop the best operators."

"Yeah, as long as the lives of the guys are worthless."

"You're in this way too deep to start with that kind of sanctimonious shit. The resources of Crepusculous make the expense of this a total nonissue. Now get your head straight and be ready for these guys on Tuesday."

Fatima handed him the documents with the mug shots of each participant. Diegert looked into their faces and saw strength and ruthlessness. He imagined facing them and visualized what he would need to do to kill each one.

CHAPTER 40

Three vehicles arrived at the Headquarters Monday night. Each transported a man who was capable of killing others and living with himself. Each man found that violence was within his comfort zone and was willing to take people's lives at the request of others without having a personal dispute with the victim. An assassin's work was to be a purveyor of death as a service to those who wanted to kill but were unwilling to take a life themselves. These men possessed that capacity and were now coming to the Proving Grounds to test their skills, strength, and determination—not against innocents and unknowns, but against men of the same breed.

Diegert's breakfast was brought to him in his room. He had never had breakfast in bed, and in fact, he sat at his desk and ate his meal in his chair. He dressed in his combat blacks and placed his gloves with the padded knuckles and open fingers in a cargo pocket. Fatima came and walked with him to the Proving Grounds. "Use your head when you're in there. Look for weapons and tools dispersed throughout the area. They will be on the ground, in the trees, hidden behind objects. Keep whatever you find, or at least make certain it is unavailable to the others."

"Thanks. Mom, I wrote my name on the waistband of my undies too, anything else?"

"Fucker. When you take a man down, check his pockets to see what valuables he's carrying."

"Alright, step back," a big guard said, moving between Fatima and Diegert. "Trainers must go to the monitoring area. Participants will come with me."

Diegert followed the big guy to the gates of the Proving Grounds. Standing outside the gates were his three opponents, each escorted by a pair of Headquarters-assigned guards. The Bulgarian MP was big and looked very strong, but he stoically looked above everyone and avoided eye contact. If Diegert had to make up a name for him, he couldn't have done better than Brutus Orilius.

The Chinese man, Shioki Wong, looked straight ahead like the soldiers of China on parade that Diegert had seen in *National Geographic* magazines. He was unwavering in his absolute discipline, remaining detached and focused on his mission.

Deiobo Mogales, however, leaned against the post of the gate. His hair, braided in cornrows, was covered by a tight black do-rag. He had tattoos on his arms and neck, which continued under his sleeves and the collar of his black T-shirt. He had a thin mustache, and his jaw was dark with the stubble of yesterday's growth. With a tilt of his head and a dismissive smirk, he looked Diegert right in the eyes and had that crazy kind of stare that people used to make others feel uncomfortable. Diegert held his gaze, raised his fist to eye level, and extended his middle finger. Deiobo's surprised chuckle produced a devious smile that revealed his crooked yellow teeth.

The guard opened the gate, and each man and his guards moved in. They were then escorted to the four corners of the fenced-in area. Diegert recalled that the swampy area was to the north, while the field of concrete blocks was in the center, and the urban movie set was to the south. Diegert was taken to the southeast corner, passing behind the buildings of the movie set.

In this far corner of the Proving Grounds was a ten-by-twelve-foot concrete block building with a shingle roof. There was a door in the center of the front wall but no windows. Diegert hadn't seen this structure when he was here with Fatima. The guards directed him toward the building. Standing in front of the structure, one of the guards unlocked the door, opened it, and motioned for Diegert to step inside. The interior of the building was pitch black, but Diegert could smell water—or rather, the foul stench of stagnant water. His hesitation at the threshold earned him a powerful shove. He fell forward hard, landing with a splash in waist-deep water.

The door closed, and the complete darkness robbed him of his vision. Being blind was very disorienting. Diegert extended his hands out in front of him and tried to get his bearings. The walls were slick and straight. He didn't know how far below ground he was, after being shoved. Touching the wall again, he recognized the feel of plastic used to create a liner for a backyard pool. He stretched and reached as high as he could along the wall, and his fingers touched a wire. Immediately, he felt an electric shock, and deafening acid rock music blared out of unseen speakers. Diegert withdrew from the wall and stood in the middle of the water.

He slowly walked forward and then turned back, keeping to the center of the pool. He was startled when he bumped into a solid structure in the middle of the water. He tested it with his hands and felt around it to get a sense of its shape. It was a square wooden box that was just barely under the water. If he stood on the box, he would be out of the water. He climbed on the box and stood up on it. When he reached his full height and all his weight was on the center of the box, he heard a great gushing sound of a large volume of water flowing into the pool. It sounded like the water was flowing in from the corner behind him, but worse was the smell. His nose was assaulted with the stench of untreated sewage. He jumped off the box and back into the water, but the flow didn't stop. He walked toward the sound of the water, and the powerful volume of disgusting waste splashed him as he sought a shutoff valve. He reached up to explore the pipe and received another electric shock and an unrelenting blast from an air horn. The eardrum-splitting sound lasted a long time. When the sewage finally stopped flowing, it was up to his armpits. He stood in it as the foul stench assailed his nostrils. He made contact with pieces of shit whenever he moved his arms and hands.

Diegert started to feel an irritation and a wriggling sensation at his ankle just above his boot and below his pants. He kicked his leg and shook his foot, but the wriggling only grew more intense. Soon he felt more and more wriggling motions against the skin of his legs. Creatures were crawling up his thighs. He put his hands under the water and pressed against his legs. He tried to stop the invaders, but when he had isolated one and tried to squish it, it delivered a bite that was sharp and painful. Diegert pulled his hands out of the water, only to feel the wriggling beings now on his arms. The slimy attackers moved up his sleeves and onto his chest and back. They didn't wait to be driven off before biting, and soon Diegert was suffering multiple bites from these aqueous aggravators.

Focus was difficult to find, but he located one of the tormentors on his forearm. He palpated it and determined he was being besieged by aquatic leeches. Their bites hurt at first, but then the pain subsided. The problem was they were blood sucking, and without counting, Diegert was afraid he already had over a hundred bites. If they all sucked a hundred milliliters of blood, he would soon lose a liter. The longer he stayed in the water, the more leeches he would be hosting.

He reached up the side of the pit again and flattened his hands so he was just able to slide under the shock wire, which was held out an inch or so from the wall by spaced insulators. With his fingers under the wire, he found the top edge of the pool liner. The plastic sheeting had been nailed to a wooden top piece, but Diegert was able to claw at the very top edge of the plastic. He curled the plastic over and pulled on a small piece of it with all the strength in his fingertips. The plastic cracked, and he pulled on one side of the separation, tearing the plastic and forming a vertical split. He managed to pull the strip of plastic below the shock wire, and then yanked it with both hands, rendering the lining and revealing the earth underneath. He kept pulling until the tear was below the water-line and the ground began absorbing the water. The liner was pushed away from the earthen wall as water widened the space between it and the underlying dirt.

The water level fell, and when it reached his waist, the flow from the corner pipe restarted. There must have been a float valve somewhere in the darkness that regulated the water level. As the surrounding earthen walls became saturated, the water level rose again, soon reaching his neck.

Diegert felt the earth through the torn plastic and discovered a section of shale rock. Shale was a sedimentary rock that formed in layers. It was very strong in one plane and quite brittle in the perpendicular plane. He dug into the softened earth and extracted several pieces of shale. One piece was rectangular, about eighteen inches long and one inch wide. Another piece was a twelve-inch triangle with a very sharp edge on one of the lengths. Diegert took the eighteen-inch piece and, using the edge of the wooden box, broke it perpendicularly into two nine-inch sections.

He searched the wall of the pit to find a span between insulators. Cutting the wire would break the circuit, stopping the shocks, and provide eight feet of current-carrying capacity. The wire lacked insulation, so it had to be kept out of the water, yet the bare wire would be useful.

He reached up and, after shocking himself a couple times, managed to impale the sharp point of the triangular piece of shale into the wall above the wire. He took the two sections of rectangular shale and placed them on either side of the wire. Using the lace from his boot, he tied the two pieces together so the wire was held firmly and could be safely handled. He then pulled down on the triangular piece, severing the wire with the sharp edge.

Now he held the live wire with the tied pieces of shale and had to make sure it didn't fall into the water. With a four-inch piece of wire extending from the shale, he touched a blood-filled leech on his arm. He felt a shock, but the leech got the worst of it and released its blood-sucking grip as it died. Diegert electrocuted leeches on his arms and neck above the waterline.

With the electric circuit broken, he investigated the sewage pipe again. Putrid sewage continued to flow, but the pipe was no longer electrified. It was very strong and extended out from the wall far enough that he could climb up onto it. He took off his belt and affixed it around the pipe. He needed to climb up while holding the live wire out of the water. Using his left arm to hoist himself, and holding the wire in his right hand, he lifted his upper body over the pipe. He shimmied forward and was able to swing his right leg around the pipe, and suddenly, he was sitting on the pipe like a horse. His feet were still in the water, but he could raise them out.

What qualified as a victory depended on the circumstances of the struggle. Diegert felt like he'd just won a world championship, even though he was still trapped in a cauldron of shit.

The stench did not subside, and he still was losing blood to leeches, but he had foiled his captors and found refuge from the tortures in the midst of their trap.

It was the first moment Diegert had to consider the other tournament participants, and he hoped they had it worse than him. Fatima had never mentioned anything about this, and Diegert reasoned that the tournament would continue as planned just as soon as the sick fuck who'd thought this up decided they'd weakened the contestants enough to now let the killing begin. Meanwhile, Diegert sat on his pipe electrocuting leeches.

After twenty-four hours in his private cesspool, a bottom drain opened and the water started to drain out of the pool. A light high up in the rafters came on, and when the water was gone, the door opened and a ladder was tossed into the pit, providing a route to the exit. Diegert tested his live wire; it no longer carried a current. He relaced and tied his boot before climbing off the pipe. The bottom of the pool wriggled with the movements of thousands of leeches. It disgusted Diegert to walk across them, but crushing them under his boots felt like evening a score. When he stepped outside, it was sunny and warm. Greeting him with assault rifles were Strakov and Jaeger.

Standing in his sewage-drenched clothes with several blood-swollen leeches still hanging on him, he looked at his dual nemeses, who offered him nothing except a bullet if he didn't comply. Diegert addressed them, "I'm done with the shithouse, if either of you has to go." Strakov stepped forward and plunged the butt of his rifle into Diegert's gut. When the exhausted assassin doubled over, Strakov drove the end of the rifle up under his chin, cracking his jaw and sending him sprawling onto the pine-covered ground. Diegert lay there, lost consciousness, and remained prone while Strakov and Jaeger chuckled on their way back to Headquarters.

CHAPTER 41

An air horn blasted, and the three other contestants, also released from twenty-four hours of torture, began actively searching for quarry. Diegert didn't hear a thing as he lay on the ground unconscious. His awareness began to return when he felt a heavy object jabbing his left shoulder. A mass was driven under his left hip, and he felt a powerful force roll him onto his back. Opening his eyes, he saw the big Bulgarian cop standing over him. He was not only imposing but hideous. His torture session must have involved fire, because he was burned over much of his body. His hair was singed back from his face. His cheeks and jaws had second-degree burns, but his lower legs, hands, and forearms were all burned to the third degree. Diegert could see the bare muscle of his appendages where the skin had been destroyed by fire. How he was able to hold onto the heavy machete in his right hand, Diegert couldn't understand.

"Brutus," Diegert exclaimed. The man was amazed that Diegert knew his name, and at that instant, Diegert realized Fatima had shared with him information the others didn't have.

"I'm glad you found me," he said as he slowly rose to his feet.

"What?" asked the confused giant.

"Goddamn, wasn't that the worst thing ever? What the fuck did they do to you?"

"Whatever I touched, it burned me. And fire"—the big guy gestured upward with his charred hands—"came up through the floor."

"Sounds like a live barbeque."

Brutus was bewildered by Diegert's sarcasm. The big guy stared at the side of Diegert's neck. Diegert followed his eyes and placed his hand on the side of his neck, where he felt a fat, fluid-filled leech. He pulled it off, leaving an oozing sore.

"I had hundreds of these things on me in that house. There's a deep hole they filled with sewage. I almost drowned in a pit of shit."

Brutus sneered at the thought, but then looked at Diegert menacingly from beneath the place where he used to have eyebrows.

"We can plan our team strategy now," Diegert said matter-of-factly.

"What?" questioned the big man, who had to put the brakes on his intent to kill.

"I think with your police skills and my communication and negotiations, we can win this thing."

"It is kill or be killed," belched Brutus.

Diegert could see the perplexed look on the man's scarred and disfigured face. "Oh, come on, you're not falling for that. That's misinformation. They're just testing to see if we are smart enough to realize that we can accomplish a whole lot more working together than apart."

"No, kill everybody."

"Oh really? Now does that make sense? Put a group of the world's most highly trained assassins together and then have them kill each other. When did that plan start making sense to you?"

"Never," said Brutus as the release of that thought unweighted his shoulders.

"Exactly! They want us to think. To demonstrate that we can use the resources available to us to do more than we could ever do alone; right now, those resources are each other."

"So what now?"

"Come here."

Diegert knelt down and brushed away leaves and pine needles, clearing some dirt. He drew with his fingers in the dirt. Brutus knelt down next to him with his machete blade in the dirt and leaned on it for support. Diegert watched how slowly the big guy moved and how each point of contact brought a wince of pain from the charred hands and arms. He could also see large sections of clothing were burned off the guy's back.

Pointing with his fingers to his drawings, Diegert began, "We're right here, and I think the other guys are over here. Now, if they are coming this way, we can isolate them in these buildings and try talking to them, and if that doesn't work, then this is a very defensible position."

"I don't know. This is very different from what they told me."

"Really?"

Diegert swung his hand back and knocked the machete out from under the weight Brutus was placing on the weapon. He grabbed the back of the big guy's neck and drove his face forward. Brutus let out a scream of pain as his sensitive skin hit the dirt. The big Bulgarian swung a powerful left arm out at Diegert, but when his fist made contact, the pain was so severe that Brutus fell to the left and rolled on his back, covering his injured left hand with his burned right one.

Diegert grabbed the machete while Brutus writhed in pain. He stood above the pitifully damaged man. Brutus swung his right leg and shrieked when his burned shin collided with

Diegert's stable leg. He closed his eyes and grimaced as the pain from the bare muscle exploded in his brain.

Diegert watched the suffering and could only imagine the infection he would develop as a result of rolling in the dirt. His skin would never grow back, and he would need several square yards of grafts to be whole again. The former police sergeant stared at Diegert with the only two spots on his face that weren't burned and said, "Kill or be killed?"

Diegert nodded his head as he held the machete to Brutus's throat.

"Don't move."

Diegert checked the man's pockets for valuables. In the left front pocket, there was a circular metallic object. Diegert pulled it out and pressed a button on the top, opening the cover to reveal a timepiece. On the inside cover was a photo of Brutus seated with his young wife and two children. Diegert looked at the boy and girl and slowly closed the watch, putting it back in the man's pocket.

"Nice family."

Brutus clenched his teeth, saying nothing.

Checking the cargo pockets on the legs, he found a fully loaded ten-round magazine of 9 mm bullets. Not much good without a gun, but he put it in his pocket. With the machete still pressed to the throat of Brutus, he stood back up.

"Get up," he told the pain-ridden Bulgarian.

With a lot of struggle, Brutus stood, stoop-shouldered and wincing. Diegert motioned with the big knife, directing Brutus to the door of the brick shithouse.

"Get in." Brutus kept his gaze on his captor as he entered the dark interior and descended the ladder into the pit. Diegert withdrew the ladder and slammed the door, locking the man inside.

CHAPTER 42

On the north side of the grounds, the blast of the air horn left Deiobo particularly unmotivated to move. He remained immobile in the northeast corner. The acid burns on his face, head, and body were painful and pissed him off.

Shioki could not be so patient. He was compelled to venture forth because he had endured twenty-four hours of refrigerated cold. Frigid unrelenting temperatures made worse by saturating water sprays whenever he searched for an escape route. When he stood still, a great fan came on, creating a deafening wind chill. He had frostbite on his fingers, ears, and nose. Heading south, he soon encountered a murky swamp, which quickly became impassable as he sank to his waist in the soft-bottomed ooze. Retracing his steps, he regained solid ground and proceeded to the east, moving with as much stealth as his soaked boots would allow. He kept an eye out for objects with which he could improvise a weapon.

Deiobo, by remaining still, hoped to be able to detect movement around him. When he employed this technique hunting in the jungles of Brazil, he was rewarded with a monkey or a capybara, his favorite bush meat. To his mind, there was a lot less wildlife in these woods than in Brazil, but he wasn't looking for animals. He did, however, painfully recall his imprisonment in the concrete hut with the acidic shower that forced him to move from one square area to another. Each attempt to escape was greeted with nozzles spraying sulfuric acid on his hands, arms, and clothing. The burns were persistent, and he had no way of removing the noxious fluid from himself. It was a relief to be out of the hut, but he would be in pain throughout the tournament.

While motionless, Deiobo sensed the movement to his right. He riveted his eyes on the moving patterns of lines in the woods, and soon he was able to see a shadow and form slowly progressing toward him.

Shioki had poor orientation to the grounds, but he believed he was approaching the northeast corner. He was unaware of the width of the fenced-in area. Each step taken to the east brought him closer to the place from which his opponent began this deadly game. Shioki was getting more and more anxious; he didn't want to walk into a trap. Deiobo felt he was adequately concealed up in the big-trunked tree. He realized there was a risk in being elevated, but he reasoned the visual advantage was worth it. The canopy of the tree also created a cleared space under its branches so the trunk couldn't be approached without exposure. He wished he had a weapon with which to shoot his enemy.

Shioki continued east until he reached the eastern fence, at which point he was afraid he'd crossed the path of one of his opponents who might now know his location. He turned suddenly with a sense of panic that he might have lost the advantage.

Deiobo watched as Shioki passed his tree. The Chinese special forces soldier never entered the clearing underneath the tree but kept to the south of the open space. Nevertheless, Deiobo was able to observe his movements, and he realized the Chinese man did not have a weapon and Deiobo distinctly heard the squishing of sodden footwear. After the soldier passed, the convict climbed down from his tree and followed on silent feet. He saw the soldier reach the eastern fence, and he closed the gap. As the soldier turned from the fence, the convict struck him in the chest with a driving head butt. The power of the blow stunned the soldier, evacuated his lungs, and thrust him into the eastern chain-link barrier. The convict followed with punches to Shioki's ribs and face. The soldier took the punishment, but his training had instilled in him a series of practiced reactions. He thrust up his arms and rotated his torso, blocking the strikes to his face and allowing him to see his opponent and counter with strikes of his own. The convict was close enough that the soldier used his legs and kicked his attacker in the shins and stomped on his foot. The pain forced the convict back. The two men now squared off, remaining in their defensive stances, circling each other and seeking advantage. The soldier had suffered the worst. He was breathing heavily to replenish his lungs, and the strikes to the face had created a wound above his right eyebrow. Deiobo's right foot was sore, but his boot had prevented broken bones. He dropped his hands and moved in the wide-ranging fashion of capoeira. The soldier remained with his fists raised and his feet perpendicular, vigilant of his enemy's movements.

Suddenly, the convict let out a loud, piercing scream, frightening the soldier, who stepped back from the strange man. The convict took the moment of surprise and ran off to the west. The soldier stood alone, looking around and trying to make sense of this erratic behavior. Needing to continue his pursuit, the soldier passed under the tree canopy and found a large fallen branch. He placed the branch between two trees and, using leverage, snapped it. He now had a club as a weapon, and he moved west in the direction of the convict. Soon he found the narrow wooden bridge without side rails that traversed the swamp. He noticed wet footprints on the boards. He stopped. There was swamp water on both sides of the bridge, and the closest vegetation that might support weight was several meters to either side. His enemy must have crossed, he reasoned, and Shioki began to make his way over the bridge.

The convict remained motionless, suspending himself above the water, clinging to the underside of the bridge. Tracking the footfalls passing over him, he reached out from under the bridge, tripping the soldier. The instant the soldier fell, the convict pulled him over the side of the bridge and into the dark water. He placed his hands on the struggling soldier's shoulders, pressing down on him with all his weight. He kneed the soldier in the groin several times, not only inflicting great pain but making the man gasp for air. Those gasps sucked in the dark swamp water, which rapidly filled the soldier's lungs, drowning him within twenty seconds.

Deiobo quickly grabbed the bridge as the soft organic matter of the swamp entombed the soldier's body. He climbed back onto the bridge, completely saturated but eager to find and kill his next opponent. Heading south across the bridge, he left the swamp behind as he walked up onto dry land. Just past the bridge, he spied an object he could hardly believe he had the good fortune to find. In the dappled light of the woods lay a Beretta 9 mm pistol. He stepped to it quickly, then hesitated. Was it a trap?

With the pistol being so obvious and inviting, he realized he might be in the crosshairs of an enemy. Pulling back, he lay down behind a fallen log. He remained still for several minutes. All was quiet. Using a long, sturdy branch, he reached out and pulled the gun to him. No booby trap. He held the gun and was delighted to have such a powerful weapon, but his happiness faded when he realized it was not loaded. Dejected, he reasoned it was better for him to have it than someone else, but it was not the lethal advantage he'd thought he'd found. Deiobo's disappointment left him when he saw another weapon lying in the weeds. With much less caution, he stepped over to a sinister-looking item and, sneering with menace, picked it up.

***

Diegert, carrying his machete, had completed an exploration of one of the movie-set buildings. Finding no enemies, he exited and crossed the street to the structures on the other side and crept around to the back. He looked north, searching for his next opponent. Beyond the buildings, there was a sparsely wooded area and then the concrete block field, which held about forty blocks of concrete, each about five feet high and five feet wide. The blocks were lined up in rows forming a grid. It was a big space with weeds growing up through the gravel between the blocks. Diegert thought it was a very strange thing to have constructed, but maybe the tactical teams used it for some kind of specific combat training. He was about to double back and head west when he saw a man moving on the far side of the block field.

Diegert watched the man move left and pick up an object that looked like a giant silver-gray lollipop. As he observed him swinging the object, Diegert realized the man had found a weapon. It looked to be a metal shaft with a cross tube at one end, upon which were affixed a sprocket gear from a bicycle and a circular saw blade. The man ducked back down, looking around.

Diegert continued to monitor the block field, seeing weeds between the blocks swaying and shaking in spite of the lack of wind. He figured the man must be crawling between the blocks, and he tracked the man's progress through the field by watching the weeds. Diegert moved north, entered the field, and then moved west to intersect with the southern path the man was taking. Moving very slowly, Diegert was careful not to disturb the weeds as his quarry was doing. When he saw the weeds wobbling just north of the intersection where he stood, Diegert raised his machete over his head.

Deiobo, crawling quickly forward now that he could see the end of the field, heard the crunch of gravel to his left. He turned and saw a figure lunging toward him. He rolled to his right and raised his weapon. Diegert's machete made a metallic clang as the blade struck the shaft of the junkyard mace. Deiobo bent his legs and kicked out with as much force as he could muster, taking the feet out from under Diegert. The assassin fell forward, landing on top of the convict. His face was inches from the saw blade, but his machete and his weight disallowed the weapon to be swung. Diegert put his hand on the back side of the machete and shoved the blade forward, catching the cross tube of the mace and forcing it out of the hands of the convict.

Once the weapon handle had left his grasp, the convict kneed Diegert in the thigh and punched him in the ribs. Diegert pushed the weapons away and sought to choke the convict, who rolled to the right and pushed up off the ground, elbowing Diegert in the gut. The convict stood up, and Diegert staggered to his feet as well. The convict lunged forward with a kick to Diegert's midsection, which Diegert blocked with his hands. The convict swung his fist, and Diegert ducked under the blow. The assassin jabbed the convict's chest and crossed with a punch to the face. The convict fell back against a concrete block, and Diegert pinned him against it, hyperextending his back with a choke hold on his throat. Diegert began to apply crushing pressure to the convict's throat, when he felt a cold steel ring on his temple. The convict had a pistol to his head.

He released Deiobo and stepped back. Deiobo coughed and sputtered as he struggled to breathe, but he kept the gun pointed at Diegert and followed his movements.

"Go ahead and shoot, you pussy. I don't give a fuck."

The convict was still struggling to breathe and couldn't say a thing.

"Come on, you lousy prick. Get it over with!" Standing with his arms wide open and his chest fully exposed, Diegert shouted, "Go ahead, shoot me, you shithead. Shoot me, you punk ass bastard."

Seeing the indecision in the convict's eyes, Diegert said, "If you don't have the guts to shoot me, then I'm gonna kill you right now."

As Diegert approached, Deiobo tossed the gun up in the air, grabbed the barrel, and threw it. The gun hit Diegert on the forehead, gashing the skin and toppling him to the ground. Deiobo ran back and grabbed the mace. He turned to go back to Diegert, who had picked up the gun and stood back up. Deiobo looked at him, laughing.

"What are you doing, you dumb shit? The damn thing's not loaded."

"I know," said Diegert as he reached into his cargo pocket, pulled out the clip, and jammed it into the Beretta. Deiobo stood in shock with his junkyard weapon as Diegert prepared to pull on the slide to chamber a round. Diegert pulled, and the slide wouldn't move. The slide was jammed, and the gun wouldn't load. Deiobo smiled as he drew his arm back and charged with his dual-disc weapon. Realizing the gun was jammed, Diegert reacted to the attack. He swerved his upper body as the mace whizzed past his face and chest. He was not quick enough, though, to avoid the saw blade digging into his right thigh. The jagged cutting tool lacerated the muscle as blood sprayed from Diegert's leg.

Deiobo tried to pull the weapon back, but it was caught in the fabric of Diegert's pants. Standing this close, Diegert crushed Deiobo's nose with the pistol. The blow dislodged the nasal cartilage and cracked the bones of the convict's nose. Blood spewed out, and Deiobo was in more pain than Diegert. With the Beretta still in hand, Diegert again pulled on the slide, which slid back and snapped forward, chambering the first round. As Deiobo staggered with blood all over his face, he looked up to see Diegert pointing the gun again. He smiled, revealing his crooked yellow teeth, just before two bullets hit his chest and a third entered his head, ending his participation in the tournament.

At that instant, Diegert didn't know if the fourth participant was still active, but having a loaded gun gave him a lot more confidence. He started to move west when the air horn, which had begun the competition, sounded. Diegert removed his belt and used it as a tourniquet on his bleeding leg. The gates opened, and teams of men entered with body bags. He was the only one going out. Outside the gate, Strakov, Blevinsky, and Jaeger looked at him but offered no congratulations. Strakov barked, "You left one alive."

"With his injuries and the shit he's in, he'll be dead by morning."

Pierre's and Gregor's smiles said much more than words. Pierre slapped him on the shoulder as he passed, and Diegert felt the camaraderie, even though he realized it was awkward for the Frenchman to be so positive in front of Strakov.

Fatima waited beyond the others, and her warm smile told Diegert that she was pleased. Also finding words difficult, she held out her hand, saying, "I'll take that."

Diegert handed her the gun and was placed in an ambulance. Fatima climbed in for the ride to medical. "I'm very proud of you."

"Killing those men was pointless. I get that it is part of this process, but those guys being dead doesn't accomplish anything."

"It showed us who is the best new operator in the world."

Diegert thought she sounded like a schoolgirl with her cheery assessment. She accompanied him to medical, where he got a shot of morphine and his thigh wound stitched up.

"One thing this did accomplish is the fulfillment of your training phase. You are no longer a trainee but an operator with all the rights and privileges ascribed to the role."

"Yeah, and what are those?" asked Diegert as he got his head wound cleaned.

"You can be assigned missions and be paid very well for completing them."

"What else?"

"Eventually, you can be assigned to a regional location and can operate independently at Headquarters' direction."

"Now that sounds like a good thing so I can get the fuck out of here."

"Right now, no one but Blevinsky can tell you what to do, and until assigned a mission, you can conduct yourself as you wish within the facility."

"You mean I get to have a staycation."

Fatima patted him on the forearm, saying, "I'll see you around, but I won't be coming to your room again to wake you in the morning."

As she walked out of medical, Diegert still couldn't deny the desire he had for her to come to his room for a completely unofficial visit.

CHAPTER 43

Four ornate offices, each with a large-screen video monitor. Four wealthy men, who quietly controlled the world's economy and influenced government policies. These four men were the members of the Board of Crepusculous. Together for two decades, they had gradually amassed tremendous wealth and, more importantly, significant power. All were born into wealth and had worked to expand their fortunes. Now they were interdependent, cooperative, and fabulously successful. They kept their profiles low, never appearing in any media. Remaining invisible, they controlled the factors that affected the majority of the world's population. They were the 1 percent of the 1 percent. Rarely were the four men in the same location, but they frequently used video conferencing to discuss business, politics, and world events as they strategically planned to increase their possessions, profits, and power.

"Good morning, gentlemen," began Klaus Panzer. "You are all looking well."

Panzer could see Dean Kellerman, Julio Perez, and Chin Liu Wei. The video screens allowed them all to see each other. The system facilitated complete communication; not only were words exchanged, but the moods and emotions of each were visually perceived.

Panzer continued, "We do have business to discuss, but first I want to acknowledge the results of our most recent tournament at the Proving Grounds."

Both Wei and Perez turned their heads, uncomfortably looking away from the camera.

"It seems the American won the contest and will become our newest asset. Well done, Dean."

"Thank you. He certainly has proven to be a tough bugger. He made a hostage rescue all by himself back in December. I believe he will be useful to all of us."

Perez exhaled a lungful of smoke before saying, "The man I sent was a last-minute submission. I had lost track of the date of the tournament; I'll send a better man next time. But my man fared no worse than yours, Klaus."

Kellerman replied, "Yes, Klaus, I was quite surprised you sent a family man."

"He had gambling debts."

"I regret the loss of Shioki Wong," offered Wei. "But the next man will be better prepared."

"Very well, our selection process is complete. We now have a new operative for mission assignments, Mr. David Diegert," concluded Panzer.

"One last thing," said Perez. "This David Diegert, is he the man who carried out my sanctions in Miami and Paris?"

Panzer nodded, adding, "He also eliminated Farooq Arindi, the man who was complicating our land purchases in Somalia and threatening the shipping lanes through the Indian Ocean."

A wry smile crept out from under the mustache of Perez, followed by a concentrated plume of smoke. "He has chosen a life of death."

Kellerman changed the subject. "Mr. Wei, I'm concerned with the disparity in the interest rates being charged to the US federal government."

"What is your concern?" asked the surprised Chinese banker.

"Are rates going up across the board or are different branches getting different rates?"

"Different rates for different customers results in better payment compliance."

"That may be so, but rates should be universal across the government so that the economic readjustment plan we've been developing will have greater impact."

"Different rates create more profits in the short term."

Panzer spoke on the subject. "Common rates will definitely facilitate more damage to the US government. I think what we need to do is recommit to the economic readjustment plan, our plan, and realize that the time for action is upon us. All of our individual efforts should be focused on making this long-range plan a success."

Wei replied, "I realize the devaluation of the US dollar will benefit us all. I did not realize the timeline was so aggressive. I will regulate one common interest rate and align all government borrowers. I am committed to the plan."

"Excellent. Are there any other questions regarding the plan for US economic disruption?"

"From readjustment to disruption just like that?" questioned the aging Spaniard.

"The downfall of the US dollar will create an economic opportunity the likes of which have never been seen before. Our digital currency, Digival, which is based on the value of our collective wealth, will improve the world's economic mechanisms and the Board's position of power."

The men eyed each other, searching for signs of reassurance that each of them was committed to the plan. Once the process of devaluing the dollar, and thus weakening the US government, was underway, there could be no turning back. These men had to trust one another to follow through with their portion of the plan.

After looking at each other for a quiet moment, Panzer spoke. "At this point in time, I am asking that each of you indicate your commitment to the plan or express any concerns that you have."

The men looked at one another with affirming nods, which was all that was needed to communicate their commitment within the intimate brotherhood of the elite group.

"Very well," said Panzer. "I do believe we have covered our agenda, and I move to close the meeting."

Each man agreed, and the video screens went dark.

***

Klaus picked up the phone and called Kellerman. "I'm glad you brought that issue up with Wei. I think he will comply."

"I hope so. We need to have the branches of the US federal government on equal footings for the plan to have its full effect."

"I know, and I think Wei knows as well, but it's hard for him to take even a temporary loss."

"Yes, but in the end, the man will own California!"

"The readjustment will work. We've been planning too long for it to fail. Besides, the US just keeps ignoring its problems and making the situation inevitable."

"We're just pushing the train over the hill so it runs away and destroys their ridiculous way of financing their lives."

"Very well, my friend, their indebtedness will be our next source of wealth."

It was the huge indebtedness of the United States that stimulated Panzer and Kellerman to develop the plan for economic readjustment. Kellerman, the actuary, calculated the unsustainable nature of US economic policy. The whole system operated on a promissory note. A use-it-now, pay-for-it-later mentality that guided car purchases, home purchases, and, in the case of the federal government, almost all purchases. The entire country was leveraged, and a requirement to pay back even a portion of the total debt would bring to a halt the system of economic figments that fueled America's culture of overspending.

When Kellerman shared his beliefs with Panzer, the German saw the vulnerability and an opportunity to correct the balance of power. The Board held a global perspective, and even though American assets like the New York Stock Exchange were important, distributing their assets across the globe was more valuable than a "Strong America" propped up by a foolishly financed system of borrowed dollars and unpaid debt.

Ironically, the US dollar remained the strongest currency upon which the value of all other currencies, and several critical commodities, including oil, was determined. Panzer sought to seize the opportunity created by the fact that the world's economy was based on a currency backed only by a promise. He determined that a currency based on the vast wealth of Crepusculous's worldwide assets, a true corporate currency, would be a better way for the world to operate. It was also determined that eliminating physical money, cash, and coins, and distributing the currency in a digital-only format, would be more efficient and secure. He successfully convinced the other Board members of his views, and they formed a plan to take down the dollar.

The plan had four phases: First, create a vacuum of leadership with a significant assassination. Second, upset the stock market by moving assets out of US holdings, tanking stock prices. Third, produce chaos and destruction the likes of which the United States had never seen. This phase would make the population feel the impact of the failure of the federal government, making it ripe for readjustment. Fourth, call in the debt. Mr. Wei held 60 percent of US federal debt financed through China. He would call in the loan, which would trigger a run on US debt obligations, and the government would go bankrupt. This wouldn't be one of those congressional showdown shutdowns. This time the government would be so insolvent that it would not be able to function, and federal services would vanish.

A period of chaos, civil unrest, and lawlessness would take place. The value of the US dollar would evaporate, eliminating the basis for the worldwide system of governmental currency. Into this vacuum, Crepusculous's public corporation, Omnisphere, would continue to promote Digival, making it a global currency with a common value throughout the world, no exchange rates based on geographic location or political ideology. It would make the globe one common market. All commerce would occur as digital transactions. The world might hesitate to adjust, but quickly those who did not participate would be left in a barter-only economy. Omnisphere's power in the global market would be unprecedented, and Crepusculous would enjoy absolute power from its position in the shadows. When things settled down, a new corporate structure would replace the US federal government. As the saying went, "Out of chaos, opportunity appears." America was still the best real estate on the planet, and this plan would allow the Board to acquire it at rock-bottom prices. The United States would become the de facto Corporate States of America.

"Dean, I want to ask you about something else," began Panzer. "Aaron shared with me the story of the Cambridge boy's rescue back in December."

"Yes, what of it?"

"What concerns me is that Michka Barovitz, a two-bit hoodlum, loan shark, and mobster, dared to extort an associate of ours and then kidnap his son. Such audacity cannot be tolerated without a response."

"We did respond. We acquired the boy right under his nose, and he lost several men in the process. David Diegert accomplished the rescue singlehandedly."

"Of course, I appreciate all of that, but what I mean is that Barovitz must be dealt with directly and eliminated, or such brashness will undermine our position."

"How can such a lowly crook be of any concern to us?"

"Aboveground, you're right, we can't be hurt, but underground, the community has a harsher code. Arms dealing and covert actions occur in the shadows, and your reputation is the only credential you carry. We are well known in the dark world. Our reputation is stark; it guarantees us full payment for deliveries. Barovitz just challenged that."

"What are you suggesting?"

"The assassination of Barovitz."

"Oh my, you are taking the hard road."

"I believe a strike team can take him out on his island in the Aegean."

"And you're seeking Board approval?"

"No, but I am letting my one true friend and confidant know I'm ordering the mission."

Pulling the receiver from his ear and giving it a look of consternation, Kellerman said, "Why did you not bring this up before the Board?"

"I did not wish to explain my reasoning to the entire group; plus, a covert mission is by its very nature secret."

"Well, I appreciate your confidence. I wish you success, and I hope your underground reputation is enhanced."

"I'll keep you better informed of the mission's progress than you did for me back in December. Have a good day, Dean."

As he replaced the receiver in its cradle, Kellerman reflected on the percentage of their wealth that was derived from illegal, unethical, and morally depraved activities. The figure was at least 20 percent. Between the arms, drugs, unregulated harvesting of raw materials, corporations that employed low-wage workshops, and hiring out operators for contracted covert action, Kellerman acknowledged to himself that he was the direct beneficiary of heinous and entrenched criminal activity. The realization left him with a nauseous ache in his stomach.

CHAPTER 44

Blevinsky's request popped up on Fatima's phone: *Meet me in my office at 0900 for a mission briefing.* When she arrived, she found a tense man cursing at his computer. Fatima knocked on the open door. "Yeah, come in," he said.

The bald, mustached man briefly looked up over his computer screen, saying, "If you want coffee, it's right there."

"No, thanks." Fatima took a seat facing Blevinsky's desk.

"I'll be right with you," he said and went back to pounding on his keyboard.

After several minutes, Fatima asked, "When is the mission?"

"Hang on, I have to finish this."

Fatima stood up. "Call me when you're really ready to meet with me."

Looking up at her from under a furrowed brow, he said, "Your time is mine. If I say wait for me, then you will wait. Now sit back down."

He stared intensely at her as she avoided his eyes and sat back in the chair. Blevinsky returned to his keyboard. Fatima fumed at being ignored in spite of being called to this meeting. After several more minutes, Fatima could see that Blevinsky's anger was growing. Whatever he was working on wasn't going very well. Suddenly, he slammed his fist on the desk, saying, "Damn it, this isn't going to work!" He pushed himself away from the desk and directed his attention to Fatima.

They both smiled at each other, their smiles being anything but genuine. "I apologize for the way this meeting began," said Blevinsky.

"You seem to be having some troubles. Is there anything I can do to help?"

Looking back at the computer on his desk, Blevinsky slowly said, "With that project, no." Turning to face her, he continued, "But I have another mission for you." Fatima focused her attention on him. "We have a CIA-directed contract to eliminate a target in Germany. I have a full dossier with mission specifics, but what I want to discuss with you is, I would like you to work with a partner on this mission."

Uncomfortable with this idea right from the beginning, Fatima protested. "Why do I need a partner? What is the danger?"

"I have a feeling that this job may involve a counterstrike on the operator." Fatima remained quiet as Blevinsky explained. "First, the longer I stay in this business, the less I trust anybody. Second, the CIA rep who set this up is the guy we usually deal with, and when I tried to contact him to verify the job, all his numbers and addresses were no longer functioning. Third, three months ago, a contract guy I worked with in the past took a CIA job and was killed after completing the hit by a counterstrike. It all adds up to a situation that makes me very nervous."

"And why are we taking the job at all?"

"There's a Board member who wants us to be cozier with the CIA and is insisting that we do the job."

"No matter what the risk?"

"Correct. So I want to send you with another operator who will be able to watch your back and expedite your safe extraction."

"Let me guess, you're sending Strakov with me?"

"No, actually, I was going to send Diegert."

"Diegert! He's fresh out of training; I don't think he could handle it."

"Oh, cut the crap! You know as well as I that he's a better operator than anyone else we've got. He's especially good at improvising during dynamic situations."

"He's careless and risky."

"He's determined and resourceful, and if you weren't so hung up on him being so good in spite of your torturing him, you would stop with this façade and start planning the mission."

"What if I refuse?"

"Refuse a mission?"

Blevinsky slid forward to the edge of his seat and lowered his voice. "If you refuse this mission, I'll send you out of the facility and have Strakov's strike team track you down and eliminate you for practice."

He leaned back in his chair and folded his arms over his chest, saying, "In the process, you might even get to find out if Alexi is actually bisexual."

Fatima looked at him with the fire in her eyes that made everyone uncomfortable. She picked up the dossier, turning as she left, and said, "I'll tell Diegert myself."

***

Fatima found Diegert target shooting on the range. She saw he was sighting in the sniper rifle she had used to rescue Andrew Cambridge, the one he had brought with him in a custom case. He was shooting at targets with tiny human silhouettes that conveyed the relative proportions of long distances. His results were impressive. She waited until he had emptied his magazine before tapping on his ear covers. Pulling off the ear protectors, Diegert said, "What do you want?"

"I need to meet with you about a mission."

"Right now? Damn, you know how much it hurts to tap on these things. When's the mission?"

"In two days."

"I'll be done here in half an hour. You could've sent me a text."

"I wanted to make sure we met as soon as possible."

"We will . . . in half an hour, in the cafeteria."

She spun on her heels and left.

Diegert ejected the magazine, disconnected the stock, and unscrewed the rifle's barrel. He placed each part in its foam cutout within the case. While putting the stock in, he noticed a rectangular cutout in the wall of the foam. As he pulled at the piece of foam, it separated from the wall, and from inside the rectangle, Diegert extracted a USB storage device. The only marking was its twenty GB capacity. He slipped the little piece of plastic into his pocket and replaced the piece of foam. At the armory, he handed the case back to Lindstrom.

"It's a pretty accurate rifle, isn't it?"

"Yeah, and the scope was easy to sight in."

"Everything's in the case?"

Diegert was slow to answer. Studying Lindstrom's face, he wondered if the armorer knew about the USB. When he saw Lindstrom's gaze intensify, he snapped the hesitation out of his response.

"Oh yeah, everything's there. Thanks for letting me shoot it. I gotta go."

Walking away from the armory, Diegert fingered the cool piece of plastic in his pocket, his curiosity growing.

American food had become ubiquitous; every lunch offered a choice of hamburgers, chicken nuggets, or macaroni and cheese. Although there were others choices, Diegert usually found himself drawn to one of these. Today, however, the menu included pizza. One of the pies featured sausage, mushrooms, and broccoli. Diegert ordered two slices. At the table, Fatima's disgust was not hidden.

"What? It has vegetables," Diegert said as the melted cheese stretched from his mouth. He hungrily chewed the warm, cheesy slice. "Tell me about the mission."

Fatima leaned forward, even though they were sitting away from other diners.

"It's a contract hit for the CIA. The target is selling some secrets. I'm posing as a representative of a Pakistani customer and will take him out at the meeting in the hotel."

"So why am I part of this?"

"You're to help with extraction."

"Why would you need my help?"

"Blevinsky's nervous about a counterstrike."

"What do you mean?"

"I mean, after the hit, somebody puts a hit on me."

"So I make sure that doesn't happen."

"Correct."

Diegert's face grew smooth as the wrinkles in his brow disappeared while he contemplated Fatima's revelation.

"OK, when do we leave?"

"Tonight."

"I'm on it. It will be worth it just to get out of this stinking place."

Back in his room, Diegert inserted the USB into his computer. The device loaded but required a password. What would Shamus McGee use for a password? Diegert started with IRISH, then IRELAND, DUBLIN, BELFAST, SHAMROCK,

LEPRECHAUN, ST. PATRICK, BLARNEYSTONE. Attempting access again was denied after so many password fails. While waiting out the time lock, Diegert remembered Barney telling him, *"Shamus was a good Irishman, he loved his Guinness."* When the computer allowed him to try passwords again, he put in GUINNESS. Nothing. DARK PORTER, DRY STOUT. No access. Bringing up Guinness on Google, Diegert studied the simple banner with the familiar name in its distinctive font followed by the logo of the golden harp. Diegert typed GOLDEN HARP in the password bar, and the device opened to reveal a series of folders. The ones labeled "Crep. Profiles" and "Crep. Plans" drew his attention. The first file he opened was titled "General Information on the Board of Crepusculous."

> *The Crepusculous Board of Directors consists of four men. I have been able to identify and profile two of them, and I continue to investigate the other two members. There is no doubt that they will be as wealthy, powerful, and secretive as the men profiled in this report. Suffice it to say, they are the upper echelon of the world's powerful elite.*
> *Shamus McGee*

Diegert's immediate suspicions upon finding the device were confirmed; Shamus McGee was a double agent. He opened the file titled "K. Panzer."

> *Klaus Panzer is sixty-two years old and very healthy and fit. He exercises regularly and challenges himself to take adventure trips to some of the most remote places on earth. Klaus is a driven man. He's the de facto chairman of the Board, exerting his influence with his lack of hesitation to forcefully speak his mind. His family's*

empire began when the Panzers became the primary arms supplier to the Nazis. Operations moved to Switzerland after the war, and the company became the world's top supplier of high-quality military armaments. Engineering and design of new weapons led them to the development of all manner of defense products, from guns and ammunition to missile defense systems, as well as digital control and communications equipment. Panzer continues to oversee a research and development program from which I have had great difficulty gaining specific operational information. I can report that the personnel are top scientists in physiology, neurology, nanotechnology, engineering, and genetics.

Panzer has never married. He does, however, have children: two daughters by two different women. Thirty-four-year-old Gretchen is an accomplished businesswoman who handles the family's real estate. The other daughter is ten years younger. Sashi has completed a liberal arts degree but has not used it; instead, she has been paid handsomely to model activewear and rep numerous adventure sports products. Klaus Panzer has no son.

The Panzer home is a huge mansion in Innsbruck, Austria. They possess other residences including a townhome in London.

S. M.

It wasn't hard for Diegert to imagine the strong, outspoken German leading this band of wealthy men to further acquisition of wealth and power. The next file was labeled "D. Kellerman."

Dean Kellerman is a sixty-year-old Englishman. He's in good health and remains active and fit. His money comes from insurance companies; however, he has also established hedge funds capable of tipping the market with the movement of money. Commodities, including oil, agricultural products, and minerals, are also controlled by the Englishman. Through the manipulation of the price of these basic raw materials, Kellerman impacts the price the world pays for every-thing. Kellerman's holdings also include large sections of European real estate and media companies that pro-vide television and Internet service to most of the world. Kellerman's wife, Felicity, passed away two years ago from pancreatic cancer. He has two children, Michael and Colleen. Michael is thirty years old and is a drug addict. Rehab programs and addiction management treatments have failed, and the goal is now to keep Michael out of jail.

His daughter, twenty-five-year-old Colleen, graduated summa cum laude from Oxford's business school. She currently manages the philanthropic activities of the family, which donates hundreds of millions of dollars each year.

The Kellerman family has several residences, but they consider Rosethorn, a 130-acre estate ten miles out-side of London, to be their home. Kellerman conducts his business from his office suite there, while Colleen orchestrates many gatherings and social fundraisers at Rosethorn so the family is never socially isolated.
S. M.

Kellerman's profile depicted a more traditional man of wealth who enjoyed his station and played the part of a British aristocrat. Diegert's opinion, though, was not swayed by this impression. This man was part of Crepusculous, so his money had blood on it.

In the folder labeled "Crep. Plans," there was only one file:

Through questioning personnel and intercepting communications, I have determined that Crepusculous has a plan for what they are calling "economic readjustment." It is a four-stage plan to disrupt and destroy a country's economy. I believe these men feel they can manipulate markets and destabilize the political structure of a vulnerable country in order to control the economy and the resources of such a nation. This disregard for social order and political process makes them more dangerous than originally perceived. It will be my priority to determine which third-world country is the target of their ruthless power seeking.

I have also discovered evidence of widespread corruption within law enforcement agencies throughout Europe, Asia, the Middle East, and the United States. Crepusculous uses its leverage within law enforcement to control the actions of agents who are moving against their interests and directs law enforcement to act against their rivals. Their influence is malignant and metastatic.

S. M.

Diegert closed the file and the folder before removing the device from his computer. He placed the device in his pocket while he thought back to Barney's story about the death of Shamus McGee. The list of possible governments, and rivals for whom McGee could've been working as a double agent,

William Schiele

was huge, but clearly the data he'd collected could prove fatal to others as well.

As Diegert packed his bag for the upcoming mission, he remembered that since winning the tournament he was allowed to make outside calls. It had been so long since he had spoken with his family, so he called his mother.

"Hello, David."

"Mom, how ya doing?"

"I'm doing very well, dear. I want to thank you for the money."

"You're welcome. Is the bank happy now that the mortgage is all paid off?"

"Well . . . not quite yet."

"Whaddya mean?"

"Your dad hasn't paid them yet."

Turning his head toward the ceiling and dropping the phone from his ear, he grimaced and felt like an idiot for not having transferred the money directly to the bank to satisfy the debt. Diegert bit his lip as he placed the phone back to his ear.

"Why didn't you pay them? I put the money in your account."

"Dad has access to that account, and he says that since we have two months to pay, we should hold on to the money and earn some interest."

Slowly shaking his head from side to side, he could see his dad saying something that sounded sensible but was, in fact, a ruse for him to do something stupid.

"Mom, if there is any way you can just go to the bank and give them the money to pay off the mortgage, I beg you to do it. Don't let Dad screw with that money."

"Oh, David, things are never easy, you know that."

324

"Yeah, I know I also worked very hard for that money, and I want it to be used to pay off the house, and if that doesn't happen, I'll be very upset."

"I understand, but I'm amazed you got that much money so quickly. How did you do it?"

"Good luck and hard work, Mom, two things Dad and Jake have never had or done."

"I'm sure it'll all work out for the best. Dad just wants to utilize all the financial time we have."

"Financial time? Mom, that sounds like Dad's bullshit. Please, I gotta go, but do me the favor of making sure the house's debt is paid. I gave you that money for that and no other reason. I want you to be secure in that house."

"Thanks. David, you're so wonderful. I miss you and I love you."

"I love you too, Mom, good-bye."

"Good-bye, honey."

After disconnecting, Diegert finished packing for the mission, grateful he would soon be focusing on something other than his fucked-up family.

CHAPTER 45

The Gulfstream streaked west, chasing the setting sun as it carried Fatima and Diegert to their first official mission together. Fatima explained what lay before them in a bit more detail.

"The target's name is Hans Klemmler. He's an executive at Zeidler-Roche, a company that contracts with the US Department of Defense to handle communications. He's selling codes on the black market. Posing as the front person for a Pakistani customer, I'll be meeting him to pay him in cash. I'll be dressed in traditional Pakistani attire, covered head to toe in order to facilitate infiltration. The hit will take place in the meeting room, and then I must be extracted."

"We'll dupe them. We'll leave that counterstrike team with no idea how they lost us."

Handing Diegert a sheet of photos, Fatima continued, "Blevinsky's mole in the CIA provided us with these photos of operatives who are tasked with being active in Frankfurt tomorrow."

Reviewing the photos, Diegert noted two women and three men. The women both looked to be in their twenties, one blonde, the other brunette. The guys were a wider range of ages. The oldest looked to be in his fifties, with gray hair and a beard. The other two were in their twenties or thirties. One had dark-black hair and dark features. The last guy had a thick, athletic neck, shoulder-length blond hair, and a very piercing gaze for an ID headshot.

Diegert folded the photos, tucking them away. He felt even more confident now that he could identify the CIA by sight.

"We've got at least another hour in the air. I brought a bottle of wine." Her voice was very seductive, but then again Diegert readily perceived everything she said as seductive.

"Is it white?"

"Of course not. It's Cabernet Sauvignon."

Fatima handed him the bottle and the corkscrew while she retrieved two glasses. Once the wine was poured, Fatima asked, "To what should we toast?"

"To the success of this mission."

"I don't like toasting the future. We should acknowledge something that has already happened."

"Like?"

"I raise my glass to you for completing your training and becoming an operator."

"Thank you," said Diegert, raising his glass, clinking hers, and then taking a sip of the deep-red wine. Feeling a bit obligated, Diegert raised his glass and said, "I want to toast you and thank you for the support you gave me. You helped me to succeed."

Glasses clinked again, and they each took a sip. Diegert couldn't hold her eye contact, and she wouldn't look away from him. "I'm not certain you believe your own words, but I thank you."

"Your methods were . . . unorthodox, but here I am."

Fatima's gaze had a questioning quality that Diegert acknowledged by taking a satisfactory sip, setting down his wineglass, and then making direct eye contact.

"Is there a woman in your life, out there somewhere?" she asked.

Diegert was surprised by the question. "No . . . no, there's not."

"Why not?"

"Because I live at Headquarters. As you know, there's very little opportunity to meet eligible women."

"Ah, but what of the past? Is there no girl at home wishing you had married her?"

"Uhh . . . no, there is no one waiting for me. My profile at home was not exactly marriage material."

"The passionate heart looks beyond, sees the man, and feels only desire."

Looking at her, he picked up his glass and took another sip of wine.

Fatima continued, "I'd think a handsome man like you would have a woman somewhere in the world who feels that way about him."

"If she exists, I haven't met her."

"You may not have recognized her feelings."

"Or no girl has ever felt that way."

"I look at you, and I know that in your hometown there were girls who dreamed of you, talked about you, and desired you."

"You've never been to Broward, Minnesota."

"I know, but I have been in the heart of a teenage girl who became a woman, who recognizes the attractive qualities of a man."

"OK, I get what you're saying, but the answer is no. I don't have a secret girl waiting for me to come home and marry her. What about you? What about Hamni? Hamni is your son, correct?"

Fatima's Cabernet-induced relaxation vanished, and her fire-and-ice face returned. Diegert was not surprised. He fully expected her to react angrily, but up here in the airplane, he figured he might actually get her to reveal what he already believed.

"Who told you this?" spat the furious woman.

"You just did," replied the relaxed man.

"I told you nothing."

"Oh, but that's not true. We speak with more than words. Tell me about Hamni, you must love him very much."

"I'm saying nothing."

"Then he's in danger. Is he being held so you'll do this work?"

Fatima's anger grew, but it started to mix with a sadness that she found increasingly difficult to control. The combination made her feel vulnerable. A feeling she would not tolerate. She looked at the confident young man and hated the fact he seemed not to have the same emotional vulnerability. She stood, picked up the bottle of wine, saying, "Finish the extraction plans before we land." She walked into the private quarters of the plane, closing the door behind her.

CHAPTER 46

The Westin Grand Hotel in Frankfurt was an impressive modern structure that looked distinctly out of place amid the antique buildings that surrounded it. Diegert drove the Mercedes E350 with Fatima beside him, dressed in a fashionable jilbab that draped her entire body. She wore a scarf over her head and neck, and a veil covered her face. All the garments were color coordinated in deep red with an embroidered border around the entire suit. The veil she wore didn't disguise the intensity of her eyes.

Diegert said, "Before we go to the hotel, we've got something to pick up."

"What?"

"I'll show you."

Diegert drove to the Sachsenhausen section of Frankfurt and slowed the car to a prowl. When he stopped at an intersection and rolled down the window, three young women ran to him. He indicated he wanted to speak to the one with dark hair and eyes who appeared South Asian.

"You want to get in and come with us?"

The young lady lowered her gaze to see Fatima, covered in Islamic dress in the passenger seat.

"Don't be fooled," said Diegert. "She's totally into it. Five hundred euros."

The dark-haired streetwalker climbed into the back. Fatima's glare burned on Diegert, who said, "You'll be glad we did this."

A block from the hotel, Diegert pulled over. Turning to the streetwalker, he handed her a hundred euros. "Go to the Westin Grand and sit outside the Danube Room on the second floor. We will meet you there in fifteen minutes."

The experienced pleasure provider was not unaccustomed to clandestine meetings, and her nods of certainty gave Diegert confidence as she stepped out of the car.

At the Westin, Fatima exited the Mercedes carrying a briefcase and proceeded into the lobby. She made her way to the Danube Room for the meeting with Klemmler. She followed the posted directions and spoke to no one on the hotel staff.

Diegert drove the Mercedes out the driveway of the hotel's covered entrance, crossed the street, and parked twenty meters away on the opposite side of the road. He sat in the car looking for the faces of the CIA observation team. Unfolding his sheet of photos, he quickly picked out the blonde woman and the dark-haired man sitting outside together in an elevated café across from the hotel. Diegert had to accept that the beard was a little longer and the man was wearing a cap, but he recognized the oldest member of the team in the window of a Brauhaus next to the hotel.

Search as he did, he couldn't find the other two observers and deduced they were inside the hotel.

The Danube Room accommodated twelve people, so there was plenty of space for Fatima and Hans Klemmler to conduct their business. Klemmler had two armed bodyguards occupying the room with him. When Fatima entered, Klemmler introduced himself. "Greetings, Fräulein, I am Hans Klemmler," said the tall, balding German, extending his hand.

She ignored his hand, stepping around him to avoid contact. Klemmler dropped his hand to his side. From behind her veil, Fatima said, "Good day, sir, shall we proceed with the transaction?"

"Yes, of course. However, I would appreciate the indulgence if you would allow my associate to ascertain that you are, in fact, unarmed."

Klemmler graciously opened his palm, indicating the way was clear for her to enter the restroom attached to the meeting space. The dour-faced, heavyset female guard followed Fatima into the restroom. Once inside, Fatima quickly undid the front of her jilbab, opening it to reveal a formfitting, full-length black body suit. The curve of her hips, the outline of her breasts, and the narrowness of her waist were all obvious yet completely covered. The guard was at first surprised at the sudden revelation of Fatima's undergarments, but she realized it made the task less embarrassing. As the woman stepped forward to frisk her, Fatima tugged on a tab that released a silenced Walther PPK that slid down the length of her sleeve into her hand, barrel first.

The guard was so intent on feeling for weapons, she did not see the arrival of the pistol. When she realized there was a barrel pressed against the base of her skull, the thought lasted less than one second before Fatima pulled the trigger. With the suppressor pressed tightly against its target, the report of the discharge was heavily muffled. Blood splattered across the room but not on Fatima. She caught the weight of the woman and guided the body quietly to the floor. She did up the front of her jilbab and stepped carefully across the floor, avoiding the puddle of blood.

Outside, Diegert stepped out of the car wearing a dark jacket and a navy-blue baseball cap. He pulled a pack of cigarettes from his pocket, shaking the pack only to realize it was empty. He played it up, appearing annoyed at being unable to smoke. After several minutes of acting frustrated, he crumpled the empty cigarette pack, threw it in a garbage can, and marched off.

When Fatima stepped out of the restroom, the male guard glanced at her. He looked perplexed when she raised her hand and fired a bullet in his face. The shot twisted his head. Fatima fired again, striking him just behind the ear and dropping him to the floor. Klemmler sat dumbfounded when he saw that the weapon was now pointing at him. So amazed was he that when the first bullet hit the right side of his chest, he still couldn't believe what was happening. The second bullet, piercing the other side of his chest, carried less surprise but more damage as it ruptured the left ventricle of his heart. His body fell back in his chair, which tipped over, dumping his bleeding chest onto the floor. Fatima stepped to him and watched the painful grimace on his face turn to the flaccid expression and dilated pupils of death. Assured her target was deceased, Fatima placed the gun into the briefcase and exited the Danube Room.

Having convinced the CIA he was searching for his nicotine fix, Diegert turned the corner and began running to the back of the hotel. He entered through the loading dock and met Fatima outside the Danube Room. She removed her jilbab and gave it to Diegert.

Diegert stepped over to the hired lover. "Here, now is the next part of the fantasy." Diegert handed the young lady the jilbab.

"Put this on and return to the Mercedes, which is parked across the street. We will meet you in ten minutes."

The girl looked a little surprised, but Diegert reasoned it probably wasn't the strangest thing she'd ever been asked to do. With the jilbab on, she wrapped the scarf around her head and drew the veil over her face.

"Excellent," said Diegert. "We'll see you at the car in ten minutes."

Diegert removed the dark jacket he was wearing, reversed it to tan, and gave it to Fatima. He took off his navy-blue cap, reversed it to white with a red Fiat emblem, and put it on Fatima's head.

From his seat in the Brauhaus, the gray-bearded man thought it had been a long time for the driver to get a pack of cigarettes. He contacted his CIA team inside the hotel. "Status?"

"Moving to the second floor now," replied the man with long blond hair.

"Clear in the kitchen," said the brunette.

Diegert went to the hotel lobby. He watched the prostitute cross the street and approach the Mercedes. When she reached the car, a Chevy pickup screeched to a halt, and a band of neo-Nazi skinheads unloaded and began harassing her. The skinheads pushed, shoved, and punched the woman in the jilbab. When they pulled off the scarf, the terrified prostitute started screaming about not being the person they wanted, but her looks were convincing enough and the beating continued.

Diegert knocked on the women's room door where Fatima was waiting. They fell into step as they traversed the second-floor hall.

The blond agent, dressed in a dull blue maintenance suit with a tool belt, turned the corner and strode down the same hall as Diegert and Fatima. They all recognized each other instantly but none gave away that fact. Immediately after passing in the middle of the hall, they all whirled around to attack. Only the big blond man was surprised.

Diegert lashed out with a series of kicks to the lower leg. The best kick forced the blond operative to stumble forward. Fatima took advantage of his awkward movement, driving a knee into his chest and striking the back of his neck. The big guy fell forward, tackling Diegert. Diegert felt his nose gushing blood after the blond guy's forehead collided with his face. The CIA agent raised his head for another strike, and Diegert blocked it with his right forearm. With his left, Diegert pulled a screwdriver from the man's tool belt and stabbed him in the rib cage. Fatima grabbed the power drill from the other side of the tool belt and drilled holes in the back of his thighs.

The torquing and tearing of flesh forced a frightening scream as the man rolled off Diegert, grabbing his wounded leg. Fatima, eyeing his vulnerable chest, drove the full length of the bit through his right pectoral. The suction of puncturing his lung held the drill in place and Fatima had to pull hard to rip the power tool from the dying man's thorax.

Diegert got to his feet, calculating the guy was in his final moments as blood flowed out of his mouth with each breath. Grabbing Fatima's hand, he said, "Let's go."

Dropping the drill as they ran down the hall, Fatima pulled her hand from Diegert's, accelerating ahead of him.

With two final strikes to the face from a sawed-off baseball bat, the prostitute's body went fatally limp. The skinhead dropped her to the ground, where she crumpled into a lifeless heap. Gray Beard contacted his team. "It's over, target is neutralized."

The blond man uttered his final words over his comm device. "Wrong person . . . target in hotel."

Gray Beard spoke to the brunette in the kitchen. "Confirm target."

The brunette inverted the kitchen knife in her hand so the blade was parallel with her forearm as she exited the kitchen.

When they arrived at the rear loading dock, Diegert saw a large truck filled with potted plants, flower boxes, and floral displays. The worker was just about to begin unloading when Diegert approached him wearing a small oronasal respirator. He sprayed the plant man with a concentrated chloroform mist known as Trank. He caught the unconscious man before he hit the floor and loaded him into the back of the truck. He motioned for Fatima to get in the driver's side. She climbed across the cab to the passenger's side and Diegert started up the truck.

The brunette arrived at the loading dock just in time to observe the loading of the driver and a woman in tight black pants climbing into the flower truck.

She contacted the team. "Target escaping in a flower truck. I'm in pursuit."

Diegert had the truck in gear and moving out of the loading dock when the brunette woman leapt on the open door step, reached in, and cut his right arm with her knife. He struggled to keep the truck straight as his attacker drew her arm back for another strike. Fatima's hand caught the woman's forearm, impeding her second stab, and held her fast. Diegert accelerated, swerving the truck toward the alley wall. Sparks flew as the bumper ground against the brick wall. Diegert straightened the steering so the entire side of the truck was scraping against the alley wall. When the sliding driver's door was hit by the wall, it shot forward into its closed position, trapping the woman by her arms. The brunette was now compressed between the truck and the wall, pinned by the door and pushed against the side-view mirror. The force of the truck abraded her back against the wall, and she was disemboweled as the mirror bracket gave way, tearing through her chest and abdomen.

Her body fell to the alley floor in large, shredded pieces over a forty-foot distance. The truck passed out of the alley and onto the street with blood and gore streaked across the side panel.

Seeing Fatima's face in the truck as it passed the Brauhaus, Gray Beard ordered the couple in the café into action. "Get moving after the flower truck."

The blonde woman and the dark-haired man pulled their Opel Astra onto the street and weaved through traffic to catch up with the truck as it moved toward the autobahn.

Gray Beard got on the phone with the skinheads.

"You have made a mistake. The actual target is getting away in a flower truck. Stop them or you won't be paid."

Diegert headed for the highway as fast as traffic would allow the big truck to move. The Opel chased the truck, making progress through traffic with its nimble handling.

Accelerating onto the autobahn entrance, Diegert moved immediately to the fast lane. The Opel and the skinheads' Chevy followed them onto the highway. Once on the expressway, Diegert could see the CIA couple right behind them. He did not want to battle them at the airport. "We're going to switch places. You ready to drive?"

Fatima nodded while climbing over the center console. Diegert let her slip under him, relinquishing the truck. Stepping into the back, Diegert was careful not to step on the unconscious plant man. He made his way to the rear of the truck and slid the door up into the ceiling. The Opel was right there, and the two CIA agents looked directly at him. Diegert also saw the big Chevy truck in the midst of the traffic on the highway. The blonde woman stretched outside the passenger window, firing her pistol. Her shots were wild, sparking and ricocheting off the truck. Diegert ducked back.

Racks of flowers and plants were lined up inside the truck. The wheeled racks were locked down for transport. Diegert unlocked two racks of plants, each ten feet long and eight feet high with a dozen shelves of potted plants. He pushed the racks out the back, sending them flying off the deck of the truck and onto the CIA Opel. The racks landed on the hood, smashing the windshield, spraying dirt and foliage all over the highway and causing the CIA vehicle to spin out of control and crash into a Volvo, setting off a chain-reaction catastrophe. The skinheads' Chevy swerved to the shoulder and rough-rode the margin of the highway to avoid the pileup forming around them.

Diegert shouted for Fatima to speed it up and get to the airport. He looked back to see the highway clear except for the skinheads. The truck carried four guys, two in the cab and two in the back. They looked like the original Road Warriors with their outrageous urban tough guy costumes and tattooed bodies.

One of the guys in the back leveled a shotgun across the roll bar and fired at the truck. The slug hit a rack of plants, spraying dirt in Diegert's eyes and lacerating his cheek with ceramic shrapnel. With his nose already bleeding and a cut on his arm, he had to take a moment to wipe the dirt and blood from his face. Up in the front of the truck's cargo area, Diegert located a large bronze planter filled with dirt and a small dying tree. The planter was on a wheeled moving cart, which Diegert unlocked. He positioned himself to push the heavy bronze ball-shaped planter, shouting for Fatima to speed it up.

When he felt the truck accelerating, he pushed with all his might, and the giant planter rolled down the floor of the truck and out the back end. The heavy spherical pot hit the pavement and started bouncing toward the Chevy truck. The pickup's driver was frozen with indecision, and the planter crashed onto the truck's hood, smashed the cabin, and rolled over the roof, crushing two skinheads. The driver was blinded by the smashed glass. He lost control of the vehicle, which spun sideways, tipped perpendicular to the road, and rolled several times before coming to a halt with two very dead neo-Nazis still onboard and two more splattered over the road.

Diegert saw nothing of what happened to the skinheads' truck. The momentum with which he'd pushed the planter had carried him right off the back of the deck. He would've been a smear of roadkill had he not caught the edge of one of the locked-in plant racks with the toe of his right boot. His entire body dangled in the slipstream of the truck. He was millimeters from having his face, hands, and arms abraded to red mist by the asphalt below him.

Fatima watched the planter knock the pickup off the road through her mirrors, but she had no idea Diegert was in trouble; she couldn't see him at all. Using the strength of his leg and abdomen, Diegert contorted himself such that he was able to grasp the edge of the truck's deck with his right hand. Fatima saw the exit for the airport and turned onto the ramp. The centrifugal force gave Diegert the chance to grasp a vertical handle on the upright edge of the truck's back end. With both hands having a grip, Diegert began to pull himself into the truck. Fatima was traveling so fast that when she hit a speed bump in the road, it violently jostled the entire vehicle and sent Diegert airborne.

Both his legs shot out behind him, and his right hand lost its grip on the edge of the deck. With only his left hand gripping the uphaul handle, the assassin was once again dangling off the back end, this time with his boots dragging on the road. Like a belt sander, the pavement was grinding the leather of his boots to dust. With all the strength that remained in his left arm, Diegert pulled on the handle. He got his right hand to the edge of the deck and hauled himself up. With a twist from his waist and a kick of his right leg, he pulled himself off the road and onto the floor of the truck.

He took one full breath, and the vehicle came to a stop. Fatima jumped out of the cab, came around to the back, and found Diegert sitting on the floor of the truck. "Quite a show with those skinheads, eh? Come on, don't just sit there, we've gotta go."

Diegert stepped down off the truck and boarded the waiting Gulfstream. The jet made an immediate departure, and the two operators were in the air when the police, with their lights and sirens wailing, surrounded the flower truck and took the groggy plant man into custody.

"That was too close," said Fatima, feeling quite satisfied with her driving. "What happened to your boots?"

"Abrasion. Hey, is there any of that wine left?"

Fatima went to the private cabin and came back with the bottle and tumblers. "I hope you'll still drink it out of these glasses?"

"Anything that holds liquid is fine with me."

Diegert gulped the first glass, and with raised eyebrows, Fatima filled it again. "I'm going to clean you up."

Diegert took a big swig of wine.

Fatima sat with her legs curled up under her while she cleaned his wounds and face. "How did you know the flower truck would be there?"

"I didn't."

"It was just luck?"

"It was improvisation. I figured some kind of vehicle would be back there. Maybe a laundry truck or food delivery, but flowers, I didn't expect that, and it didn't matter."

"Well, it certainly worked," said Fatima as she wiped away the black potting soil. "That was pretty clever of you to use that girl as a decoy."

"Yeah, more fortunate for us than her."

"I like working with you. This mission wouldn't have worked if we weren't together."

"You're right, being a team is important, and I'm going to ask you about something I think we can work on together. Tell me about Hamni, and don't go locking yourself in the back."

The fire and ice began to form on her face.

"You have a son, and he does not have his mother. I can tell you that my mother was very important to me when I was young. I relied on her way more than my father, and I was able to grow up OK because she was there."

Diegert slid forward on his seat, deepening his voice and looking into her eyes.

"You're important to him, and I want to help you get him back."

"By inserting yourself into this situation, you can only make things worse."

"Crepusculous has him, don't they? They have him, and they make you work for them."

"The best thing you can do is drop this and stop trying to be the hero to a little boy you've never met."

"I'm not trying to be a hero, but I am trying to help. Tell me what you know about the Board members of Crepusculous."

"I don't have anything to tell you."

"I can tell you two of their members: Dean Kellerman and Klaus Panzer."

"Good for you. I'm sure you'll have a seat at their table just as soon as you make a trillion dollars."

Chuckling, Diegert said, "That shouldn't take long."

"That will never happen," Fatima snapped. "These men were rich before they were born. Their power and money make us all their servants. You can deceive yourself into believing that you can do something to affect them, but the truth is, you're powerless. Hamni won't be back with me until I fulfill my obligations."

"And what are your obligations?"

Fatima took a long sip from her glass and struggled with her answer. "The requirements are always changing. First I am led to believe one thing, and then I'm told another. All the while there is a threat to my son if I do not comply. I love my son!" shouted Fatima. "By doing what is asked of me, I'm protecting him. If I fail, he dies."

Diegert remained silent for a moment. "I can see the devotion you have for him. But I can also see how Headquarters is manipulating you. Your strength and your determination are admirable, but they are also allowing you to endure this unfair situation too long while Hamni grows up without you. He won't know you if this continues. When did you last see him?"

Fatima was now choking back tears. She hated displaying her vulnerability and was torn between her belief of superiority and her feeling of camaraderie. She answered his question matter-of-factly. "I last saw him four years ago."

"How old was he then?"

"Five years old."

Diegert paused, thinking of the years. "We had better get that boy back soon."

Fatima fired, "Do you think I don't consider that every day?" She looked away from him. "I have him in my mind and in my heart every minute of every day until it becomes so heavy a burden I collapse under its weight. I sit and cry under its force, but I do not want the burden removed for fear I will then feel nothing for my son and he will be totally lost to me."

Fatima's eyelids could no longer hold back the tears that now streamed down her face. She did not sob, bellow, or blubber, but the tears rolled down her cheeks and dripped off her chin. Diegert handed her a napkin, witnessing the emotional turmoil with which Fatima lived.

She dried her tears, saying, "These men are light-years ahead of you. There is nothing you can do."

"I do not think like you. They are men, they are human, and they have weaknesses."

"Oh, cut the crap, men who crave and amass power cannot be stopped by their servants."

"You can't know how to defeat them if you do not know who they are. Tell me who you know on the Board, and we'll learn things about them."

"What do you mean you will learn things about them?" asked the skeptical lady.

"I can tell you that Dean Kellerman resides in a 130-acre English estate. His son is a drug addict, and his daughter runs a family-funded charity foundation. Klaus Panzer is not married but has two daughters. He's the true leader of the Board. I look at him like the kingpin in a drug cartel. Both of these guys are well protected and censor any media profiles. Kellerman always comes across as a devoted philanthropist, although his name is not on any buildings. Panzer is never in the media, but if we want to influence the Board, he's the one to be manipulated."

"How did you get this information and how do you know it's accurate? Anyone could post that bullshit on the Web to smear these guys."

Diegert felt the USB device in his pocket. He hesitated as he thought about trusting Fatima with the source he held between his fingers. He started this, so he figured he had to press forward.

"You're right, but this information comes from an insider."

Diegert pulled out the USB.

"What's that? You want to impress me with a piece of plastic?"

"On this device is the work of a mole who is no longer active. I have read the files, and this person was collecting data on the Board members and their plans."

"So what does it reveal?"

"I just shared with you two identities you would otherwise have never known. Now it is your turn to share something with me. Who do you know on the Board?"

Diegert could see her hesitation and waited while she struggled with her words until finally she spit out a name. "Julio Perez," she said, nearly choking as the name she'd shared with no one fell out of her lips. "He practically owns South and Central America."

"Very well, then, we'll see what we can learn about Mr. Perez and start the process of recovering your son."

Diegert relaxed back in his chair, stretched out his legs, and took another swallow of wine. He'd finally gotten her to crack, and he could now help her. Fatima looked surprised and disappointed. "Well, what do we do now?"

From his position of repose, Diegert said, "Whoa, there, cowgirl. We can't search for Board members at thirty thousand feet on my smartphone. It requires proprietary software, which I have on my computer in my room but not up here."

Leaning over and smiling at her, he said, "Don't worry—in my room I'll show you everything."

"In your room, you will show me only what I want to see, and that's the use of intelligence rather than bullets to get Hamni back so he won't grow up without me."

CHAPTER 47

"We may have a problem here," said Jake Diegert after reading a news story about the establishment of a digital currency by the corporate giant Omnisphere.

"What? What's wrong?" asked his father.

Digival was a new corporate currency being introduced around the world as an alternative to traditional government-issued money. It was independent of all countries and governments, and was sponsored by the world's largest and wealthiest corporation. Available in a digital-only format, it undermined the need for cash and created a digital record of every purchase. The replacement of cash as a means of making purchases concerned Jake.

"Dad, this new Digival stuff is a digital-only means of buying stuff."

"You mean like a credit card."

"Well, yeah, but it's not the card—it's the money behind the card. Instead of dollars, the thing of value will be Digival. Digital units that you have in an account that you shift to whoever you're buying stuff from."

"So?"

"So . . . when people buy drugs from us, they pay us cash. That way there is no record and people are anonymous. That's kinda important for what we sell."

"When does this stuff go into use?"

"It's already in use. So far, not too many people are using it, but the news says they expect use to grow quickly because Omnisphere is promoting Digival with huge incentives."

"Like what?"

"They'll increase your money ten percent when you switch from dollars to Digival."

"Wow, maybe we should change some of our cash."

"Negative. We are not changing to any form of money that can be tracked. We are so far under the radar that our business is practically invisible until we start making digital records of every purchase with every customer. No way are we going Digival."

"Do you have to buy a machine to do Digival?"

"No, it's all handled through an app on a smartphone."

Tom Diegert grabbed the chain connected to the belt loop on his pants and pulled his fat wallet from his pocket. Opening the thick black leather fold, he pulled out a wad of bills and flipped them with his finger, saying, "Well, then, fuck them. It's cold hard cash for me. Fuck them and their digital bullshit. As long as I have dollars, they will have to accept them, 'cause they're backed by the US government and nobody can take that away."

Jake, watching this display of patriotic delusion, deepened his frown as he said, "Yeah right . . . whatever, Dad."

***

In his room back at Headquarters, Diegert fired up Tor on his computer, input the required passwords, and began searching the darknet. The darknet shielded the accessing computer from network detection. This convenience allowed Diegert to search through it without arousing the attention of Headquarters' IT specialists. Julio Perez had an information file on the darknet, which meant facilitators had collected information on him but no contracts had been activated. Julio had a son named Julio Jr., who was born in 1963 but had died in 2003, when he'd crashed a Ferrari F430 in the countryside of Spain. Julio's first wife had divorced him when he was thirty-seven years old, and he remarried at age forty-five. He had two more children with his second wife: a daughter, Gabrielle, and a second son, Javier. Both of these children were living.

To find more about the two Perez children did not require the darknet. Instead, access to Facebook was granted through an intrusive app called frenemy. The program provided access as a friend on Facebook without having to ask. Both of the Perez children were clearly enamored with Facebook and YouTube. In fact, Gabrielle Perez had her own channel where she interviewed celebrities and other people she found interesting. She posted the videos and had enough of a following to have some advertising mixed in. She wore fashionable clothes and drove expensive cars, but she was rich, so what else would she drive? After watching some interviews on her YouTube channel, Diegert found her not as annoying as he'd expected. Her interview questions were interesting, and she let the people answer without interrupting. Not all the topics were significant, but she didn't seem as shallow as he'd anticipated.

Javier's Facebook, however, painted the perfect picture of the rich, partying playboy. The locations were exotic, the vehicles were big or fast or both, and everything was expensive. Cars, SUVs, yachts, he had them all and he photographed everything. His Facebook albums were organized under "Places," "Parties," "Toys," and "Girls." Diegert scrolled through the "Girls" gallery, which was organized by year. It looked like 2012 was a very good year. All the women were young, sexy, and gorgeous. 2011 was the same but with a few more Asian beauties. Year after year, this guy was never without the company of beautiful women. Diegert scrolled down to 2004. He looked through the pictures and suddenly stopped at a picture with Javier smiling and looking a little drunk while his arms were wrapped around a strikingly beautiful, dark-haired, spaghetti strap–dressed Fatima Hussain. Her face was unmistakable. He leaned back in his chair, saying to himself, "Fatima, you naughty girl."

CHAPTER 48

Returning to her room from a workout, Fatima was approached by Blevinsky. "Excuse me, I would like to speak with you," he said.

Fatima stopped and stood at attention, ready to listen to the Headquarters' director. Blevinsky recognized the respectful posture and told her, "Relax. Please walk with me."

They went outside to the grounds in the rear of the building. "I see the mission in Germany was a success."

"Collateral fatalities notwithstanding, I agree, we succeeded."

"Diegert was helpful?"

"Yes, he's an effective operator and has a keen capacity to improvise."

"What do you mean?"

"He turns obstacles into opportunities, and he has the skills and guts to try dangerous things and succeed. All traits which I believe are prerequisites for this type of work."

"Do you believe he's ready for a solo mission?"

"Is it an assassination?"

Blevinsky nodded his head, turned, and headed back toward Headquarters.

"Yes, I believe he is, and I'm confident he will accomplish the task and extract himself no matter what the circumstances."

"Thanks, I appreciate your candor and the training you have given him."

"Thank you, sir, I intend to fulfill my obligations."

At the entrance to the building, Blevinsky made one last remark. "Oh, by the way, I have heard from London, and Hamni has learned to ride a bike."

He smiled when he said it, as if he were some loving uncle bringing news from a summer vacation. Brooding on the false kindness in his voice, Fatima grew angrier as she walked back to her quarters. She burst into her room and slammed the door. She paced frantically and looked in the mirror at her angry reflection. She saw her own pain, her frustration, her maternal love withering on the vine. She was exhausted. The hurt turned into sadness, and the crying took control of her. She fell to the floor sobbing, convulsing, and releasing years of pain as she grieved the undelivered love for her son.

***

Much later that night, Blevinsky received a call from Klaus Panzer. "Aaron, are we ready to enact the initial phase of the plan?"

"Yes, sir, we are prepared."

"Indeed. How are the preparations for the third phase progressing?"

Blevinsky was afraid this question was coming. The third phase consisted of thermobaric explosives detonating simultaneously in several US cities. It required a single source of ignition that was free from the Internet yet operated by remote signaling from Europe. The ignition system had to be one that couldn't be interrupted or jammed by electronic countermeasures. A single source of satellite detonation was risky, but if implemented properly, it would undermine the electronic safety net upon which the US government relied. It was an audacious plan that would be devastating to the United States, but the logistics, the technology, the communication, and the coordination were all proving very difficult and time-consuming. Blevinsky found himself constantly tied to his computer and often having to come up with alternate plans when the originals failed. Worst of all, though, was the fact that the Board had put this project in the hands of an up-and-coming new member, the son of Julio Perez, Javier.

Blevinsky hadn't disliked the thirty-year-old playboy until he didn't answer his communications for days and any request for a phone conversation received only a text in response. Javier had a sense that being in charge meant you touched something once and it was done. The complexity of the explosives and the placement of them by confederates whose silence was absolutely necessary, as well as the sophistication of the signaling and detonation process, meant that this project had to be addressed and handled on a daily basis. Blevinsky was doing all the heavy lifting, but Javier had to be involved regarding expenses and major plan alterations. When these issues interrupted Javier's pursuit of fucking forty women in forty days, Blevinsky lost patience with the irresponsible son of a man who failed to instill any discipline in his heir apparent.

With all that in mind, Blevinsky responded to Panzer, "The project is proving very difficult, and changes are constantly being made to accommodate necessary adjustments."

"Are we on schedule? Now that we have begun, we must be ready to carry out each phase in a timely manner."

"Yes, of course. We are still on schedule, but, frankly, one of my biggest frustrations is with the man in charge of the finances."

"Javier," said an unsurprised Panzer.

"Yes, sir. He proves himself less interested in the business of the Board than the pleasures of his prick! If you will excuse my expression?"

"No . . . that's fine," replied Panzer. "Like many young men, that guy is distracted by sexual pursuits. He is the future leader of the southern hemisphere, though, so we do want him to develop."

"Sir, the success of the whole third phase hangs in the balance."

"I appreciate your concerns, Aaron, but I want Javier not only committed and responsible but culpable as well. I want his skin in the game when his father dies and power passes to him."

"Now I see, sir."

"With him activating the single-source detonation device, I'll have the kind of control that makes me welcome him to the Board of Crepusculous."

"Yes, sir," said Blevinsky, realizing once again that Klaus Panzer's actions always fulfilled a manipulative goal.

"If we start to fall behind, you let me know. Otherwise, take full charge. I'll see to it that all expenses are covered."

"Thank you, sir. It is a relief to have you aware of the situation and to have your support."

"Excellent! Proceed with the plan. One more thing, Aaron. I'd like to set up another job."

Blevinsky froze on the phone as he listened to Panzer.

"I'd like you to task a team with killing Michka Barovitz. I believe he's on his island in the Aegean this time of year."

Blevinsky still had no words as he contemplated the audacity of this man to ask for another job in the middle of preparing for this long-awaited primary mission.

"Do you think we have a window of opportunity now?" asked the German.

Going against his best tactical judgment, yet following his sense of Panzer politics, he replied, "Yes, of course, sir, we can carry out this sanction."

"This operation is not sanctioned by the Board. You're to carry it out directly under my orders and to keep the whole mission and all its information completely black."

"I understand. I'll gather the intelligence and put together the team. I'll inform you when the mission has been completed."

"Thank you, Aaron. I knew I could rely on you," Panzer said before disconnecting the call.

Although he presented a confident and reassuring demeanor to Panzer, Blevinsky knew that completing this mission without interfering with the other would require immediate action. He called Strakov.

"*Da.*"

"Alexi, I've just received orders for a priority sanction. Assemble a four-man team and report to the armory."

"*Da.*"

Blevinsky e-mailed Carl Lindstrom a directive indicating the kit required for each operator, as well as the vehicles the team would need. The knock on the jamb of his open office door drew his gaze to Diegert standing on the threshold. Neither man spoke for a moment until Blevinsky said, "You knocked, so why are you here?"

"I have something to ask you."

"What is it?"

"As a full operator, I believe I'm supposed to be paid for missions."

Directing his full attention on Diegert, Blevinsky asked, "Where'd you hear that?"

"Fatima."

Throwing his body back in his chair, Blevinsky said, "She's right, and so are you. If you don't ask, I won't pay you. It's a Balkan custom."

"Then I'm asking for a hundred grand."

Chuckling as he leaned forward, Blevinsky maintained eye contact with Diegert. "That's a little steep."

"That's what I got before I was brought here for training."

"Yes, but as a contractor, many of your expenses are your own. Now we are providing everything. You're not getting that much, try again."

"Seventy-five thousand dollars."

"Too much . . . again."

"Fifty thousand, and that's going low."

Blevinsky looked down at his desk and started speaking to the wood grain, "I'll pay you fifty thousand, but you have to do something more." Turning up to Diegert, he continued, "I have a mission that's taking form right now with Strakov leading a team. You join them, and fifty thousand dollars will be in your account when you return."

"If I don't?"

"You'll only get five thousand for pissing me off."

Diegert leaned against the doorjamb with his arms crossed over his chest.

"And I imagine Strakov doesn't know I will be on his team."

"He doesn't yet, but I'll take care of that."

"What's the mission?"

"If I tell you, you'll know before Strakov."

"I feel sooo special."

Blevinsky's brow wrinkled at Diegert's wisecrack, making his forehead look like a wide staircase leading to a bald spot.

"You're going to assassinate Michka Barovitz."

Diegert remained stoically still as his eyes narrowed at the mention of the Romanian mobster.

"Why didn't we kill him when we rescued the kid?"

"We didn't have orders."

"You want me on this because I know the casino?"

"No, Barovitz has a private island in the Aegean. We'll hit him there."

"Then why do you want me on this?"

"Because you proved to be resourceful in Germany, and you're the best fifth man I've got."

"Being on mission with Strakov and his gang, he'll probably take me out."

"Listen, you can't be afraid of anyone. This business requires bravery like no other. You have to bypass the fear and find a way to get the job done. Strakov will stay on mission. He isn't going to fuck around with you."

"Strakov makes decisions with a head full of hate. Your reassurance gives me no confidence. If he fucks with me, then he doesn't come back, agreed?"

Curling his lips into a bemused smile, Blevinsky replied, "It's a deal, and you two will both come back still hating each other."

CHAPTER 49

At the armory, Strakov arrived with Jaeger, Pierre, and Enrique. Lindstrom had their kits ready. Each man was outfitted in the latest generation of body armor. The suits incorporate RDP-composite materials into the garments. This material *reacted* to forces, *dissipating* energy to provide *protection* against trauma: RDP. The fabric was as comfortable to wear as cotton and could be fashioned into clothing of any design. When the fabric was exposed to sudden trauma, such as a bullet, it would stiffen by a factor of three hundred, providing projectile penetration protection. The four men were dressed in identical suits. The pants had kneepads built into them, as well as integrated thigh straps for the attachment of gun holsters and knife scabbards. The upper body jacket provided extra protection at the shoulders, and the sleeves had integrated gauntlets covering the forearms. The clothing was sleek and formfitting, not baggy or binding. Each man buckled on a utility belt with pouches carrying extra ammunition, explosives, Minicams, listening devices, and infrared infiltrative viewing mechanisms. Black tactical boots and gloves completed the outfit, complementing the thundercloud gray and black trim color scheme of the rest of the uniform. The weapons Lindstrom issued were H&K MP5 submachine guns with integrated laser sights. The weapons were outfitted with sound suppressors and extra-large magazines. An additional Glock 9 mm occupied the thigh holsters, so each operator was armed with a second weapon.

When Diegert walked into the armory with Blevinsky, the room turned silent as eyes looked at the American with surprise, curiosity, and disdain. Diegert could feel the derision with which his presence was being judged. He hoped that Blevinsky could see what a bad idea this was; instead, the operations director instructed Lindstrom, "Carl, I need you to put together one more kit for Diegert here."

Strakov exploded. "No fucking way! We're not adding him to the team now; we leave in thirty minutes."

Blevinsky's hands went up as he approached Strakov. The heavy bald man wrapped his arm around the big guy's shoulder and walked with him to the back of the armory. Away from the others, he told Strakov, "Relax, Diegert is good, you know that. You're going to assault with a four-man team; you'll need someone to guard the boat."

"We've got other men who could be added to the team."

"There's not enough time now. Diegert is it, and I want you to lead him like any other operator. Treat him as a team member and bring him home safe."

"You've really pissed me off."

Blevinsky's hand snapped out, grabbing a section of Strakov's beard between his thumb and forefinger, and he pulled the taller man's face down to his.

"You will treat him with respect or I'll have the next class of recruits hunt down your naked ass in the Proving Grounds."

Blevinsky slapped Strakov across the face with his other hand. "I don't care that you're my nephew, you will conduct yourself as a professional when you are on a mission. You will follow orders as they are issued and operate with the team that is assigned."

"*Da*," offered Strakov, who was still bent forward with his beard in Blevinsky's grasp.

"Good, now get back over there and get ready to go," said Blevinsky as he released Strakov's chin.

Strakov and Blevinsky returned to the staging area just as Lindstrom unzipped a black cloth bag and extracted a set of clothing for Diegert. The pants were black canvas with cargo pockets on both thighs. The shirt was a black Under Armour compression garment, and the vest was a Kevlar model that looked like it had already stopped several bullets.

Diegert's thoughts were spoken by Blevinsky's words, "Hey, where's Diegert's RDP suit?"

"We only have four of the new suits," replied the disappointed armorer. "This is the best we have. Just last month, we would have sent the whole team out in these."

Blevinsky's face softened, but Diegert's annoyed and disappointed expression deepened.

Strakov approached Lindstrom, Blevinsky, and Diegert. "Mr. Lindstrom," said the big Russian as he raised his hand to reveal a tactical night-vision scope. "Can I put this on Diegert's weapon?"

"You think he'll need night vision?"

"Yeah, I think it will be best for him to be prepared for any contingency."

"Alright, you can install it on his rifle over on the bench."

Diegert turned his head to watch Strakov walk to the workbench. Blevinsky slapped him on the back. "Go get changed; you're leaving right away."

At the workbench, Strakov installed the NV scope on the rifle's rail system. He sighted it and was able to see targets in the darkness. Then he opened the breech of the chamber and extracted the firing pin. This act of sabotage rendered the weapon useless in spite of the cool NV scope. He left the weapon on the bench as he stepped away with the small metal firing pin tucked in his pocket.

Wearing the black outfit, Diegert joined the others as they boarded the Sikorsky X2 helicopter. The aircraft had a dual rotor design overhead that provided tremendous stability and hovering capacity. A perpendicularly mounted rear rotor provided exceptional pushing power, making the X2 the fastest helicopter in the world. With a cabin capacity for six passengers, the helicopter accommodated all five of the operators. Once the team was secured, the craft took off. One and a half hours later, the helicopter delivered the team to the Aegean coastal port of Keramoti, Greece. There they loaded into a Zodiac for the thirty-minute ride to the island of Thesalonas, which Barovitz owned. The Zodiac had a unique seating system specially designed for riding through rough seas. The seats were designed to be straddled. They looked like little horses with a grip handle in front and a padded backrest. The boat could accommodate a crew of nine, so the team easily fit into the craft.

On board the Zodiac, Enrique stepped to the controls of the craft and fired up the 225 hp Honda outboard engine. For such a big, powerful engine, it was amazingly quiet, especially at low rpms.

The sky had darkened about an hour before, allowing the team to depart into the blackness of the night. As the boat progressed, a light rain began to fall.

The island of Thesalonas had a history of being owned by criminals. Slave traders, pirates, opium merchants, and now a mobster had all laid claim to the beautiful and secluded retreat. The exchange of the island had never occurred through a sale but rather a change of possession to fulfill a debt. Barovitz had gained control through the indebtedness of a particularly unlucky Greek gambler. To keep it protected, he had two guards occupying the island at all times, along with a full-time care-taker. When he traveled there, two additional guards accompa-nied him, along with two to three young women. Blevinsky had shared this information with the team, preparing them to take out four men along with Barovitz.

Enrique slowed the engine to a quiet purr as they approached the dock at Thesalonas. The rain was falling harder, but the lack of guards at the boat dock was a welcomed surprise. Barovitz had traveled to the island on a twenty-five-foot yacht, which was secured to the dock and currently unoccupied. As the Zodiac pulled up to the dock, Diegert jumped out and tied the ropes to the mooring cleats. The four Crepusculous opera-tors immediately formed into two-man attack teams and pro-ceed to the island. Diegert, with his assault rifle slung over his shoulder, prowled up the dock to inspect Barovitz's yacht.

The unguarded vessel beckoned exploration. Stepping onto the gangplank, he crossed the threshold and stole into the hold. Passing by the luxury seating, bar, and bedrooms, he made his way to the engine compartment. The big boat was powered by a truck engine, which Diegert disabled by remov-ing the distributor cap, leaving the spark plugs without the capacity for ignition. Back up on deck, he tossed the distrib-utor cap overboard, ensuring the vessel could not be used for an escape. With the rain persisting, Diegert decided to stay on board the yacht under the second-floor overhang.

Approaching the big house, Enrique and Pierre went north as Strakov and Jaeger proceeded to the south. When the teams could no longer see each other, they checked their comms.

"Bravo, this is Alpha," said Strakov.

"Copy," replied Pierre.

The main entrance to the house was to the south, and Strakov grew nervous when they were able to creep right up to the landscaped foliage and not encounter any guards. *Could we have been detected?* he thought. He was concerned their cover was blown and they would be walking into a trap. "Bravo, talk to me."

"I see two tables, four Tangos per table. Barovitz is here; they're playing cards."

Strakov realized that eight men were more than they had expected but not more than they could handle.

"Execute the plan."

"Copy."

Pierre and Enrique drew blocks of C-4 from their utility pouches and pasted them to the doorknob and the hinges. Igniting the volatile dough sent the door crashing inward, blowing the north entrance wide open.

The shock wave as well as wood shrapnel and metal hinges hit the first table of card players, knocking all four men to the ground. Enrique fired his weapon, ending their lives with four precision shots, before squatting on the floor, closing his eyes, and covering his ears.

The second table suffered ear-splitting decibels and sudden blindness when the flashbang Pierre tossed detonated amid the pot of poker chips. Uncovering his ears and opening his eyes, Pierre took aim at the disoriented men. He took down two with bullets to the head and neck. The third man raised his gun, firing at Enrique and striking him in the chest and shoulder. It was the third bullet, though, that pierced Enrique's neck, spraying blood across the room. Pierre saw Enrique fall as he shot the man who had wounded his comrade.

Barovitz recovered enough of his bearings to see that Enrique was down and that Pierre was moving toward the injured man. Stumbling to his feet, the mob boss awkwardly ran out through the north entrance around the west end of the house toward the dock.

Pierre called on the comm, "Man down, requiring medical assistance."

Strakov called back. "Target status?"

"Barovitz is mobile, moving in your direction."

"Copy," said Strakov as he and Jaeger crept closer to the south entrance, anticipating Barovitz's exit onto the veranda where they would lay waste to the arrogant mobster. As they trained their attention in front of them, Barovitz ran behind them toward the dock.

Being the team medic, Pierre rushed to Enrique in time to see a stream of blood pumping out of his neck. As he moved closer, he could see that the distance the blood spurted was declining with each beat. Enrique's life was exiting his body as Pierre pulled open his medical pack and stuffed the wound with gauze. Adhesive tape and manual pressure were not enough, though, to overcome the lacerated trachea and the torn carotid artery and jugular vein. Enrique's life was ending, but Pierre held pressure against the wound and fought death's pull on his comrade's soul.

From under the rain-protected overhang on the yacht, Diegert heard the flashbang and saw the shooting. After the violent firefight, he expected the strike team to return. The man who came running onto the dock was quite unexpected. Dressed in black pants and a white silk shirt, Barovitz was soaked by the rain, which had intensified as the attack ensued. Diegert ducked down behind the bulkhead of the galley, leveled his weapon, and focused on the target of Barovitz's chest through his NV scope. As the man came closer to the yacht, Diegert's confidence grew. When he pulled the trigger, he expected to see Barovitz go down, but instead, he only felt the compression of the mechanism with no reaction. With the target still in the scope, he tried to fire the weapon again, only to once again have the system fail. He unslung the weapon and checked its functions.

Arriving at the yacht's side, Barovitz moved his formerly athletic body as quickly as he could, untying the moorings and jumping onto the deck. He climbed the stairs to the second floor, making his way into the control room. Turning the key produced only an unproductive run of the starter motor. "Fuck!" shouted the frustrated man as he turned the key again, hoping to hear the ignition of the engine. *"Shisa,"* he cursed to no one but Diegert, who had crept up the stairs without his ineffective weapon and approached the doorway of the control room undetected. As Diegert looked in the entrance, Barovitz noticed the break in the line of the doorway and kicked the door. Diegert pulled back and blocked the door with his foot. He pushed the door back in with such force that it hit Barovitz in the head, lacerating his forehead.

Bleeding, Barovitz turned to face Diegert, who was ready to fight. He circled Barovitz, sizing him up, looking for vulnerability. Barovitz stepped past the boat's controls, reached his hand alongside the console, releasing the fire extinguisher, which he flung at Diegert. The heavy canister struck the forearm and the forehead of the American. Diegert staggered back but regained his composure only to see Barovitz extract a pistol from a drawer. The bullets whizzed past Diegert as he exited from the control room with the most evasive movements his instincts could produce.

Diegert sprinted to the top of the stairs. He grabbed the rails and slid down to the first floor. Barovitz rushed to the stairs, firing down. One of the bullets struck Diegert in the left shoulder, knocking him to the floor, where he crawled under the overhang. Barovitz descended the stairs with his gun in front of him.

Strakov and Jaeger, hearing the gunshots from the yacht, sprinted to the dock, arriving in a joint tactical approach. Strakov signaled Jaeger to reattach the yacht's ropes.

Barovitz searched the first floor. The blood trail was difficult to follow in the darkness, but he knew this boat better than anybody. He stepped into the luxurious quarters, turned on the lights, and fired into the front wall of the polished cherry bar. Splinters flew as bullets pockmarked the finish. Having spent half a clip, Barovitz stepped to the bar and peered over the heavily lacquered top. Diegert, grateful for the solid construction of the handsome bar, swung a liquor bottle from his hiding place below the bar's surface. The bottle smashed on Barovitz's head, showering him with glass and expensive liquor. As the stunned mobster stumbled back, Diegert vaulted over the bar, only to land on the piercing base of the broken bottle. The upward-projecting shards of glass tore into his boot and ripped through his foot. Diegert bellowed as the unexpected injury radiated pain throughout his lower leg.

Strakov and Jaeger entered the room. Barovitz grabbed Diegert, stepped behind him, and pointed his pistol at the two arrivals.

"Drop your guns and move the fuck back."

Strakov and Jaeger stood their ground, pointing their MP5s at Barovitz.

Moving the barrel of his pistol to the base of Diegert's jaw and shoving it hard enough to twist the American's head, Barovitz said, "Get the fuck out of here or I blow his head off."

Strakov fired two bullets into Diegert's chest, sending him backward and spinning out of Barovitz's grasp. Jaeger fired at Barovitz, hitting him in the forehead and imploding his skull, nose, and eye sockets. Barovitz fell back on the floor. Blood began to pool in the concavity that had replaced his handsome face.

Pierre appeared at the entrance. Strakov spun, turning his weapon on the man.

Raising his hands defensively, Pierre said, "Hold on, it's me, brother."

As Strakov lowered his barrel, Pierre stepped forward. "Enrique is dead." The Frenchman could see that Barovitz's wound was fatal, since his face looked like a bowl of sangria. Diegert was on the floor gasping for breath next to the bullet-blasted bar. Pierre assessed his medical condition, determining that the bleeding shoulder needed attention first; the foot required dressing, as well, but the worst thing affecting Diegert was his traumatic pneumothorax.

"How is he?" asked Strakov.

"He's bad. He's got at least one collapsed lung. I need the first aid kit from the Zodiac."

Strakov remained impassive, looking directly at Pierre. "Well, then, you better go get it." Pierre held the stare as he stood up and left the yacht.

Strakov felt the hate he had for the hotshot fucking American coalesce with the adrenaline pumping through his body as he placed his laser sight on Diegert's head. His finger trembled on the trigger as the desire to kill fought with what little sense of team cohesion he had. As he stiffened his arm and tilted his head to focus on the laser point, Jaeger stepped forward, placing his hand on Strakov's arm, saying, "Come on, let's go get Enrique."

Pierre passed his departing teammates as he returned to the yacht. At Diegert's side, he opened the kit and dressed both of his wounds, stopping the bleeding. Pierre looked at the white-and-black leather amulet with the footprint spanning both halves that was around Diegert's neck. Examining the reverse side, he was perplexed by the Ojibwa inscription. In spite of being fluent in French, English, Spanish, and German, he could find no meaning in the unfamiliar letters.

The force of Strakov's bullets had collapsed Diegert's lungs. The Kevlar vest had stopped the bullets from penetrating, but the concussive force separated the lung tissue from the inside of the chest wall. Tears in the lungs allowed air into the chest space that was compressing the lungs so they could no longer ventilate. Diegert was slowly suffocating as his lungs continued to deteriorate. Pierre knew he had to act fast.

CHAPTER 50

At the big house, Strakov and Jaeger surveyed the dead and realized there was a lot of money on the floor. Some of it was stained with blood, but it was all valuable and unaccounted for. Both men picked up bills, folded them into wads, and placed them in their pockets.

Strakov noticed the door movement first. Jaeger picked up on the sudden weariness of his partner, who signaled him to train his attention on the door to their right. Both men quickly stepped to opposite sides of the door. Strakov was on the entrance side. He could see a descending stairway beyond the door. Signaling Jaeger to pull the door open, he trained his rifle to shoot into the stairwell. When Jaeger pulled the door open, a woman's shriek blasted into the room. Strakov fired his weapon, but the bullet went high as he diverted the aim at the last second. The screaming continued down the stairs as the woman retreated, while more screaming echoed up from the building's basement.

The two baffled men looked at each other with relieved smiles as they stepped into the stairwell. The women were huddled in a back storage room. A woman of medium height with a shock of dyed pink hair stepped out from the storeroom, while a taller woman with shoulder-length dark hair and defiant dark eyes took a position in the storage room doorway.

"How many more of you are there?" asked Strakov as he flipped a glowing switch that turned on the hall lights.

Squinting against the sudden brightness, the woman with pink hair replied, "There's no need to hurt us. We're not the type to speak to the police."

Strakov leaned closer to her and peered beyond the taller one. "How many?"

The defiance slackened as Strakov's infectious menace diluted their bravery.

"There are five of us all together," stated the tall, dark-haired one.

"Get them all out here."

The women responded, and Strakov lined them up along the wall in the harsh light. They were all in their twenties with trim bodies featuring ample T & A.

"Do any of you have a weapon?"

Several said no, while others just shook their heads for fear that any speech would overwhelm their emotions, bringing on fits of crying.

"Give me your phones," ordered Strakov as he held out his hands and collected all five devices.

"You're the girlfriends of the men upstairs, aren't you?"

"We would've been . . . at least for tonight," answered the tall one with dark hair.

A sardonic smile crept over Strakov's lips.

"My partner and I'll be leaving this island. I don't want any of you coming out of this basement for two hours. You got that?"

The two invading tough guys turned to climb the stairs.

"You can't just leave us here," said the girl with pink hair.

Strakov stopped on the third step, turned back, and placed his laser sight on the girl's cleavage, saying, "You can stay down here and live or come upstairs and die."

The girl looked to the floor and stepped back in line against the wall.

Reaching the top of the stairs, Strakov directed Jaeger, "Set the charges."

Strakov reinvestigated the corpses by the overturned card tables. Looking at their firearms, he picked up a Taurus 24/7 tactical .45. The grip felt right in his hand, and a full magazine was an extra bonus. The next man's weapon was an HK P2000. This weapon was commonly carried by police officers. Digging into the dead man's coat pocket, Strakov pulled out his wallet to find his police badge. Officer Hiro Eliglanis, Athens Police. Strakov pocketed the weapon and the badge.

"The charges are all set," announced Jaeger upon his return. The two men walked out the south entrance, stepping onto the veranda where their attention was drawn to the field in front of the docks. They both looked up at the whirling rotors of the X2 helicopter that had taken them to Keramoti as it lifted off the island and turned north, heading back to Greece. "What the . . ." was all Strakov could manage to say.

***

Pierre had acted fast; he knew Diegert was tough, but even the toughest would die without sufficient oxygen. Calling the helicopter to evacuate them back to Headquarters seemed like the most prudent and appropriate action. Diegert was unconscious, and his breathing was becoming more shallow and irregular. He needed the staff and equipment of a true medical facility. *Fuck Strakov,* thought Pierre.

CHAPTER 51

In flight, Diegert's skin began to turn grayish blue. His life was ebbing away as the helicopter sped toward Headquarters. Although he lay on a stretcher unconscious, a dark, cold sensation ran over Diegert, making him aware of someone's presence. He looked around in the darkness and could see no one. He couldn't see or feel his own body, but he was able to move and look in all directions. The darkness seemed to be in front of him, but it had a distant, faded aura around it that made him feel like there was a huge black circle in front of him. *What is this?* he questioned. *What's going on? Where am I?* From the left, he saw a man appear, dressed in black clothing. The man's face and body emerged as he walked right by Diegert without acknowledging him. The face was old and lined in deep crevices, but the walk was brisk and powerful.

"You're a conflicted man, David Diegert," said a voice from behind him. Turning to the right, Diegert was startled to be spoken to, yet now he saw nothing but darkness. "You're blinded by greed and obstinacy." Diegert turned to the voice immediately in front of him and looked into the dark eyes and skin framed by thick gray hair parted in the middle and pulled back into a ponytail. The face was aged, but the energy of this man radiated into Diegert and commanded his attention. The mouth did not move, but the message was as audible and clear to Diegert as any words ever spoken. "You have a spirit you do not recognize, and it is fighting for you. It will not give up on you, but you are pushing it away and challenging its loyalty."

Confused and angry, Diegert shouted, "Fuck this spirit bullshit, what does it want?"

Pierre looked at Diegert, surprised to hear him speaking while he remained unconscious.

The motionless face answered Diegert's question. "Acceptance is what the spirit has always sought. You must ask it into your life."

"I don't want it," retorted Diegert. "Who the hell are you?"

"I am the Anishinaabe, and I can only guide those who are willing to follow."

The face faded into blackness and spoke to Diegert again from behind.

"I'm afraid you have many dark deeds ahead of you, David."

"Does that mean I'm not going to die?" asked Diegert.

"Not today, but if you die as you are, living in darkness, your spirit will never find the light, never join the Anishinaabe."

Diegert turned to the voice behind him, but the face was not to be seen.

"Your amulet's inscription, 'A man must travel through the darkness to find the light,' implies that you must seek the light and not get lost in the darkness."

"Show me the light, then, give me the directions," demanded Diegert.

The voice replied, "You have been given all you need, but you must accept and look through eyes of hope rather than fear. *Ondaas minawaa.*"

Diegert opened his eyes into the blindingly bright light of the cabin interior. The sound of the rotors and the movement of the helicopter entered his sensory neurons, informing him he was still alive and inside an aircraft. Turning his head, he saw Pierre, who placed a reassuring hand on his shoulder. "You're going to be alright. Did you have a bad dream?"

Diegert nodded and laid his head back down for the rest of the flight.

***

On the dock at Barovitz's island, the zipper pulled together the sides of the body bag enclosing Enrique's remains. Grasping the bag's handles, Strakov and Jaeger lifted their fallen comrade into the Zodiac. Before setting off for Keramoti, Strakov ignited the charges Jaeger had set around the house. The explosions blew out the critical support structures of the first floor, collapsing the entire second floor and roof. Several fires broke out, and soon the once-grand house was a conflagration of flames and smoke.

The Zodiac's engine accelerated, and the inflated boat pulled away from the island, leaving behind the dead and dying. Strakov radioed Lindstrom and ordered a van to be sent to the port. He and Jaeger would drive back to Headquarters transporting Enrique.

***

In medical, Diegert was recovering under the care of Physician's Assistant Henry Bellsworth, whose supervising physician was in London and communicated with Henry only when absolutely necessary. Henry enjoyed his job because he got to practice as a doctor and only had to go to school for four years.

"How are you doing today, Mr. Diegert?"

Opening his eyes to a groggy sense of awareness, Diegert squinted as he adjusted to being conscious.

"I'm alright."

"Your vitals are looking good, how's your ventilation?"

Taking a careful breath, Diegert replied, "I can breathe, if that's what you mean."

Placing his stethoscope in his ears, Henry instructed Diegert, "I want you to sit up so I can listen to your lungs."

Diegert slowly rose to a seated position while Henry placed the bell of the stethoscope on his back. "Take a deep breath for me."

Diegert drew in a deep breath, and when he began to exhale, he started coughing so violently that Henry had to help him lie back down, and it took several minutes until his breathing returned to normal.

"Mr. Diegert, you've suffered two collapsed lungs, a dual pneumothorax. I have corrected the immediate condition, but your lungs are not yet healed. You also have a gunshot wound to your left shoulder and lacerations to your right foot. The healing challenges you face are substantial."

"You mean, I'm going to be here awhile," Diegert croaked.

"In a normal situation, that would be true, but we have treatments not available to the typical patient. Crepusculous funds a venture called Creation Labs. It is a biotech facility specializing in the science of human enhancement."

Diegert nodded.

"I'll be administering a treatment called Healix. This medication is a form of rapid reactive stem-cell therapy. You have heard of stem cells, right?"

Diegert nodded again, although he really knew very little about cells.

"The stem cells are sensitive to cytokinetic signals your body is releasing from all the injured tissues. Reacting to these signals, the stem cells differentiate into the type of proteins necessary to complete the healing process. Having stem cells turn into the right kind of cells right at the site where they are needed speeds up the healing process tremendously. The quicker you heal, the quicker you're back to normal without so much down time for recovery."

Diegert shrugged his shoulders and gave an affirming nod but not a smile.

Henry continued, "Creation Labs makes the kind of medicines everyone could have if people weren't so bunged up about stem cells. Crepusculous has enough resources that it funds its research without any government money. You're lucky to be on the right side of this issue, and you'll see how good you're gonna feel when Healix has done its job."

Healix hadn't started its job just yet, and Diegert felt like shit. "Hey, until Heal-afix starts working, you got something to take off the edge?"

Henry administered a dose of morphine into Diegert's IV, and within minutes, the pain and discomfort disappeared and the aching man fell fast asleep.

***

In Blevinsky's office, Pierre sat waiting for ten minutes. He contemplated the conversation he was about to have and realized the truth was on his side and Strakov was the one who'd fucked up. Although he knew Strakov had shot Diegert, he had no evidence, so he would share only the facts. Blevinsky walked in and took his seat behind his desk. He pulled up Pierre's report on his screen and began. "So tell me in your own words what happened on the island that led you to request the helicopter?"

"While still at the house, I heard shots coming from Barovitz's yacht. I arrived to find Barovitz dead and Diegert injured."

"Injured by gunshots?"

"Yes, and he also had a lacerated foot."

"Who shot Diegert?"

"I do not know; perhaps it was Barovitz."

Blevinsky cast a doubtful look, but Pierre refrained from reaction.

"Then what?"

"I administered medical treatment to Diegert, dressing his wounds and stabilizing his collapsed lungs as best I could."

"Collapsed lung?"

"Yes, both lungs, actually. The bullet strikes to his chest were not penetrating, but they damaged the underlying lung tissue and he was suffocating."

"Where were Strakov and Jaeger?"

"They'd returned to the house, and I was unable to contact them. Diegert was dying, and I knew he wouldn't survive a boat ride. I radioed the helicopter, which arrived in minutes, and loaded Diegert. If we'd not flown straight here, I'm certain he would've died."

"But you did leave your teammates on the island."

"They had the Zodiac, and I know the two of them to be very capable men who can adjust to circumstances and succeed no matter what the challenge."

"That's quite an endorsement."

"I hope they would say the same about me, and if similar circumstances ever require it, I would gladly stay behind in order to save an injured comrade."

"Diegert is a comrade, now is he?"

Pierre looked at Blevinsky with quizzical surprise. "Of course he is; he was on the mission with us, and I believe he was the first to confront Barovitz, and he suffered for it."

"Well, I'm glad teamwork is the name of the game, and I'll be sure Diegert knows who he has to thank for his life. That'll be all. You've got no duty call tomorrow. Take it easy."

"Thank you." Pierre rose out of his seat and asked Blevinsky one more thing. "Has there been any contact from Strakov and Jaeger?"

"That's nice of you to ask. Mr. Lindstrom sent a van to the port at Keramoti; the two of them'll be driving back with Enrique's body. I imagine they'll be here tomorrow."

Pierre nodded as he left the office, walked down the hall, and pulled out his phone. He texted Strakov: *You're in the clear with Blevinsky. Diegert has survived, drive safe.*

Strakov replied: *Thanx and FU.*

***

After a good night's sleep, Diegert woke up feeling surprisingly better. While he'd slept, the pluripotent stem cells contained in the dose of Healix responded to the chemotactic signals released by the injured cells in his body. Following the trail of signals, the stem cells traveled to the areas of injury and transformed into the specific cells needed for damage repair. The specificity of this process allowed Diegert to heal at a rate ten times faster than he would have in an untreated state. His muscles, blood vessels, and skin were repairing themselves in an accelerated fashion. Even the inside lining of his lungs, damaged by the concussive force of the bullets, was reattaching itself to the chest wall, improving his breathing by the hour. When Henry Bellsworth checked in on him, he was very impressed.

"Damn, boy, you are healing fast. The stuff I gave you is good, but you're going to be up and active in record time."

"Not fast enough for me."

"You really have no clue, but today you're staying here in medical. Is there anything I can get for you?"

"I'd like a phone to make a long-distance call."

"*Long distance?* I never took you for being that old. I'll get you a phone."

When Henry returned and gave him the phone, he also gave him privacy by closing the door to his room.

After failing several times to get his mom on her phone, Diegert reluctantly called his brother. "Yeah?"

"Hey, Jake, it's me, David."

"David Dipshit, David Douche Bag, David Dickhead. What the fuck are you doing calling me?"

"Look I tried to reach Mom, but she isn't answering. Where is she?"

"You're such a fuckup. How do you think it's going here in this town with my dishonorably discharged brother on the news for murder and running from the law, huh?"

"Screw you, you fat fuck. Where's Mom?"

"It's killing Dad, ya know. He can't go anywhere without people asking him about you or just plain avoiding him. The tow-truck business is drying up because of you."

"Look, are you going tell me where Mom is or what?"

"She's not here."

"Shit . . . when will she be back?"

"We don't know because . . . we don't know where she is."

"What do you mean you don't know where she is?"

"She didn't come home from work three days ago, and we haven't heard from her."

"Three days! You've called the police, right?"

"We reported it late yesterday, but believe me, the mother of America's Most Wanted isn't a high priority with the Broward County cops. You're a real selfish bastard to call her."

"Don't call me that."

"I'll call you whatever the fuck I want, but a *bastard* is what you really are, and now the half-breed whore from whom you spawned is probably out getting knocked up again."

Diegert remained silent as the urge to crush the throat of his idiot brother boiled inside him.

"Hey, David . . . David Dog Shit . . . You still there? I'm sure the county sheriff would be very happy to hear from you about this case. In fact, it might be kind of suspicious not to hear from you regarding your missing mother. I guess you'll just have to keep an eye on the news and learn what happened to the slut when everybody else does. I'll let Dad know you called, and fuck you, you bastard."

Diegert heard the call disconnect, and he slid his phone away from him across the top of the bedside table. Holding his forehead in his palm, he scratched his scalp and gripped a handful of hair. He tugged on it till it hurt and then slammed his fists on the bed frame. Staring across the room, he realized how little he could do. His mother was smart. His mother was resilient. But what if Jake or his father had harmed her? Jake called her such awful names. Could they have hurt her? He accessed the Internet on his phone and searched for the Broward County police blotter, but there was no report of a missing woman. Why would her disappearance remain unreported? Had they really called the police? He couldn't call the police himself; they would trace his call and track him down. It was frustrating to have the one person he really cared about, and who cared about him, missing. That good feeling he'd had when he'd woken up quickly dissipated.

After twenty-four hours of resting in bed and worrying about his mother, Diegert had a visitor. Fatima strode into the hospital room dressed in black, looking strong and fit.

"I heard you were cleared for visitors."

Diegert couldn't keep from smiling, and his lips cracked a bit since he hadn't curled them up in such a long time.

"Thanks for coming," his unused voice croaked.

"You're looking better than I thought you would . . . physically, anyway."

"Yeah, they've got great medicine here."

"Well, then, what's bothering you?"

"What do you mean? I'm fine."

"You sure there isn't something bothering you?"

Being revealed by her made him uncomfortable, which she quickly picked up on.

"If you don't tell me what's wrong, I can't help you."

Diegert struggled with what to say while Fatima waited patiently.

"Alright, you know how important my mother is to me."

Fatima nodded her head.

"She's missing, and I can't find anything about where she might be, and I'm afraid my dad and brother might have hurt her."

Fatima pulled out her smartphone. "Denise, right?"

"Yeah."

Fatima tapped and stroked her screen. "Minnesota?"

"Uh-huh."

"What's her cell phone number?"

Diegert gave it to her. Quiet and focused for the next several minutes, Fatima concentrated on her screen. Diegert was restless with anticipation. He wanted to know where his mother was, but he feared the only thing Fatima would find was a report of a dead body.

"I can see a lot of activity on her phone in Broward County."

"Right, that's where she lives."

"The last recorded activity was in Minneapolis."

"Minneapolis? That doesn't make sense; she would never go there."

"If your father and brother were going to hurt her, would they have taken her there?"

"No way; the two of them would never go to the cities."

"Well, then, they probably didn't do anything to her."

"Probably."

"What do you think happened?"

"I don't know, but it's weird for her to be in Minneapolis. Can you see who she called? Can you tell how long she was there?"

"No, this software is not that sophisticated. It only traces the GPS locator on her phone. It can't tell if she's there, but her phone is."

Diegert leaned back against the pillow, brought his fist to his chin, and thought that, while Fatima was very helpful, he really couldn't draw any conclusions from what she had discovered.

"Thanks, I appreciate your help. I think I'm going to get out of here in two more days."

"Good. It'll be good for you to get back on your feet, back in the game."

Diegert nodded as Fatima squeezed his hand, gave him a little smile, and left. As she exited the room, he couldn't help but think how unlike a game this all was.

***

Two days of driving brought Strakov and Jaeger back to Headquarters. They turned over the van to Lindstrom, who also took care of disposing of Enrique's body. The muscular Spaniard's death would go unreported and unrecorded outside of the compound. The industrial furnaces that provided the complex with heat also served as a crematorium where the temperatures were so hot that there would be no remains to scatter.

After submitting his after-action report and eating a good dinner, Strakov was relaxing in his room. The big Russian's room was larger than the one Diegert occupied. The extra space afforded Strakov room for a couch and a large-screen TV. The TV was connected to the Internet so that entertainment was not limited to just a laptop. As Strakov streamed his favorite show, he was interrupted by a knock on the door.

Through the narrow space created when opening the door, Strakov was perturbed to see Blevinsky's face. Blevinsky pushed the door open, pressing his hand into Strakov's chest as he entered the room.

"What are you doing here?"

"Just a welcome-back visit. Actually, I've read your report and I'm just seeking clarification," said the round, bald man as he looked around the room. Strakov hated the way this intruder was tacitly inspecting his private quarters.

"I'd like you to tell me what happened on the yacht."

"Jaeger shot Barovitz."

"Did you provide any assistance?"

"Like it says in my report, I removed the shield the coward was hiding behind."

"How did you remove this shield?"

Strakov bent his elbow, pointing his hand like a gun, saying, "With propulsive force."

Blevinsky tilted his head, put a smirk on his face, and bore down on the bigger man with his unflinching eyes.

"Look, I knew he had Kevlar," admitted Strakov.

"It's only thanks to Pierre that he's not dead," Blevinsky said.

"If he had died, I would happily consider the mission a complete success."

Blevinsky straightened his gaze and narrowed his eyes. "We've been planning an important mission for a long time now, and in this folder"—Blevinsky raised his hand, in which he held a manila folder—"is your briefing." As he handed the folder to Strakov, he stepped over to a small table at the side of the couch. Blevinsky picked up the Taurus pistol and the HK P2000. "What are these doing here? There are no weapons in the complex outside of the armory. You know that."

Strakov averted his vision to the ceiling, rolling his eyes and sighing.

"Where did these come from?"

Strakov brought his head down but kept his eyes diverted from Blevinsky's.

"Collateral acquisitions."

"You mean the guns of dead men."

Blevinsky pulled back the slide on the Taurus, emptying the chamber, and snapped out the clip. "Fully loaded as well."

Strakov closed his eyelids, slowly turning his head while reopening his eyes to direct his gaze on Blevinsky, but said nothing.

"The rules of engagement inside Headquarters disallow fratricide."

"I don't consider him a brother."

Leaning in, Blevinsky replied, "I don't care." Pointing his finger into his own chest, he continued, "You are in my house and will follow my rules."

Tilting his head back and looking down on his upset uncle, Strakov asked, "What about outside of your house?"

Picking up the two pistols, Blevinsky crossed the room, saying, "Read your mission briefing and be ready." At the door, he stopped to say, "And stay off the gay porn."

CHAPTER 52

After being released from medical, Diegert returned to his small room, slept in his narrow bed, ate in the cafeteria, worked out in the gym, and presently was shooting on the target range. He assumed the role of a trained operative without a mission. It was strangely satisfying and frustrating at the same time. All the training was fun but had little meaning without a mission, but having a mission meant he was going to have to kill someone. Damned, both ways. He distracted himself by rattling off three-round bursts on the MP5. Later that night before falling asleep, Diegert got a text from Blevinsky.

Meet me in my office tomorrow morning 0800.

Diegert got up at 0530, which gave him time to exercise and eat breakfast. When he arrived on time, Fatima was already sitting across from Blevinsky. "Good morning," began the director.

Diegert just nodded and sat down. Perturbed, Blevinsky chastised him, "It is customary to return a greeting."

"Oh . . . good morning, sir."

"Thank you."

Looking at Fatima and back at Diegert, Blevinsky continued, "I am assigning you a mission that is crucial to the

Crepusculous business plan, and requires your skills and abilities."

"OK, what's the plan?"

"That's on a need-to-know basis."

"Yeah . . . but aren't we the ones who need to know?"

"You are, but you only need to know when it's necessary."

Quickly deciphering what Blevinsky was saying, Diegert replied, "You mean, I don't get the whole picture. I only get to know what to do just before I do it?"

Blevinsky smiled, realizing he wasn't going to have to explain it to him. "Correct. Fatima will be accompanying you, and you will have to see the armorer and go to medical for special equipment. One piece is particularly interesting." Blevinsky was excited to tell Diegert about whatever it was. "You will be fitted with a tympanic transponder. This nanotechnology communication device is a microparticle that, when affixed to the tympanic membrane, your eardrum, can transmit waves directly into the ear without an audible signal to be heard by others. The transponder can also transmit your voice through the interpretation of bone vibrations."

Blevinsky looked like a kid with a new game app. "Medical will fit you with the device, and we will be in constant communication."

"Great."

"You will leave the day after tomorrow, and remember, when you're operational, it is always mission first."

"Yes, sir, you got that last line right off the cob, didn't you?"

"Forget the wiseass shit, you were brought here and put through this training specifically for this mission. It is your destiny here, and I expect you to perform with excellence. Now you're scheduled in medical at 1030 and at the armory at 1300. Get going and have a good day."

Walking with Fatima from the office, Diegert asked, "So what do you know that I don't?"

"I know that you won't know until I tell you. That is all I'll tell you." She smiled with obvious satisfaction.

He rolled his eyes, turned the corner, and walked away from her. At the cafeteria, he got a hot cup of coffee and walked down to the armory. Lindstrom was reloading bullets.

"I have you scheduled for 1300."

"Well, here I am, and here's a hot one for ya."

Diegert put the coffee down on the bench next to the skinny gray-haired man.

"I'll take over the bullets if you tell me what you've got for me."

"Deal. You get started. I'll get the hardware."

Diegert had reloaded nearly a hundred bullets before Lindstrom came back. "That took a while."

Lindstrom, holding a hard plastic case in hand, looked at Diegert's production. "Oh . . . I thought you'd be further along."

"What's in the case?"

Lindstrom opened the cover, revealing a Desert Eagle .50-caliber pistol cushioned in custom foam. Immersed in the surrounding foam were ammunition magazines and another piece that Lindstrom extracted first.

"This sighting mechanism is a computerized decision-maker. It calculates all the data regarding the probability of a projectile to strike a target, and it chooses the time to fire the bullet. All we need is an agent to get in range of the target."

"I've actually used this sort of thing before, but it was controlled remotely from a tablet."

"Oh, yes, the True-Shot system," said Lindstrom. "We have that, but it has not been deemed functional for this mission. This works similarly, but you will have to aim at the target. Once locked on, the computer will alert you when it's time to take the shot." The armorer handed Diegert the device. Holding it by the mounting clip, he looked through the small optical lens next to the cube-shaped plastic box that housed the computer. Lindstrom continued, "The ammunition is unique as well. Inside the projectile is a guidance chip that seeks the target. Both the gun and the bullet are guided by an invisible laser. The laser is so small that human eyes can't see it, but its signal can be detected by the computer and the chip in the bullet."

Lindstrom looked up at Diegert. "Lasers, computers, microchips; you can't miss with this thing, and the force of the .50 cal will completely destroy any human target."

"Do I get to practice?"

Lindstrom tilted his head down and looked at Diegert from above his glasses. "Practice what? All I'm going to do is show you how to assemble it, activate it, and point it; the thing does the rest."

Diegert brought the sighting mechanism back to his eye and pointed it at a drill press across the room. The computer indicated a lock on the target, and when Diegert moved the mechanism, the reticle in the telescopic sight remained aimed on the drill press. After watching it function through the eyepiece, he looked up at Lindstrom.

"Any questions?"

"Is this the unit I'll be using?"

"No, a duplicate will be supplied to you when you need it."

Lindstrom returned the sight to the case and closed it up. "Back to bullets, please."

Diegert stood up from the reloading station. "Sorry, I've got an appointment in medical. Thanks for seeing me early. Enjoy the coffee."

"Hey . . . good luck on your mission."

In medical, the insertion of the transponder only took a couple minutes. The medic tested the reception, and Diegert could hear incoming communication easily, and the technician heard his voice with no difficulty. "Hey, how do I turn this thing off?"

"You don't."

"Is there some kind of a program that controls its transmissions?"

The medic thought for a moment and then looked at his tablet. "Well, yeah, there's an app here that I use to measure and adjust things."

"Great," said Diegert. "Please send the app to my phone."

When the app popped up, Diegert scrolled through it. With a satisfied look on his face, he thanked the medic and left.

***

Unlike other missions, when they left with all their gear and flew on the Gulfstream, Diegert and Fatima boarded a commercial flight and flew to London. At Heathrow, they boarded a flight to Montreal. Diegert carried a Canadian passport that identified him as Jacques Le'Prue. When asked, he said he was a resident of Chibougamau, Quebec. Fortunately he had practiced saying the town's name a few times. Fatima had made certain they were not sitting together on either of the flights, but avoiding Diegert wouldn't be so easy on the next leg of their journey, a nine-hour drive to Windsor, Ontario.

Diegert didn't understand why they hadn't just flown to Windsor, but then again, each leg of this entire mission was not revealed until he needed to know about it. He'd only found out they were going to Windsor because Fatima hadn't shut off the voice on the GPS system fast enough. They shared the driving, switching every couple of hours. During Fatima's stretch between Kingston and Toronto, Diegert began, "When we were discussing Hamni the other day, I failed to ask you one very important question."

Fatima looked at him, saying nothing.

He continued, "I didn't ask who Hamni's father was."

It seemed as though Fatima had anticipated this question, because she had no reaction at all. She had learned that Diegert got information by asking probing questions and relying on emotional reactions for answers. So this time she gave none.

Diegert tried another angle. "When I was in school, seventh grade, one day I stayed late working on a science project or something. Anyway, I was waiting for my ride home outside the school and these older boys, high school seniors, were there. They started picking on me. There were four or five of them, and they were having fun bullying me. The biggest one suggested a wedgie. Do you know what that is?"

Fatima shook her head.

"It's when someone grabs the back of your underwear and pulls it up out of your pants and over your head."

Fatima squirmed uncomfortably at the thought. Picking up on her reaction, Diegert said, "Yeah . . . it hurts. But it's also humiliating."

Diegert was quiet for a moment as he relived the memory. "There I was, though, other kids coming around laughing or scurrying away so they wouldn't be next. I was all alone with my tormentors. Then my mom pulls up. She sees what's going on, and she marches up to the biggest one, who was yanking on my pants. She yells at him to stop and pushes him away from me and slaps him across the face. Not just once, but, like, four times. The other kids were in shock, and so was I. The big guy ran away and we drove home. That night she took me to the YMCA and signed me up for a karate class. I was so grateful. She gave me the opportunity to develop the skills to defend myself, and that really boosted my confidence. I hadn't even realized what a scared little person I was until I took those classes and learned what it meant to face my fears."

Fatima asked, "Where was your father during all this?"

"My father really didn't like me. I didn't know why until years later, but I always knew he didn't. He preferred my brother, and his dislike for me was demonstrated on a regular basis. Neither my mom nor I ever mentioned the incident. He didn't care about the YMCA thing as long as I got all my chores done. She was my protector. She was my parent, and I owe a lot to her for making sure I survived my childhood."

Both of the car's occupants were quiet and contemplative. Diegert thought of the fact that his mother was now missing and there wasn't much he could do about it. He had faith in her resilience, but he doubted his brother's and his father's innocence in her disappearance. The conflict gnawed at him, but he knew that soon he would have to focus on his mission.

Fatima broke the quiet. "Hamni was born premature. Four weeks early. He may not have gotten the best prenatal care, so out he came not quite ready for the world. In the emergency room, they put him in a special box so he could breathe and gave him medicine to help his lungs. The doctor in charge knew I didn't have insurance or any money. He suggested that I consider the baby's future. Would I like to just hold him and let him pass peacefully?"

The determination began to show on Fatima's face. "I told him I had a mother's love and that he had better do everything possible to save my child's life. That if my child died, I would not only sue him but track his family down and hurt them."

She felt the strength of that long-ago threat and realized now how outrageous it was, as well as how desperate. "That doctor's eyes popped open, and he went right to work ordering medicines and procedures and everything they had to help Hamni."

She smiled and almost giggled, thinking back to her feisty younger self. "I was there every day at the hospital. Taking care of him and making sure he got what he needed."

"Giving him his mother's love."

"He ended up with some developmental delays and continued to need medical care after we were discharged from the hospital."

"Where was his father during all this?"

Fatima could feel the manipulation, and she could see what Diegert had done to ease into getting the information he wanted. Still, it felt good to talk about Hamni and the challenges of his early days. "He was out where he always was, with a hundred other women. He was a very irresponsible man and was completely unaware of Hamni's birth. I know you want me to tell you who he is, but I suspect you already know. The world no longer allows the keeping of secrets."

Diegert could see there was no advantage to continuing the ruse. "Javier Perez," he said. "How did you meet him?"

"At a wild frat party. He was so handsome, so confident, and every girl in the place wanted him. It becomes an unconscious competition when a man that desirable is in the presence of several women. You begin pursuing him just so you get him before the other girls do. It's stupid, and you will do stupid things, but you want to win. I won that night. We had sex upstairs in someone's bedroom. He was good. He would come and get hard again and fuck me again and again. I had never been with a man who could recover so quickly and get hard again, you know?"

Diegert barely nodded.

"When he was finally done, that was it, he said good-bye and walked out. He left me undressed in some stranger's bed. I realized right then what a mistake I had made. I wanted to forget the whole thing. I wanted to pretend it hadn't happened.

As I dressed, I noticed a watch on the nightstand next to the bed. It was engraved on the back: *To my dear son, Javier, may time always be on your side. Love, Julio.* The watch was a Rolex, of course. I put it in my pocket and left the party. A month later, I realize I'm pregnant, and soon my parents are furious with me. They are not strict Muslims, but Pakistani culture does not tolerate promiscuous sexuality, and an unwed pregnancy was absolutely shameful. My father wanted to perform an abortion himself. I had to leave. I lived with friends until the birth, and then I lived in a shelter. It was awful being homeless with Hamni, and his special needs were very expensive. Debts were mounting. I had to do something. Javier lived in a grand home in Sussex. It was fenced, guarded, and under camera surveillance. I got past all of that and into his private quarters. I told him we had sex, I got pregnant, and he now had a son. I showed him pictures of Hamni. He laughed and said it was all a lie, and that's when I quoted his watch: 'May time always be on your side. Love, Julio.'"

He realized I wasn't lying and asked what I wanted. I told him I needed money for his son's medical bills. I didn't tell him how troubled Hamni was, but I figured this guy had no clue about medical expenses or the needs of a special child. I told him how much money I needed, and only then did he ask how I got into his place. He was amazed that I was able to bypass all his security and get to him. He agreed to help me, but I would have to do something for him. We agreed to meet the next day, but he insisted I leave and exit his home without being detected. Which I did. The next day we met, he had set up an account I could use for Hamni, and he introduced me to Blevinsky. Headquarters had been looking for female operatives. Blevinsky gave me some trials to perform and had me shoot at a range, and soon I was recruited into service. Hamni was placed in a home where he receives the special care he requires."

"A deal made with the devil."

"Maybe, but, you see, I had to do what was necessary for my son."

"How about Javier? Do you have any communication with him?"

"Not very often, but at least he knows who I am now."

"Julio's the man, though. He's the member of the Board you told me about."

"Yes, but he is old and in poor health. Javier is the one who will take over the business."

"Business? It's more like an empire. Is he up to the job?"

"Hopefully, he has matured. Otherwise, it will be a mess."

"Somehow I don't think the other Board members are going to let things become a mess." After pausing, Diegert asked, "Does he ever visit Hamni? Does Hamni know who his father is?"

"For your first question, I don't know. He does know where Hamni is, and it's not that far from his home in London, but whether he ever visits, I don't know. I have never told Hamni who his father is. I'm not certain he understands the concept."

"I see."

"Look, we've got a couple more hours before Windsor; let's switch, I want to sleep."

CHAPTER 53

Diegert finished driving the last hour and a half from Dutton, Ontario, to Windsor. He followed the GPS coordinates precisely, arriving at Riverside Park. Fatima woke up when the car's engine turned off. Diegert smiled at her sleepy face, and she made a cute crinkle with her nose as she had a little yawn and stretched her stiff body. Diegert's phone rang. Blevinsky was on the other end. "I'm going to activate the device in your ear." Diegert heard a small electronic tone, then, "Diegert, do you read me?"

"Yeah, I hear you."

"Remove the black bag from the trunk."

Diegert got out and found the bag in the car's trunk.

"Change into the black clothes."

Diegert put on the black combat fatigue pants like they had at Headquarters. He put on a black turtleneck and laced up a pair of black tactical boots. There was a small black toque for his head. A black jacket with a dark diamond-patterned exterior was also included. Curious, Diegert read the inside label to learn that the jacket was a thermal-suppression garment. The jacket would reduce his heat signature, so he could avoid the thermal scanners used to secure the border. "Alright, sir, I'm dressed."

"Proceed to the water's edge near a grove of large willow trees. You will find a tarp covering a kayak. Inform me when you locate it."

As he walked down to the river, Diegert looked at the ragged skyline of Detroit, Michigan. He was going back to the USA. It was quite puzzling to him that he was going to assassinate somebody in this recently bankrupt city. Glancing back at Fatima, he waved good-bye. She nodded her head slightly. Diegert found the kayak; it, too, was black. "Got it, sir."

"Launch the vessel, paddle across the river, and land at the William G. Milliken State Park. Conceal the vessel and inform me when you have crossed."

Diegert had been in a kayak a few times in Minnesota, so he wasn't worried. At the moment he launched, a large container ship slowly passed by. Diegert paddled next to the vessel, then tucked in behind it, finally paddling into its wake lines on the opposite side to complete his crossing. In the late-afternoon darkness, his movements were unobserved, and he found a grove of trees to stash the kayak. He had stuffed the black tarp into the storage hold and now used it to conceal the kayak's presence. He informed Blevinsky, "I'm in the US."

"Good. Proceed to the parking area on the east side of the park and locate a white van with the markings 'Motor City Electric.' You will be expected."

Diegert saw the van. As he approached, the side door slid open. He stepped inside. The man in the back of the van introduced himself. "I am Abraham."

Indicating the driver, he said, "He's Mohammed."

"Right," said Diegert.

The van started moving, but Diegert could see no land-marks or street signs from the back of the solid-sided van. Blevinsky came back on. "Open the black bag."

Diegert saw a big black bag and unzipped it. Inside was a navy-blue nylon jacket with "Event Security" written across the back in big yellow letters. The coat had a smaller version of the same statement on the left chest. He would also be wearing a baseball cap of the same colors with the same identifier embla-zoned across the front brow. His credentials were on a lami-nated magnetic strip card with his picture. The card was on a lanyard, and it identified him as Matthew Wilcox, an employee of Eagle Talon Security.

Sewn into the left panel of the jacket was a holster with the Desert Eagle pistol Lindstrom had shown him. Diegert took a moment to look over the weapon. Abraham's curiosity couldn't be contained, and he watched Diegert intensely as the gun was being inspected. Satisfied the weapon would operate, Diegert placed it back in the holster. He slipped the jacket on and zipped it up. He donned the cap and the lanyard just as they arrived at his insertion point. The van came to a stop, and Blevinsky was back in his ear.

"You will exit the vehicle and walk north on Concord Street. Blend in with the other security guards who are man-ning an outer perimeter."

While listening to the instructions, Diegert slipped his finger under the phone in Abraham's belt holster, pushing the phone up and into his hand. *It's always handy to have an extra,* he thought.

Diegert stepped out into a very strange environment. The urban landscape was dominated by the decaying edifice of an old industrial facility that had been abandoned long ago. The surrounding area was comprised of vacant lots with weeds, small trees, and windblown trash entangled in the unmanaged growth. There were small buildings that suffered the same blight as the mammoth old factory. Diegert took all this in with a brief turn of his head. What was so strange was all the people, bright lights, security, television broadcast towers, limousines, and activity. The juxtaposition of desertion and occupation was striking and intriguing. Something big was going on in a place where nothing good had happened for at least a decade. He walked toward the building and saw other security people dressed like him and started acting like them.

Blevinsky instructed him, "Proceed to the third floor on the northeast side of the main structure."

Diegert thought it very strange that he might be here to put a hit on a rock star or some other celebrity. As he moved through the abandoned factory, he noted all the destroyed interior materials hanging in loops and shreds, making it look like a rotten urban jungle. He couldn't understand why a big event would be put on in such an unsafe and unkempt area. Diegert felt a buzzing in his right jacket pocket. He hadn't realized he had a company-issue walkie-talkie. When he pulled it out, a voice message instructed him, "Arrival in fifteen minutes. Please take your final positions."

Diegert found the third floor and was on the northeast side in an area where there were stairs to the ground just behind him.

Blevinsky came on again in his ear. "Proceed forward to the support structure in front of you."

Diegert looked about. He stood behind a stained support structure where he had an unobstructed line of sight to the central platform.

"Remain in position and await my instructions," Blevinsky directed.

Fatima, sitting in the car across the river in Canada, received a text from Blevinsky: *Drive to Toronto, catch Flight*

485 to Heathrow. Communicate with no one. This was strange, but she reasoned that there must have been a change in the extraction plan for Diegert. Another three hours of driving. At least she didn't have to go all the way back to Montreal.

Diegert really didn't think about what he was about to do. Instead, he was planning his route back to the van and his extraction once the deed was done. It never made him feel good to think about the target except as a mission to be completed. He heard fast-moving, powerful footsteps coming in his direction. He stepped out from behind the concrete support pillar and startled the big man he heard coming.

"Oh shit . . . you scared me, man. I was afraid no one was guarding this stairwell."

Diegert noticed the "Supervisor" title on the right chest of his navy-blue jacket.

"Don't let anyone up or down it. No one should be using those stairs, you got it?"

"Yes, sir," replied Diegert before the big guy enthusiastically walked on, continuing his rounds.

"Arrival in two minutes, look sharp, people," crackled the walkie-talkie. Diegert returned to his position, where he was able to see the central platform around which everyone's attention was focused. The platform was covered by a tent with an awning extended out over an area where a car would arrive.

"Arrival," the walkie-talkie chirped. "The president has arrived."

As Diegert was listening to the walkie-talkie, he thought he heard "the president," but he wasn't sure. As he looked out on the scene in front of him, a big black limousine arrived under the awning. After a minute, the limousine drove out from under the tent awning. The canvas that covered the driveway and the platform was pulled back. Revealed to everyone was a stage with a podium upon which was affixed the seal of the president of the United States. Standing at the podium was President Peter Carson.

Diegert was the only one in the building, perhaps the only one in the entire world, to be surprised to see the president in this venue. The leader of the free world stood on a stage in a dilapidated Detroit factory to deliver a speech. Diegert's predicament was now clear to him. He thought about all that the Board had on him, the killings in Miami, Paris, and Mogadishu. He reasoned he didn't have to do this. He could avoid capture and evade the law; hell, he had done that before. He could paddle back to Canada and live in the mountains. Yes, the Board had an expectation that he would complete this mission, but that didn't mean he had to carry it out. Blevinsky spoke, "Look at the video on your phone."

Diegert looked at his phone, and on the screen was his mother with a gag in her mouth and a gun to her head. The realization that Crepusculous had kidnapped his mother flashed across his mind.

"We won't hurt her as long as you fulfill your obligation. But if you don't shoot the president, she will be hurt and humiliated before she dies slowly and painfully. Get ready."

Diegert's head was spinning: kill the president or sentence his mother to rape and torture. He looked out at the man surrounded by Secret Service and speaking on a national broadcast.

"Good evening, ladies and gentlemen, thank you for coming tonight to Detroit! Motor City!" the president said with enthusiasm as the audience thundered their applause. "Look where I've brought you," he began. "Look at what has been left behind. The people who built this and ran it are very wealthy. One is a billionaire, and the other has over seven hundred million dollars in personal wealth. The average pensioner from this workplace receives less than twenty thousand dollars a year and no health care. This type of disparity is what I'm calling economic feudalism. When the leader of a company is paid five hundred times what the average employee earns, income disparity grows. America is becoming an imperial feudal system with powerful, wealthy overlords taking indecent incomes for themselves while the hardworking, educated, dutiful employees are paid proportionally less and less each year. The erosion of the middle class means that even well-educated workers are earning salaries that do not allow them to maintain their modest lifestyles."

Carson's style of dynamic speaking captivated audiences, and the theater of this venue made his point even more salient and profound. With emphatic hand gestures and a knack for seeming to address each member of his audience individually, the president carried his point forward.

"Earning five hundred times less than your boss does not represent your economic worth. There is no way one person does five hundred times more work than another. No corporate leader has five hundred times more responsibility than the average worker, and any lifestyle that requires five hundred times more money to sustain is absolutely excessive and morally repugnant. Corporate kings and feudal serfs, that is what America is becoming, and I will address this issue legally, socially, morally, and personally."

"Engage the target," commanded Blevinsky.

Diegert drew the .50-caliber pistol from the holster. He pointed the barrel toward the president. Looking through the sight, he could see the reticle hovering on the president's head. With the grip firmly in his hand and his index finger extended outside the trigger guard, he steadied the pistol so the reticle remained still. Suddenly, the gun fired.

Diegert hadn't pulled the trigger, but the bullet was on its way. The shot, though sound suppressed, startled Diegert because he thought the mechanism still required him to pull the trigger. The bullet followed its laser-guided path and struck the president in the head, creating an image of blood and brains exploding off his shoulders like a video-game graphic. The moment of stunned silence didn't last long before the screaming, the hustling of Secret Service agents, and the sirens began to wail. Diegert had to move and follow his extraction protocol. He reholstered his pistol and descended the staircase. On the ground level, many of the other security guards were confused now that something had actually happened. In an authoritarian voice, Diegert shouted, "Stay at your posts. Don't move from your positions. Maintain the security of your designated areas."

Diegert said this several times as he moved south toward the point where he was to meet the van. Bewildered guards seemed relieved to be told what to do. It reduced their anxiety and reassured them as the word spread that the president had been shot.

Diegert arrived at Bellevue Street and East Grand Boulevard, but the van wasn't there. Bellevue Street was lined on both sides by decrepit, decaying factory buildings like the ones on Concord Street. While Diegert looked to see if the van had been stopped by the police or had to park elsewhere, his eyes caught sight of the dazzling light of a laser sight. He immediately ducked and rolled on the ground as a round whizzed by and struck the pavement where he had just been. He regained his feet and sprinted into the destroyed interior of another deteriorating factory.

Bullets pockmarked the ground as he ran and then the walls of the building as he continued deeper into its interior. He kept moving until he found cover behind a solid brick interior wall.

The shots stopped, and it remained quiet for several minutes, giving him a moment to think. *Sniper fire? There's no way the Secret Service could be firing at me already. I've been set up.* He realized he was about four miles from the river where the kayak was. *If the kayak is still there,* he thought. *Crepusculous has set me up to take the fall.* He heard footsteps crunching through the dry debris on the building's floor. He was being pursued. The night's darkness made the building's interior a place of shadow and dappled light. He peered around the wall behind which he was hiding and saw two figures moving cautiously toward him. He pulled back behind the wall and reached out his hand, searching for debris. He felt a small pile of broken bricks. Taking a chunk of brick into his hand, he heaved it across the building perpendicular to the direction the pursuers were coming. The brick hit a piece of sheet metal, making a very loud clang. He threw more pieces of brick, making it sound like there was movement. The pursuers crept close to the wall behind which he was hiding. He heard one of them say, "We're getting closer to his signal."

Diegert realized how they had found him. He slipped out his smartphone, activating the app for his tympanic transponder, and shut it down.

"Shit . . . I just lost the signal."

"Let's follow those earlier sounds."

The two men passed the wall behind which Diegert was hiding as he relocated himself around the back side of the wall. Diegert thought for a moment he had recognized the voices. He squinted in the darkness and watched the men move away from him. As they proceeded, the one in the lead banged into an obstruction.

"Shit."

Together they tried to find a way around the obstacle. Eventually, one of them turned on the flashlight attached to his

HK45 pistol. Doing so created silhouettes in the ring of light. Diegert drew the Desert Eagle, placed the reticle on the first guy's neck, and pulled the trigger. The bullet ripped through his vertebrae and tore open his throat. The guy's body fell to the floor, and the light beam from his weapon illuminated the building's interior to the west. The second man scurried to the east, leapt through a window space, and crashed through the brush and weeds that grew outside the building.

Diegert sat motionless, listening. He would have to move. Whoever it was that had run off would surely be back, and this old building would be overrun. He could see that the light beam still shone from the fallen man's pistol. He crept down to the body and took the gun and an extra clip of ammunition. He shone the light on the man's face before turning it off, and was both surprised and not surprised to see the dead man was Curtis Jaeger. The Board had a counterstrike team after him, and the presence of Jaeger gave him a pretty good idea as to the other man's identity.

Diegert removed the combat vest from Jaeger and put it on under his jacket. The vest had a communication device clipped to it. He quickly moved to the north, making his way through the debris and clutter of the former factory. The comm unit crackled, and he recognized Strakov's voice. "He's on the run, and he's killed Jaeger."

The reply came from Blevinsky. "Look, we need to button it up. Backup is several minutes away. Continue your pursuit."

At the southernmost end of the factory building, Diegert scrambled through a vacant weed-covered lot and collided with a three-foot granite block. He hit his knee hard on the solid stone and limped a bit before encountering another large block of granite. The weeds were at least three to four feet high, and so were the stones. As he moved about, he realized he was walking on graves. This weed lot was a cemetery. Even the dead in Detroit had been abandoned.

The irony of escaping from being killed by hiding in a graveyard wore off instantly when he was hit in the back of his right shoulder by a shot without sound. The force of the projectile didn't penetrate the vest, but it spun him to his right, knocking him forward into a gravestone. He tumbled and fell in the weeds between two graves.

Strakov saw him go down and quickly advanced with his gun, ready to fire again. Diegert rolled onto his hands and knees and crawled behind a line of gravestones. He peered up and saw Strakov coming. Diegert raised the HK45 and fired. Strakov fell to the ground. Diegert moved immediately, crouching low and running across the graves and between the lines of gravestones, his shoulder throbbing. Shots whizzed by him, ricocheting off the stones. He hit the deck and hugged the ground for a moment, then rolled over and fired. Strakov had to take cover from the bullets sent in his direction. Diegert was the one to escape the game of pistol tag as he burst through a line of bushes that defined the border of the graveyard.

He hopped over a chain-link fence and sprinted through an empty neighborhood of small houses, heading toward the river and a busy street with shops and high-rise apartments. His sense of safety in numbers immediately dissipated when he saw angry mobs of people on the street. The president's assassination had people upset, and they were outside expressing their outrage.

Diegert kept his hat low and his eyes downcast as he walked the streets. He hoped his security jacket would lend some authority to his presence. As he passed a sports bar with a big-screen TV in the front window, he saw that the screen was filled with a picture of his Eagle Talon Security identity card. The card identified him as Matthew Wilcox, but the graphic underneath scrolled his true name: David Terrence Diegert. The scroll indicated he was armed and dangerous and that citizens should report sightings to law enforcement. The manhunt was on. With the technology of Crepusculous and the reach of the Internet, Diegert had suddenly become the world's most wanted man. The president's death was so much bigger than his other jobs, and he realized his chances of escape were growing slim.

Two dudes working the front door of the bar gestured to one another, and one of them got on his phone while the other stepped forward for a better look. "Hey, dude?"

Diegert never looked at him; he just turned and started running. The bouncer shouted out, "It's him . . . It's the guy who shot the president."

Diegert caught the looks of people as he sprinted past them. Just running through the streets with a security coat was enough to draw attention, but with the shouting added in, Diegert knew he was in trouble. He ran by a small park with a big graffiti-covered statue. The park was dark and, for the moment, unoccupied. On his smartphone, he searched for a place he reasoned would provide safe haven from Strakov and the vigilante mobs forming on the angry streets of Detroit. Survival was often achieved by knowing when to avoid a fight you cannot win. His search revealed the address 1300 Beaubien Street, which was only four blocks away.

"Hey, there he is!" Diegert heard the shout and saw a group of people running through the darkness into the park. He bolted from the statue and ran toward Beaubien Street. He sprinted down the middle of whatever street he was on, dodging oncoming traffic and causing cars to slam on their brakes. Angry motorists blew their horns and shouted out their windows. The more fit members of the mob continued their pursuit. Diegert continued down the street until he hit Beaubien

Street. He saw an address on a building: 939. As he ran, the address numbers increased: 998, 1005. Looking back down the street, he saw the mob gaining on him. He stopped, and as they approached, he pointed his gun and fired over their heads. The pursuers ducked for cover and cleared the street. Diegert continued—1180, 125—and at the corner of Beaubien and Clinton was the address he was looking for. Diegert dashed up the steps of the Detroit Police Department station at 1300 Beaubien Street.

It was eerily quiet as he walked through the station doors. Alone in the reception area, he had to call out twice before an older, overweight woman, not dressed in a uniform, approached the counter. "Look, we're kinda busy tonight. Is your problem an emergency?"

"My name is David Terrance Diegert. I'd like to speak to an officer."

"What about? All our officers are on emergency assignment."

"What is your name, ma'am?"

"Helen Mitchell."

"Ms. Mitchell, I'm here to surrender for the assassination of President Carson. Please call in an officer."

Under her breath, Helen grumbled, "*Nutjob.*" In a serious tone, she addressed Diegert. "I'm sorry, sir, but you'll just have to have a seat over there and wait for an officer to return."

"Have you been on the Internet tonight?"

"Tonight's events have kept me plenty busy on the radio. I don't have time for Web surfing!"

With a disdainful shake of his head, Diegert walked over to the wooden bench in the lobby and sat down. Over Jaeger's comm unit, he heard Strakov's voice. "I lost him in the city near the river."

Blevinsky said, "He turned off the GPS tracker in his phone, and he somehow turned off his ear implant. Hey, I thought you said Jaeger was dead."

"He's definitely dead. Diegert shot him right through the throat."

"Well, I've got a position on his transponder not far from the river."

"Maybe that fucker took Jaeger's comm unit."

"He's probably listening to us right now."

The moment that last statement was made, the comm unit went silent. Diegert realized his location had been tracked. He pulled off the comm unit, walked to the men's room, and flushed it down the toilet. Walking back into the reception area, he pulled out his phone, dialed 911, and shouted, "They're shooting in the station. The police are being attacked at 1300 Beaubien. Help!"

The emergency dispatcher asked, "Please, sir, may I have your name?" Diegert let out as loud a scream as he could and hung up in the middle of it.

Diegert shouted at Helen, "Where's the interrogation room?"

Perturbed, she looked up at him, replying, "We don't have an interrogation room; it's a secure cell."

"Fine, I want to be put in there."

"You can't go in there until you've been arrested."

Diegert pulled his pistol and pointed it at her. "I don't care if I've been arrested or not; you're going to put me in that cell."

She looked at him stunned and confused.

"Get up, get the keys, and lock me in," demanded Diegert.

Helen walked slowly over to the cell, removed the keys from her pocket, opened the door, and stepped aside.

With the touch of an iron grandmother, Helen laid out the palm of her hand and said, "I'm required to confiscate your weapon."

Looking into her unblinking eyes above her granny glasses, Diegert found himself torn between two conflicting instincts. Submitting to authority was not comfortable, but resisting would result in his death. He slowly turned the pistol over and placed the gun that had shot the president into Helen's hand.

Diegert stepped into the cell and watched as she locked the door, put the keys back in her pocket, and placed the pistol in a drawer of her desk.

***

The president's body was placed in an ambulance and sped off to Detroit Receiving Hospital. Anyone who had seen the images realized they had witnessed a fatal moment. The head injury was so complete, it was obvious the president was dead.

Dick Chambliss was the Secret Service's chief of mobile security. His job was to oversee the prepping of sites and secure the president's environment at his public appearances. Now, in the midst of this catastrophic failure, he was directing the Secret Service's immediate reaction protocol. It surprised him how quickly pictures of the shooter went viral on the Web. The shooter's identity and an alias were already scrolling on screens before law enforcement had convened a task force to begin the investigation. No one wanted to catch the culprit more than Chambliss, but he was cautious about the identity of the shooter being so rapidly available and broadcast with such certainty. Dick recalled the false information that was broadcast after the Boston Marathon bombing. Inaccurate identities derailed the investigation and wasted valuable time, which ultimately resulted in more mayhem and death. Due process was still required, even for a presidential assassin.

CHAPTER 54

Following the information from Jaeger's comm unit that Blevinsky had extracted, Strakov arrived at 1300 Beaubien Street. Reading the building's sign, Strakov thought Diegert must have been arrested by the police. This complicated things, but he reasoned he might still be able to carry out the Board's plan with swift action. Bounding up the stairs, he burst through the doors of the police station and strode into the reception area, booming, "Federal agent. I need to speak to the officer in command."

Helen looked up from her desk just as the phone rang. With an eye on the man at the front counter, she answered the phone, "Detroit Police Department, how may I help you?"

"This is the 911 operator, what is the nature of your emergency?"

"There's no emergency here," replied the confused woman. "Why are you calling me?"

"Ma'am, we received a report of a shooting at the station," stated the emergency services operator.

Frustrated at being ignored, Strakov shouted, "Hey . . . I need to talk to the officer in charge."

Helen, with the phone still to her ear, waved off the shouting man. "I don't know what you're talking about. There is nothing going on here."

"Ma'am, if you're certain there is no need for emergency assistance, I'll cancel the call, but I believe officers are already en route."

"Yeah, yeah . . . cancel the call. Things are fine here."

Hanging up the phone, Helen walked up to the front counter.

Strakov spoke as she approached. "I need to speak to the officer in charge."

"All officers are on emergency assignment this evening. What do you need?"

"I'm a federal agent, and I'm here to take the assassination suspect into custody."

Helen, whose mind was a lot faster than her body in spite of her technophobic nature, said, "What suspect are you referring to?"

Strakov, feeling the pressure of time and wanting to bully this old lady, said, "A suspect in the presidential assassination is here in this building, and I'm here to take him into custody."

"What makes you think it's a man?"

Strakov showed her a picture of Diegert on his smartphone.

"That doesn't explain why you think he's here," said Helen with her mother-knows-best tone, looking at him through her glasses.

Strakov met her with a steely glare. "Are you trying to obstruct me from taking this suspect into custody?"

"I'm neither confirming nor denying that there is anyone in custody here at the station. If I did have someone here, how would I know that you're not an accomplice? You're dressed in that space-age SWAT suit. You say you're a federal agent, but you show me no ID. We already have a federal liaison who is an FBI agent, and he looks and acts nothing like you."

Frustrated with her assessments, Strakov walked around the end of the counter and searched the room signs.

"Hey!" yelled Helen. "You can't go back here."

He saw Diegert through the small pane of thick glass in the door of the secure cell. Turning the doorknob, he found it locked. "Where's the key?" he said as he walked over to her.

"You're not authoriz—" Helen's words were trapped in her throat when Strakov jabbed two fingers into her suprasternal notch. She choked as he continued to apply pressure where the bones of her chest met the base of her throat.

"I want that key."

Helen was terrified and struggling for air but was determined not to give in.

"Hey, Helen, what's going on?" The voice of Ben Hoffman punctured the tension of the moment, and Strakov took his fingers from Helen's chest.

As the scene became clearer, Ben stepped between Helen and Strakov. With genuine concern, he looked Helen in the eyes and asked, "Are you OK?"

Helen nodded while rubbing the base of her throat.

"What the hell's going on?" asked the young officer who had rushed back to the station. "Dispatch put out a frantic call saying there was trouble."

Hoffman looked at Strakov, dressed in his tactical suit with an HK MK 23 in his holster. "Who are you?" he asked.

Helen jumped in. "Says he's a federal agent, but he sure ain't FBI."

"My name is Brian Stratton, and I'm an agent with the Secret Service."

"Not without ID, you're not," said Hoffman with Helen nodding her head.

"Look, I'm taking the suspect locked in that room into custody . . . now."

At the conclusion of his statement, he drew his MK 23 and pointed it at Hoffman. Reflexively, Hoffman went for his weapon. Strakov fired, piercing the young officer's abdomen, felling him. A stream of blood poured from his wound. Helen screamed, and Strakov fired at her as well, hitting her in the upper chest. She collapsed across her desk, scattering the clutter that covered the work space. At that instant, the doors opened and half a dozen officers entered the station. Strakov wasted no time as he exited the office through the rear, descended a back stairway, and made his way to the street through the garage.

The officers entering the station were stunned and began treating Helen and Hoffman. Two of the officers pursued Strakov but were too late to apprehend him. Ben Hoffman's wounds were serious, and he was unable to give an account of what had happened. Helen died on the office floor as a result of the attack, and capturing her killer became a personal cause for the officers of 1300.

Almost an hour had passed before someone realized there was a suspect in the secure cell. Officer Nathan Sawyer looked through the window of the cell and stared in disbelief at the suspect within: David Terrance Diegert.

"Holy shit! Captain, you gotta get over here."

Captain Desmond Thompson joined the younger officer and peered through the window. He was astonished when he saw the man whose face had been broadcast around the world. Here in their cell sat the assassin of the president of the United States.

Trying the door, Captain Thompson found it to be locked. "Get the key," he told Officer Sawyer. While he waited, he thought of whom he should contact to deal with this suspect.

"It's not in the cabinet," shouted Sawyer.

"Check Helen's pockets—you know she never puts the keys back." Helen's body was still awaiting transport by the medical examiner's office. Sawyer retrieved the keys.

Captain Thompson unlocked the door. Feeling like a monkey in a cage, Diegert rose when the door opened. Thompson began by asking, "Who was your arresting officer?"

"I surrendered myself, and Helen put me in here."

Thompson took a moment to process this surprise before replying, "Helen is now dead, and one of our officers has been shot. Who the hell was that guy who was here when we arrived?"

"Is he in custody?"

"No, he is not, but you better answer my question."

"His name is Alexi Strakov. He's part of a kill team that my former employer has activated to terminate me."

"You're the guy who shot the president."

Diegert held his reply while considering the gravity of his response and the immediate effect it would have on the situation. He realized that, even though he did not actually pull the trigger, only he and whoever was operating the computer that controlled the gun knew that.

"Yes, I am," he said, "and that makes this a federal case, so I believe you better call in the FBI."

Thompson, repressing the urge to beat the man who had shot the best president this country had ever had, realized the son of a bitch was right. Never softening his hateful glare, the captain stepped out of the cell, instructing Officer Sawyer, "Get Jim Donovan down here."

***

At Pearson International Airport in Toronto, Fatima returned her rental car. She had been listening to music while driving but now realized that there was a lot of security at the airport. Walking through the terminal, she stopped at a TV displaying a video of President Peter Carson being shot in the head. Following the graphic image, the video cut to images of David Diegert with a pistol pointing from an elevated position. The next image was the corporate security badge with Diegert's picture and the name "Mathew Wilcox" on the card. Below the image, the graphic read: *AKA—David Terrence Diegert*. The twenty-four-hour news cycle turned the event into a nonstop search for the president's assassin.

On her phone, Fatima called Blevinsky. "Hey, David's in trouble. The hit's gone worldwide, and he's been ID'd. What do you want me to do?"

"Is your flight on time?"

"Yeah . . . it leaves in forty-five minutes."

"I want you on that plane, and I'll meet you in London. Someone will pick you up at Heathrow. If your flight's on time, you can visit Hamni. Would you like that?"

"Of course, but what about David?"

"Don't worry about Diegert. I know there's been some publicity, but we have his extraction under control. You'll get to see him in London. Have a nice flight."

What bullshit, she thought. *Have a nice flight?* Blevinsky would never say that. *Visit Hamni?* That wasn't an invitation; it was a threat. On the television, the video was being replayed and patrons were cursing Diegert's image. In a quiet corner of the gate, she turned her phone camera on herself and recorded: *"Hey, I know you're facing some tough decisions, but I . . . I believe in you. I look forward to seeing you soon."* She sent the video to Diegert and hoped he wouldn't take it the wrong way.

As she walked to the board area, she found herself wondering if David Diegert would suffer the same fate as Shamus McGee.

***

The vice president, Lydia Stanwix, was rushed to the White House, where she was secured in the Situation Room. The national security advisor, the joint chiefs, and the directors of both the CIA and the FBI, along with the chief justice of the Supreme Court, were all assembled for the administration of the oath of office. A somber ceremony transferring power to the shocked and grieving vice president was broadcast to a nation reeling from surprise and frazzled with frustration. President Stanwix spoke to the nation from deep below the White House but also from the depth of her very heavy heart.

"My fellow Americans, I grieve with you for the loss of a man who dedicated himself to the well-being and freedom of all Americans. President Peter Carson embodied the very best qualities possessed by human beings. His goodness and generosity will stand as a testament to the man he was. I want to express special condolences to his wife, First Lady Mary Carson, and his son, Jason, and daughter, Ashley. Their loss is even more personal than ours. The fact that his life has all too soon become a legacy is a pain we will all have to bear as we progress forward into the world Carson left for us. It has been over fifty years since this great nation faced such a devastating loss of a charismatic and caring leader. For us now, the emotions are raw and the same as those experienced fifty years ago. We, however, have much more sophisticated technology, and we will apprehend this criminal and have him face the justice he deserves. I ask you as a nation to remain calm and vigilant while being cooperative with law enforcement. God bless you all as you grieve this loss, and God bless the United States of America."

Jim Donovan was the director of investigation for the FBI in the Detroit area. The fifty-two-year-old had the look of a classic G-man: gray hair cut short and a slightly soft belly under a midgrade dark suit. He had a reputation within the DPD as a very cordial and cooperative agent who kept his focus on resolving cases instead of controlling turf. The events of this evening had him absolutely overwhelmed. Captain Desmond Thompson had to call him three times before Donovan took the call. "Desmond, what's going on? I'm getting my ass kicked tonight," said the usually polite Donovan.

Thompson replied simply, "We got him. We got Diegert. Come to 1300 but keep it quiet."

***

Strakov called Blevinsky as he walked the streets of Detroit.

"Diegert's in police custody. He's being held in a station house."

"I have a four-man assault team heading to your GPS location. Stay where you are. Their ETA is ten minutes."

"What's the mission?"

Annoyed, Blevinsky retorted, "The mission is the same. There has been no change in the mission just because you've failed three times! Take the assault team and kill Diegert. Leave no loose ends."

Strakov felt like he had just been kicked in the ear. He replied, "Yes, sir, mission first."

"Make certain it is."

After Strakov had waited impatiently for ten minutes, a white SUV pulled up. Strakov climbed in to find four operators wearing black combat gear including tactical helmets. The driver asked Strakov for directions, and the big Russian placed his smartphone in the tech dock. The GPS-guided route came up on the vehicle's dash screen, and they drove off to Diegert's location.

When Donovan arrived at 1300, Captain Thompson met him and shook his hand. "Where'd you find him?"

"He turned himself in."

Donovan's surprised look and abrupt halt expressed the *holy shit* sentiment he didn't need to say.

"I know," said Thompson as they continued. Donovan was again surprised when he saw the condition of the familiar office. Yellow tape, splattered blood, and busy forensic techs made the office look like so many crime scenes he had worked throughout his career. "What the hell?"

"Helen is dead, and Ben Hoffman is wounded."

Getting the shocked FBI man to focus, Thompson directed him toward the secure cell.

"Diegert's over here. Let's see if we can get some answers."

Donovan was reeling from the news of Helen's death. She was a big old battle-ax of a woman, but she'd had a soft spot for Donovan and had always treated him kindly. He and Thompson entered the secure cell together.

"This is Jim Donovan. He's the FBI agent in charge of Detroit."

"I know who you are, Mr. Diegert, as does everyone in the world with an Internet connection."

Diegert watched the men cross the room. Donovan stood behind him while Thompson circled back to stand by the door. Diegert shifted his chair so he could see them both.

Diegert began, "I realize the pressure you're under to inform the public that the president's assassin has been caught. I'm not denying I am that person, but I believe you should be concerned about the forces behind this and how this event ties to what's coming next."

Donovan and Thompson sat down in hard metal chairs; the FBI agent said, "Go on, Mr. Diegert."

"I am an agent for a group of powerful elites known as Crepusculous. They possess tremendous wealth, and they use it to manipulate governments, markets, and whole economies. Today's assassination is part of a plan to destroy the US economy."

"How the hell do you know that?" asked Thompson.

"At the Crepusculous training facility, I discovered electronic records from a double agent. They revealed a three-part plan to destroy a nation's economy. I figured it was some third-world country, but killing the president was about destroying the United States."

Both lawmen looked at Diegert with a mix of contempt and curiosity.

Diegert continued, "That means at least two more actions are planned."

"What are they?" asked Donovan.

"I don't know exactly, but the Board's actions are always multilayered with subsequent missions building on previous successes."

"And why are you telling us this?" interjected Thompson.

"I've been trained by them. When I'm on an operation, the exact nature of the mission or the identity of a target is not revealed until absolutely necessary. I didn't know the target was the president until he stepped out onto that stage."

Diegert looked back and forth, noting the two officers' intense interest before continuing.

"After I completed the assignment, there was an extraction plan. When I acted on that plan, two attempts were made on my life. When those failed, my identity was released for worldwide broadcast. It wasn't the police or the FBI that released the information; it was Crepusculous. They want me dead. The man who was here, who shot Helen and the officer, is part of a hit team that will continue to try to kill me." Holding up his smartphone, he said, "The blogosphere is fomenting vigilantes to kill me, and the Board has posted an anonymous reward for my death. The last thing they want is for me to be in custody talking to honest law officers like you."

"Certainly your arrest was a distinct probability," observed Donovan.

"Crepusculous has corrupt agents in every branch of law enforcement. When you announce my custody, the first officers to arrive will be their agents who will assert control, remove me, and terminate me."

Donovan shot a look at Thompson, who, with his chin in his hand, raised his eyebrow. Diegert continued, "The fact that you haven't shot me already convinces me you're not corrupted."

"Don't think that I haven't considered doing exactly that," said Thompson with steely restraint in his voice.

Speaking slowly, Diegert said, "Soon they will broadcast fabricated reports identifying me as a radical loner with a vendetta against the president. It will all be disinformation so the Board can control the message and manipulate public perception."

After the two officers sighed and considered what was said, Donovan remarked, "So you're the fall guy, and all this is coming down on you, even though you're the guy who shot the president."

Diegert wanted to explain about the remotely controlled system on the gun, but he could tell these two were looking for a reason not to believe him. He had to keep his story simple so he could convince them that Crepusculous had turned on him and was trying to kill him while also getting them to value him as a source of information regarding the next terrorist attacks.

"Yes, sir, you're right on both accounts, and I want to help you stop the next attack."

CHAPTER 55

On Beaubien Street, the white SUV pulled up in front of 1300 and disgorged its five-man assault team. Alexi Strakov led them up the steps. The four operators, all dressed in black combat gear, carried H&K MP5 submachine guns. Upon entering the office area, Strakov bellowed, "Federal agents." All the cops looked at the black-clad team with tactical helmets, balaclavas, and automatic weapons and felt quite certain these were not federal agents. Strakov started firing, and the rest of the team opened up as well. Some of the officers dived to the floor and crawled toward the back hall. Others took fatal bullets in their upper bodies and heads, falling to the floor and splattering the squad room with their red, American blood.

The officers who made it to the back tactical room grabbed M4 carbines and combat shotguns. In the squad room, Strakov and his team fired their weapons at the secure cell door. Donovan, Thompson, and Diegert backed away from the door as it resisted the barrage of bullets. Donovan looked at Diegert. "This is all because of you?" Diegert tilted his head while shrugging his shoulders.

Strakov called off the futile gunfire and directed two team members to place breaching charges on the door. When the detonators were set, the team converged on the far side of the room. Just before the detonator was engaged, a spate of bullets hit the assault team, killing two of them. The cops were firing from the back hallway. Two of the remaining assault team members moved to cover and returned fire. From under a desk, Strakov saw the detonator in the hand of a dead team member. He crawled out from under the desk, reached out, and activated the detonator.

The explosion was massive, with the majority of the force directed into the squad room, killing the two other remaining assault team members. The cops were blown back into the hall by the concussive force, which produced blast burns and shrapnel wounds. The door of the secure cell was twisted into the room with its top hinge ripped out and the lower hinge still attached by a twisted piece of steel framing. The gaping entrance was clouded in dust and smoke. Inside the cell, all three men coughed and convulsed as they grappled with orienting themselves.

Their ears were deaf and they could hardly breathe with all the dust in the air. Donovan was unseen behind the destroyed door. Thompson took up a position on the left side of the open doorway. Diegert moved to the back right corner and got behind the overturned steel table, using it as a defensive shield.

Strakov rose from his refuge and walked through the dust and smoke, approaching the blasted entrance of the secure cell. With his Springfield Armory .45 leading the way, he entered the room. Thompson reacted first, firing on Strakov and hitting him in the torso. Strakov's tactical suit prevented the bullets from penetrating, but the force spun the big Russian so he was facing Thompson. Strakov fired on the department captain, striking him with several fatal rounds. Diegert, seeing a service weapon on the floor, grabbed the gun, stood up from behind the table, faced the man he hated, and fired at Strakov.

He first struck him in the hip and then, using automatic fire, progressed up the midsection until he put three bullets in the head of his nemesis. Strakov's big body fell to the floor with a loud thud and a plume of dust. Diegert stepped over to look at the corpse of the man he was so very satisfied to see lying dead.

Diegert pulled back the broken steel door to find Donovan covered in dust with a bleeding cut on his head. He helped the dazed man to his feet, brushing the dust off him. Peering through the clouded air, Donovan saw Strakov's body. Diegert explained, "He's the guy who led the kill team. He was one of the best operators the Board had working for them. I think this is yours." Diegert handed the service weapon to Donovan.

Reaching for his holster and finding it empty, Donovan took the gun and replaced the hot weapon under his suit coat.

"Come on," commanded Diegert.

Before following Diegert into the squad room, Donovan stopped at the corpse of his friend Desmond Thompson. He closed the eyes of one of the best men he had ever worked with, and he thought of how the man's close-knit family would be devastated.

In the squad room, Diegert opened the drawer of Helen's desk and took out the gun that had shot the president.

Diegert placed the gun in Strakov's empty holster.

"What are you doing?" asked Donovan.

"I'm setting up our own disinformation campaign. Let's go," said Diegert.

While crossing the squad room, Diegert removed a helmet and a pistol from one of the assaulters. He and Donovan stepped outside, and the cool night air made both of them cough and spit. The coughing made Donovan's head wound bleed even more.

"Have you got a first aid kit in your car?" asked Diegert.

Donovan, caught in a spasm of coughing, pointed to a blue Malibu parked across the street. Diegert put on the tactical helmet and led Donovan over to the car. He took the keys from the FBI agent, put him in the passenger seat, and drove off. A few blocks away, he pulled over, got out the kit, and bandaged Donovan's head. With the bleeding stopped, he drove on.

***

Aaron Blevinsky hesitated when he saw Klaus Panzer's name on his phone screen. "Yes, sir."

"What is the status on the elimination of Diegert?"

"I cannot report success at this time, sir, but Strakov's team knows his location and they are assaulting the site as we speak."

"Very well, keep me apprised of developments."

"Yes, sir."

When Panzer concluded the call, Dean Kellerman remarked, "We do seem to be in a bit of a pickle."

"Yes, but we must move forward. Any retraction at this point would be a waste."

"Is Diegert really so important? We've already initiated the media campaign against him. He did it! What could he say that anyone would believe?"

"Ah—you see . . . that's just it. He can't get everyone to believe him, but he might get someone to, and that person could do us harm."

"And when he's dead, the story is ours to tell."

"Precisely."

CHAPTER 56

Diegert drove through Detroit not really knowing where he was going but avoiding the closed roads and traffic control roadblocks by staying on side streets and deserted avenues.

"Hey, you better get on the phone and call some people or do something," he said to Donovan, who sat in the passenger seat recovering from dust and smoke inhalation.

Donovan looked at Diegert, and he wondered how much truth there was in his story. He contemplated what would have happened if Lee Harvey Oswald hadn't been gunned down. Wouldn't we have learned more about the plot behind the JFK assassination? Diegert's story might be just to save his own ass, but Donovan knew he could've easily been killed back at the station, and that hit team was no figment.

"Hello," said a calm, warm female voice when Donovan's call connected.

"Carolyn, it's Jim Donovan. Things are nuts, can we meet at a safe house?"

"Safe house? I was hoping for a cup of coffee."

"No, I need a secure address."

"OK . . . meet me at 2113 Locust Circle in thirty minutes. You gonna tell me more?"

"Trust me, when we meet, I'll tell you and show you every-thing at the center of what happened tonight." Donovan dis-connected the call.

"You were smart not to say anything more. Crepusculous owns the means of communication."

Carolyn Fuller was the CIA counterterrorism analyst for the Detroit area and had known Jim Donovan for over ten years. As the senior agent for Detroit, Carolyn had developed a collegial, cooperative, and professional relationship with her FBI counterpart. Their ability to work together proved crucial in 2009 during the underwear bomber incident. The Christmas Day terrorist threat was quickly made safe while the evidence and the suspect were held in an unquestionable chain of legal custody.

Establishing a safe house in Detroit required simply choos-ing an abandoned structure out of the seventy-eight thousand available, keeping the neighborhood's electricity and water on, and locking it up tight. The house on Locust Circle was a sturdy brick structure on a truly dead-end street. All twenty-four of the houses leading up to it were abandoned. Nature was tak-ing over, and the plant growth was prolific. Weeds and over-grown trees would one day hide this street's existence. Carolyn had chosen this house specifically because the garage was in the back. The automatic door opener still worked, so once the car was inside, the place retained its abandoned appearance. Inside, the furnishings were sparse and mostly what the pre-vious residents had left behind. The boarded windows denied any natural light; there were, however, enough electric lights to make the place functional.

CHAPTER 57

Panzer didn't like it, but he had to think like David Diegert. He imagined himself in the position of a powerless, publicly identified criminal on the run from superior adversaries. He could barely stomach the conclusion, but he would have to turn to the authorities. He called Blevinsky and directed him to activate Crepusculous agents in the CIA, NSA, DIA, and FBI. He also reiterated to the director of Headquarters how vital it was he apprehend Diegert. Blevinsky could hear the threat through the airwaves. "Yes, I'm doing everything I can to find him."

Waiting for a response, all Blevinsky heard was the line go dead.

Klaus Panzer placed another call. This one reached Javier Perez in his luxurious town house in London. "Javier, I am so pleased you will be ascending to your father's chair on the Board soon."

"Thank you, it will be an honor to work with you."

"Change is happening all around us. I trust you've made the necessary arrangements for our third phase of the operation?"

"Yes, I have. All components will be in place in two days."

"Excellent! The trial run of the initiation sequence was successful?"

"Absolutely . . . single-source satellite initiation worked wonderfully. We had some challenges, but recently Blevinsky and I resolved the barriers, and all our practice runs have been successful."

"The thermobaric charges are ready?"

"Seven of them, yes; the last two are being placed as we speak. Placing the volatile compounds in proximity to each other without spontaneous combustion is a problem our engineers struggled with but solved."

"You have faith in the system now?"

"Certainly. One signal, and the compounds activate and ignite."

"Your father will be proud, and I'm glad it's you who'll have the honor of activating the detonation device. It's only right that the next generation of Crepusculous plays that role."

"I'm looking forward to furthering our partnership."

"Very well, we'll speak again soon."

"Good night."

After the call concluded, Javier reflected on a comment his father had made referring to Klaus Panzer as the world's most ruthless man. When he'd first heard this, he thought it was a compliment, but now he reconsidered.

Javier also took a moment to reflect on himself. He really didn't like thinking very deeply about himself. He found that just under the surface of the success he projected was a man filled with doubt and fear. Fear of failure, fear of exposure, fear of real intimacy. The money, the wealth, the good looks were a façade behind which he hid. He was good at so few things and bad at so many. He lacked the true self-confidence that was possessed by those who worked hard to develop themselves.

He was uncertain as to where his talents lay beyond screwing women.

Women made it so easy for him to feel successful. If the only goal in life were having sex with a woman on the first night, he would be world champion. His relationships, though, were hollow. They always ended with the girl's feelings hurt and him feeling nothing. The intensity of a new sex partner was an emotional sanctuary where he could feel really good for a while, share that with a woman, and then avoid any true commitment. This pattern had worked for him since he was a teenager. Now, at the age of thirty, he was afraid he couldn't relate to a woman in any other way. Seduce, consume, discard was the way he experienced relationships with women. If he was ultimately a failure with women, then he really had no talent at all.

At this point in his life, he also began to contemplate the fact that he was a father. He certainly wasn't a good one. He had only been to visit Hamni just once. Rather, he didn't "visit" but went to the facility where Hamni lived and observed. The young boy's special needs were a challenge, but the spirit and perseverance he demonstrated through his activities impressed Javier. His son had guts. The little guy was not going to let his difficulties define him. Why, with so many challenges, was this kid more confident than his father, who had so much and was still capable of so little?

Julio Perez's empire was Javier's destiny, but it felt like a curse. How much does a man need? How far will he go to acquire and retain all that he seeks? Javier really didn't understand why Klaus wanted to destroy the United States, and the bombs he was in charge of placing—he had no clue. Blevinsky set it all up, and Javier just nodded and spoke his lines to Panzer. What they were trying to accomplish made no sense, but he was afraid of the consequences if he didn't play his part. He hadn't even bothered to Google "thermobaric bombs." Nine cities in the United States, though, were going to have one of these things go off. Klaus wanted catastrophic devastation across the country. Javier, as a sign of his commitment to Crepusculous, was to "oversee" the procurement, placement, and activation of the explosive devices. Without Blevinsky, absolutely nothing would've been accomplished. Javier, by position of birth alone, was being credited with setting up an incredibly complex and destructive attack that would bring violent changes to the structure of the United States of America, and he alone possessed the triggering device.

All these thoughts were upsetting and befuddled his mind. He didn't want to think about these problems; besides, he had a Thai teenager, with bleached blonde hair, upstairs waiting to be fucked.

CHAPTER 58

Thirty minutes after speaking to Jim Donovan, Carolyn watched his blue Malibu pull into the driveway on the camouflaged security camera feed. She activated the garage door, and Diegert parked next to her Honda Accord. With the garage door closed, Donovan stepped out of the passenger side and greeted Carolyn. "Hey, it's good to see you."

"Yeah . . . It's good to see you too. Now what the hell's going on?"

"I have a suspect in the car, and I'd like to get him inside."

"I can see your suspect was driving the car!"

"I know . . . Let's get him inside."

Carolyn was taken aback when the suspect stepped out of the car with his helmet on. Donovan grasped his left arm and led the man up the steps and into the kitchen.

"Take the helmet off," ordered Donovan.

When Diegert removed the helmet, Carolyn recognized him immediately. She struggled to stifle her emotional surprise and relied on her professional stoicism so as not to reveal her reaction.

Donovan said, "Yeah . . . I know, I can hardly believe it either, and I know we're in big trouble with this one, but you've got to hear the story."

Donovan and Diegert spent the next thirty minutes telling Carolyn all about the events of the day and the power of Crepusculous. Listening carefully, Carolyn offered that she was aware of Crepusculous. The Agency had a watch protocol, but what was observed seemed very philanthropic. Nevertheless, the CIA was concerned because the power the Board could wield was significant enough to affect markets and even governments.

"Exactly!" said Donovan. "And that's what they're trying to do in the United States. Diegert here says there's more to come."

"When I was training in Romania at a Crepusculous facility, we planned covert operations that were always multilayered. Each action contributed to the completion of the next, until the final objective was revealed and typically easily achieved because of the preliminary work that had already been done."

"You think the president's assassination was just the first step in a broader plan?" asked Carolyn.

"Yes, I do, and I think the next thing is going to happen very soon. I acquired an electronic record from a mole who was working undercover inside Crepusculous. It revealed a four-stage plan for economic readjustment."

"So what's the next phase of the plan?" asked Carolyn.

"The record doesn't indicate that. I only know that four stages have been planned."

She continued, "I'm aware that the Perez family are members of the Board."

"They are," confirmed Diegert.

"I read that the father is quite old and in poor health. It is speculated that his son, Javier, is in line to take over."

"That's interesting. I know of Javier, but I didn't think he was ready to take control of the empire."

"Why do you say it that way, with all that doubt?" questioned Carolyn.

"The guy's a playboy. He's spending his wealth, not contributing to it."

"His father's failing health must be forcing his hand."

"I know that Klaus Panzer and Dean Kellerman are also Board members. The mole's documents included profiles on both men."

"What did they have to say?" asked Carolyn.

"Panzer is a real disciplinarian with a strong German heritage. He's the self-appointed leader and sees to it that the Board bends to his will. He has two daughters, one who is involved in the business, and a younger one, who is not."

Donovan asked, "Does the Agency know the full membership of the Board?"

"No, but there may be even more members," said Carolyn.

"I have a plan to find out what's next," said Diegert.

Both agents looked at him as he sat on a stool at the linoleum counter.

"I know someone who can get access to Javier Perez. Her name is Fatima Hussain. She's an agent for the Board, and she has a history with Javier."

"You mean you want her to spy on her ex?"

"Fatima has a son who is held by the Board. She's denied access to him unless she serves as an operative."

"She's being blackmailed," offered Carolyn.

"I plan to acquire her son and convince her to infiltrate Javier's place and steal intel to share with us in exchange for her son."

Both agents were quiet for a moment, and then Donovan said, "Interesting, but there are so many holes in your perforated plan that I can't see the possibility of success."

"You don't know the personalities," said Diegert. "I know what Fatima is capable of, and I also know she will do anything for her son."

Carolyn spoke up. "You're suggesting kidnapping a child and holding him hostage to force his mother to extract information from an ex-boyfriend that you're not even certain has valuable intel."

"Alright, I can see your hesitation, but it makes sense that Javier should take an active role in this process as an up-and-coming Board member. You two can shoot holes in my plan, but I'm telling you that it'll work and we'll stop whatever attack is coming to the United States, and neither of you has a better plan to do that."

Carolyn and Donovan looked at each other with exasperated bewilderment.

***

Blevinsky was pleased to find the Board's mole in the FBI was already in Detroit. Special Agent Stanley Talbot had been immediately dispatched to Detroit and was active in the investigation. Blevinsky informed him of the kill order on Diegert and told him of the incident at Station 1300. Talbot arrived at the police station and was informed that Jim Donovan had been seen leaving with the assassination suspect. Talbot found Donovan's contact info in his Bureau smartphone and activated a GPS app to find Donovan. Accompanied by his two junior agents, Steven Peterson and Andrew Gates, the special agent began following the trail to Donovan's location.

At 2113 Locust Circle, Carolyn Fuller was taking notes and trying to make sense of everything that a man she knew and trusted had told her, along with what the admitted assassin of the president had to say. She made it clear to Donovan that the risks they were taking were huge, and the penalties permanent. Donovan agreed with her, but based on his experiences, Diegert was telling the truth and cooperating when he could've easily killed them and escaped. Carolyn continued to struggle with accepting everything she was told.

As Talbot turned the tan Chevy Malibu onto the abandoned Locust Circle, he informed his agents, "Lock and load boys, these people are armed and dangerous. We take them dead if we have to."

"Yes, sir," replied Peterson and Gates as they checked their weapons.

While the three occupants of 2113 Locust Circle sat contemplating their situation, a vehicle emerged on the security camera screen. The car doors opened, and three agents stepped out of the vehicle. The driver of the car spoke into a PA system. "Attention, Agent James Donovan. I am FBI Special Agent Stanley Talbot, and we're here to assist you. Please reveal yourself and allow us to help you."

"It's a hit squad," said Diegert. "The FBI wouldn't send so few agents."

Looking somewhat doubtful, Donovan replied, "You're getting paranoid, the Bureau is on a skeleton staff tonight. They're here to help us."

Carolyn said nothing but nodded at the man in whom she believed. Donovan opened the side door and stepped into the driveway. Diegert and Carolyn watched the security camera's feed on her laptop. Donovan stepped into the field of view in front of the car. He had his hands raised, and although they couldn't hear the conversation, Diegert and Carolyn could see that Donovan and Talbot were talking. Suddenly, Talbot drew his weapon and shot Jim Donovan three times.

The senior FBI agent fell to his knees and collapsed on his side as his life poured out in a large puddle of blood on the driveway. Carolyn was shocked, but Diegert grabbed her hand and bolted for the garage. They escaped through the rear door of the garage and ran through the backyards of the unoccupied houses of Locust Circle.

Talbot and his agents entered the kitchen through the side door. They cleared the rooms and returned to the kitchen. The laptop continued to project the scene on the driveway with Jim Donovan's dead body. Talbot stepped to the garage door and saw the back door of the garage wide open. "Alright, we're on a rabbit hunt. Let's cover both sides of the street. Keep your comms open."

Diegert and Carolyn were crouched under a deck in the backyard of a house two doors down from 2113. He signaled for her to remain silent. It was important to listen and determine if the three agents were sticking together or splitting up.

With a hand signal, Talbot directed Gates to take the west side of the street. He indicated that Peterson should start searching the east. Both agents proceeded as directed.

It was a dark night with only a crescent moon. The backyards, having been neglected for several years, possessed both the trappings of human inhabitants—patio furniture, picnic tables, swing sets—and the consequences of unmanaged growth—fallen limbs, layers of leaves, and tall grass. Fences were also an obstacle, and the chain-link variety was especially difficult to detect on this opaque night.

Diegert and Carolyn listened as Agent Peterson clanged into the fence that surrounded the yard they were in. He climbed over the barrier and proceeded with his weapon drawn. Beyond the deck they were hiding under was a swimming pool filled with algae-laden water covered in a rotting layer of leaves. Diegert watched the shadows extending in front of Agent Peterson as he passed between the deck and the pool. Carolyn was field trained as a CIA agent but inexperienced. Fear jangled her nerves as she struggled to keep her composure. The tension of this life-and-death game made it very difficult for her to keep from crying out.

Diegert, on the other hand, knew how to play this game well. He wanted to see how good Agent Peterson was at cat and mouse. Diegert definitely felt he was in the role of the feline. After Peterson passed their hiding spot, Diegert stepped out and crept behind him. He reached out and struck the agent on his elbow, flexing the arm and drawing it back. With his other arm, he placed a choke hold on Peterson's neck. He swept down the right forearm forcefully, stripping the gun from the FBI man's hand. The pistol dropped to the pool deck. Peterson's reflexes were good; he rotated his torso and drove his elbow into Diegert's abdomen, delivering several painful blows. Diegert hung on, twisting Peterson's arm behind his back. The FBI agent kicked Diegert in the shin and stomped on his foot, sending searing pain through his metatarsals. This maneuver forced Diegert to reposition his footing, which slackened the choke hold. Peterson grabbed Diegert's hand and pried it loose, releasing the hold and freeing his airway.

Carolyn watched the battle in front of her, shocked at the speed and violence of the two men. She saw the pistol by the side of the pool and retrieved it but remained under the deck. Peterson was now able to pivot and turn into the hold Diegert had on his right arm. Anticipating Peterson's move, Diegert held the man's hand tight and kicked his opponent's knee with a lateral blow. The kick produced a snapping crack as the ligaments in the vulnerable joint gave way to the precision force. Peterson cried out and fell to his right. As he collapsed on the crippled knee, Diegert hit him in the jaw with a palm heel strike. The blow awkwardly twisted Peterson's neck, compressing his brain stem, making consciousness difficult to maintain. The FBI man was still able to see and perceive, but motor control of his body was failing. Diegert grabbed him by the lapels of his gray G-man suit and flung him into the brown-green water of the neglected pool. The sudden immersion into the cold water was startling; it forced Peterson to find his footing and stand up. Diegert descended the pool steps, entering the water up to his waist. Peterson was wiping pond scum from his face when he heard Diegert moving toward him. The agent faced his tormentor, who unexpectedly splashed two handfuls of filthy water into the eyes of the G-man. Capturing the moment, Diegert grasped Peterson's throat with his right hand. Placing his right leg behind the injured leg of the agent, Diegert kicked Peterson's leg out from under him while forcefully pushing his upper body under the water. Peterson's hand clamped on to Diegert's arm while his other arm reached up and out of the water and pounded on Diegert's chest. Diegert increased the pressure on Peterson's throat while the determined man threw several ineffective blows. Diegert grabbed the flailing right hand of his adversary, hyperextended the wrist, and held it out away from an effective strike zone. The surface of the water convulsed from the struggling movements of the desperate man held below. Diegert knew it would be over soon, and he steeled himself for the inevitable conclusion.

Peterson's mind was frantically racing through a million thoughts as his neurons fired survival sequences that failed to change their deteriorating physiologic state. The final image projected on the mind's eye of the dying agent, as water replaced air in his lungs, was the beautiful sight of his young wife, Sarah, dressed in sexy lingerie smiling at him in the doorway of their bedroom.

Diegert saw a large bubble of air break the surface of the water as the thrashing subsided and the tension in Peterson's arm disappeared. Diegert gently lowered the arm to the water and released the throat of his lifeless foe. The body calmly floated in the murky fluid. Diegert exited the pool.

"Oh my God, are you OK?" exclaimed Carolyn.

Diegert raised his finger to his lips and made a hand gesture, indicating that two more agents were still active. Carolyn composed herself while Diegert began searching the ground for something. She tapped him on the shoulder and held up Agent Peterson's pistol. Diegert nodded and took the weapon. He was surprised it was a Viper 9 mm, not the Glock 23, standard issue for the FBI. They exited the yard through the northern gate, moving away from the safe house and toward the entrance to Locust Circle. Entering the next yard, Diegert found a storage shed in the back corner of the property. The shed had a concrete floor and a wood frame, while the walls and roof were made of aluminum. Carolyn and Diegert entered the structure. The building did not have electricity, so as Diegert searched in the darkness, Carolyn turned on her phone's flashlight. There was an old lawn mower, a rolled-up garden hose, hand tools hanging on a rack, and shelves with typical things for the maintenance of a backyard. When he discovered an enticing combination of items, Diegert realized he could take the fight to the agents by drawing them into a trap.

In a whisper, he explained to Carolyn what he planned to do.

"Shh, just listen. I'm going to mix this bag of fertilizer with the gas in this can and ignite it with this extension cord. You will draw the agents into the building before I blow it up."

Carolyn followed him through the bomb-making part of the plan, but a look of doubt resided on her face in response to the second part of the plan. Reading her emotions, Diegert stepped to the back corner of the shed and, without much effort, pressed out an aluminum panel, creating a backdoor exit. Using hand signals, he pointed at her and gestured that this was her exit.

"When the bomb is ready, I want you to scream outside as loud as you can. Then come in here and bang on the walls, exit out the back, and run."

She looked at him with fear and suspicion, but he didn't acknowledge it. He smiled at her, patted her on the shoulder, and got to work.

He first took a three-tined hand rake and ripped open the bag of fertilizer that lay lengthwise on a shelf. He then jammed one of the metal tines from the hand rake into the receptacle end of the extension cord. This combined piece of equipment was then buried in the bag of granulated ammonium nitrate. A rusty coffee can on a shelf contained old nails, screws, small hinges, and other bits of metal hardware. The can's contents were dumped on top of the fertilizer. Diegert opened the gas can and poured gasoline into the fertilizer, making sure it penetrated into the depth of the bag and thoroughly mixed with the granules. The smell of gasoline permeated the shed and made Carolyn feel kind of sick.

Holding up the three-pronged plug, Diegert whispered, "I'm going to the house to find an exterior outlet to plug this in." Pointing to her wristwatch, he told her, "In four minutes, you scream long and loud. Leave the door to the shed open. Bang on the walls like you're in a fight, then go out the back and run like hell." He waited for her reply. She seemed puzzled but then looked directly into his eyes, nodding her head.

Diegert tied off a section of the extension cord so it wouldn't pull out of the fertilizer. On a shelf, he found a hose nozzle spray gun and put it in his pocket. He exited the back of the shed and made his way to the rear of the house, rolling out the electric cord behind him.

Carolyn sat in the shed looking at her watch and feeling like four minutes was a very long time to be alone with Diegert's improvised explosive device. The smell of the gas made her nauseous, and she wanted to get the hell out of there. She realized, though, that she shouldn't rush her actions since the agents could be some distance away. Finally, the fourth minute passed, she cleared her throat, opened the shed door, and stuck her head outside. Like an actress auditioning for a horror movie, Carolyn let out a high, piercing scream. She screamed again and again before ducking back into the shed.

Diegert heard it. Talbot and Gates heard it as well. Over their comm unit, Talbot, who remained at the safe house, instructed Gates and Peterson, "Converge on the sounds to the northeast of your original position."

"Copy," Gates replied and moved toward the house from which the sounds were emanating. Cautiously, he rounded the corner of the house and heard a struggle coming from a small shed in the corner of the yard. He heard another scream from inside the shed before it went silent. With his gun extended, he crossed the overgrown lawn. Diegert was crouched on the back deck next to an electrical outlet, ready to insert the plug. Gates stepped to the side of the shed's entrance and quickly peered in to determine if the space was clear. He flipped on his mini Maglite, illuminating the shed's interior. When Diegert saw the flashlight's beam, he inserted the plug, sending electricity across the lawn. It sparked when it hit the fork, igniting the fertilizer-and-fuel mixture, creating an explosion that ripped the building apart while dispersing ten thousand pieces of Gates's body all over the abandoned backyard.

Carolyn had underestimated the force of the explosion. She was struck by both the heat surge and a piece of aluminum shrapnel, which gashed her right shoulder. Stunned and bleeding, she moved along the hedgerow toward the street.

CHAPTER 59

An unexpected explosion of such magnitude shook Talbot as he turned to see the night sky lit up by an intense fireball. He immediately put out a call to his agents, which got no response from either of them. Proceeding cautiously down the street, he needed to investigate the situation.

Stepping onto the street from the yard where the explosion had occurred, he saw a woman who appeared disoriented. Talbot closed in on her quickly, grabbing her from behind and taking her down to the ground. She struggled, but he quickly had her hands bound behind her in flexicuffs. Carolyn screamed from the pain in her shoulder. Talbot could see the injury, and he forced a second scream when he lifted her by the injured arm.

Diegert had pulled the plug and crept south along the back of the house. He heard Carolyn scream and continued in the direction of her painful shrieks. At the corner of the garage, he could see Talbot in the street tormenting Carolyn Fuller. Talbot shouted, "Diegert, get your ass out here now or this pretty lady pays in pain."

The belligerent FBI agent stood at the edge of the driveway, scanning the area for Diegert's movement.

"Throw out your gun or I shoot her in the leg."

"Alright," shouted Diegert.

He tossed the hose spray gun out onto the dark driveway, where it landed with a loud clatter.

"Now you walk out real slow."

"I can't . . . I'm injured, I can't walk."

"Bullshit, fuckin' crawl out onto the driveway."

"Fuck you, you dishonest prick."

"Ha—look who's insulting who."

Diegert crawled slowly and convincingly onto the pavement of the driveway.

In the darkness, Talbot could just barely see Diegert appear on the driveway from around the corner of the garage. He walked up the driveway with Carolyn as a shield in front of him. When he was halfway up the driveway, a motion sensor triggered two bulbs, which flooded the asphalt with blindingly bright light. Carolyn ducked down from the brightness. Talbot let go of her, shielding his eyes with his left arm. Diegert had Agent Peterson's pistol ready and used the moment of illumination to fire a bullet into Talbot's shoulder. The shot spun him to the right, and Diegert fired again. The force of the second projectile penetrated Talbot's ribs, causing him to lurch forward and drop to his knees. Diegert's third bullet opened the FBI agent's cranium, and his brains spilled out when his big body fell forward onto the blacktop.

Diegert ran over to Carolyn and guided her out of the light and over to the edge of the driveway. He stepped over to Talbot's corpse and slipped his smartphone out from his jacket pocket. Crossing back to Carolyn, he looked at her wound and put some pressure on it. "Come on, Donovan has a first aid kit in his car."

Walking back to the safe house, Carolyn began, "That's it? You just killed three men and now we walk away and bind our wounds?"

"What do you want me to do? Call the police so another hit team can be sent? Those guys weren't going to arrest us; it was us or them. Now I'm going to fix you up, and then we're getting the hell out of here."

"I've just never seen people killed like that before. I've been with the agency a long time, but I've never fired my weapon. It's just so sudden."

Diegert held the door for her as she stepped into the safe house. He set her in a kitchen chair and retrieved the first aid kit from Donovan's car. In the trunk, Diegert found a change of clothes in a luggage bag. He took both things back inside. His clothing was saturated in cesspool sludge, stinking like raw sewage. He changed his clothes and cleaned himself up before tending to Carolyn's injured shoulder. The wound was through the skin but not the muscle. The kit contained a local anesthetic and a fully threaded suture needle. "I'm going to stitch your cut."

Diegert injected the pain-blocking agent, and when she was numb to the touch, he sewed up the gap between the edges of her skin. He covered the wound with antibacterial ointment and bandaged it up.

"Thanks," said Carolyn as she looked up into Diegert's eyes.

"Thank Jim; he's the one with the kit."

Carolyn rose from her seat and stood close to Diegert. "I want to thank you. Not just for the stitches but for everything you did tonight. I wouldn't have survived if . . ."

Carolyn's voice broke off; she could no longer speak. Her tears choked off her words and she began to cry. She leaned into Diegert as the sobs burst forth from her. Diegert held her and felt his own sadness, which had been building since Romania.

The men he killed in the tournament, the hit in Germany, the president of the United States—and now his mother was in the hands of Crepusculous. He felt the grief well up in him like the bubble of air from Peterson's lungs. Even though he wanted to hold it in, it had to come out. He wrapped his arms around this warm and vulnerable woman. He wanted to protect her while he also revealed his vulnerable side. Tears filled his eyes as the eyes of dying men played across his mind. The windows to the soul, whose light he had extinguished, now made him feel the pain he had inflicted not just on their bodies but on their psyches, their families, and their friends.

Carolyn was crying and sobbing, but she was quite bewildered when she felt Diegert crying and bellowing with the greatest anguish and despair she had ever witnessed in a man. The two of them filled the house with sounds of emotional turmoil. Carolyn couldn't support his weight, and they collapsed to the floor. They held and hugged, fully clothed, each lost in their private world of grief, shared but not revealed.

Carolyn's negative energy gradually dissipated, but Diegert was still releasing the pain he held inside. Carolyn found herself compassionately soothing the grieving man. She stroked his head and wiped his tears. She kissed his forehead and told him it was going to be OK. Her ministrations eased Diegert back from the tortured place his mind had traveled to. He stopped crying and returned her caresses. They gently stroked one another on the head, face, and neck. Their bodies were entwined, hips pressed against one another, the pressure fueled by a primal urge. It was Diegert who was afraid of what might happen next between two adults in an emotionally charged moment. He reasoned that what might feel satisfying right now could compromise their survival. Always pragmatic when in danger, he knew they had to leave this place now. He avoided looking into her eyes; he also did not want to see her moist lips so close. He moved his hips away from hers, yet he could feel the heat of her body radiating between them when he separated from her.

Carolyn was aroused and confused. She was afraid she had misconstrued the emotional closeness for something more. She was attracted to this man and was experiencing a sexual desire that now felt awkward and out of place. She knew they were still threatened and had to leave right away. Still she felt his erection against her, and the feeling filled her with lust. She was both dispirited and grateful when Diegert said, "We gotta go."

CHAPTER 60

Ballistics testing performed on the gun found in the holster of Alexi Strakov matched it to the bullets that had killed President Peter Carson. This revelation changed the thinking about who was guilty of assassinating the president. Preliminary data revealed that Strakov was an international freelance operator who was sought for questioning in several high-profile killings in Europe. The focus on Diegert was still active, but the public was now being fed conflicting stories. When this information began disseminating across the Web, Blevinsky had to move quickly to purge any records that connected Strakov to the Board. His fail-safe program dropped Strakov like a bag of garbage in a skyscraper's chute. The moment he presented a possible liability, he became a piece of discarded refuse.

Dick Chambliss called a conference with the FBI, CIA, and DPD. The absence of Jim Donovan and Carolyn Fuller made the meeting practically useless. The chief of police treated the Secret Service man like a houseguest whose dog had just taken a crap on the living-room carpet. He was furious that the security was so slack, that the most important and imperiled man in the world was shot in his front yard. Detroit would never recover from the damage this would create for the city's reputation. He wanted to know what the Secret Service was going to do to publicly take all the blame for this colossal failure. Chambliss didn't anticipate the public-relations attack. He dismissed the chief's concerns as shortsighted and unpatriotic. The two men left the meeting without even discussing the investigation. Their only outcome was an entrenched animosity on both sides.

***

Untangling from each other and getting up off the floor was an awkward moment for Diegert and Carolyn. They both felt like embarrassed teenagers who'd experimented with carnal passion and now wanted to be as far away from each other as possible. All the regret with none of the joy.

"We've got to get out of here, and I have to find a way across the Canadian border."

"I can help you with that."

Diegert looked at her quizzically.

"I work for the CIA—and espionage is our business. I've got what we need to cross into Canada."

Diegert had to pull Donovan's body across the driveway so Carolyn's car could exit the garage. She looked through the car's window at her friend's lifeless body being carefully dragged through a puddle of his own blood. The harshness of this business started to weigh on her again. Diegert came to the driver's side window. Carolyn gestured with her thumb to the back of the car. Diegert rolled his eyes and stepped to the rear. Carolyn popped the trunk and joined Diegert, who was feeling claustrophobic looking into the cramped and uncomfortable luggage space.

"Just a minute," said Carolyn before she ran back into the house. A moment later, she returned with two couch cushions.

She placed them in the trunk, and with an enticing flourish of her hand, invited Diegert to climb in. She closed the compartment and double-checked to make sure the magnets securely held the Ontario plates to the trunk lid.

Carolyn took Highway 75 to the Ambassador Bridge. US customs was performing an exit check before vehicles were allowed to cross. With her Canadian passport, windshield registration sticker, and Ontario plates, all she had to do was be polite and she would pass for a resident of the northern neighbor returning home from a business conference. Traffic moved at the expected but annoying crawl. Once she was lined up to cross the border, there was nothing to do but observe her fellow motorists. Diegert tried to sleep, but he was afraid he might not wake up, since a lot more exhaust fumes permeate the trunk than the cabin of a car. When Carolyn was second in line for the customs agent, she carefully watched the car in front of her. The car had Michigan plates and two male travelers. It was driven by a European-looking man with a salt-and-pepper beard. His passenger had brown skin, jet-black hair, and a scruffy beard. The agent took their documents, and after some time, another agent arrived with a sniffer dog who was allowed to circle the car. After the benign canine inspection, the agent asked the men to open the trunk. Carolyn could see the men were objecting to this request, and it looked like they were refusing to comply. Two more agents came to the scene, one standing by the passenger door, while the other took a position by the opening of the driver's door. The motorists were shouting and gesticulating inside the car, which only made the agents place their hands on their weapons. Carolyn was feeling the tension. As an intelligence agent, she could see the warning signs that concerned the customs agents, and the jerks in the car weren't making things any easier. Finally, the lead agent directed the car to drive to the inspection area. Two of the agents escorted the car behind a concrete wall, where the situation would be resolved without public observation.

Carolyn pulled her car up. The agent with the dog stood next to the primary agent, who asked Carolyn for her passport. While inspecting the document, he asked, "Where do you live?"

"Dutton, Ontario."

"The reason for your visit?"

"A business conference."

The dog rose from his seated position and began enthusiastically wagging his tail. The agent looked surprised to see his canine partner behaving like a happy puppy. He leaned forward to Carolyn's window and asked, "Ma'am, do you have a dog?"

"Not in the car, but I do at home."

"OK, thank you. He's still young," said the agent, referring to his dog. "He has a great nose for contraband, but he still gets excited when he smells another dog or someone with whom he wants to make a friend."

Carolyn looked up at the agent and just smiled.

"Is she OK, Mick?" he asked his human partner.

Handing back her passport, the primary agent said, "Yeah . . . you're all set."

Carolyn crossed the bridge, breezed through Canadian customs, and drove to a dark lot in a public park and let Diegert out of the trunk. As he stretched his body, he said, "I'll never volunteer to ride in a trunk again."

"You're here and you're free, so don't complain. What happens now?"

"Now?" He paused. "I've got to get to Montreal, where my fake documents will get me on a flight to London."

"I'm coming with you."

"What?"

"You're still a wanted man, and even though there is some truth to what you've told me, you still shot the president. I helped you leave the United States, but I am not letting you fly off to Europe without me."

"Well, good, because I had no idea how I was going to get to Montreal, but I want to ride in a seat this time."

***

Thermobaric bombs destroy with their initial explosions and then continue to kill people by consuming oxygen with super-high temperatures. If people survive the explosion, asphyxiation kills them. The Board planted nine bombs in nine cities in the United States. Only Klaus Panzer and Aaron Blevinsky knew the cities and the exact locations within those cities. Javier Perez, who was supposedly in charge of the operation, didn't even bother to ask Blevinsky which cities were targeted. The bombs were timed to go off in simultaneous triplets. Each group of three was separated by one hour. The plan was to have the United States attacked nine times within three hours. The inflicted damage to infrastructure and transportation would cripple areas of the country. The chaos and confusion brought about by the disruption of communication would create disinformation and uncoordinated emergency responses. The multiple attacks on a wide variety of communities would create psychological fear and eviscerate America's sense of security. Americans would become refugees in their own homes. They would experience the ravages of war on their own soil like never before. Panzer was completely convinced that America would implode. The devastation would be too great for the weak fabric of the gluttonous nation. In its anemic state, the country would no longer be able to call itself the greatest nation on earth; instead, it would have to face the consequences of its decline. The overweight, in debt, morally bankrupt nation would, Panzer believed, turn on itself and fracture into battling tribes loosely associated along regional lines. Even these groups, though, would have such vast ideological differences that it was possible that the country—that was all about "me"— might very well degenerate into small warrior groups geared for survival like in a postapocalyptic dystopia. He could only hope it would be so, because his plan for dominance would be most effective in a society that was fractured into a multiconflict civil war.

Blevinsky was getting impatient waiting for a status report from Talbot. He wanted current information, and hopefully good news, to give Panzer when he asked for an update. He texted Talbot: *Status report?*

***

While traveling east toward Montreal on Highway 401 with Carolyn, Diegert felt Talbot's phone buzz. Aaron Blevinsky's name popped up with a request for a status report. He replied: *We have Diegert. What action do you want taken?*

Blevinsky was ecstatic when he got Talbot's text. He replied: *Terminate him and send me a photo.* Diegert was not surprised by the answer, but he was surprised at how much the terse reply hurt. Blevinsky had never been a friend, but he'd been like a coach. Diegert wanted the balding man's approval for the missions he had completed. To be so completely and fatally rejected left him with a feeling of failure. He replied to Blevinsky: *Yes, sir.*

Diegert looked up from his texting and asked Carolyn to pull over at the next exit.

A tractor route into a hayfield provided the privacy they needed. Diegert lay on the ground, tilting his head to the side in the most uncomfortable and unnatural position he could manage. Carolyn took his picture. Reviewing the image, Diegert convinced himself he looked pretty dead. Carolyn told him to drive the car. By the time they got back to the 401, Carolyn had Diegert's image in her computer and was editing the photograph with a photo app so the assassin really looked dead. She made his skin pale, darkened under the eyes, and added a touch of jaundice. Carolyn added blood dribbling out the nose and smeared at the corner of his mouth, which gave the impression that Diegert's death was a violent one. She showed the image to Diegert, who asked, "Is that my future?"

"I hope not."

***

When Blevinsky received the photo, he was as happy as a kid on Christmas morning. He published the image on the Web, announcing that Special Agent Stanley Talbot of the FBI had killed the assassin in a violent gun battle. Talbot's bravery and dedication to the investigation were to be commended, and the American people should be proud of this federal law-enforcement agent.

***

After reading Blevinsky's posting, Carolyn was glad they were already past Toronto on their way to Montreal's Mirabel International Airport. She had switched places with Diegert and drove a lot faster than he did.

"How much do you make?" Diegert asked in a pointed and rather abrupt manner.

"You mean, what's my annual salary?"

"Yeah."

"Why do you want to know that?"

"Because I wonder what all this is worth to you?"

"Eighty-two thousand dollars a year, but that is not why I do this job."

"Why, then?"

"This will sound stupid to you but patriotism, loyalty, service to others."

"Did you get that out of a Marvel or a DC comic?"

"Shut up, you're in no position to judge me. You shot the leader of the free world, killing a great man. You've disrupted the entire country, and except for crying on the floor, I don't see a smidge of this weighing on your conscience. I don't think you're feeling this enough."

"Conscience: Right or wrong? Innocence or guilt? I couldn't consider these with the decision I had to make."

"Had to make? Or chose to make? You did not have to kill the president. You were alone and could've aborted the mission. You can't tell me there isn't a place in your heart that says that was wrong."

"A decision has to be assessed within the context of the situation. You think you understand this, and me. You have no idea, which surprises me, since I thought the CIA was better than that. The obvious and the easy always have to be investigated more thoroughly. Isn't that true?"

"You wanna convince me this was necessary, somehow unavoidable? Why did you pull the trigger?"

"That was the mission."

"Bullshit, you're hiding behind that. Why didn't you change the course of history and let the president live?"

Diegert didn't reply as he swiped the screen of his phone. His thoughts were swirling with a confused sense of needing to have Carolyn understand his actions while also wanting to remain in control of his problems.

Carolyn grew impatient. "You have to answer my question; you're not getting a pass. You tell me why you shot the president."

Diegert scrolled through images on his phone until the picture of his mother, gagged with a gun at her head, appeared on the screen. With trembling hands, he looked at the image.

Through a shaky, choked-up voice, Diegert said, "I'm going to show you why I shot him. Pull over; I'm gonna drive."

Diegert took the wheel with Carolyn next to him as they got back on the highway. Diegert's phone lay on the center console.

"Look at my phone."

Carolyn examined the screen, then said, "Who is she and who's holding her?"

"She's my mother, and Crepusculous has her. That image popped up on my screen as the president took the stage. If I didn't shoot him, she would be raped, beaten, and killed. That was my dilemma."

Carolyn grew silent. She hung her head, ran her hand through her hair, and sighed.

"Then I guess you've got more than one reason to be going after them."

"Damn right."

"Where is she now?"

"I don't know, but they still have her. They could be doing whatever they want to her."

Diegert slammed his fist on the dashboard.

"OK, OK, I'm sorry to have asked, but let's stick to our plan, because I think it will help you find her."

"You really think so?"

"I do."

"You know, I didn't tell you about this before, but I didn't pull the trigger on the gun that shot the president."

Carolyn turned her head, peering at Diegert with a *don't give me that bullshit* look.

"I swear to God. That gun was equipped with a remote sensor so someone else could fire it. You must've heard of this kind of technology?"

Carolyn nodded, but the doubt never left her eyes.

"I've heard of remotely operated weapons, but I've never seen them demonstrated or worked on a case in which they were involved."

Diegert continued, "When I saw it was the president, I decided I couldn't go through with it. After my mom's picture showed up on my phone, I had to point the gun in his direction, but I couldn't pull the trigger. The instant I failed to act, the gun fired automatically. Crepusculous controlled it."

Carolyn's doubt softened just a little, but she was confused about something. "You mean, you didn't know the target was the president beforehand?"

"No. Everything for the mission was on a need-to-know basis. I was instructed where to go, what to wear, and what weapon to bring, but nothing else. Crazy, eh?"

"It's a little bit hard to believe, but it also makes sense if you're sending someone to do a job for which you're afraid they're not fully committed."

"It's total deceit and manipulation."

"So you really didn't kill him, you're an agent who's been used and was then targeted for elimination."

"I'm still targeted for elimination," said Diegert as he scanned Carolyn's face for some clue that she believed him. Her expression was dispassionate.

"I planted the remote-controlled gun on Alexi Strakov's body."

"And who is that?"

"Strakov was the leader of the Crepusculous tactical team. He was one big, mean motherfucker they sent to kill me after I killed the president."

"But that's not what happened, correct?"

"I killed him when he attacked the police station where I met Jim Donovan."

Carolyn put her head down and stroked her forehead as she recalled the death of her friend from the FBI and tried to keep all of Diegert's story straight.

Diegert continued, "By putting the gun on him, I started a disinformation campaign to make it look like he did it."

She pulled her head up and gave him a sidelong glance.

Diegert jumped in. "Look, Strakov was a very bad guy, and he deserves to be pegged as the president's assassin. He's going to be found dead with the gun in his possession, and when they search his background, they'll find out he's an international assassin with multiple prior crimes."

"So you're OK with someone else taking the blame for what you did?"

Diegert thought for a moment as they progressed north on the 401, passing a tractor-trailer loaded with Canadian logs headed to a lumber mill. "If I'm identified as the president's assassin, my life is over. But if a man whose life is already over is seen as the assassin, then I am free to leave this violence behind and live a peaceful life. So, yeah, I'm OK with that."

"I don't exonerate you from the president's death. Even if I believe all that you've told me, you still entered the United States with the intention to kill someone, and that makes you a criminal."

Her words chilled Diegert's marrow. Was she going to turn on him here in Canada? Was she reconsidering helping him? Calling him a criminal, was she now going to be a cop? Diegert looked up as they passed under the sign indicating they were two kilometers from the Prescott Exit off the 401. It was open, desolate country; there would be dirt roads running into big fields separated by woodlots. He could do her, dump her, and just drive away, preserving his freedom. He looked at her, feeling a dark menace rising, but the thought made him sick. He felt regret and guilt for just thinking about it. The conflict was clouding his decision, and the exit, veering off to the right, was now visible.

Carolyn's words broke his frustration. "I think the fact that you are a criminal is actually going to be very useful to us."

Diegert twisted his head in surprise at what Carolyn had just said. He tweaked the wheel to the left, keeping the car on the highway.

Carolyn went on to say, "I can't promise a miracle, but there's a mechanism by which I can use you in the investigation."

"How? What do you mean?"

"At the CIA, we deal with bad people all the time. The little fish leads us to the big fish; that's how we topple large organizations. We call these little fish special field assets or SFAs."

Now Diegert's face was filled with doubt as he asked, "So when you catch the big fish, do you go back and take out the little fish too?"

"Yes, sometimes. But if the little fish continues to be useful and doesn't commit more crimes, we'll work with 'em for years, and they're never arrested."

"You think I could be one of those?"

"It's the mechanism by which I can justify what we're doing. But you better produce something big on Crepusculous."

Diegert thought about working for the CIA. It would be even cooler than the Special Forces, which was what he'd secretly hoped he would be able to do while in the Army. Now that that was never going to happen, perhaps this would be better. "Does it come with a salary?"

Carolyn looked at him in utter disbelief. "You don't get paid. You're not an employee. You're a double agent, a mole, an inside man who dishes on the organization in which you are embedded. The CIA is not going to hire you, but they aren't going to arrest you either, as long as you cooperate and provide good intel."

"Oh."

"You're not an agent, you're an asset, and your position within Crepusculous is what makes you valuable. You get it?"

"Yeah, but it's really no different than what we're doing right now."

"Correct, only I have to submit a profile and request permission to designate you as an SFA."

"If you submit a profile on me, they'll say either arrest him or shoot him."

"Actually, assets are most helpful in the early stages of an investigation before things become entrenched. It wouldn't be unprecedented to request this now."

Through the windshield, Carolyn saw a sign indicating a rest stop in five kilometers.

"If I'm hungry, you must be too," she said. Diegert nodded with enthusiasm. "OK, let's stop and eat."

As Diegert drove into the rest area, Carolyn directed him. "Drop me at the entrance and go fill up the gas, then park over there by those semis." She pointed to a dark, distant area of the parking lot where tractor-trailers sat. "I'll bring the food."

"Yeah, but you don't know what I want," said a petulant David Diegert.

"Too bad, you'll eat what I bring." She flung the door open and bolted out of the car.

Diegert put on his baseball cap and kept his head down so the gas cam wouldn't catch his face. After parking the car on the edge of the lot away from the building but not too close to the trucks, he took a piss in the weeds. Waiting for Carolyn in the car, he thought maybe he should just drive away. He still had impulses to run, to be alone, to be independent, but he realized all she'd have to do is call in the license plate and he'd be pursued. No, he would not run from her; she seemed to want to work with him to battle Crepusculous and help him get his mom back. Although it was hard for him to trust her, and believe she trusted him, he was going to have to ride this out. The passenger door opened, and Carolyn climbed in holding white paper bags exuding the warmth and greasy aroma of deep-fried fast food. Diegert smiled as he popped french fries into his mouth before taking big bites of a cheeseburger. With his mouth still full and smiling, he said, "You chose well."

Carolyn's Caesar salad wrap came with an apple.

Sitting in the car with the interior lights on, Carolyn was able to look at Diegert's face. She wanted to see his eyes while they spoke. Diegert sucked up soda through his straw.

"You gotta stop doing the dirty work of liars and untouchable thieves."

Diegert turned to her but kept drinking through the straw.

Carolyn continued, "When you work for the CIA, even as an asset, you work to protect people, and that's a purpose worth the risk."

Diegert nodded his head as he took another bite.

"Killing people must be a burden on your conscience. You do have one, don't you?"

Diegert chewed as he considered his answer; he felt she was reaching deep inside him, asking him to reveal his darkness, but he swallowed and looked her square in the eyes when he said, "I have a conscience. I feel the pain of my actions, but I've also had little choice under the circumstances in which I've been forced to kill."

"That sounds like an excuse."

"It's an explanation. I have killed to keep from being killed. I have killed in order to remain free. You've been the benefactor of these actions, and I wonder how you deal with the weight of it on your conscience?"

"Don't turn this back on me. I have a code and clearance sanctioned by the CIA. If I ever kill someone, it'll be in the line of duty under the rules of engagement associated with a mission."

Diegert allowed a smirk to curl across his lips. "Well, I hope every encounter you have fits within your rules, because every time I've pulled the trigger, there were no rules to guide me." He reached into his bag and gobbled a handful of fries.

"You need to develop your own code, David. You can't wield deadly force with no personal code. How do you decide if it's right or wrong to kill someone?"

Feeling pressed like never before, Diegert responded, "I don't shoot women or children, and the targets I've taken out were all guilty of crimes."

Carolyn locked her eyes on him as she chewed a bite of her wrap. With a measured tone, she asked, "And what was the president's crime?"

"Hey, I already told you I didn't shoot him."

"OK, no women or children, and you'll only shoot criminals."

"Right, that's what I've done and will continue to do."

"I'm going to make sure you do, David. I'm going to make sure you live up to that pledge."

Diegert pulled his gaze away from her and looked out onto the parking lot. He felt ambivalent about his pledge because a promise to act in a very specific manner was a promise he knew he'd be unlikely to keep. A loud slurp reverberated through his cup as he sucked the last of his soda.

Back on the road, Carolyn pulled out her computer and began typing up a profile and permission request for Diegert to become a special field asset.

As the miles persisted, Diegert thought about betraying the people at Headquarters. They were not trustworthy people. They were murderers, hackers, and unethical scientists pumped up on corporate power. It would be honorable to take them down, close the shop, and end their unique type of terror. Diegert figured his crimes would be justified if he now used his position to reveal and destroy the secrets of Crepusculous. Wasn't the hero the one who put himself in danger to help others? Wasn't that what he'd been doing? Helping Carolyn and the CIA stop Crepusculous from destroying America would certainly be the work of a heroic person. Diegert began to see himself and the things he'd been doing from a different perspective. Instead of seeing a sad failure, clawing his way through survival, he began to realize that he was in a unique position to thwart the dark intentions of a criminal enterprise. If a poor boy from Minnesota could stop an evil empire from destroying the United States, then he should do so without fear or hesitation. Diegert caught himself before he allowed his thoughts to go overboard when the theme from *Rocky* started playing in his head. Nevertheless, he had a lot to think about and the time to do it as the road to Montreal stretched out in front of him.

After they passed the exit for Route 416 to Ottawa, the agrarian countryside of central Ontario gave way to the granite outcroppings of the Canadian Shield. Diegert was impressed with the cliff faces formed by the demolition of mountains of granite. Rock had been cleared to make the road, and the debris was crushed and dumped into the swampy hollows to level the bed upon which 830 kilometers of asphalt had been laid, creating Highway 401. Carolyn had been typing for nearly an hour.

"David, what unit of the Army were you with?"

"You better not tell them that."

"Look, I'm trying to make you look good, and I don't have a lot to work with. What was the unit?"

"1st Cavalry out of Fort Hood, The First Team."

"Your rank?"

"Private first class."

"OK, you know your Strakov theory might just be working. I've been monitoring a CIA information site, and Strakov's record is convincing certain people that he is a much more likely suspect than you. One of the assistant directors went so far as to say, "A dead bird in the hand is better than one on the wing."

"His legend will grow with this crime," Diegert thought out loud.

"It's a long way before you're cleared, but that was a clever move to plant the gun on him."

"Well, that's a trick I learned from my brother; he was always pinning the blame on me."

Carolyn smiled and chuckled. "My brothers were always joshing around with each other. My older brother would set up my younger brother, and Mom would fall for it every time. Patrick would come out smelling like roses, while Michael took the heat and got in trouble. I developed my powers of observation watching those two."

"Sounds like fun. What about the rest of your family?"

Carolyn closed her computer and slid it back into its case as she turned in her seat to face Diegert. A comforting smile lit up her face, and a warm glow started to rise in her cheeks.

"OK, so my two older brothers, Patrick and Michael. They're both married. Pat has three kids, two boys and a girl.

Mike has a son and a daughter. I have a younger sister, Laura. She's twenty-eight and, like me, not yet married. Boy, do we get it all the time about why aren't we married yet."

"Why aren't you?"

"That's another story. My dad's a dentist and my mom runs the office. They've worked together as long as they've been married. We just celebrated their fortieth anniversary. We kids sent them on a cruise through the Caribbean, and they had a great time. My parents' marriage is, like, the ideal. I want a relationship like they have, and it's hard to find, but I'm lucky to have a great family; they're the rock of my foundation."

Glancing over at her throughout her story, Diegert could see the pride and happiness her family inspired. The disappointment and dysfunction of his own family hung in his mind like an all-day rain cloud.

"What about you? Tell me about your family."

Diegert glanced over with a wan smile and turned back to concentrate on the white lines zipping past the car, saying nothing.

"So tell me some more about your brother," persisted Carolyn.

Diegert scratched the back of his head and ran his fingers through his hair. He wondered if he should lie and make his family sound nice. Carolyn had something about her, though; he didn't want to lie to her. Diegert was usually very suspicious of anyone who made him feel this way, but it had been a very long time since he'd felt the beginnings of a sense of trust.

"My brother, Jake, is a drug dealer. He's short, fat, and loud. He's my dad's favorite, and he uses that fact to his advantage on a daily basis. He makes sure my life is as miserable as he wants it to be. I never trusted him the whole time we were growing up."

Carolyn's smile and jovial expectation faded. "I'm sorry to hear that."

"Well, you're going to love this. My dad is a drunk. He has a tow-truck business in northern Minnesota, which makes no money. He hates me, but at least he has a reason. The man's never been a father to me, and I will be glad if I never see him again."

"Gee, that's harsh. You said he had a reason not to like you; what do you mean by that?"

"That would be my mother. She's tall, beautiful, half white, half Ojibwa Indian."

"Yeah, yeah, I saw the picture on your phone. In spite of the dreadful circumstances, I could see she's a beautiful woman."

"Her beauty is exotic, but it has never been anything but trouble for her. She's emotionally crippled and struggles with a lack of confidence. Her self-esteem is assaulted on a regular basis by my dad, who treats her like a domestic slave. She works her ass off waitressing at a local diner where she's happy to put in extra shifts just to avoid being home. The two of them are financially dependent on each other, but they live on opposite sides of an emotional canyon with jagged rock walls that are a hundred feet high."

"I still don't see why he should hate his own son."

"Because I'm not."

"What?"

"I'm not his true son." Diegert let that statement hang in the air. As he watched her struggle to reenter the conversation, he could see the CIA investigator in her want to ask the probing questions. This was not an interrogation, though, and she did not pursue the question. Diegert recognized her dilemma and offered the answer.

"My mom got knocked up through an illicit affair, but they stayed together and the bastard son was tolerated but never accepted or loved by Tom Diegert."

Diegert looked her way, and Carolyn caught his eyes and held his gaze. She started to nod very slowly, and Diegert felt that simple gesture carried more meaning than any other communication he'd ever had on this topic. That comfort, that sense of acceptance and belief she seemed to have in him, was a feeling he couldn't recall with anyone else. Part of him wanted to stop the car and run away, the other part wanted to drive forever with Carolyn and leave the real world behind.

"You love your mom, though."

"Yes, I do. She's the one person I can count on to help me and who loves me no matter what. I hate how I was conceived, but I love that she didn't give up on me. I know she sacrificed and struggled to raise me as best she could."

Carolyn's warm smile broadened to hear this man speak so reverently and respectfully of his mother in spite of being the product of a passionate transgression.

"You're part Ojibwa, then, that's cool."

Diegert shot her a look as sharp as shattered glass.

"No. Definitely not cool."

The silence amplified their distance on this topic as Carolyn was unable to disguise her surprise. "I'm sorry, I mean, having a different culture as part of your heritage is very interesting."

"Oh, fucking bullshit. Different cultures tend to hate each other, especially when one invades and dominates the other. People think racial prejudice is only in the South, but that's because they haven't spent time in the North. The Indians and the white people do not get along, and a half-breed is an affront to both sides. I was abused by both cultures; that's how fucking interesting it was growing up as a *halfsy* in Broward, Minnesota."

Carolyn sat silently, keeping an eye on him with a sidelong glance. Diegert stewed in his anger over his biculturalism, gritting his teeth and knotting up his jaw muscles. He eventually spoke again.

"Look, I'm sorry to go off on you, but you hit a nerve, and I have a lot of baggage from the past."

"Yeah, I can tell. Don't you want to let that go? Wouldn't it be better to move beyond it?"

The perplexed look on Diegert's face pleaded for further explanation.

Carolyn continued, "We all have bad experiences from the past. Growing up, you have to experience some bad things so you can tell the difference and find your place on controversial issues. Now, granted, it sounds like your situation was especially bad, but you're an adult now. Don't you want to progress past your childhood?"

Diegert said nothing; he just nodded.

"I remember learning about the Ojibwa people in school," offered Carolyn. "They are very spiritual, with . . . I think, seven principles by which they live."

"The seven gifts of the Anishinaabe: love, respect, bravery, honesty, humility, wisdom, and truth."

"Whoa! That's impressive. If you can commit those to memory, can't you incorporate them into your life?"

"That's easier said than done."

"Everything's easier when it's only said. In training, at the Farm, we ran five-mile obstacle courses that made a Tough Mudder look like a day in the sandbox. They wanted us to push ourselves through adversity and find the determination to never give up."

Diegert countered saying, "At Fort Benning, we rucksacked ten miles a day for seven days, slept on the ground, and avoided an op force the entire time."

"I'm not trying to say who's tougher, and I know you can withstand pain, but living by principles is also tough. But it produces good things just like difficult training."

Diegert looked at her as she waited for him to respond. He reached under his collar and pulled his amulet out from under his shirt. The seven colored beads strung on both sides of the medallion caught Carolyn's eye. Diegert told her, "Each bead represents one of the seven gifts, and the medallion has an inscription on the back."

He pulled the necklace over his head and handed it to her. She received it with delicate care in her open hands. The leather was soft and warm; it retained the heat from Diegert's body. The dark bottom half of the circle contrasted with the white top half, and the human foot that traversed both halves almost seemed to be in motion. Carolyn turned the amulet over and saw the inscription.

"This is written in Ojibwa," Carolyn said.

"It says: 'A man must travel through darkness to find the light.'"

"So that's what you're doing? Seeking the light? Traveling through darkness and killing people along the way?"

"Kind of a twisted vision quest, eh?"

"More like a criminal quest. You've got to get a focus and follow a principle, or you'll never even find the light switch. As a field asset, you can help us because you're already in there with the criminals."

"Don't forget the criminals are trying to kill me."

"You're still in their dark world, but maybe fighting them will help you find that light."

Carolyn handed him back the necklace. Diegert clutched it in his hand.

"You're a complicated and conflicted man, David Diegert."

"Yeah, I've heard that one before."

"You have skills and abilities that the agency trains men for years to develop, yet you have no guiding principles to discipline your actions. You're like a wild mustang, strong and fast but unable to be of any good in a civilized life."

Diegert looked over at her, fighting the urge to neigh like a horse. He held up the amulet, saying, "I want out of the darkness, and I'm humble enough to ask for your help finding the light."

Carolyn's expressionless reaction left Diegert wondering if she believed him or doubted his sincerity.

"Alright, David, you're on. I want you to come out of the darkness, but you'll have to follow my lead to the light; I can't force you to go."

Diegert strung the necklace over his head and left it hanging outside his shirt. "I'm with you."

"How much farther to Montreal?"

"About forty miles."

Carolyn tilted the seat back and rolled up her jacket on the headrest, turning away from Diegert to take a nap.

Diegert thought about the seven gifts. He'd memorized them but rarely considered their meaning. Carolyn got him to contemplate the role of the gifts in his life. He thought of humility and how one must recognize that there is much you do not know and be willing to be taught. Honesty, defined as the habit of being truthful. The truth for Diegert was not always clear; it was dependent on the situation.

Bravery, though, brought his thoughts to an uncomfortable place. He wanted so much to believe he was brave. He thought he was brave when he went on missions by himself behind enemy lines and battled attackers without any help. But the Ojibwa definition was not about individual heroics. Ojibwa beliefs on bravery dealt with the fact that you are terrified that you are not good enough and that others will find out. Bravery is to look at your innermost self and face the fact that you consider yourself unworthy and then find the way to true inner strength and acceptance.

Unworthy and not good enough were two feelings Diegert knew very well. How could he not, since this was all he felt from the time he was a little boy, bashed about by his father and brother. Feeling that he was a valuable person was a figment of vapor. He had no context in which to place such a concept, yet he was beginning to realize that without a belief in one's own worth, it was impossible to see the value in anyone else. Now he had to find a sense of self-worth and value while escaping from several law enforcement agencies and stopping Crepusculous from carrying out the rest of its plan.

CHAPTER 61

Making her way through Heathrow, Fatima saw the image of a dead David Diegert on a television in one of the terminal's pubs. She gasped out loud, startling the people around her when the grisly image registered. David was dead. Her student, her pupil, her protégé was now deceased and pilloried in the worldwide media, hung up like big game to bleed out. She was overcome with the despair she felt for the loss of someone she had grown to admire and respect. That image of his injured face was disturbing, but a hopeful thought took form that perhaps Diegert was pulling a ruse and might not actually be dead. The indifference and delight with which people were celebrating his death left Fatima feeling conflicted.

***

Carolyn bought tickets to Heathrow on an Air Canada flight under a Canadian identity as Marnie and Ian Taylor from Chelsea, Quebec. Carolyn provided Diegert with a disguise from the espionage kit in her car. With the skills of a theater makeup artist, she had turned his hair gray and given him a beard and mustache. The look matched the Canadian passport she fashioned for him, and Diegert couldn't believe how well the change in appearance worked as he cleared customs for the London-bound flight.

They waited together in the terminal for the flight to board. "We need to rent a place, preferably one outside the city," Diegert said.

Carolyn opened her laptop and found a site featuring cottages in the English countryside. "This one's only twenty minutes from central London."

"OK, rent it for the whole week. Then rent a car, and we'll be ready."

"Are we still going to kidnap that kid?"

"We are liberating him and returning him to his mother."

"You can convince yourself of whatever you want, but it's not right."

"Look, I'm an expert at convincing myself of things."

Over the PA, their flight was called for boarding. Diegert stood up with his bag and could see the doubt in Carolyn's face. "I'll see you in London."

As he walked to the gate, Carolyn wondered if his statement was one of hopeful expectation or a question. She sat for a few moments, realizing she could end this right here. She could skip the flight, report him to authorities, and have him taken into custody right now. His arrest would fulfill her CIA obligations. But then she thought of the bigger plan Diegert was determined to stop, and she realized she could save many more Americans by helping him stop whatever was happening. What she had to deny was that any of this was being done because she was attracted to him. She had to convince herself that any desire for David Diegert was delusional and not the motivation for her actions. She got up and boarded the flight.

***

The assistant director of the FBI in charge of national investigations was Madeline Anderson, a fifty-four-year-old seasoned agent who was director of the West Coast Division of the Bureau from 2001 to 2010 before taking the national position. Dick Chambliss had her on a secure Skype call, and the usually polite, levelheaded Secret Service officer was summarizing for the FBI the problems as he saw them.

"We are not in charge of this investigation. We're being overrun with unsubstantiated media that is broadcasting unconfirmed information as evidence. We are reacting to these things rather than conducting an investigation as we all know we should."

"What do you see as our primary issues at this time?" asked the perturbed assistant director, who was not used to being dressed down about the operation of the Bureau.

"We need clarity on several issues: the report of the David Diegert/Matthew Wilcox character being dead; the location of Agent Talbot, from whom we need an official statement; and the identity of the dead man with the gun that shot the president. These are all issues which have risen from the Web but need to be cleared by authorities."

Chambliss observed Anderson lower her face and scratch her forehead. He continued, "Simultaneously, we need to interview the supervisors on the scene for Eagle Talon Security who handled the outer perimeter and review all available video surveillance within one square mile of the president's address. We need eyes and information so we can understand the conditions at the time of the shooting."

Having listened to his summary, the assistant director stated, "Dick, I will personally direct this investigation, and I will update you each hour."

Chambliss replied, "Thank you, this is the most substantial crime of our lifetimes. We want to get it right."

***

Sitting in the deep leather chair in Kellerman's London office, Klaus Panzer couldn't take his eyes off the image of David Diegert's dead face. Mysteriously, there was something familiar about his features that was welling up memories so faded and dusty that Panzer couldn't tell if they were figments or actual recollections.

"Really, Klaus, it is a bit morbid the way you're transfixed by that gruesome sight."

"Forgive me; I'm a bit preoccupied with this man's death."

"Diegert was a cheeky bastard. He was the one who single-handedly rescued Andrew Cambridge from the Baltic mob." After deeply inhaling and swallowing another aromatic sip of his brandy, Kellerman continued, "Perhaps we'll be able to find another one like him soon."

Panzer turned to look at the screen again, and the instant his eyes were on it his brain went to work trying to match that image with one of the millions and millions of memories stored in his cortex. Not being one who tolerated unresolved issues, Panzer secretly hoped that Diegert was not dead so he could confront the man and determine the source of his conjecture.

CHAPTER 62

At Heathrow, Carolyn and Diegert moved through customs without incident and secured their rental car. As Diegert drove to the cottage, an exasperated Carolyn muttered under breath, "Damn it."

"What's wrong?"

As she looked at her phone screen, Carolyn explained, "Back in Montreal, I sent my request for you to be classified as a special field asset."

"They're not buying it."

"No. In fact, they insist I arrest you immediately and call in FBI agents to take you into custody."

"They still think we're in the US."

"Well, I didn't give them any reason to think otherwise."

"So we proceed just the same as if they had said yes. I'm a CIA asset, and I'll act like one."

"If you don't, the message authorizes me to use deadly force."

Her statement shocked him back to the harsh realities of what they were doing. "Alright, then, let's hope it doesn't come to that."

Arriving at the cottage, they found the little house well-appointed and comfortable. The bathroom was clean and stocked with thick, soft towels.

"Look, I've had to smell you for the last thirty-six hours, and it's time for you to get rid of the gray hair and fake beard. Hit the shower, would ya?"

When a sniff of his armpits produced a wrinkled nose, Diegert nodded and began peeling the beard off as he headed to the bathroom.

Carolyn opened the computer and connected to the Internet. She was searching maps of the area to get her bearings. As she looked up from the screen, she noticed light emerging from the short hall that led to the bathroom. The level of light told her that the door to the bathroom was still open. She knew she should be polite and stay where she was, but the curiosity was too great—besides, she should check and make sure David didn't need anything. She stepped toward the hall quietly, and as she neared the corner, she could see through the open door. In the mirror, she saw Diegert drop his black combat pants and pull down his underwear. His buttocks were reflected, and she reacted to the strong-looking muscles of his ass with a gulp in her throat. David kicked his clothes into a pile and turned around to face the mirror. Carolyn was able to secretly see his entire body in the mirror's reflection. Diegert was fit, muscular, and handsome. The long scar on his thigh looked nasty, and he had bruises on his ribs, which he turned toward the mirror to inspect. He winced as he pressed on the darkest areas of injury. His abdomen was lean and rippled. The muscles converged from his hips down to his crotch where his penis hung.

Diegert spun away from the mirror and turned on the shower, adjusted the temperature, and stepped in. Carolyn stood there with all intentions of going back to the computer, but she lingered, drawn to the possibility her mind couldn't let go. She knew Diegert was a criminal, but his mission was redemptive. She hadn't been with a man for so long, and no man she had ever been with had a physique like his. The masculine frame and muscular contours created erotic images in her mind, which were arousing her body. The hug and cry, and the memory of his body on the safe house floor, converged with her thoughts to produce a flow within her. She stepped to the threshold of the bathroom, and the sound of the cascading water pulsed in her brain like the coursing of her blood. Crossing in, she removed her shoes, unbuttoned her blouse, and undid her pants. With her outer garments on the floor, she looked in the mirror and the reflection of him moving behind the translucent shower curtain, his form tantalized her to remove her bra and panties. Feeling bold and fully aroused, she slid the shower curtain back, surprising Diegert with her naked body.

He stopped rubbing the soap between his hands and stepped back, making room for her to step in. She locked her gaze onto his eyes and loved the way his lids pulled back. She smiled at him and giggled a little as the water splashed on her back and ran over her shoulders, dribbling off her nipples. She leaned her head back under the showerhead to wet her hair. With her eyes closed and her face turned up to the ceiling, she could feel Diegert's eyes inspecting every inch of her. She exercised regularly to keep her thirty-two-year-old body in top shape in order to qualify for the CIA fitness standards. She was also an avid cyclist and swimmer. She knew her athletic curves drew admiring looks from appreciative guys.

Soaking her hair darkened her brunette locks, which she smoothed away from her face as she opened her eyes and looked at Diegert. She reached a hand out and tenderly caressed his injured ribs. He tensed as she touched the painful bruises but relaxed when he felt how gentle she was. She made a sad pouty face that told Diegert she was sympathetic to his pain. Looking deeply into each other's eyes, they brought their bodies together in a close embrace. The feel of skin on skin under the flow of warm water was delightful to both of them, and they stayed like that for several quiet minutes. Carolyn began stroking Diegert's body, running her hands up his back, down over his buttocks, and onto the back of his thighs. Likewise, Diegert caressed her body, following the flow of water over the contours of her hips, back, and thighs. Their mutual exploration aroused and excited them both.

Carolyn was relieved to find that Diegert was a patient lover, which made her feel safe and more erotic. She turned her face to his, and they kissed deeply and passionately. They were both overtaken by the lustful feelings that blossomed when their mouths touched. As their bodies pressed tightly against each other, their passion found an undulating rhythm. Soon Diegert lifted Carolyn, and she positioned his shaft inside her. The two lovers celebrated the pleasure they felt in their strong, fit bodies, following their passion to an orgasm that left them both shuddering, satisfied, and momentarily exhausted.

When Carolyn's feet returned to the bathtub floor, she leaned in against Diegert, and they hugged each other warmly while they relaxed in their sexual denouement.

"That was wonderful," said Carolyn.

"I think we both needed that."

She hugged him tighter and pressed her face into his shoulder. She then looked up at him, saying, "Honestly, I stepped in here for the sex, but I didn't know it would be that good."

"You're a beautiful woman, and I appreciate your boldness. It was good for me too."

Reaching for a bottle of shampoo called Botanical Bouquet, Carolyn started washing her hair.

Diegert coughed.

"What's wrong?"

"That stuff smells really floral."

"*Floral!* Well, I think it's nice. It's the only shampoo in here, so you used it already, didn't you?"

"Well, yeah, but only because there was no other choice."

"I think maybe deep inside you like Botanical Bouquet," teased Carolyn.

"Yeah, I like it so much I'm getting out of here right now."

Diegert pulled the curtain, climbed out, dried himself, and left to get dressed.

Carolyn rinsed her hair and stood in the hot water contemplating the complications of what she had done. It had felt so good, but as the passion subsided, she knew it was so wrong in so many ways.

CHAPTER 63

All four Board members were in attendance at the video conference. Klaus began. "This is an auspicious day: the day when Crepusculous will assert its strength. The work to make this second phase of our plan a success has been done, and we will now commence."

The other three men sat in front of keyboards in their respective offices and awaited the signal for the simultaneous initiation of the greatest plunge in value the New York Stock Exchange had ever seen. The simultaneous initiation was necessary to bypass fail-safe software that would automatically shut down the stock exchange when massive movements were attempted. The Board controlled 20 percent of the value of the stock market. This was accomplished through so many subsidiaries and diversified portfolios, as well as hedge funds and amalgamated property funds, that its reach and penetration were unseen by regulators. Additionally, they had corrupted significant people in the U.S. Securities and Exchange Commission. The dishonest regulators needed only to be slow at responding. The initial action would precipitate a cascade of panic selling so that the majority of the losses wouldn't be directly associated with the Board's actions but rather only instigated by them.

In an earlier meeting, Julio Perez had asked about the wisdom of this act, and he was told that the end product of this action would have all the currency in the world under the control of Crepusculous. Mr. Wei's fears were similarly allayed when he was reminded that China already embraced several forms of digital currency, all of which were pegged to the dollar. Digival would replace all of them and keep happy all the customers already convinced of the convenience of digital currency.

Klaus looked at the three pairs of eyes on the screen and the lights at the bottom, which would indicate that the member had actually pressed the "Enter" key, and said, "Gentlemen, let's change the world."

All four "Enter" keys were simultaneously depressed at eleven thirty a.m., Eastern Standard Time, and the transactions put into play removed 20 percent of the value of the New York Stock Exchange. The clamor was immediate; people were both frantic and completely dumbfounded as the proverbial rug was yanked out from under them. Brokers and traders, fund managers and regulators watched as the irrational become reality. The wealth they had so painstakingly worked to build vanished into the ether. The regulatory delay allowed the exchange to free-fall for thirty-five minutes before all trading was halted. In that period of time, the Board had grabbed all their marbles and gone home. Wall Street was awash in confusion as money men tried to figure out what just happened. Business journalists started reporting before they really knew what had taken place.

Suspicions and possibilities were broadcast as probabilities. Computer glitches were blamed, which gave people immediate hope that the glitch would be fixed and everything would return to normal. Terrorism was reported, and the NYPD Emergency Services Unit was dispatched to see if guys in cool uniforms with automatic weapons could change the situation. The chairperson of the Securities and Exchange Commission, Katherine Smithfield, was called away from a meeting and informed of current events. She reviewed with her subordinates the list of all the stop-action procedures they had and was assured they had all eventually been enacted. The president, who was meeting with her cabinet restructuring the government, was informed of the crash, forcing her to change the focus of the cabinet meeting.

Presidential staffers compiled statistics of the impact while projecting possible ramifications for both the economy and national security. To the president, this disaster so close to the assassination was starting to look like an act of economic terrorism. As the hours passed, the blogosphere predicted economic Armageddon and the end of the world as it was known. The president had to make an appearance and send a calming message. From the Rose Garden, President Stanwix told the American people, "We have suffered an unprecedented drop in the value of the stock market. All federal officials involved in the regulation and management of not only the market but the entire economy are working on nothing but figuring out what happened and how we can move forward. I want the citizens of the United States to know that the full efforts of the federal government are working to understand this event and secure our economy and our nation. Many of you, like me, are still caught in the emotional shock wave of the loss of President Carson. I hope you find in his legacy the strength and resolve that inspires me to face this challenge with determination and fortitude. For most of you, your day-to-day personal finances are separate from the stock market, and thus you still have funds at your disposal to continue your lives. I ask you to reflect on that fact and remain calm and civil while we figure this out and report back to you. Thank you for your time and attention. God bless the United States of America."

The panic removed 60 percent of the value of the NYSE, producing a drop in the Dow Jones Industrial Average of 80 percent. The Dow dropped from 18,567 to 3,113. The evaporation of wealth exceeded the drop that had triggered the Great Depression of the 1930s, and the public was angry that technology was not able to stop the run. People were dismayed at the possibility that they might have actually lost all their investments: retirement funds, pension plans, and college tuition accounts. With the presidential assassination still an open wound, this disaster was nothing short of a saline rub on raw flesh. The sun was going to rise tomorrow, but for many Americans, that was the only thing of which they were certain.

***

"I have Hamni's address," stated Diegert. "If we're there in two hours, we'll arrive during a shift change, and I can extract him. Here, you can study the map."

Carolyn looked at the map with the route to the address where Hamni resided and could see that it wasn't far. The place was called St. James Home. The website described it as a home for children with developmental needs.

"What kind of needs does Hamni have?" she asked.

"I don't know."

"Maybe I should be the one to pick him up."

"You think so?"

"I don't think you're someone the staff would trust or Hamni would feel secure with. It's all about you being a tough guy; people don't instinctively trust you."

"Well, OK, but take my phone, there's a convincing video of Fatima you can use."

As they drove through London, Carolyn read a newsfeed on her phone. "My God, the New York Stock Exchange just crashed."

"Really? How much?"

"They aren't sure, but a lot. It says here more value was lost than in 2008, and that this could be worse than the 1929 crash that started the Great Depression."

"It's phase two," said Diegert. "Crepusculous is behind it. They're destroying the US economy. We better hurry."

The staff of St. James Home changed shifts at six p.m. after the children had their evening meal. The dining hall was connected to the residence halls by interior walkways, but when the weather was nice, the children could also get there by walking through the sylvan grounds of the 110-year-old facility. Today was a beautiful, sunny day. Carolyn walked through the wrought-iron gate after showing the guard her British driver's license. Once inside, she reviewed the picture of Hamni that Diegert had lifted from Fatima's phone. Dressed in business casual attire, she walked the grounds carrying a briefcase.

A line of children emerged from the dining hall, but the expected enthusiasm of running and shouting was replaced with shuffling gaits, awkward faces, and hands occupied by nervous tics as the children walked on the concrete paths. No adults appeared until three exited pushing wheelchairs. Scanning the children, Carolyn didn't see Hamni. Only after all the rest of the children emerged did a boy and a girl slowly step out into the warm autumn weather. The boy had black hair and very dark eyes. He had a dark-olive complexion and walked with a stiff upright gait and his head held high like an ostrich scanning the Serengeti. Carolyn recognized him in an instant and initiated her plan.

Approaching Hamni was a tricky first step. Carolyn smiled at the adults pushing the wheelchairs as she passed them. She was friendly yet purposeful, which gave the adults a sense that she seemed to know what she was doing. Hamni's observant mannerism was just that, a habit without the expected outcome; he would, in fact, not make eye contact with anyone.

"Hamni," said Carolyn. "I'm here to take you to go visit your mother."

The boy listened but did not respond. Carolyn pulled out her smartphone and played the video Fatima had sent Diegert. The video was a selfie of Fatima saying, *"Hey, I know you're facing some tough decisions, but I . . . believe in you. I look forward to seeing you soon."*

When Hamni saw his mother's face and heard her voice, he immediately got so excited he began gesticulating and vocalizing in ways that surprised Carolyn. His actions also drew the attention of the staff. The three adults, two women and a man, stopped pushing the wheelchairs and looked back at Hamni's expressions and the woman who was speaking to him.

"Can I help you?" asked the man, who was of Middle Eastern descent.

"Yes, thank you," said Carolyn. "I'm here to pick up Hamni, because his mother is in the hospital and she wants to see him. She told me it was important for Hamni to be told of this first. Can you direct me to the control desk where I can sign him out?"

All three of the staff members looked at Carolyn quizzically as she waited for directions. Hamni was excitedly looking at the picture of his mother on Carolyn's phone and anxiously pulling on her sleeve. The Middle Eastern man was torn between escorting them and abandoning the child in the wheelchair.

"Hamni knows where to go. He is a very smart boy; he'll take you to Gibson Hall."

"Gibson Hall?" Carolyn repeated as Hamni led her away by the sleeve. "Thank you," she said as Hamni waved to the staff, who returned to pushing the wheelchairs and gossiping.

The control desk was staffed by Mildred Faber, who could see that Carolyn had the right papers from the hospital indicating that Fatima was admitted and requested Hamni's release to come visit. Diegert had forged these documents on the flight.

"The last thing I'll need," said the efficient Miss Faber, "is your ID."

Carolyn was so very grateful for the time she had invested in putting together her CIA alternative documents package, which was always in the trunk of her car. She handed Miss Faber her British driver's license, and when it was returned, she walked out holding Hamni's hand.

Diegert pulled up as they exited the front gate of St. James. When they got back to the cottage, Diegert called Fatima.

"Hello," she answered.

"This is David."

"Diegert?"

"Yes."

"What about being dead?"

"A gross exaggeration. I used an opportunity to throw Blevinsky off my trail. Please don't divulge my survival?"

"I won't. Where are you?"

"First, I want to thank you for the video message you sent me. I really appreciate what you said, and it certainly was exactly what I needed to get me through this ordeal."

Fatima felt a sudden softness in her heart that hadn't been there for a long time.

"You're welcome. I could see that Crepusculous turned on you, and I thought you were probably feeling betrayed. I want you to know I wasn't in on the betrayal."

"You know, when you said you believed in me, that really meant a lot and helped me out. Thanks."

"So where are you?"

"I'm in London."

"London! How did you get here? That's amazing!"

"Fatima, I have someone with me. Get ready to receive a picture."

Pointing his phone at Hamni, he said, "We're going to send your mum a picture, OK?"

Hamni didn't actually look directly into the camera, but his face was unmistakable. Diegert sent the picture to Fatima. Her voice came through the phone like an acidic flame.

"I am going to kill you, David Diegert. I am going to see your life end. What are you doing with Hamni? You know he has special needs. If you have him out of his home environment for long, he won't be able to handle it. You idiot, what are you doing?"

"Fatima, I want you to believe in me like you said you did. I know Crepusculous has plans."

Fatima screamed her interruption. "Crepusculous! Fuck them—what are you talking about? You've made a terrible mistake, and Hamni is going to suffer. I'm gonna hurt you so bad, Diegert. This is not a game; you have violated my family."

"Fatima, please hear what I have to say."

"I'm going to hear what you have to say, and then I'm going to kill you anyway."

"Crepusculous plans to attack the United States. I don't know exactly how, but it is going to be big and we need to stop them."

"Oh great . . . now we're heroes saving the whole damn world, and you've kidnapped my son in the process. This makes absolutely no sense!"

"Fatima, I believe Javier Perez has critical information about the next phase of the attack."

"Phase—what phase?"

"The assassination of the president, the stock market crash, those were phases one and two, and the next phase will be bigger, affecting more people."

"So fucking what? What are you asking me to do?"

"I want you to infiltrate Javier's place and acquire intel about what's next. We need to know what the plan is so we can interrupt it."

"You're acting on a hunch. You have no evidence that Javier knows anything about this."

"You're right, but it makes sense. Javier is going to inherit his father's seat. This is the biggest thing Crepusculous has ever done. It makes sense that the up-and-coming guy would have an important role to play."

"OK, I see it makes sense to you, but it could be totally wrong, and you're forcing me to do something or else you're going to hurt Hamni."

"I'm asking you to get information from Javier, and I'll reunite you with Hamni. You can have the mother-child relationship you've been wanting for so long. He is free of Crepusculous and wants to be with you. Call me back after you've got information from Javier."

Diegert ended the call and turned to Hamni. "Your mum has been delayed. We're going to stay here while we wait for her. OK?"

Hamni's wondering eyes avoided Diegert's face as he started swaying his head back and forth.

"You're a real bastard, you know that?" said Carolyn.

"Yeah, more than you know."

CHAPTER 64

"Now that Diegert's dead, what do you want me to do with his mother?" Blevinsky asked Panzer. Leaning back in his leather chair, the German tapped his phone against his chin.

"I want her here in London," he told his *chargé d'affaires.*

"Excuse me," replied Blevinsky. "Did you say London, sir?"

"Yes, I want her here in London and held in comfort. She's not to be mistreated."

On the other end of the phone, Blevinsky was mouthing a litany of silent curses as he had to figure out the logistics of yet another complication in this circus of disasters. Back on the phone, he replied to Panzer, "Yes, sir, I'll inform you of her arrival."

"Good man, Aaron, thank you."

***

Fatima dressed in her black operations outfit. The clothes fit snugly and were made of Kevlar-reinforced fibers, so they were tough and resistant to tears, abrasions, and bullets. She wore a belt with pouches for necessary items like Trank, extra ammo, incendiary devices, and formed explosives. Hung over her shoulder was a thirty-foot length of superstrong, ultra-light climbing line. Sneaking into Javier's place would involve a stealth entry and quite likely some rough encounters for which she would be well prepared with her Beretta M9 on her hip.

The Perez town house was surrounded by a high wrought-iron fence and patrolled by two guards at night. Under the cover of ten p.m. darkness, Fatima found access by zipping across the power lines, scaling the wall, and dropping onto a balcony from the roof. The balcony serviced an unoccupied bedroom on the third floor. Fatima picked the lock and stepped inside. She crossed the room and entered the hallway. She recalled that Javier had an office on the second floor. She crept to the staircase and waited at the top of the stairs to be certain no residents saw her descent. Going down the stairs left her feeling very exposed, but she saw no one and moved very quickly. The office door, as she remembered it, was big and made of dark mahogany. She turned the knob, stepped inside, and closed the door behind her. She stood quietly, letting her eyes adjust to the dim light that filtered in from the street through the sheer curtains in front of the French doors that led to the office's balcony.

Fatima approached the desk located in the middle of the room. She stepped around to the chair, which faced the room's entrance. She slid out a keyboard from under the desk's surface, and a monitor screen rose out of an inlaid slot in the desk. Fatima inserted her hacking device into a USB port while the computer was booting up.

The office's motion detection system was designed to be disabled by an arriving inhabitant who submitted the proper code in the keypad within the top right-hand drawer of the desk. If the code was not submitted within five minutes, a silent alarm was sent to the company in charge of security. Fatima had been in the office for more than five minutes, and the security guards were converging on the office. Two of them met at the office door. Another accessed the office balcony from an adjacent room. A fourth guard went to Javier's room to be certain he was unharmed.

When the guard entered Javier's room with his key card, he interrupted the *Kama Sutra* lessons Mr. Perez was receiving from Anisha and Geeta, two beauties from New Delhi. "Hey, what the hell's this?"

"Sir, there's been an intrusion to the premises. I'm here to ensure your safety."

The security company informed the two guards at the office door that a single female intruder could be seen on the office camera. The surveillance system was equipped with an audio broadcast capability, over which the security guard at the company headquarters was able to speak to Fatima.

"Attention, you are intruding on this property and must surrender."

The sudden voice startled Fatima, who had just begun to hack into the log-in encryption. Her jolting reaction was visible on the camera and almost humorous if the company was not supposed to stop people long before they got this far.

"Security guards will enter the office to arrest you. Please submit peacefully."

Fatima pulled her device out of the USB and fired her pistol at the entrance door. The hard wood splintered as bullets passed through, leaving large exit holes. The guards wisely remained to the sides of the door behind thick walls.

Fatima grabbed a statue of a beautiful naked woman off Javier's desk and threw it through the French doors. The smashed glass became a jagged portal through which Fatima stepped out onto the balcony. The street below would allow her to escape, but before she had a chance to tie her rope, she was hit with forty-two hundred volts of Taser-induced electricity.

The two wires fired into her by the guard on the balcony conducted so much voltage that Fatima was completely immobile under the electric assault. Her muscles were no longer able to function as the electricity disrupted her motor neurons. When the tasing stopped, she collapsed and was quickly handcuffed and taken back in the building.

"Suspect is in custody," the guard in Javier's room heard over his communication unit.

"What's going on?" asked Javier.

"They have the intruder in custody."

"I want to see the guy. Don't take him away before I get to see him."

"Sir, it's a woman."

"Then I definitely want to see her."

Javier, dressed in a robe and wearing sandals, marched to the second-floor office. He strode into his private study and saw three armed guards and Fatima Hussain wearing handcuffs. He stood quietly for a minute before saying, "Leave the intruder with me. Please close the door and stay in the hallway."

The guards hesitated and looked to one another for direction.

"I know this is unusual, but please, do as I ask."

Mr. Perez seemed calm and relaxed, and they would be right on the other side of the door, so the guards acquiesced to his request and left him in the office with the intruder.

Javier looked at Fatima and saw that she was quite uncomfortable. "What are you doing here? What are you trying to steal?"

Fatima gave no reply.

"You can see I have upgraded the security since you broke in eight years ago. I have better security guards as well. You impressed me last time you trespassed into my home, but this time, you rudely interrupted something I was enjoying."

Fatima remained silent, but her eyes were riveted to Javier as he walked to the desk, typed on the keyboard, and dimmed the red lights on the surveillance camera.

"If you're not going to talk, then I'm just going to have you taken to jail to be prosecuted."

"I'm here because of our son," shouted Fatima.

Javier's glare receded slightly.

"He's been kidnapped and is being held by the man who assassinated the president of the United States."

"*What?*"

"You heard me."

"Yeah . . . but it's a little far-fetched to believe."

"Oh, is it? Crepusculous ordered the assassination of the president, then turned on the assassin and tried to kill him, but he survived and he's pissed and wants to know what's next. What is the next phase of the Board's plan? What is going to happen to the United States?"

Fatima, with her hands still in cuffs, stepped up and shouted in Javier's face. "You know . . . and so he took Hamni from St. James and forced me to break in here to find out what's next."

Fatima fell silent as tears welled up in her eyes and sobs tried to escape her throat. "I need you to help me. I need you to help get our son back. I know you don't think of him as your son, but he is, and he needs your help."

Javier looked at this woman and thought about the extraordinary efforts she had made to help her son. He thought about the time he visited St. James and watched Hamni. It hurt inside to be such a neglectful father. His own father had always done so much for him. Javier realized that all he did was take. He never gave to anyone, especially of himself. He was insular, selfish, and quite lonely. Here was this woman who knew what it meant to care about someone and put herself in danger just to improve the life of a little boy he could so easily care for if he only would. These thoughts were like a dam breaking, a great release of pressure that had been denied for far too long. Javier Perez needed to grow up and take responsibility for his life, his son, his family, and right now was the moment it was going to happen.

He stepped over to the computer and brought up a file that described the Board's plan for America. He had never fully read it, but he knew the answer Fatima wanted was there. He also knew that the second right-hand desk drawer contained, in a locked box, the device necessary to initiate the next phase of the plan. "Look at this."

Fatima stepped over to the desk. She read the screen and learned that Crepusculous planned to attack nine US cities with thermobaric bombs. The bombs were already in place, and a single-source device would trigger detonation. The device's signal was sent via a dedicated satellite, and single source meant the signal could not be interrupted, intercepted, or corrupted.

Fatima looked at him. "Where is that device?"

"When I tell you, I want you to guarantee that you and Hamni will come live with me."

Fatima's eyes widened as she gasped at this request. She stepped back from the desk, shaking her head, saying, "I can't believe you just said that while I'm still in handcuffs."

Javier walked to the office's entrance and was disappointed to see that the door had bullet holes through it. He stepped out into the hall and returned with the handcuff keys. Fatima rubbed her wrists after the metal binds were removed. "Thanks," she said.

With Javier standing just behind her and to the right, she kicked him in the shin and drove his head onto the desktop. She grabbed his right shoulder, turned him to his back, and pinned him to the desk by the throat.

"I'm to believe that after all the shit you've put me through for the past nine years that you've had some kind of epiphany and you now want to be a family man? But first you're going to blow up the United States!"

Fatima put her weight on his throat, and the additional force made him squirm. She lifted off and let him breathe.

She got close to his face and said, "You had better choose your next words very carefully, because I could still kill you and get out of here."

She released him and stepped back. Coughing and sputtering while drawing big breaths of air, Javier rolled on the desktop and twisted into a seated position on the desk. After a few more breaths, he began, "I can see why you're upset, but I've been thinking about this for a long time. I just haven't acted. I've come to realize that the wealth I live within steals the ability to recognize the difficulties of others."

Fatima crossed her arms in front of her, rolled her eyes, and looked away.

"But going and watching Hamni and seeing his difficulties . . . he has made me feel it. I could feel his struggle and perseverance, because he is my son. I want to help him, but I need your help to do that. Fatherhood should be so natural, but I need help to be a good father, and that's what I want to do with you, learn to be a good father."

Javier became very emotional while he spoke; he kept sniffling as tears drained through his nose. Fatima looked at him but did not uncross her arms.

"You want to start acting like a good man? Where is that device? Give it to me."

Javier pulled out the second drawer on the right, unlocked the metal box, and removed a satellite phone. He handed it to Fatima.

"There is just one preprogrammed number; just turn it on, press send, and all the bombs in the US will detonate according to the plan."

Fatima looked at the phone and held it up between them, saying, "This is going to get our son back."

CHAPTER 65

Hamni found the cottage and the people and the food and the routine all so unfamiliar. He knew things would be different whenever he saw his mother, but she understood his needs and made him comfortable wherever they were. These people were not doing that, and he was getting anxious. Hamni first began to rock back and forth in his chair. He then stood up in front of the big picture window that faced the road. He placed his right foot in front of his left and rocked back and forth from one foot to the other while he looked out the window as if searching for something. He began vocalizing, saying, "Hun-goo, hun-goo," over and over with an escalating crescendo until he screamed out loud, leaning all his weight forward on his right foot and elevating his left behind him. After emptying his lungs into a high-pitched, piercing scream he put his foot back on the floor and started the whole process over again. He repeated the pattern several times as Diegert and Carolyn watched with perplexed amazement at the intense behavior of this little lost boy. Looking at Carolyn, Diegert said, "Do something."

"Like what?"

"I don't know. You're a woman—comfort him." Diegert turned to walk out of the room. "Calm him down."

Carolyn followed Diegert, saying, "Look, I'm not the babysitter here. Taking him was your idea; he's your responsibility."

"Well, I don't know what to do with him."

"Neither do I."

The crash of breaking glass jolted both of them out of their argument. They were drawn back to the front room where Hamni stood with a gash on his forehead from a jagged shard he'd created when he'd smashed his head through the window. He was still rocking back and forth, but now he had blood pulsing out of his head and streaming down his face. The room was quickly becoming a crimson mess, splattered with hemorrhaging fluid. Carolyn stepped forward and grabbed Hamni, who struck back at her and started screaming. She struggled with him while blood sprayed all over her. Diegert ran to his duffel bag and, from an internal zippered pocket, retrieved a small aerosol can.

He returned to the front room to see Carolyn covered in Hamni's blood and struggling with the small boy, who possessed the crazed strength of a grown man. Diegert stepped up to the two of them, placing his hand over Carolyn's nose and mouth. He sprayed Hamni in the face at close range, and within seconds, the boy was unconscious. "I should've done that a long time ago."

Carolyn felt Hamni go limp in her arms, and she took him to the kitchen, placing him on the table. Diegert grabbed a towel from the rack, tore it in half, and put pressure on the gash. "Go to the bathroom and find whatever first aid you can, and I need a needle and thread."

Carolyn passed through the front room on her way to the bathroom where she encountered a very nervous but inquisitive overweight middle-aged woman who must've lived close by. With a startled reaction to the blood-drenched appearance of Carolyn, the woman steeled herself to ask, "Oh dear God . . . do you need help, love?"

Carolyn didn't hesitate. "Yes, our son has special needs and he has just injured himself by smashing the window. Do you have a first aid kit with a needle and thread?"

The bewildered woman gathered her thoughts and repeated, "Needle and thread—first aid. I will be right back, love."

The woman waddled away as fast as she could. Carolyn went to the bathroom and grabbed a roll of toilet paper and another towel and found a small box of old Band-Aids. She looked at herself in the mirror and saw what a hideous sight she was. That woman certainly was a caring person to have not turned and run away. She splashed water on her face and rubbed it on a towel, leaving a bloody smear on the cotton cloth. She rummaged in the cupboard under the sink but found nothing useful. She walked back through the front room just as the neighbor returned with a plastic first aid case and her sewing kit. Carolyn took them both. "Thank you so much. Please don't consider me rude, but could you wait out here? My husband is a doctor, and he will be able to treat our son with these."

Carolyn continued to the kitchen; over her shoulder, she said, "What a tough start to our vacation."

Diegert had kept constant pressure on the wound, and the bleeding was stopping. The gash was right at Hamni's hairline about two inches in length, but the tension of the skin had caused it to spread to about an inch and a half in width. Looking at the items Carolyn had brought with her, Diegert exclaimed, "Holy shit, you found these in the house?"

"No."

Carolyn opened the first aid case and handed Diegert a sterile gauze pad and some antiseptic fluid. He began washing the wound. Carolyn opened the woman's sewing case and found the typical things used to mend and sew clothes. She threaded a needle with some plastic thread that resembled fishing line. She handed the needle to Diegert, who said, "It's a good thing I tranked him, because this is going to hurt."

With quick, even strokes, Diegert had the wound edges back in contact. He tied the sutures tightly so the cut no longer bled. The dressing was preceded by an application of antibiotic ointment, and although a typical bandage for a wound like this would've wrapped around the small boy's head, Diegert sufficed to cover it with a sterile gauze pad and tape it in place. Carolyn stepped in and washed all the blood off the boy's face, hands, and arms. His clothes, as well as hers, were covered in blood.

Carolyn closed up the sewing kit and the first aid case and returned to the front room. The neighbor was outside on the front steps. "Thank you again so very much; you are very kind. I'm sorry for the frightening appearance of the situation."

"It's alright, love. Many people suffer with the needs of family members."

Carolyn handed the kit and the case back to the helpful woman.

"Is there anything else you need, love?"

"His clothes are rather . . . distasteful, and his luggage was lost on the flight. You wouldn't happen to have any clothes for a small boy, would you?"

"Just a minute, love, I think I may have something."

In the cottage, Diegert washed his hands and was drying them when his phone went off. "Hello," he answered.

"Crepusculous has at least nine thermobaric bombs set to go off in US cities, and they are all tied to a single-source detonation device that I have in my possession."

Fatima's icy voice sizzled over the phone and cut through Diegert's cochlea, searing into his brain a fearful realization of the consequences of Hamni's injuries. He needed to gather his wits quickly. "You got this from Javier?"

"Yes."

"How do I know it's authentic?"

"You don't . . . how do I know Hamni's alright? I don't. We have to trust each other, because we've both got what the other wants."

"OK, let's arrange the exchange. I'll send you GPS coordinates in an hour."

"Alright, but if Hamni is harmed, I will kill you and blow up the United States."

Diegert disconnected the call.

The neighbor returned to find Carolyn sweeping the broken glass from the sidewalk in front of the house. She handed Carolyn a paper bag. Carolyn opened the bag and withdrew a pair of soccer shorts and a numbered jersey. She looked at the woman, who, with a wan smile, said, "It's Manchester United. I bought it for my grandson's birthday."

"Oh, that's so sweet . . . We couldn't take it."

"You are in need, and I can get another set."

"Well, then, you must let us pay you for it."

"No, love, I will not take money from those in need."

"Thank you so much. Your kindness is truly so very touching."

The gentle woman patted Carolyn on the forearm and turned to walk back to her house. Over her shoulder, she said, "Just see to it your son becomes a fan of Manchester."

CHAPTER 66

"We've got to go," said Diegert impatiently.

"Right now?"

"Yeah . . . What have you got there?"

Carolyn slid the clothes out of the bag. "From the neighbor."

"You stole them?"

Shoving the clothes back in the bag, Carolyn replied, "No . . . there are actually kind people in this world. A generous neighbor gave them to me because we need them. If you will excuse me?"

Diegert stepped to the side and Carolyn went to dress Hamni.

***

When Fatima put her phone down, Javier said, "You let him dictate the meeting place."

"It's not important. We have to be ready to take Hamni back safely."

"You're sure he has him?"

"I called St. James earlier, and they admitted Hamni left the premises with a woman."

Javier scratched his head and ran his fingers through his thick black hair. Fatima addressed him sternly, "Don't attempt anything that will put Hamni in jeopardy. Diegert is resourceful and ruthless, but I know he will give us our son in exchange for the device."

"You believe that because you want to believe it."

"Yes, I do," said the very quick and highly agitated woman, who then kicked Javier in the hip and twisted his arm around his back as she took out his knee from behind, pressing his face to the floor.

"You want to show me you're a changed man, you show me by making our son a priority."

She stepped up and away from him. He rolled to his side, saying, "You know it's only because you're a girl that I let you do that to me."

"Yeah right. Go get me a gun from one of your guards and then lock them in their office. I don't want any heroics endangering Hamni."

***

Diegert and Carolyn changed into their last set of clean clothes, and Hamni was now wearing a number-ten jersey for the Manchester United Football Club. The young lad was still unconscious, and both Diegert and Carolyn were grateful for that. While Carolyn drove, Diegert searched Google Maps for a suitable meeting place.

"When we get the device, I take custody of it," said the CIA agent.

"You're going to turn it in to the agency?"

"By turning it in, I have a chance of making a deal for leniency."

"You're going to arrest me?"

"I suggest you turn yourself in. The hunt for you will continue, and it will go international. Once that happens, the stakes get higher and your chances of survival plummet."

"I've been hunted before."

"I don't think you understand the intensity with which you will be pursued. But I also don't want to see you dead."

"You think you can get me a lenient deal?"

"I don't know. Maybe we can appeal for a commutation of the death penalty and negotiate the charges you'll face."

"Maybe, but I hope they appreciate the fact that we stopped the US from being destroyed. Hey . . . turn left here."

Carolyn pulled the car onto the street to her left. Diegert explained, "This is Mackenzie. It connects to Remington, and it's on Remington that I've found what I'm looking for."

***

When Blevinsky's ID appeared on Panzer's phone, the wealthy German activated the speaker. "Is she here in London?"

"Yes, sir, the Gulfstream landed a short time ago. She will occupy the secure suite at the Royal Ambassador Hotel."

"Excellent. Thank you, Aaron."

"Will you be seeing her, sir?"

"I'll inform you of what you need to know."

"Of course, sir."

***

"Park here," instructed Diegert. Carolyn pulled into a vacant lot with pavement that was crumbling into gravel. The weeds weakened the surface by seeking the soil beneath the cracks. The whole neighborhood was devoid of inhabitants. The buildings were undergoing rehabilitation. Each old structure had scaffolding rising up the sides and tarps wrapping the outside, keeping the weather from the interior construction work. The reclamation of these buildings would one day produce a gentrified community of new residents. It wasn't too hard to imagine this place having a cool future, but right now the conditions reminded Carolyn of Detroit decay.

"Now here's the plan. I'm going to find a location in that building."

Diegert pointed to the building across the street that had a large external foyer overgrown with weeds.

"I plan to access an upper floor that's open enough to give me a sight line back to here. I will draw her up to me. Fatima won't allow the exchange until Hamni is secured. So she will come back down to the car. You will be concealed in the dark, out of sight, and when I signal you on your phone, you'll unlock the car with the remote. Once Fatima has Hamni, she will leave and we'll have the device."

"Why this elaborate plan to get her up to the work site?"

"She may very well have an additional attack plan or a Crepusculous hit team in play with her. I want to spread things out and keep her guessing about Hamni's location. This way neither of us has to actually be there when she gets him back."

Nodding her agreement with a look of doubt, Carolyn capitulated to his plan.

"I'm going to find my place in the building, then I'll send my GPS coordinates to Fatima and wait."

"I just stay down here?"

"Keeping Hamni calm and quiet is critical to the plan."

"Well, we've really had no success with that."

"Here," Diegert said, extending his hand and giving Carolyn the can of Trank.

"I'm not spraying him with that again."

"You might have to."

Again expressing an indignant sense of surrender, Carolyn took the tiny aerosol can.

"This whole thing is crazy. You're hoping your manipulations work, but if they don't, then what?"

"Look, stopping people with criminal intent always involves craziness. You know that. When this is all over, the US will be safe, and you and I . . . can take another shower."

"With Botanical Bouquet?"

"I sure hope not."

Diegert stepped out of the car and disappeared around the corner of the building across the street.

***

Fatima's phone chirped, and she opened the message from Diegert. The GPS coordinates indicated a location in the Brentwood district on Remington Avenue. "Come on, Javier, it's time to go."

***

After waiting ten minutes, Carolyn checked on Hamni again. He was unconscious, but he looked like he was peacefully sleeping with his seat belt on and his head leaning against the side of the car's interior. His dark-brown shoes and black socks did not complement the striking red of his Manchester United soccer suit. She opened the car door and stepped out into the soft rain that fell from the dark sky. Not far from the edge of the parking lot was a hedgerow of overgrown bushes that fronted an overhanging roof. Carolyn concealed herself behind the thick foliage and began to shiver as the wet evening grew cool. She tested the remote, confirming that the car remained within the key's operating range.

CHAPTER 67

The sixth floor was totally gutted. Only the studs and the construction materials remained. The wiring, plumbing, and ductwork were all being upgraded, and only a few bulbs, hanging in protective cages, provided what light there was. Diegert walked to one of the window spaces. They were all devoid of glass and had plastic sheets hanging over them. He drew back the plastic and could see the car in the lot where he had left Carolyn. Crossing the building to the opposite side, he looked out, anticipating Fatima's arrival. He'd purposefully given her directions that wouldn't have her passing the area where the car with Hamni was parked.

The silver-gray Mercedes was a bit garish, but it didn't surprise Diegert. The car parked alongside the deserted street, and Fatima stepped out. Her sleek, lean figure was familiar, and he could see her face in the streetlight. Fatima lifted a leather hood over her head against the rain. Diegert called her cell. When she lifted her phone to her ear, he said, "Sixth floor of the building across the street on your right."

She disconnected, turned her head, and looked directly at him. She began walking toward the building, and when Diegert saw her enter, he stepped over to the stairwell to greet

---

her arrival. Diegert observed her ascent up the stairwell, which was the only entrance to the floor. She was still wearing the black leather hood of her coat. Her pants were black and tight and tucked into sturdy but fashionable leather boots. She stepped off the last step and crossed to the center of the floor. "I don't see my son," began the woman who sought to control the situation.

"You do have the device?"

"You don't get to see it until I see my son."

"Hamni is so cute. You never told me what a darling little boy he is, and he's incredibly smart."

"Shut up. What's your plan?"

"Did you know he could play chess? He took two straight games off me."

"Stop talking about him. Where is he?"

"He's safe and secure and nearby."

From the stairwell, another figure rose from the hole in the floor. The dark-haired man crossed the top stair and stood in front of the stairwell, removing his black leather gloves. Diegert's gaze projected from his dark eyes like that of a cornered panther. Fatima said, "Javier has the device. He will give it to you when I have Hamni."

"This sucks, you untrustworthy bitch."

"You're telling me. Now where is he?"

"You two are very tense. Let's just calm down for a moment," said the handsome Spaniard. Diegert's weariness lost none of its intensity. Fatima continued to watch his every move. Javier Perez continued, "I've heard some interesting things about you, Mr. Diegert. I've been told you're the best killer of men in the world. This, of course, was delivered as a warning, not a compliment. I appreciate the world's finest things. It has been my life's experience to be surrounded by only the best in the world. Food, cars, yachts, clothing . . . entertainment—always the best. But an experience I have not had is to be in the presence of the best assassin in the world!"

Diegert looked at him and felt like the panther was now in a cage at the zoo.

"You killed the president of the United States and got away with it. Here you are!"

Javier removed his black leather jacket, revealing a fine white linen dress shirt under a black leather vest. He wore black jeans, and his ankle-high boots were also black.

"The cunning, the grit, the willingness to kill, you must feel like a powerful predator, choosing how and when your victims will die and watching their lives end at your direction. Now that's a powerful experience I have never had."

"Will you shut up? Let's exchange the device and get our son back," barked an impatient Fatima.

Diegert raised his eyebrows and looked into Javier's eyes. He saw the mounting displeasure of a man who was not used to taking orders from a woman. Diegert wanted to see if he was going to make the mistake of not listening to Fatima.

"Hamni's in a car," said Diegert. Pointing behind him, he continued, "Look out this window. You will see a car in the lot below."

"You left him in a car by himself?" Fatima threw the plastic out of the way, thrusting her head out the window.

"He's secure. It's locked."

As she turned away from the window, Fatima's fury erupted. "God damn it, that's not good enough for him. Goddamn you, Diegert. You should know he can't be left alone."

"Then give me the device, and the two of you can go get your son."

As Diegert finished his statement, his sight fell directly upon Javier, who cringed at the mention of his shared parenthood with Fatima.

"Give me the device, and I'll remotely unlock the car for you."

***

Hamni opened his eyes and blinked a few times. He felt a slight chill. The rain on the car windows made what little ambient light there was diffuse and heavily shadowed. He scratched his ear and realized he wasn't dreaming. He realized he didn't recognize anything. He looked at the clothes he was wearing and didn't recognize them either. He was quiet for another moment, and then a scream burst out from him that expressed all the fear and anxiety of a boy dependent upon routine to make order of the scattered world in his brain.

Being all alone in unfamiliar surroundings was extremely frightening. He struggled with the seat belt. When he finally unclipped it, he was unaware of the automatic retraction and felt the strap was trying to rebind him. He fought with the belt until it snapped out of his hand, freeing him to the full space of the car's interior. He pulled on the door handle, but it was locked. He began rocking back and forth, chanting his personal mantra, "Hun-goo, hun-goo," with escalating intensity. From her place in the bushes, Carolyn could hear the muffled chant and see that he was moving. When he first smacked his head into the window, Carolyn was startled by the tremendous force thrust into the glass by this already injured boy. She fingered the canister of Trank as she approached the car.

***

"Alright," said Fatima. Directing her instructions to Javier, she said. "I'll call you when I get down there. The exchange will be simultaneous."

"OK," answered the wealthy playboy.

Fatima descended the staircase and made her way to the ground floor. She had to walk a block to get to the other side of the building where Hamni was waiting for her in the car. She flipped the hood over her head against the rain.

Javier continued to speak with Diegert on the sixth floor. "As I was saying, taking a man's life must feel incredible."

"It's a feeling of power like no other, Javier. It's the power of life. It's not based on wealth or family position or anything material. It comes from your inner strength and personal resolve."

"Yes . . . I can imagine it does. You know, you and I are alike in many ways."

With a doubtful smirk on his face, Diegert replied, "I don't think I see it that way. Give me the device and call Fatima."

"In due time."

"Now."

Diegert stepped forward with his hand out and his look hardening into his fight face. Javier shifted into a defensive stance. Diegert advised him, "I don't think that's a good idea."

"You won't be the first guy I've had to beat down. I can't get away with fucking over two hundred women a year without pissing off some husbands and boyfriends. Bring it on, you wuss."

Diegert lowered his center of gravity and widened his base of support as he circled around Javier in a clockwise direction. The Spaniard rotated, keeping his eyes locked on Diegert's. The assassin struck first. He jabbed with his right and kicked with his left. The jab failed to distract. Javier reacted to the left leg kick with his right, striking Diegert in the thigh, forcing him to spin to keep from falling. Knowing he was vulnerable while his back was turned on his adversary, Diegert rapidly repositioned himself to face Javier.

"The best in the world! That's who my tae kwon do teacher was. Master Kim Le Pac. Now I get to see if my black belt is a match for the world's best assassin."

Stepping away and rising out of his ready stance, Diegert said, "If you got all that on me, then I guess we're done here and your son is going to die."

Diegert pulled from his pocket the keys to the car. "The car is rigged, and the detonator is tied to the remote. This way I get rid of Fatima as well."

"No!" shouted Javier, and Diegert threw the keys across the room into the darkness. The assassin closed quickly with a flurry of punches to the head and neck as the Spaniard struggled to regain his defensive stance. It surprised Diegert how well this wealthy pretty boy weathered the blistering punishment. Diegert attempted to deliver a fatal blow, but Javier fended off the deadliest strikes while reestablishing his fighting position. His face was battered and the corner of his mouth was bleeding, but there was still plenty of fight in him.

***

Hamni remained in the back seat on the driver's side. His head was bleeding again after striking the window. Carolyn opened the rear passenger door, and the instant illumination frightened the boy, whose wide eyes met Carolyn's. She smiled and hoped he would recognize her. He did not. He screamed, backing away from her, pressing himself against the locked door.

"Hamni, relax. Shhhh, settle down. It's OK. It's OK."

Her words were ineffective, and the boy continued to scream. Carolyn raised the can of tranquilizing spray, hesitating because she was unsure if he would overdose from another blast.

The force she felt on the belt of her pants was not only surprising but incredibly strong. The back of her head smacked on the doorframe as she was pulled out of the car and flung onto the wet ground. She looked up to see a black-clad figure with a hood. Fatima knelt down, pressing her thumb on the trachea of Carolyn's throat. The pressure was extremely painful and made it difficult for Carolyn to breathe. Fatima had her full attention. "Give me the keys."

Carolyn removed the keys from her pocket and handed them over. The angry mother stood up and pointed her Sig Sauer P320 at Carolyn, who raised her hands and sought to make eye contact with the face under the hood. Fatima, from the angry place in her soul and hidden beneath her dark shroud, fired into the right side of Carolyn's chest.

Hamni froze when he heard the shot. His next sight, though, was his beautiful, loving mother pulling a hood off her head, revealing a smiling, comforting face, one he knew so well and longed to be with every day. The confused and bewildered boy thrust his arms out and embraced his mother like he did no other person in the world. He was excited, exhausted, and so very happy to be with her. Fatima hugged the boy, kissed him, and was so relieved to have him back. She held him tight and released all the anxiety she had been feeling for his safety. She looked at his head bandage and the sports uniform and was disappointed the woman outside would not be answering questions. She belted Hamni in the front seat, and with the joy of being reunited with her child, drove away from the Brentwood neighborhood.

CHAPTER 68

Javier bounced on his feet and danced in a circle as he cleared his head and got back in the fight. "Sex and violence both stimulate the same part of the brain," shared the man who was testing Diegert. "So fighting is a lot like sex. It's best one-on-one. It's an adrenaline rush, the outcome is uncertain, and there is both pleasure and pain."

Eyeing his adversary for damage from the earlier attack, Diegert replied, "Well, I can't wait to fuck you."

As the two combatants warily eyed each other seeking an advantage, Javier stepped in and struck Diegert's jaw with a quick right jab. Simultaneously, Diegert plunged a powerful fist into Javier's abdomen. The strike caused the Spaniard to double over. Diegert grabbed the back of his enemy's head and powerfully drove Javier's face into his flexed knee.

Javier collapsed on the floor. Diegert moved toward him to search for the device. With his right leg, Javier hit the assassin's left leg, toppling him backward to the floor. Javier found a jagged shard of wood. With blood streaming down his face, the desperate son of a billionaire charged Diegert. From his supine position, Diegert kicked Javier in the hip. As Javier fell forward onto the ground, he stabbed Diegert in the thigh.

The pain from the impaled piece of wood seared Diegert's leg muscles. Diegert rolled toward Javier and punched him in the temple. The blow cracked Javier's skull and wrenched his neck. Diegert pulled the wooden spike out of his leg and grabbed a handful of powdered grout from a nearby bag. Javier returned to his feet and came at Diegert, who was now on one knee. As Javier approached, Diegert threw the grout into his face. The dusty material coated Javier's eyes, nose, and mouth. It mixed with the blood on his face, becoming an adherent paste. The Spaniard gasped, breathing in even more of the dust. He then coughed in an uncontrollable spasm. Diegert rose, grabbed Javier's right arm, twisted it behind his back, and drove him forward into a hanging sheet of plastic. He wrapped the plastic around Javier's head, kicking out his legs, forcing him to suffocate. Diegert applied force with fatal intent.

Javier retrieved the satellite phone from his vest pocket. With the push of one button, he activated the phone's initiation code. He held the phone aloft and Diegert saw the screen light up with green letters: "ACTIVATED—00:30." Javier tossed the phone across the open space. Diegert saw the phone on the far side of the room and realized he couldn't finish off Javier and stop the phone from detonating the United States. Releasing Javier, Diegert raced over to the phone. The screen indicated that there were nineteen seconds remaining. Diegert, recognizing the satellite phone as similar to the one on the *Sue Ellen*, entered the shutdown code. The screen went black. It remained black for a very tense moment before red letters appeared on the screen: "D . . . E . . . - . . . ACTIVATED."

Diegert looked back to the hanging plastic, but Javier was gone. Bruised and bleeding, with a deep wound in his leg, Diegert shuffled to the window, pushing back the tarp to see that the car was gone and Carolyn was lying on the ground in the rain.

Descending the stairs as fast as his injured body could go, he struggled to run around the block to where he had left her. Diegert knelt beside her and looked into her frightened eyes. He held her head and slid his hand under her back. Carolyn gasped for breath in ragged, guttural jolts.

"That bitch . . . shot me."

Running his hand underneath her, Diegert felt no exit wounds.

"It didn't go through. You're gonna live."

"It . . . doesn't . . . feel that way."

On her phone, Diegert dialed 999. He gave the dispatcher the address and left on the GPS signal for them to follow.

Carolyn clutched Diegert's arm. "Give . . . me the . . . device."

"Shh, just relax, the ambulance is coming."

"Give it to me," croaked Carolyn.

Taking off his jacket, rolling it up, and placing it under her head, he said, "You need to stay calm and relax."

"Don't make a fool . . . of me for . . . trusting you," said Carolyn, rolling to her side and grabbing Diegert's arm.

"Don't worry, I'll keep the device safe," said Diegert as he looked over his shoulder in the direction of the wailing sirens.

Tightening her grip on his forearm, Carolyn commanded, with as much force as she could muster, "Don't leave."

"I've got to."

"Don't abandon me," said Carolyn as she succumbed to her failing strength, rolled onto her back, and let her head sink into Diegert's coat.

"I won't, I'm your asset."

"I should never have trusted you."

Squatting next to her, Diegert pulled the sat phone from his pocket and began striking the keys. "Listen, I'm turning on the GPS tracker on the sat phone." Continuing to type on the keys, he said, "I'm creating an access code in order to turn the

GPS off, and I'm hiding the code so that anyone who tries to turn off the GPS won't be able to, so the phone will continually broadcast its location."

"So what?"

"Wait." Diegert picked up Carolyn's phone. "I'm placing the number of the sat phone into your phone, and you'll be able to track the phone's GPS signal twenty-four seven. You'll always know where I am."

"Just give me the device."

"I can't do that. I'm going deep into Crepusculous. I'll be an even more valuable asset. We'll bring them to their knees."

Carolyn's breaths became shorter, and she could no longer speak. Her eyes though shone with the fire of frustration as she helplessly watched Diegert stand up as the ambulance arrived. He moved off into the shadows, watching as the paramedics ran over to Carolyn. As they worked on her, a thought flashed in his mind: Had he found his Sue Ellen? When he was sure she was getting proper treatment, he disappeared into the night with the power to destroy the United States in his pocket.

CHAPTER 69

Shuffling into the night, Diegert used his belt as a tourniquet around his leg to reduce the flow of blood. Moving along a deserted concrete walkway beside the River Thames, Diegert searched the satellite phone's history, retrieving two numbers from the trash bin that had not yet been permanently deleted. Conference calling both numbers, he steeled himself for the confrontation.

"Hello," came the hesitant but familiar voice of Blevinsky.

"Hallo," came a distinctly German voice he had never heard before.

"Gentlemen, this is David Diegert. Based on the caller ID, you should be aware of the device in my possession. I know what this is programmed to do, and I know how valuable it is to you. The only way you get this back is to release my mother."

"You're in no position to be making demands," shot Blevinsky.

"Wait a moment," interrupted Panzer. "Mr. Diegert, I am very impressed with your determination. You seem to have the ability to return from the dead," said the German lightheartedly.

"I'd be happy to see if you could pass that test."

Chuckling uncomfortably, Panzer replied, "Perhaps another time. We can, however, arrange for you to see your mother. Aaron, would you please assist our young man's reunion? I look forward to making your acquaintance shortly, David." Panzer disconnected. Blevinsky got Diegert's cell phone number and sent him directions to the Royal Ambassador Hotel. Diegert demanded, "I want to speak to my mother."

"Alright."

Diegert grew tense during the wait. What if this was a trap? What if she was injured? What would he do with her once they were free?

"David?"

"Mom, are you OK? Where are you?"

"I'm fine, I'm in a very fancy apartment at some fancy hotel."

"Are they hurting you?"

"No, but they won't let me leave. The men have guns."

"Mom, I'm on my way to come get you."

"David, it's not safe. Does this have anything to do with the money you sent me?"

"Mom, I know you're scared and this is serious business, but it's not about that money. I'll try to explain when I get there. I won't be long."

"It's not safe, David, you shouldn't come."

Blevinsky disconnected Diegert from his mother and connected him to a conference call with the guards at the Royal Ambassador. "Gentlemen, when Mr. Diegert arrives, you're to treat him with nothing but courtesy and respect. Is that understood?"

"Yes, sir," said several voices simultaneously.

"Alright, men, disconnect." When all the guards had hung up, Blevinsky spoke just to Diegert. "I don't care how you did it, but I'm not happy you're back in Europe."

"Not only Europe, Aaron, but London. And your boss has to be wondering why his operations manager isn't on top of it, when I'm calling him from the single-source detonation device for your elaborate plan. Fuck you, Blevinsky."

It was a long walk on an injured leg, but he found the private entrance for the penthouse at the Royal Ambassador. The guard on the street patted him down for a weapon but made no attempt to take his phone. Inside the entrance, he was directed to the private elevator, which he rode with a guard straight to the top of the hotel. The elevator doors slid open, revealing the interior of the penthouse with its rich décor and luxurious furnishings.

A guard greeted him as he stepped off the elevator into the foyer of the penthouse apartment. "If you would please follow me, Mr. Diegert."

His limping gait put an ache in his hips while he left bloody footprints every step of the way. The guard stood before wide double doors and slid one of the panels into the wall. Diegert watched as the door retracted into its pocket, revealing his mother standing in the middle of the room. She smiled when she saw her son, but her facial expression passed through surprise and shock before revealing horror. Diegert looked down at himself to realize his pant leg was soaked in blood, his boot covered in a crimson sheen, while his thigh was encircled by a cinched-up belt. His shirt was torn and dirty, his face bruised, his hair a mess, and his hands smeared with blood. Denise Diegert's gape-mouthed inability to speak led Diegert to begin. "Mom, I'm alright. The leg will be fine." While his body shook from the blood loss, he held his hands out to her. She rushed across the room, wrapped her arms around him, and held on tight. Diegert melted into her, with a sense of relief to have found her safe and unharmed. She pulled back from him, feeling his weakness as the blood loss depleted him. "David, you need a doctor."

The guard at the door interjected. "Mrs. Diegert, a doctor has been called and will be here in seven minutes."

"Seven minutes?"

Looking at his phone screen, he said, "Yes, ma'am."

"David, you've got to lie down."

Leading him to the couch, she said, "What happened to you? Tell me what's going on. I need to know, honey."

Looking at her frightened eyes and stressed face, Diegert said, "Mom, I'm so sorry you're involved in this. These people are dangerous. I don't want to scare you, but we're in deep trouble."

Diegert closed his eyes and drifted into a semiconscious stupor. Denise knelt on the floor next to him and looked back at the guards with even more suspicion and fear.

Right on time, a doctor arrived with a backpack full of equipment. He ordered the guards to move Diegert into one of the bedrooms. Diegert's wounds were treated, he received an IV transfusion, his thigh was stitched, and he was then cleaned up and dressed in a loose-fitting pair of black pants and a gray T-shirt. The doctor administered a dose of Healix, and soon Diegert was feeling better. When he exited the treatment bedroom, his mother beamed.

"David, you look so much better."

She hugged him and could feel that strength had already started to return to his sturdy frame. They sat together on the couch.

"You were saying we're in danger."

"Oh, Mom, I was delirious. We're going to be fine."

He reassuringly patted her shoulder and squeezed her forearm.

She clutched his hand and locked on to his gaze. "I'm not comfortable with your change of opinion. Why would we now be safe?"

Diegert smiled, seeking a way to get her to relax. He struggled with lying to her but wanted her to be calm and not so concerned. "We're going to be fine because . . ."

As the words stumbled over his lips, the elevator door opened and from it exited a distinguished man with a full head of gray hair and piercing blue eyes set in a handsome face, wearing an impeccably tailored gray suit on his trim, tall body. He walked with a powerful stride that belied his years and quickly carried him into the main room where Diegert and Denise sat. Although he had never laid eyes on this man, Diegert needed no introduction to realize that Klaus Panzer had just entered the room. The bold man exuded confidence, projecting an expectation of getting whatever he wanted simply by exerting his sense of inalienable rights.

Diegert and his mother rose to their feet. Between them and Panzer was a long, rectangular coffee table on which stood a vase filled with soft white baby's breath and a dozen red roses. Diegert observed a change in the look on Panzer's face. The sense of control gave way to an expression of surprised recognition. The man seemed unsettled as he looked at Diegert's mother. Glancing at his mother's face, he saw the same look. She knew this man. These two knew each other, yet they were both absolutely stunned to be in one another's presence at this moment.

Neither Panzer nor Denise spoke, but their faces revealed the presence of their history. Panzer stepped to the side, coming around the coffee table to stand before the tall, dark-haired woman. She held his gaze, unblinking with a slight defiance in the set of her chin. "Denise," said Panzer with enthusiastic familiarity. He looked at David then slowly turned back to

Denise. With a tone of resolution, he said, "Diegert." The tall, debonair man reached for her hand, gently lifting it to his lips and placing a kiss just past her knuckles.

What the fuck? raced through Diegert's head as he watched the man he considered his archenemy fondling the hand of his mother. The protestations clogged Diegert's throat, and his only expression was an open-mouthed look of disbelief.

Panzer broke the silence as he turned to Diegert, saying, "Young man, this may come as quite a surprise to you, but your mother and I shared a night of passionate intimacy a long time ago. Twenty-six years ago, to be exact."

Shocked, Diegert cast a piercing eye upon Panzer. "Twenty-six years?"

CHAPTER 70

Everything fell into place in Diegert's mind the instant the words were spoken, but accepting the fact was not so sudden. He struggled with the puzzle piece, unable to place it into the empty hole in his life where a father's love was supposed to fit. The man he had often fantasized about meeting was certainly not standing in front of him. His mother had known all along and never said a word, keeping hidden the name of his real father. Loving her and trusting her were two things he struggled to do simultaneously.

Diegert felt Panzer's gaze weighing upon him as the man scanned him curiously. Panzer stepped closer, approaching Diegert as though he were a recently acquired and long-desired possession.

"You could be my son," said the man, who was accustomed to getting absolutely everything he wanted.

Diegert stood toe-to-toe with him. A well-placed series of strikes would take this jerk down and end his life within thirty seconds. Diegert looked into the ice-blue eyes, which he found unsettling yet also strangely calming. Panzer spoke again. "You are something that can never be bought but which I have wanted for decades."

"Why do you think I'm your son?"

Flustered for a moment, Panzer said, "In 1991, your mother was on the catering staff at the Deerfield Lodge . . . in Minnesota. I was a guest there, demonstrating some of our very best hunting rifles. We met, we made love, and if my seed found fertile ground, then I could be your father." He looked at Denise. "I trust her to know."

Distraught, Denise cast Panzer a look of fury. She swung her gaze to her son, and her eyes now pleaded for release from this forced revelation of her deepest secret. The expressions of both men demanded a response. Denise looked at David and nodded her head.

Glaring at his mother until she turned her eyes to the floor, Diegert struggled to keep himself from lashing out at both of these thoughtless people . . . his parents.

Panzer continued, "I think we both have a lot to process, but I feel like I have been given a gift I never thought I would receive."

"Yeah, well, I feel like I've just been kicked in the head. Only to find out that the one person I should be able to trust withheld the truth from me my whole life."

Diegert stepped away from Panzer, who crossed back to stand next to Denise.

"You fucked her and walked away, leaving her to raise a bastard son with no idea I even existed."

Unaccustomed to being dressed down, Panzer searched for words. "I . . . if . . . if she had contacted me and let me know . . . but I never heard from her."

"Of course not, you shithead, she was a poor country girl married to an alcoholic scumbag who controlled her with deprivation and violence. Why do you think she was attracted to you? Did you even pay her?"

Panzer and Denise looked at each other.

Diegert let them contemplate their actions from so long ago. "I'm a bastard from a free fuck."

Diegert spun away from them and walked to the window. "I can see that both of you don't think about other people." Stepping away from the window and whirling to face them, Diegert raised his voice as he crossed the room.

"Mom, because you're so scared of being abandoned, you're unwilling to be responsible. And you, Klaus Panzer, who the hell knows what you think? But the kind of work I've been doing for you tells me you don't give a shit about other people." Leaning in close, Diegert said, "I've killed for you."

Panzer replied, "Thank you, son."

With an instant rage, Diegert shoved Panzer in the chest, forcing the trillionaire to stumble backward.

Three guards all drew their weapons and moved in with barrels trained on Diegert.

Denise stepped between them, raising her arms. "Wait, wait, don't shoot." She turned to Diegert and embraced him while speaking in his ear. "I love you, David, more than anything, and I'm sorry for hurting you, but I have always loved you."

"I know, Mom, but I don't know what to do."

Pulling back and looking into Diegert's face through tear-filled eyes, she pointed at Panzer. "He's so rich and powerful, let's see what he can do for us. He could give you a good job."

"I don't think you get what this guy does, Mom."

"I don't care. It can't be that bad. Look at Jake and Dad; they're both criminals."

"The order of magnitude makes those two look like first-offense shoplifters."

"I'm tired of living poor. I want to live better. I've lived a lousy life while others have walked all over me. Maybe I have to step on somebody to live better. I'm OK with that."

"She's right, you know, son," interrupted Panzer as he waved his hand, directing the guards to holster their weapons. "I can offer both of you opportunities within my organization. Denise, I could see you working in our philanthropic branch making high six figures."

Denise smiled at him. "Six figures?"

Diegert rolled his eyes. "I already work for you."

"Yes, I know, son, but I see an expanded role for you in management. A position that is . . . not so tactical. It would be a promotion."

"See, David, this could be good."

Diegert passed between the couch and the coffee table, bumping the table leg and jostling the vase of roses and baby's breath. Instinctively, he reached out to steady the solid ceramic vessel. He grasped the narrow neck of the vase and swung it like a club into the face of the guard to his left. The flowers and water sprayed across the room as the guard tumbled to the floor with imploded teeth. As the second guard reached for his gun, Diegert threw the vase. It flew end over end, striking him in the head. Turning back to his left, Diegert grabbed the first guard's pistol and shot him. He swung to the second guard and shot him as well. The third and final guard came running from the elevator with his weapon drawn. As he entered the room, Diegert leveled three bullets into his chest, dropping him to the floor.

With the gun still hot in his hand, Diegert cast his sight on Panzer, who now held Denise in front of him with a freshly cut rose stem pressed against her neck.

Diegert smirked. "You're going to stab her with a rose?"

"The end is sharp, and the stem is stiff." He pressed the shaft to her neck, which drew blood and a squeal from Denise. "I'll drive it right through her throat."

Diegert pulled out the satellite phone, dropped it onto the coffee table, and pointed the pistol at it. "You let her go right now."

Panzer's eyes diverted to the phone, and Diegert fired the pistol into the floor, startling the man. With a quick move, Diegert punched Panzer on the jaw, knocking him to the floor, forcing the release of his mother.

Panzer slowly rose to his feet while Diegert picked up the satellite phone.

Denise moved to the side, placing her hand on her neck wound.

Panzer and Diegert faced each other like combatants in a ring. Diegert's pistol made clear his advantage. He spoke first. "So where do we go from here?"

"Remember what I told you: there is a future for you in my organization. You will be successful beyond your wildest dreams."

"That's fucking bullshit."

Diegert lifted the pistol, placing Panzer's face in the iron sights.

Extending his hands and backing away, Panzer said, "Before acting rashly, you should consider all your options."

"Yeah, I will. I could kill you right here." Panzer continued backing up, making his way through the apartment. "I could kill you in the bedroom." Panzer passed the bedroom door. "I could kill you in the bathroom." Panzer stood in the door-frame of the bathroom. "Get in there." Panzer stepped into the bathroom as Diegert stood outside with the pistol steady in his hand.

Panzer pleaded, "Son, I'm the only person on earth who can show you a father's love."

Diegert's steely gaze and fatal focus softened for an instant.

Panzer continued, "Let me share my wealth, power, and love with my one true son. Won't you give me that chance?"

Diegert hesitated but did not lower the pistol as he contemplated his reply. "I can see the wealth and power, but I don't believe in the love."

Keeping his father at the end of his pistol, Diegert reached out and slammed the door. He wedged the door closed with a sturdy straight-backed chair jammed against the knob.

Returning to the main room, he grabbed the medical backpack and dressed his mother's puncture wound.

"David, I'm so sorry I never told you, but I never imagined I would ever see that man again."

Folding her into his arms, he hugged her, saying, "Shh, it's OK."

Breaking into a sob, Denise said, "A mother should never have to share such shame with her son."

Patting her shoulder, Diegert said, "It's OK, Mom. You're the one person in this whole world who I love."

Gazing up at her son, Denise said, "Oh, David, it's good to hear you say that again."

The water of love, sadness, joy, and grief seeped from the windows of their souls, spilled over their lids, and rolled down their faces as they looked at each other with emotions for which there were not words. Diegert's tension and trepidation were giving way to relief now that he had secured her freedom.

"David," his mother said. "I think we're still in big trouble."

Wiping his eyes on his sleeve, he picked up his pistol and said, "Come on, Mom. We're getting out of here."

With his arm around her shoulder and the satellite phone in his pocket, he walked with his mother to the elevator. He instinctively placed himself between her and the doors before pressing the call button. While waiting, he thought about how they would have to escape . . . somewhere, anywhere. He had enough money to lay low for a while, so he could figure out a way to get her home.

The metal panels of the elevator separated, revealing the interior of the cabin and the presence of Pierre and two other men. Diegert's pistol immediately rose, but his hesitation at seeing the one friendly guy from Headquarters cost him dearly when Pierre pulled the trigger on his Taser, releasing forty-two hundred volts of muscle-paralyzing electricity into Diegert's legs and torso. As he fell to the floor, Diegert fired his weapon, but the spasms in his arm sent the bullet harmlessly into the ceiling. He felt all muscular control vacate his body. Looking up, he watched as the two men flexicuffed his mom's hands behind her back, covered her mouth with duct tape, and shoved her into the elevator.

Pierre barked the orders, "Hold her in the elevator. You, go find Mr. Panzer."

Convulsing on the floor, Diegert turned his eyes to see Pierre open a small case and extract a syringe. "You're a foolish idiot for taking the hard way to learn how this business works. I'm sorry to do this, but you've forgotten we are servants to the powerful."

The second man returned with Panzer. The gray-haired tyrant stepped over to Diegert, knelt on his chest, and took the satellite phone. He then bent forward, looking straight into the wide eyes of his terrified son, and growled, "Now I will show you a father's love."

As he stood up, Panzer nodded to Pierre, who pressed the syringe into Diegert's thigh. The injection sedated the consciousness of David Diegert, fading his world to black.

ACKNOWLEDGMENTS

Writing a novel is an audacious and electrifying challenge. My efforts have been supported and encouraged by many fine people, and I want to thank them.

My wife, **Leah**, is the most amazing person who has believed in me and my writing when there was no other reason to except that she loves me. I love her back with all the strength in my heart, and I am so thankful for having her in my life. My three children, **Brandon**, **Korina**, and **Talia**, all encouraged me while being patient during the long hours I spent writing. I love you guys.

Patrick Anthony Johnson is a very talented and inspiring storyteller with whom I am very fortunate to share brainstorming Skype sessions, a twisted sense of humor, and a penchant for the use of contractions. His creative contributions are on practically every page of this novel, from editing to character traits to generationally corrected dialogue. He also helped me set up my website. I owe a Patrick a huge debt, which I look forward to repaying by helping him succeed as a filmmaker. Keep it creative, Patrick.

John Reitano is a friend who has made me believe in myself for the past thirty-five years. He is a published author and an exceptionally inspirational public speaker. In spite of not being a thriller fan, he swallowed hard and read through my manuscript. He drew insights I hadn't even considered but which allowed me to deepen the development of many of the characters. He pushed me to complete the project, and for his unwavering support I am eternally grateful.

John Robert Marlow gave me a professional editor's opinion of my first draft; it needed a lot of work. I appreciated his candor and followed his advice. By the third draft, he gave me the hesitant thumbs-up of an accomplished editor who holds the belief that there is always something to be improved. John showed me that perseverance in the editing and rewriting of a story is where the magic is. His lessons will remain with me and influence all my future writing. He is an excellent teacher.

A writer needs readers, and I am very fortunate to have a group of people who have been generous with their time, constructive with their criticism, and tolerant with their patience. Their remarks and observations of my beta drafts have been incorporated into these pages, and I want to thank them: **Chris, Ed**, **Paul**, **Mark**, **Ken**, and **Anne Brewer**, siblings who were not afraid to criticize the writing of their biggest brother; **Kennan Keating**, who shared a perspective that was much appreciated; **Elaine Sanzel**, who shared her encyclopedic knowledge of the genre to help me mold the characters; **Steve Dora**, whose eye for details in editing the first beta draft dramatically improved the readability of the story; **Rob Dick, Joe Bortle, Matt Shue**, and **Jeff Wilcox**, lifelong compatriots who stepped up and helped a friend who needed their opinions; **Reid McLachlan**, an incredibly talented person who not only provided me with great insight into plot and character development but also created the book's cover—he is a consummate artist, and I am his humble and grateful fan.

Turning this manuscript into a book took the support, technical platform, and inspiration of **Inkshares**. With their help, I was able to reach out to all the people I know and a whole lot of new people in order to demonstrate that there was interest in my story. I am so very grateful to all the people who showed their faith in this project by preordering a copy. It is only through their collective strength, and the dedication of the people of **Inkshares**, that this project has succeeded. I am thankful beyond expression, and I look forward to continuing the story and keeping my readers entertained with the adventures of David Diegert. Thank you.

ABOUT THE AUTHOR

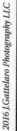

© 2016 J.Gattelaro Photography LLC

William Schiele is married and has three grown children. He is a professor of anatomy and physiology and lives in upstate New York. *Tears of the Assassin* is his debut novel. Mr. Schiele will neither confirm nor deny any involvement in acts of assassination.

For more information, please visit www.williamschiele.com.

LIST OF PATRONS

This book was made possible in part by the following grand patrons who preordered the book on Inkshares.com. Thank you.

Charles Edic

Edward J. Brewer

Heleene Brewer

Joanne S. Ernenwein

John Reitano

Kenneth G. Brewer

Kevin Fitzpatrick

Leah McLachlan

Michael Broski

Michael Mclachlan

Minerva Francis

Patrick Anthony Johnson

Robert Dick

Tom Hennessy